THE
VANISHED

D1390079

THE
VANISHED
LOTTE AND SØREN
HAMMER

Translated from the Danish
by Martin Aitken

B L O O M S B U R Y

LONDON · OXFORD · NEW YORK · NEW DELHI · SYDNEY

Bloomsbury Publishing
An imprint of Bloomsbury Publishing Plc

50 Bedford Square	1385 Broadway
London	New York
WC1B 3DP	NY 10018
UK	USA

www.bloomsbury.com

BLOOMSBURY and the Diana logo are trademarks of Bloomsbury Publishing Plc

First published in 2011 in Denmark as *Ensomme Hjerters Klub* by Gyldendal
First published in Great Britain 2016

British Library Cataloguing-in-Publication Data
A catalogue record for this book is available from the British Library.

ISBN: TPB: 978-1-4088-6030-4
ePub: 978-1-4088-6031-1

2 4 6 8 10 9 7 5 3 1

Typeset by Integra Software Services Pvt. Ltd.
Printed and bound in Great Britain by CPI Group (UK) Ltd, Croydon CR0 4YY

To find out more about our authors and books visit www.bloomsbury.com
Here you will find extracts, author interviews, details of forthcoming events
and the option to sign up for our newsletters.

*To Merete Borre – a wonderful
person and a brilliant editor*

CHAPTER 1

The date was Wednesday 13 August. In Copenhagen the weather was bleak and windy. For Police HQ last night in the city centre had passed relatively peacefully: there had been a couple of bar brawls, an attempted stabbing resulting in only superficial injuries, a handful of drunks now sleeping it off in detention, a prostitute junkie OD'd and dead, but nothing serious or out of the ordinary. The worst had been a drunk driver tearing through the streets in the early morning in an attempt to shake off two patrol cars in hot pursuit. Eventually, he succeeded: with tyres squealing he had turned off Sydhavnsgade towards Sluseholmen doing about a hundred K, after which he had veered right along Ved Stigbordene, putting his foot down with a triumphant look back in the rear-view before plunging straight into the harbour. Now the divers were out looking for him, but the current was strong there, so the search was going to drag on. Everyone hoped he had managed to get out in time and had got himself back on to dry land, but it didn't seem likely.

The boy making his way over Polititorvet was seriously overweight. At the pedestrian crossing in front of Police HQ he carefully looked both ways before venturing out into the road, his progress laboured and slow. Reaching the other side, he stopped to wipe his cheeks and brow with the handkerchief he pulled out of his trouser pocket, then continued on his way along Niels Brocks Gade. His feet were hurting and he still had a fair way to go before arriving at school. The odd passer-by looked at him with concern, others sending him fleeting glances of pity before hurrying on. Most ignored him.

The boy's clothing was as wretched-looking as he himself was. His parents were by no means short of money, but this was his own form of protest. He was wearing white, worn-down trainers, bought on special offer last year in the local supermarket, faded jeans that drooped beneath his stomach, and a fawn-coloured windcheater zipped halfway down, one hand tucked inside as if his arm was broken and the garment was a sling. The jacket made him sweat even more, and with his natural padding he could easily have dispensed with it, the weather wasn't cold. But he needed it: the hand inside clutched a submachine gun.

It was 8.16 a.m.

If Detective Superintendent Konrad Simonsen had got up from his chair and looked out of the window at the right time, he would have been able to see the boy as he passed by below. But he didn't. Instead, he stared at the Deputy Commissioner while she talked on the phone. She was known for her abysmal dress sense, and today was no exception. That much was plain, even to Konrad Simonsen. She was wearing a snug-fitting, blue-and-green-checked jacket with striped trousers that were almost, though not quite, in the same colours. Konrad Simonsen found himself thinking that all she needed was a dead animal thrown around her neck – a fox fur, for instance – and the hideous effect would be complete.

It was his first day at work in eight weeks and he had felt oddly on edge clocking in that morning. Now his nerves, at least, were gone. He glanced restlessly at the portrait of the queen that adorned the wall behind the Deputy Commissioner's seat and tried to stifle his annoyance. After a long while he sent the sovereign a grimace as though she were an ally, then glanced back at the case folder on the desk in front of him. It looked thin.

At long last, the Deputy Commissioner finished her call. She smiled warmly at him in a way that was either meticulously rehearsed or genuine, and began to list all the different people who had been in touch with her during his illness, to see how he was doing.

'Quite a few even called me at home.'

'Well, I'm touched, I must say,' he felt obliged to respond

'And so you should be. Don't pretend you're not bothered, you should be glad you've got colleagues here who care about you.'

She was right. He said he was glad. She carried on:

'I've decided not to alter your formal status. You're still in charge of Homicide, but in practice you'll leave the day-to-day running to Arne Petersen...'

'Arne Pedersen. His name's Pedersen, not Petersen.'

Arne Pedersen was one of Konrad Simonsen's closest colleagues, a highly competent, quick-thinking man in his early forties. It was more or less understood that he would take over from Simonsen as head of the Homicide Department at some point, when the time came, and quite naturally he had stepped in during the two months Simonsen had been away.

The Deputy Commissioner replied:

'Indeed, my apologies. Anyway, he'll continue in charge as de facto head until I deem you sufficiently recovered to take over. And to begin with, you'll stick to three hours a day, four at most. Am I understood?'

He nodded and repeated her words slowly out loud: *three hours a day, four at most*. After which she informed him that everyone in his vicinity was under strict orders to report to her in the event that he failed to observe her instruction.

'And if you feel tired, you don't come in. Remember, the cemetery's full of people who couldn't be done without.'

'Of course. Do I have any say in when I'll be in, or do you decide that, too?'

The sarcasm was lost on her. She answered him in earnest:

'You can start by deciding for yourself and we'll see how it goes.'

'Thanks. Do I get my new case now?'

She ignored this.

'We've had your office refurbished while you've been away. There's an extra little room for you now, with a sofa in it for whenever you need a lie-down.'

It was obvious she'd been looking forward to telling him that. He thanked her again, awkwardly, feeling ancient. And then at long last she opened the case folder in front of her. Her eyes avoided his as she spoke.

'This isn't a case as such. It's more me wanting something closed in an orderly manner.'

She slapped a hand down on the folder before running through its contents for his benefit. He listened with increasing dismay and realised she was serious: it wasn't a case at all. He enquired indignantly:

'You mean the vice-chairman of the Parliamentary Legal Affairs Committee went straight to you in person, interfering in police matters? I've never heard the like.'

'It's not exactly by the book, Simon, I know. But can't you interview some witnesses and... well, just put yourself in the picture? Write a report I can...'

She hesitated; he finished the sentence on her behalf.

'... show the vice-chairman and make her happy?'

The Deputy Commissioner nodded.

'You're free to delegate, and I won't poke my nose in as to how you go about it, only to make sure you're not overexerting

4

yourself. I just thought it might be a good place for you to start. To get you going again.'

Konrad Simonsen pulled the folder towards him, feeling disgruntled.

'But it's not a case.'

And then suddenly he heard music. Indistinct tones, like those that had drifted into his ears when he woke up in the hospital eight weeks before. He was momentarily gripped by panic, paralysed by it as he had been many times since the operation.

'Is something the matter? Aren't you feeling well?' asked his boss, immediately concerned.

He summoned the energy to reply:

'Can you hear music, too?'

She laughed heartily, and for a couple of near-endless seconds he had no idea if she was hearing the same thing or just indulging him in his delusions. But then she got to her feet, stepped up to the plasterboard wall and thumped her fist against it a couple of times. The music stopped.

'It's resonance, that's all. We've got a new intern in the secretariat and she's got one of those squashed-up little tape recorders with earphones… iPods, I believe they're called. Anyway, when she leans her head back against the wall, her skull and the partition work together like a loudspeaker.'

He sighed with relief and at once felt exhausted. It was the familiar pattern: first fear of dying, then fatigue.

'Why don't you ban her from using it?'

'I have, but it seems her relationship to authority is… how should I put it?… strained. I was thinking…'

But Konrad Simonsen had stopped listening.

The boy with the submachine gun had reached his destination. The school was on Marmorgade, a short street that lay tucked between H. C. Andersens Boulevard and Vester Voldgade, and comprised a three-winged red-brick building of four storeys, dating back to the early 1900s. The playground faced out on to the street, separated from the pavement only by a chain-link fence. The main entrance was at the rear of the building, imposing steps of granite leading up to an oversized pair of double doors that were painted green and seemed oddly out of place in this setting. The boy headed slowly towards them.

Through a window in the north wing his class teacher spotted him. She had already resolved to speak to the boy about his habitual lateness: it had been dire before the summer holiday, and the new school year had kicked off quite as badly. Moreover, she had a stack of handouts for his class, and if she had a word with him now, she thought, she wouldn't have to go all the way up the stairs to the second floor. Two birds with one stone. She opened the window and called out to him but to her astonishment he failed to react, though he was no more than a few metres away. She sighed. It wasn't like him at all, but then being him probably wasn't always that easy, poor lad.

After battling his way up the stairs and along the corridor to his classroom, the boy sat down on a bench outside to get his breath back. The pause lasted longer than he had anticipated, but he was exhausted and racked by nerves, badly needing to collect himself. Not until a few minutes later, when he caught sight of his class teacher coming towards him with her papers under her arm and a determined smile on her face, did he get to his feet and go inside.

None of his classmates seemed to notice him come in, not even when he crossed their line of vision to get to his chair. He heaved for breath, but did not seat himself. Instead, he remained standing beside his desk with his back against the wall. The substitute teacher who stood at the board conjugating irregular verbs in English appeared undisturbed by the boy's late arrival. He turned his head to look over for a second, casting a brief and disinterested glance in his direction before carrying on as if nothing had happened. The boy studied him for five long seconds and felt the hatred well inside him, delivering courage.

The substitute was a fair-haired, rather foppishly dressed man in his early thirties with an appealing demeanour and a classically handsome profile, popular with boys and girls alike, and an excellent teacher as well. As though by some premonition, he turned his head once more and looked over his shoulder. It was then he saw the weapon, the short, black barrel pointed straight at him. Tunnel vision, pumping adrenalin. He reacted with impressive speed, reaching the door in three seamless, athletic bounds and managing to grab the door handle before the gun spat out its rounds.

Thirty-seven shots in less than half a second.

Later, each would be classified: eleven struck the victim in the back, three in the head, one in the upper arm. The man was dead before he hit the ground. The remaining twenty-two rounds had all gone through the door, most of them at a height of more than two and a half metres above the floor, presumably because the boy was unfamiliar with the firearm and had failed to take account of the upward pull of the barrel during operation. However, three rounds had penetrated the door at a height of around a metre and a half, one of which had struck his class teacher, who at that moment had approached the other side. A bullet had gone through her hand. Another had ripped a shard of wood from the door, this having struck her in the right eye, lodging itself between the orb and her cheek, though causing only superficial damage.

She felt no pain at these injuries, only astonishment. In a reflex action, she immediately reached up to her eye and pulled out the shard; then, after staring in bewilderment at her injured hand, she fainted. She suffered from haemophobia, an irrational fear of blood.

Inside, the students panicked. Most screamed and huddled together as far from the fat boy as possible. One pupil jumped resolutely from an open window at the rear and was more than fortunate not to land on the tarmac of the playground below, but on the roof of a van in the process of unloading deliveries. He got away with a broken wrist and a nasty abrasion on his cheek. One girl crawled inside a cupboard and managed to close the door from inside. There she cowered, curled up like an embryo, as quietly as she could. The rest of the class clumped together in the corner furthest from the blackboard, some lying down or seated on the floor, others clinging to the wall as though it might help if they were to be shot at. Their screams faded and became intermittent sobs. All stared in terror at the killer, frightened eyes following each movement of his weapon. The boy himself flopped down on a chair, stunned and confused. He, too, was crying.

Following his meeting with the Deputy Commissioner, Konrad Simonsen adjourned to his office with the case folder under his arm. On his way, he decided he was all right about starting off slowly and with something that didn't really matter much, a thought that both perplexed him and put him at his ease.

Just as his boss had said, he found his office had been revamped in his absence, the room next door now having been incoporated into it. Previously it had been a storeroom, with mostly pens and stationery at one end and discarded computer equipment at the other. Now it was a kind of informal anteroom, newly painted and decorated, with wall-to-wall carpeting and a leather sofa that had seen better days. It was equipped with a fridge, a coffee maker and a 50-inch TV he assumed must have been inherited from Poul Troulsen, a former close colleague, now retired. On a low, rectangular table in front of the sofa, coffee and bread rolls had been set out, as well as a splendid vase of flowers, and up against the walls stood a handful of colleagues waiting for him, among them the Countess, who besides being one of his closest co-workers also happened to be his life-partner. They lived together in her house in Søllerød. It had been more than a year now since he'd moved in with her, though he still kept on his flat in Valby and slept in a separate bedroom in her house, ostensibly because of his heart condition. She greeted him with a kiss, a gesture that was seldom made during working hours. He looked around him and said:

'Well, you certainly kept this a secret.'

'Yes, it was meant to be a surprise. Arne's on his way, too, he just had to deal with a phone call.'

Simonsen greeted those who had come and noticed Pauline Berg, a woman in her late twenties, another of his closest colleagues. At least, she had been. This was the first time he had seen her in almost a year. The previous September she had been abducted while investigating a case on which Homicide had been working. A seriously disturbed individual had held her hostage together with another young woman in a bunker in the Hareskoven woods. The other woman had been slaughtered in front of Pauline Berg's eyes and Pauline herself left to rot in captivity, before being rescued at the last minute. Since then, he had received sporadic bulletins as to how she was getting on: she had sold her house in Reerslev and bought a flat on the sixth floor of a high-rise in Rødovre, where she lived alone. For long periods following her stay in hospital she had been too fright-ened to go out, and any number of things, from cats to cellars, could send her spinning into anxiety. Moreover, she suffered from severe changes of mood and found it difficult to deal with people she didn't know, especially men, unless she sought their company of her own accord. She must have started work again while he'd been ill. As soon as he saw her, he felt guilty. As her immediate superior he ought to have monitored her progress more diligently. But he was no good at that kind of thing, and more recently he'd had his own problems.

He greeted her warmly and noted that she now wore her hair short and that her clothes were informal, not to say slovenly. She straightened up on the sofa and smiled at him, a sad, almost apologetic smile, followed by a shrug that told him far better than words that she wished everything could have been different. That went for both of them, he thought to himself, before addressing everyone in the room.

'Thanks for the kind reception, and for such lovely flowers.'

It was all he could think of, adding awkwardly almost as an afterthought:

'Maybe we should have some breakfast. It looks just the job.'

At the same moment the door to the office was flung open and Arne Pedersen burst in with a wild expression in his eyes. He grabbed Simonsen by the arm and barked out:

'Everyone, now! We've got a shooting just round the corner at Marmorgades Skole.'

He waved his free arm in the air, then swept it in a sixty-degree arc in what was actually the opposite direction from the school.

'One of the kids has gone berserk with a submachine gun. It's a massacre.'

When Konrad Simonsen arrived in the playground of the Marmorgade school everything was chaos. No one seemed to have any kind of grip on the situation, and it was hard to find out what had actually happened. Worse than that, the evacuation of the premises was sloppy and unco-ordinated, children and adults alike running around in confusion. Someone had set off the fire alarm, so a lot of the teachers thought it was a fire drill, and as procedure dictated were busy getting the pupils to assemble in the playground and trying to count heads. Outside in the street a crowd of inquisitive onlookers had gathered, pressing their noses to the fence, and in the building opposite people were leaning out of their windows to get a glimpse of what was going on. Police were there in numbers, but the efforts of the rank and file seemed quite as disorganised, and most of them seemed merely to be standing around waiting, staring up at the windows.

Having consulted a number of teachers at random, none of whom knew anything at all, Konrad Simonsen was eventually more fortunate. A secretary at the school had spoken to a pupil who had jumped out of a window to get away from his class. The boy in question had already been taken off to hospital, but the secretary's account of what he had told her was the closest Simonsen could get to hard facts. It seemed a pupil in Year 11, Robert Steen Hertz, had shot and killed two teachers and that he was in possession of an automatic firearm. At present, the boy was in his classroom on the second floor, where he was holding his classmates hostage if he hadn't already killed them – no one knew. The classroom had four windows facing the playground. The secretary pointed them out. They were approximately in the middle of the building.

Konrad Simonsen's knowledge of school shootings was some-what limited, but one thing he did know was that in every case with which he was familiar, the perpetrator had run amok in a frenzy of bloodlust and made sure to kill as many people as possible, just for the hell of it. He looked around the playground and a shudder ran down his spine. An automatic weapon fired from one of those windows would leave dozens dead, at least.

His priorities were therefore obvious. They needed to clear the playground as quickly as possible, then move the onlook-ers away and ensure all occupants of the building opposite stayed back from their windows. He instructed Arne Pedersen to get the road cleared, almost yelling the order into his ear: '*Get it cleared, then cordon off at both ends.*' After that, he collared two of the nearest constables and a number of teachers for good measure and hectically explained to them what needed to be done. Everyone in the street to be moved on. Quickly and efficiently, but no running, and most importantly no one anywhere near the fence. Simonsen repeated his orders, after which he ran into the middle of the playground and rounded up a new group of officers and teachers whom he instructed in the same way.

A constable handed him a loudhailer. His voice echoed between the buildings: *'Everyone out into the street, away from here immediately! Walk with haste, but don't run. Older pupils help the younger ones. Keep access free. No running, no pushing. Use truncheons or mace if necessary, access* must *be kept free.'* The latter order was of course directed at the police officers present, and while he would surely have won no prizes for unambiguous communication, he was nevertheless understood. He repeated: *'Out into the street. Move away. Do not run. Do not shove. Older pupils help the younger ones. Access to be kept free, access* must *be free.'*

His orders worked, the situation stabilised. Astonishingly quickly, the playground emptied, and after it the street outside. Konrad Simonsen let go of the loudhailer. It fell to the ground where it rolled back and forth for a while in a semicircle. Only when he realised he was now standing on his own in the middle of the playground did any thought for his own safety occur to him.

'We should get out of here, Simon.'

The Countess appeared behind him, wearing a bulletproof vest and holding another in her hand. Her eyes were fixed on the second-floor windows as she spoke. He barked again:

'Where the hell's the Special Intervention Unit? Have you heard anything? They're supposed to be rapid-response, what the bloody hell are they doing? It's situations like this...'

She cut him off with a hand on his shoulder.

'They'll be here within five minutes.'

He glanced at his watch and could see he'd only been here himself for ten. It felt like an hour.

'We've got more pupils inside the building.'

'They're being led out through other exits. Come on.'

She bundled him away at a trot. He turned to her as they went.

'Have you learned anything about what happened?'

'Indications are we've got at least two dead, both teachers. We've got the second-floor corridor sealed, but we're not going in, we're leaving that to the professionals. The body of the class teacher is in front of the classroom door. She's been shot in the head, so we can assume she's dead. We're leaving her where she is for the moment.'

'What about the kids?'

'No one knows.'

'How many?'

'About twenty-five.'

They found cover behind a patrol car parked on the street in front of the school. The Countess handed Simonsen his bullet-proof vest. He put it on and realised to his surprise that it was a perfect fit.

Confusion still prevailed. The Special Intervention Unit had arrived in two vehicles, but were experiencing difficulties getting through the police line on Vester Voldgade. Two badly parked ambulances and a crowd of curious onlookers were blocking their way. Simonsen turned his head in surprise. Behind him, a journalist from Denmark News had commenced an on-the-spot report, jabbering excitedly into her microphone about the bullets that any minute now could be flying about in all directions, and commenting that no one would feel safe as long as the killer was still on the loose inside the school buildings. She, too, had found cover behind the patrol car, while her cameraman fearlessly stood

13

up as he filmed her. Simonsen ordered a constable to get rid of them, then asked the Countess:

'Are we sure he's got an automatic weapon?'

'No, but everything points to it.'

'What a bloody mess.'

The boy was crying. Having killed his substitute teacher he had sat down apathetically on a chair by the blackboard without knowing quite what to do next. He hadn't thought this far on. Twice he had risen to his feet, once to look out of the window into the playground where everyone was running around in a frenzy, and once to overturn a table – an action without logic, yet one that caused his classmates at the back of the room to huddle even closer together, as though their terror could in some way be shared. Most held someone's hand, all followed his every move-ment with wide and fearful eyes. He got up again, walked through the room and halted a couple of metres in front of them. Many covered their heads, a few began to whimper pitifully. He jabbed his gun towards a girl and issued a command:

'Go away, Maja.'

The girl he had selected did not at first understand what he had said, and he repeated the order, this time in a desperate shout:

'Get lost, Maja! You can go… go to hell!'

He went back to his chair by the board, in a laboured waddle, and watched as the girl, slowly and with eyes that begged and pleaded, crept along the wall towards the door. She had to pull hard on the handle before the body of their substitute teacher allowed her to squeeze through. As she did, she slipped in the blood on the floor and almost crawled across their class teacher who lay in the corridor. Outside, she began to wail. Immediately, three other girls tried to follow her, only for the boy to deliver a volley of rounds into the ceiling. The girls screamed and ran back to their places at the rear of the room. He had no idea himself why he hadn't allowed them to leave, too. Perhaps it was because their attempted escape represented a change he had not sanctioned, a lack of control. Or perhaps it was because he simply didn't care for them. He fired another brief volley into the body at the door, though he felt no pleasure in doing so. And then he began to cry again, and to wish it would all be over soon.

Konrad Simonsen and the Countess received the girl as she came running. She had lost one shoe and was smeared in blood from head to toe. Her white blouse, tight jeans, face and fair hair were crimson. It took a while for the two investigators to realise she was unharmed. The Countess wrapped a blanket around the girl's shoulders. She was trembling and clearly in need of medical attention.

They were standing behind the Special Intervention Unit's group vehicle, now referred to invariably as the Gulf, though in this case it was a Mercedes Vito. It was armoured, and anyway there was no longer a danger of their being shot at from the windows. Not for long, at least, the operational commander having just received confirmation that his marksman was in place in the apartment building behind them. Cautiously, the Countess began to question the girl.

'What happened? How did you get out?'

The reply came in frightened little bursts, and the Countess realised that more than three or four questions would hardly be reasonable.

'He let me go... but then he shot the others who came after me.'

'So some of your classmates have been shot?'

The girl put her bloodied hands to her ears and lowered her head.

'He shot them down in cold blood, that fucking psycho! They never had a chance. Just because they wanted to get away as well. In cold blood...'

The Countess held her gently, shaking her ever so slightly to maintain the girl's focus. The operational commander and Konrad Simonsen, standing beside them, exchanged glances.

'How many of your friends are alive?'

'Some are alive, some are dead. I don't know how many. He's going to kill the rest of them soon. He's going to mow them down like rabbits.'

'Is that what he said?'

She didn't seem to comprehend the question, and the Countess repeated:

'Did Robert Steen Hertz say he was going to kill your classmates?'

'He doesn't say anything, he just pumps bullets into people whenever he feels like it. The fat bastard! Why isn't anyone doing anything? Can't you blow his head off or something?'

The Countess frowned. Arne Pedersen, who had just joined them, muttered:

'She's not much use.'

Simonsen intervened.

'Get her into an ambulance, Countess.'

The operational commander narrowed his eyes and peered up towards the windows of the classroom, as though it might afford him a clearer picture of the situation inside. It was up to him what was going to happen, whether his men were to go in and neutralise the killer, whether he should try negotiating, or whether the marksman should be given orders to shoot on sight. He was far from convinced by what the girl had said. She was clearly in a state of shock, and the way she talked about it was less than credible, more like something out of a Hollywood movie she'd seen. He did not feel inclined to order the marksman into action on that account. On the other hand, storming the classroom might easily result in more dead. Again, he peered up at the windows, and then he made his decision.

'A stun grenade and then in. I only hope we're in time, that's all.'

At the same moment, the main door of the school opened and a woman gingerly emerged. Even from a distance it was plain that she was covered in blood. She wobbled down the steps, seemingly badly injured, an apparent confirmation of what the girl had told them. A few steps into the playground the class teacher collapsed and fell to the ground in a heap. The operational commander nodded to two of his men, indicating the woman he thought to be a pupil. The men ran out to bring her in. As they did so, the commander gripped the lapel of his jacket and spoke into the microphone that was fastened to its rear.

'This is Lima. If you get a decent crack, Palle, kill him.'

And then he shouted out loud:

'Get an ambulance!'

The marksman had been lucky. After arriving at the scene with his unit he had quickly identified the ideal spot, on the third floor of the apartment building opposite, that would afford him an unimpeded view of the windows on the second floor of the school's main building, behind which the incident was unfolding. He took his rifle from the Gulf, ran quickly to the front door he had picked out and proceeded up the stairs. There were two flats to choose between, but the door of one was already ajar. Inside, a police officer was explaining to the occupant that he was to keep back from the windows facing the street. This was when he struck lucky. The occupant turned out to be a retired army officer, who despite his almost eighty years was quick to sense the gravity of the situation and the needs of the marksman.

The police officer opened one of the living-room windows, lifted it carefully from its hinges and put it down on the floor. The marksman cleared the window sill. Together they lifted the retired officer's heavy mahogany dining table and carried it over to the window. It was no more than a couple of centimetres shorter in height than the sill. The marksman lay down on the table and prepared his rifle. It was a Heckler & Koch PSG1 A1, one of the most precise rifles ever manufactured, and using it an experienced marksman could hit a target up to eight hundred metres away. That wouldn't be necessary here, the flat no more than a hundred and fifty metres from the classroom. It was as perfect as could be. He informed his commander that he was in position.

Three times he identified the target in his sights, each time only fleetingly. The first time, he saw the boy upend a table, the second and third times he passed in front of the window, first one way, then the other. Unfortunately, he had moved too quickly for the marksman to be able to identify his weapon. And then the order came, the order he had hoped would never come at all. He requested confirmation and received it immediately.

In the classroom, the boy with the submachine gun had finally decided that the best thing for him to do was to let his classmates go and give himself up. He was exhausted, frightened and hungry, and he wanted out. It didn't matter where, as long as it was out. Then it was that he heard the ambulance and went over to the window closest to the blackboard, cupping his hand to the pane to eliminate the reflected light as he peered out into the street to see what was going on.

The bullet hit him square in the forehead above his left eye and exited from his lower skull, after which it continued on its path, striking the leg of an overturned desk, ricocheting diagonally downwards, piercing the door of the classroom cupboard and the knee of the girl who cowered inside it, then passing through her neck and spine, before finally embedding itself in the wall. Both children died immediately.

Outside, the shot echoed between the buildings. Simonsen automatically looked up towards the source and then back at the

Countess, solemnly and without words. The operational commander approached them.

'It's over.'

It was almost noon and the situation at the Marmorgade school was under control. The Special Intervention Unit had left the scene, forensics were at work in the classroom and counsellors had been summoned. The mood was oppressive, conversation between the officers present clipped and businesslike.

Konrad Simonsen's first day back at work was over, Arne Pedersen was insisting on driving him home. In the meantime, the Countess would have to take over. Pedersen would be back within the hour.

In the car Simonsen asked:

'Haven't you got better things to do than play chauffeur?'

'Yeah, but I need to run some decision-making by you.'

'It's pretty straightforward, isn't it? We'll have a fairly good idea of what exactly happened by the end of the day, then all you need is a motive and to find out how Robert Steen Hertz managed to get his hands on a submachine gun. You'll have to deal with the press, but apart from that I'd focus mainly on making sure the boy was on his own. Because if he's got mates with the same ideas and the same sort of weapons, you're going to need to know as soon as possible. And one more thing: if you're anticipating funding issues, now's the time to put in for more.'

They discussed matters for a while. Arne Pedersen had a number of questions, Konrad Simonsen answered them. By the time they turned off towards Søllerød they had no more to say on the issue, and Pedersen changed the subject:

'What about you anyway? How did it go with the Deputy Commissioner? Did she give you something to be getting on with?'

It was obvious he was only asking for the sake of politeness. His mind was still on the school shooting.

'Of a sort, I suppose.'

Arne Pedersen said nothing, and Simonsen added:

'Then I heard music.'

'Music? What sort of music?'

'Something that'll make you smile.'

He explained about the resonance. Arne Pedersen was puzzled.

'Is this important?'

Simonsen shook his head. No, it wasn't important at all.

When he woke up after collapsing it had meant everything.

The cheerful, inciting overture from the fairground, where everyone was welcome. French horns tearing the old world apart and drawing the marvelling audience into the future. The singer whose optimistic vocals gripped his soul and for a moment dulled the pains in his chest. It was as if he had been allotted another chance, an opportunity to change his mind, alter his life, perhaps even understand it. And then the light intruded, he had felt the weight of his body and everything hurt. In vain he reached out to the music as the final notes drifted away, and the movement caused him to wince. Someone took his hand, and he opened his eyes.

Konrad Simonsen was on the job early, far too early for his own liking, but he came in with the Countess and she had more than enough to think about with the ongoing investigation into the shooting at the school. His schedule would have to bow to hers if they were to go in together. She smiled and was chirpy. *The sooner you go in, the sooner you can go home again, think of it that way.* She was right, of course, but going home early wasn't actually an inviting prospect. Time spent on his own in Søllerød dragged, and the Countess herself probably wouldn't be home until late.

He felt pitiful and was annoyed with himself for the same reason. He still hadn't properly rearranged his life after the heart attack, he thought to himself, and tried to think about something else instead.

Arriving at his office he found Pauline Berg there. She was lounging on the sofa in his annexe, as the little anteroom had swiftly been dubbed, watching TV. He dumped his briefcase on the desk and went in to join her. She switched it off and they said hello, though with little warmth. He studied her for a moment, still standing, long enough for her to look away. He sat down at the other end of the sofa.

'You look like a dosser.'

He was right. She was wearing a pair of ragged old jeans and a grey man's shirt whose sleeves and collar were all but threadbare. Her sandals were worn down, the leather in disrepair.

'If you want to work for me, you can come in properly dressed,' Simonsen told her.

'I think I've got a pair of UFO pants at the back of my wardrobe, I'll wear them tomorrow, if you like.'

Seeing that the threat cut no ice, she growled at him:

'I wear what I want.'

'No, you don't. As from tomorrow, you wear what *I* want. Otherwise, you're out of here. It's your choice.'

She flashed him an angry look, but remained seated. He handed her the case folder the Deputy Commissioner had given him.

'Jørgen Kramer Nielsen, born 1951, Copenhagen. Unmarried, worked as a postman. Lived in Hvidovre, died falling down a flight of stairs in his home somewhere round the twentieth of February, which is to say about six months ago. Exact time of death unknown, deceased not having been found until some considerable time after the event.'

21

Pauline Berg replied in a rather disinterested tone:

'Tell me about it. These things happen.'

He looked at her in annoyance before going on.

'On the afternoon of Friday the twenty-ninth of February, a downstairs neighbour finds Jørgen Kramer Nielsen's body on the shared staircase. The man's been dead for quite some time and the corpse has started to stink. Neighbour calls an ambulance, and we're brought in as a matter of routine. A patrol car with two officers arrives at the scene, then shortly afterwards the district medical officer as well. He sends the two officers away, investigates the circumstances of death and writes out a certificate saying Jørgen Kramer Nielsen broke his neck in an accident falling down the stairs. In other words: no criminal police, no forensics, no pathology, just away to the morgue with him and then into a coffin.'

'What a tosser.'

'Indeed. But there's an explanation. The district medical officer came straight from a slap-up dinner with the lads, stinking like a distillery. He could hardly walk straight.'

'You mean, he was pissed?'

'As a newt. No contention about that. So far, so bad. But it gets worse. One of the two officers called to the scene, a Hans Ulrik Gormsen…'

He sent her an enquiring glance to see if she knew him. She shook her head and Simonsen carried on.

'This Hans Ulrik Gormsen says he had an idea that Nielsen had been murdered the moment he set eyes on him. And I'm afraid that's a quote. His suspicion was due to the position of the body, along with the fact that the staircase down which Jørgen Kramer Nielsen ostensibly fell is only seven stairs. He took a number of photos of the body and the stairs with his mobile, measured up as well as he could and questioned the neighbour, apparently having cause to threaten the man with arrest. The neighbour, by the way, is a priest. It seems he wound up the medical officer the wrong way, too, which might be one reason why the case was closed so peremptorily.'

'I'm with you, but where do we come in? It may be a mess, I'll give you that, but people found dead with a broken neck at the bottom of a flight of stairs have only very rarely been murdered.'

'True, nor is there any indication that Jørgen Kramer Nielsen was either, which Hans Ulrik Gormsen, to his great resentment, was told in no uncertain terms when he presented his photos to the police prosecutor. After that, nothing more happened for a month or so, until Gormsen moved on to a new job as security executive in a private company. At this point he decides to pick up the postman case, as he calls it, and lay it out for his mother-in-law. And she was a lot easier to convince that a crime had taken place. Unfortunately, his mother-in-law happens to be vice-chairman of the Parliamentary Legal Affairs Committee.'

'Oh, Christ.'

'My sentiments exactly, but the bottom line is we're expected to spend a couple of days, maybe a week, on Kramer Nielsen's death, after which we write out a report confirming the man died as a result of a simple domestic fall.'

Pauline Berg guessed:

'A report the Deputy Commissioner can present to Gormsen's mother-in-law with a clean conscience?'

'Exactly, yes. Are you still interested? Or do you want me to tell Arne you'd rather be on the school shooting with everyone else?'

Pauline threw her hands up in annoyance.

'The fat kid? No, thanks. That case is too depressing.'

She ignored Simonsen's admonishment to *be respectful* and stared into space for a while. He waited patiently, and eventually she spoke.

'What do we know about this postman? Any previous?'

Simonsen shook his head.

'We know practically nothing apart from this. It's all we've got.'

He handed her a sheet of paper from the folder.

On 5 March 1996, Jørgen Kramer Nielsen was attacked and beaten up on his postal route. His assailant was a forty-year-old fitter from Rødovre, no criminal record. Jørgen Kramer Nielsen had the stuffing knocked out of him, and the attack only stopped because a patrol car happened by. He was taken to Hvidovre Hospital, but afterwards neither man wished to make a statement, and Nielsen had refused to press charges. The assailant was detained, only to be released later.

Pauline Berg read the report through twice. It was quickly done. She handed it back and said in a wistful tone:

'The others see me as some kind of untouchable. The Countess doesn't know where to look, and no one really knows what to do with me. They treat me like an unwanted gift, something no one really likes, but which can't be discarded either. What I'd really like is a case of my own, but Arne won't give me one.'

'I see.'

'When I get up each morning I feel like it's going to be the last day of my life. And as for the clothes... well, I don't like my old stuff any more, the stuff I wore before... before it happened. It makes me afraid.'

'Then wear your uniform. I can't take you anywhere in that get-up.'

All of a sudden, she smiled at him warmly. Optimistically, almost.

'OK, so tell me where to start.'

Arne Pedersen had allocated considerable resources to uncovering what might have been behind the shooting at the Marmorgade school, and their efforts quickly paid off.

The teacher who had been killed turned out to have been an *arsehole*, as Pedersen himself put it. Tobias Juul was thirty-two years old with a sideline in drug-dealing, supplying mainly to young teenage girls, among them a couple from the Year 11 class he taught. A search of his home revealed a wide selection of narcotics: ecstasy, amphetamine, methamphetamine and cocaine. But he was involved in other shady activities too. Once his girls, as he had referred to them, had become sufficiently addicted and had worked up a sizeable debt, he exploited them sexually. First, for his own pleasure, then later as a money-maker.

Arne Pedersen informed Konrad Simonsen of his findings. Not because Simonsen was a part of the investigation, he wasn't, but more as a sparring partner, someone he could lean on. He elaborated on Tobias Juul.

'That said, it was all small-scale. Juul was no big fish.'

'So where does the shooting come in?'

'We could basically be dealing with a common-or-garden crime of passion. We're thinking that Robert Steen Hertz, the boy with the gun, might have been trying to help one of his classmates, a Maja Nørgaard. It seems she was one of Tobias Juul's girls, to stay in the vernacular. Hertz may have had a crush on her, but of course he'd never have stood a chance with all that weight he was carrying. Maybe he wanted to save her, or whatever you want to call it.'

'It sounds like you're closing in on a motive. What about the gun? Where did he get it from?'

'Good question. How does a sixteen-year-old Danish lad get hold of a nine-millimetre ArmyTocx SA-5 submachine gun? I've no idea, not yet. And your optimism as to the motive might still be a bit premature, I fear. These two girls, Maja Nørgaard being one, aren't helping us one little bit. Both of them are denying any knowledge of events at all. It doesn't matter what we're asking them, they haven't a clue, so they say. At the moment it's all uphill. The parents are backing them, of course, especially Maja Nørgaard's mother. She's even hired a solicitor. I'm telling you, she's a bloody nightmare, built like a barn and arrogant as hell. The truth of the matter is it's the mother who's obstructing the inquiry, but there's not a lot I can do about it. The only alternative is to give her the swerve and piece things together as best we can based on second-hand accounts.'

'Why is she being like that about it?'

'I don't know for sure, but most likely she's afraid word's going to get out. Her little diddums involved in drugs and prostitution. How the kid feels about it seems to be beside the point. Anyway, how's the postman case coming along?'

Pedersen chuckled as he asked this.

'It's coming along.'

'What about Pauline? Any problems there?'

'None whatsoever.'

Konrad Simonsen had begun with the priest, the downstairs neighbour of the deceased postman Jørgen Kramer Nielsen, partly so as to have a look at the house in which the death occurred, partly to speak to the witness whose statement he assumed to be the most reliable. It would give him something to write in his report.

The priest turned out to be an amicable sort, a man in his late thirties who guessed Simonsen's thoughts the moment he noticed the policeman's somewhat surprised expression on seeing his white dog collar.

'That's right, I'm Catholic. It always seems to throw people a bit if they aren't expecting it, so let me start by saying I don't bite.'

He laughed warmly. Konrad Simonsen laughed, too, and they shook hands.

The man's recollections of what had happened on 29 February were quickly dealt with. He had returned home from holiday to find his upstairs neighbour dead on the staircase. Simonsen moved on to the heart of the matter.

'And you're sure you didn't move the body or alter its position in any way before the ambulance arrived?'

'Why on earth would I do that? Jørgen was obviously dead, so there was nothing I could do.'

'Quite. What about the police officers who came? Did any of them change the way the body was lying compared to how you found him?'

'You mean, before the ambulance people took him away?'

'Of course.'

The priest thought back, before answering with some measure of uncertainty:

'The young detective placed a matchbox next to the head before taking photos with his mobile phone. To give an idea of relative dimensions, I suppose. I remember thinking it odd for him to have a matchbox at hand. I mean, who carries matches around with them these days? But he didn't touch the body.'

'You're sure of that?'

'Yes… yes, quite sure.'

'He wasn't a detective, by the way.'

'Well, that's a comfort.'

'My sentiment exactly. Is the front door usually kept locked?'

'Always.'

'Who's got a key?'

'I have, naturally. And my new tenants upstairs. Jørgen had as well, of course. Two sets, I imagine, though that would be a guess.'

'And no one else? A cleaner, anyone like that?'

'Not as far as I know.'

'Talking about cleaners, how often does the staircase get cleaned?'

'Once a fortnight. That's the agreement. We take turns, but… well, if you're thinking about forensic evidence, or whatever you call it, I'm afraid the stairs have been scrubbed more thoroughly twice since February. I'm sorry about that. First, I made rather a point of it myself, vacuuming and washing the carpet. The body could have been there for some time.'

He paused, seeming ill at ease. Konrad Simonsen leaned on him.

'And secondly?'

'Well, my new tenants said there was a smell. Or rather, no, that's a bit unfair. The woman thought there was, but only after she heard what had happened to Jørgen. Her husband and I shared the cost of getting professional cleaners in. They came and gave it the works. It was mostly to be neighbourly, if you understand?'

Konrad Simonsen sighed.

'It can't be helped. Do you mind if I have a look round on my own?'

The priest didn't mind at all.

The entrance looked like entrances do. The main door opened on to a small, tiled hall, from which three steps led up to the first landing where the door to the ground-floor flat was. The staircase then continued up to the next landing, where Jørgen Kramer Nielsen's body had been found. Finally, there was a short flight up to the top landing, where there was a wardrobe and the door to the upstairs flat. The whole lot was carpeted, except for the tiles inside the entrance. The banister looked like it had just been painted, in shiny gloss, while the walls appeared white and pristine, hung with a couple of nondescript framed reproductions by an artist Simonsen didn't recognise. A large, white glass pendant lamp hanging from the upstairs ceiling could have done with a good dusting, and the floor-level window on the upper landing, with its leaded, stained-glass panes, broke with the general impression of unerring suburban chic. Konrad Simonsen walked slowly up and down a few times, trying to focus his mind and senses, though with no other return than sore legs.

* * *

Pauline Berg had looked into Jørgen Kramer Nielsen's personal documents, an inquiry that had not been unproblematic. She reported back to Simonsen:

'His stuff was in store with Express Move, at their premises on Peter Adlers Vej out in Hvidovre. Only when I got there, they were being picked up by a buyer. I had to threaten them with all sorts, then whizz out to the probate court in Glostrup and get the receiver to tie up his estate again. You can imagine the red tape, and you might as well prepare yourself for complaints coming in, since I had to give them a mouthful in court and else-where before they gave in. But that's the fault of the Deputy Commissioner, she should have told them long since.'

'Did you give her a mouthful, too?'

'Yeah, but she wasn't the worst. Those dithering suits in the probate court were. Would you believe I found his will? Or at least a yellowed envelope that said *Last Will and Testament* on it. Don't ask me what was inside, because I left it unopened. Though not without ringing the receiver and telling him what I'd unearthed. Was he glad, do you think? Or even just a bit embar-rassed by his own carelessness? Was he hell. And what's more, he even had the cheek to expect me to drive over and drop it off with him in Glostrup. I told him where he could shove it, of course.'

'Of course you did.'

She smiled, sheepishly.

'So I had an angry day, I can see that now. But what would you have done?'

'Dropped it off with him in Glostrup. But what I would have done is beside the point. I'll deal with it, if anyone kicks up a fuss. Since you've put on some decent clothes for a change.'

Pauline Berg was in a neat, knee-length skirt and a simple poloneck sweater, both in shades of grey and eminently suitable had she been a librarian in her fifties, but definitely an improvement on yesterday's get-up. She smiled again, wryly this time, he thought.

'Did you come up with anything interesting?' he asked.

'There were far too many documents to get through in any detail, so basically all I could do was skim the surface. He had like a million exercise books with all sorts of sums in them… calculations, I think it must have been a hobby of his. He kept all his receipts from the local Netto as well, little bundles going back eleven years, with two figures written on the back. One for the amount and another that didn't make any immediate sense. Apart from that, I don't think there was anything interesting at all. But then we weren't really looking for that, were we?'

He agreed: no, that wasn't really what they were doing. She went on, hesitantly this time:

'There's always something you wonder about, though, isn't there? I suppose it's just people, isn't it?'

Jørgen Kramer Nielsen owned an old-fashioned camera, for instance, and an enlarger with various equipment belonging to it, but she hadn't come across any developed photographs at all. Moreover, from his bills she could see that Nielsen had bought pay-as-you-go SIMs, and there was a phone charger, too, but no phone. Her take was that it had probably found its way accidentally-on-purpose into the funeral director's pocket. Simonsen was doubtful, but chose not to pursue the matter.

'Anything else?'

'He used a lot of window cleaner, looking at his Netto receipts. No idea why, anyone would think he had a greenhouse, which he didn't. He had money, though, lots of it. At the time of his death there was almost one point seven million kroner in his account, money he got out of selling the house to the priest in nineteen ninety-nine. No unusual withdrawals or credits the last five years, though, apart perhaps from four hundred and forty kroner each month to his local Catholic parish.'

'He was Catholic, then?'

Pauline nodded and looked at her watch.

'I'm sorry, but I've got an appointment with my therapist in half an hour and you'll be getting picked up soon anyway. What do you want me to do on Monday?'

He had no idea and promised to call. After she went, he looked at his own watch and realised she was right, it was time for him to be collected. They took turns driving him home, maybe they had a roster worked out, he didn't know and hadn't asked, but he hoped it was going to be the Countess today. They weren't seeing that much of each other at the moment; she worked until late and had often already gone in again by the time he woke up in the mornings. Now it was the weekend, but most likely she still had her hands full with the school shooting. He gave a sigh and looked forward to being allowed to drive a car again. And then there was a knock on the door, the appointed time, right on the dot. They were certainly looking after him. It was a young constable this time. Simonsen had never seen him before.

On the Monday afternoon, Simonsen wasted his time interviewing the two ambulance men who had removed the body of Jørgen Kramer Nielsen from the staircase in February. Tracing them took a while and the statements they made were of no use at all. A phone call to the doctor who'd written out the death certificate had likewise drawn a blank. He said he couldn't even remember the case, and Simonsen believed him. He was unable to get hold of Hans Ulrik Gormsen, and besides that there wasn't much more he could do that day. It was astonishing how quickly four hours could pass.

The next day, a delightful Tuesday with sunshine and clear blue skies, began with Simonsen sounding out Hans Ulrik Gormsen's former partner on the job. The female officer turned up looking spick and span in her uniform, with her cap under her left arm in a somewhat exaggerated display of correctness. She marched in and halted in the middle of his office, where she stood to attention like a tin soldier, sweating visibly, until he offered her a chair in which she then sat quite as rigidly and by the book as she had stood.

Simonsen asked her to outline what had happened, without expecting any other information than he already had. But then she mentioned a detail he realised he'd overlooked. It was about blood. Or rather, the lack of it.

'Well, he was just lying there dead, without any real blood or anything, just dead.'

'He hadn't bled at all?'

'Not really. I didn't see blood, as such.'

'As such?'

'Yes, sir.'

He felt the urge to shake her into a more relaxed posture, though it would hardly have been possible had he tried.

'Did you see something that resembled blood, but wasn't?'

It was a stupid question, but he couldn't think of anything better.

'No, sir, I didn't.'

'Try and close your eyes and think back to that staircase, then tell me what makes you think you saw something that wasn't blood *as such*.'

She closed her eyes, then said:

'Because there was a wound on one of his hands. Like an abrasion, only it hadn't bled. It was just the skin that had been grazed away, probably during his fall. You might be able to see it on the photos Hans Ulrik took with this phone. I'd definitely think so.'

Simonsen grabbed a ring binder from the shelf behind him, pulled out the printouts and saw that she was right. The abrasion on Kramer Nielsen's right hand was visible on about half the images. Rather clearly at that, once you knew it was there.

'May I open my eyes again, sir?'

'What? Oh, yes, of course. And thanks, you've been a great help.'

'Am I done?'

He saw how she almost trembled with nerves, her frightened eyes glued to the floor. He had never seen a police officer as tense before. He folded his hands in front of his chin, considering her for a few seconds, before saying:

'Yes, you're done.'

She was gone before he could say 'knife'. He called Pauline Berg and told her what the female officer had said.

Pauline Berg knew the officer in question and had worked with her before moving on to Homicide. When Berg and Simonsen met up the next day, she said:

'I don't get it. I've never seen her like that at all, nothing like.'

'Then it's a pity you weren't here, because I've never seen anything like it either. What did Melsing say anyway?'

He had asked Pauline to go over to the National Centre of Forensic Services and get the department's director, Kurt Melsing, to go through the photos of the dead postman, just to hear his immediate reaction. Pauline said:

'He grunted a bit and flicked through them, then he said there were all sorts of ways you could fall down a flight of stairs.'

'And that was it?'

'Just about. If we want it looked into properly, he said he'd have to send people out to the scene and would probably need the original photos... and besides that we'd have to wait six months. They've bought this software from the US that might be able to help us, but no one's really learned how to use it yet. You and Arne are to give him a ring if we want it doing officially.'

Simonsen shook his head.

'No, it doesn't matter.'

'I told him we probably didn't. Anyway, it's my turn to drive you home today and we'd better get going.'

They hardly spoke in the car, except for a few brief exchanges.

'They've found out how the fat kid got his hands on that submachine gun. Arne's going to give you a call later on.'

'Be more respectful. How many times do I have to tell you?'

Then shortly afterwards:

'Are you sure she was actually shaking? It doesn't sound like her at all,' Pauline observed.

'If I said she was shaking, she was shaking.'

'Do you mind if I have a word with her?'

Simonsen turned and looked at her.

'About Jørgen Kramer Nielsen's phone?'

'Yes.'

As Pauline Berg had said he would, Arne Pedersen called Simonsen that afternoon. He was half dozing, half daydreaming, and sounded miles away when he answered the phone.

'I didn't wake you, did I?' Pedersen asked.

'No. I was just thinking about a girl I used to know a long time ago.'

Pedersen apologised for having interrupted, a bit embarrassed by Simonsen's frankness. It wasn't like him to share that sort of thing. He told his boss about the submachine gun.

Robert Steen Hertz, the boy who had shot Tobias Juul at the school on Marmorgade, had a good friend in the States, a lad by the name of Russ Andrews, from Burlington, Vermont. Hertz had met him just over a year ago when his class had been over there in Year 10 on a school trip. It turned out both boys shared an interest in weaponry and were obsessed by guns. After Hertz returned home to Denmark, the two of them chatted regularly online, always on the subject of guns. In March, Russ Andrews turned eighteen and was legally able to purchase firearms in his home state, Vermont, together with Arizona and Alaska, under the most liberal gun laws in the United States. Andrews bought everything he could afford, including a submachine gun for his new friend. The problem of getting it to Denmark was overcome by Hertz first sending a parcel to a non-existent address in Burlington, a parcel weighing about the same as an ArmyTocx SA-5 and four boxes of ammunition. Approximately one month later, the postal service delivered the parcel back to Hertz, informing him that the address given was unknown. The same day, Hertz sent off a new parcel, this time by express delivery. This one contained the cardboard packaging from the first parcel, complete with all the appropriate stamps and return labels, and was addressed to Russ Andrews. On receipt, Andrews placed the gun and the ammunition in the packaging from the first parcel, which then for the second time was sent return to Denmark with a little help from Andrew's elder brother who worked for the private company Burlington's council had contracted to deliver the city's parcel post. Just as the boys had calculated, their parcel went through all security screenings without problems, having already been scanned once the first time around, and after about a month Robert Steen Hertz took delivery of his submachine gun, this time with his postman's admonition to take care better care with the address when sending parcels to the USA.

Arne Pedersen wrapped up the rather convoluted explanation:

'The rest was a piece of cake for Hertz. Using an Allen key, a metal file and a set of instructions off the internet, he modified the gun, converting it from semi-automatic to fully automatic.'

Konrad Simonsen grunted:

'The customs lot are going to have red ears.'

'It seems they're now changing their procedures about returns, here as well as in the States.'

'What about money? Or was the gun a present?'

'Dad's credit card. The father's a stockbroker at the dubious end of the scale. Profitable business by the looks of it, he didn't notice the money was gone from his account. Four thousand kroner. Peanuts, not worth bothering about. That's what he said, I kid you not.'

Simonsen thanked him for the information, though it could all easily have waited until the next day, and then hung on patiently for Pedersen to get round to the real reason he was calling. It took him a while, but when eventually he did get on to the subject it was, as Simonsen had guessed, to do with Maja Nørgaard, whose lack of co-operation had become a major hindrance. Without her help Hertz's motive would most likely never be identified with any certainty. Arne Pedersen had run out of bright ideas. Simonsen agreed to take part in a meeting about the problem the next day, though he found it hard to see what difference his presence would make.

Barely a week after starting back on the job after his illness, Konrad Simonsen finished up his report to the Deputy Commissioner on the death of Jørgen Kramer Nielsen. The unsurprising conclusion was that the postman's demise was due to an unfortunate fall rather than any criminal act. Simonsen printed it out and read it through one last time, making a couple of minor corrections before printing it out again and taking it with him to his meeting with Arne Pedersen. Handing it over, he said:

'It's your shop for the moment, do you want to send this in?'

Pedersen didn't.

'No, thanks. The less I have to do with her, the better. Better you submit it personally.'

He was referring to the Deputy Commissioner. Simonsen frowned, but refrained from passing comment.

Shortly afterwards, the others who were taking part in the meeting arrived: four officers, among them the Countess, all involved in the school shooting. Arne Pedersen kicked off, the subject being Maja Nørgaard, and his briefing was mainly for Simonsen's benefit.

'As you know, we're assuming Hertz's motive for the killings was simple jealousy. It seems the lad had a crush on Maja Nørgaard, who he'd known ever since they were in kindergarten together. She was the reason he carried on in Year 11 instead of going straight on to upper secondary, which was easily within his capabilities. The lad wasn't daft. He knew perfectly well he didn't stand a chance with her, so he made do with admiring her from a distance, if we can call it that. But then when she fell into Tobias Juul's clutches, as we're strongly assuming she did, the lad flipped his lid, though it did take him a while to suss it out, piecing information together bit by bit. Then...'

And that was as far as Arne Pedersen got. Pauline Berg burst into the room and interrupted him. In her hand was a mobile phone, which she held out in front of Konrad Simonsen without bothering at all about the disgruntled looks she received from around the table.

'It's Jørgen Kramer Nielsen's.'

Simonsen composed himself.

'Can't it wait, Pauline?'

She said nothing, but pressed a couple of keys until the display showed a photo of a young woman, blonde and smiling. She pressed again and a new image appeared. The same girl, standing in a living room, TV and chandelier visible behind her. She was naked, and this time she wasn't smiling.

'Maja Nørgaard?' Simonsen exclaimed in surprise.

'It was half question, half statement of fact. Pauline Berg confirmed:

'On Kramer Nielsen's mobile!'

It wasn't the first time the Homicide Department had seen apparently unconnected cases intersecting; far from it. It happened once in a while. The phone went round the table and Pauline Berg filled them in.

'These MMS photos were sent by Tobias Juul on the twenty-third of January this year with the accompanying text, *Sunday 10 a.m.* Nothing else. But I don't know where they were taken.'

The Countess, however, did.

'Tobias Juul's living room, I recognise the chandelier. But where did Juul and Kramer Nielsen know each other from?'

Arne Pedersen smiled broadly.

'I don't know, but what I do know is that Maja Nørgaard is going to be very eager indeed for her mother not to see these photos. All I need is a word with her on my own, without the solicitor or the mother present. How are we going to do that, Countess? You know her habits.'

The Countess was in no doubt.

'Friday between six and eight p.m. at the bar called the Goose's Eye. It's on Balle Allé, just opposite Enghave Station. She and her mates like to warm up there before going off clubbing in the city centre.'

Konrad Simonsen dropped his report discreetly into the wastepaper basket.

'I'll deal with her myself,' he offered.

There were no protests.

The Goose's Eye was a drinking establishment of the old-fashioned kind. A single room with a bar at one end and a row of flashing fruit machines at the other. The eight tables with accompanying chairs were of heavy, dark wood, and matched the room's head-height mahogany panelling. There were beer mats on all the tables, the majority sporting burn marks from dropped cigarettes. An antique copper ventilation fan on its last legs rotated on the ceiling, and the music was low, light-weight Danish pop.

The place was half empty, populated mainly by men in their mid-fifties and upwards, apart from three teenage girls who occupied the rear table furthest from the bar, clearly uninterested in mingling with the rest of the clientele.

Konrad Simonsen slid rather inelegantly on to a bar stool and ordered a beer once the bartender had dragged himself moment-arily away from the game of dice in which he was immersed with two somewhat worse for wear customers. Simonsen poured the contents of the bottle into his glass and took a cautious sip. If he was going to break with his regimen he certainly wasn't going to do it here.

Shortly afterwards, there was a lull in the game and Simonsen waved the bartender over. He was a man in his forties with ener-getic movements and a friendly smile, attentive and sober-looking. Simonsen flashed his ID discreetly, then leaned over the counter.

'Homicide Department,' he said in a low voice. 'I'm not inter-ested in bothering you or your business. Certainly not if you co-operate.'

The bartender didn't hesitate for a second.

'I'm co-operating.'

Simonsen nodded towards the girls at the back of the room.

'Not exactly your usual clientele.'

The bartender explained: the redhead's uncle had a half share in the place, which meant drinks on the slate, and cheaper at that.

'I'm going to go over to them in a second. When I do, can you make sure the two girls with their backs to us are shown the door?' Simonsen asked.

'Sure, if that's what you want.'

'I do, and I want them well out of the way, not hanging around outside.'

The bartender hesitated.

'I reckon all of them are under age. Your licence could be in jeopardy...'

Simonsen left the words hanging in the air, and the bartender capitulated with a smile.

'Well, out of the way it is, then.'

Understandably, the girls kicked up a fuss when Simonsen sat down on the spare chair at their table. Ignoring the insults they hurled at him, he studied Maja Nørgaard in silence and was glad she was seated against the wall. If she wanted to get out, she would have to crawl under the table. The rest of the customers watched what was going on, while the bartender kept his word and with a minimum of drama ushered the girl's two friends out on to the street and into a taxi.

Maja Nørgaard spoke first:

'Are you police?'

She was quick on the uptake. Simonsen showed her his ID.

'I'm only going to talk to you if my solicitor's with me.'

Jørgen Kramer Nielsen's mobile was ready in his inside pocket, all he had to do was press a single key to activate the display. He did so, pushed the phone across the table and waited. A moment passed before she hissed at him:

'Have you been slobbering over a picture of me, you old creep? How about getting a life instead?'

'You can go if you want, Maja. But I don't think your mum's going to be very pleased once she gets to know there's a photograph of you naked doing the rounds, to whet the appetites of old... creeps.'

'You dare!'

Simonsen kept his cool.

'I might. And then again, I might not. It's entirely up to you.'

He could tell she'd already caved in, she just didn't realise it herself yet. Her hand was shaking as she took a gulp of her

Breezer, Smirnoff Red Ice. He gestured to the bartender, who came to the table immediately.

'We'd like to swap these for a Coke and a mineral water.'

He indicated their glasses, and the bartender removed them. Maja Nørgaard didn't protest, but said in a feeble voice:

'What do you want me to do?'

'First I want you to talk to me, then I want you to talk to Arne Pedersen and the Coun... Nathalie von Rosen. You know them both already. And after that I want you to talk to a school counsellor. And in each instance I want you to tell not just the *truth*, but the *whole* truth.'

'And if I do, you won't show that photo to my mum?'

'If you do, I won't show that photo to your mum, that's correct.'

'What if you're lying and you show her anyway?'

'In that case I'm lying. All you can do is trust me.'

She thought about it for a second and accepted the logic.

'Why should I talk to that counsellor guy?'

'Because you drink too much, not to mention snorting a line or two when you can afford it. You keep all the wrong company, Maja. Moreover, if you need money, you prostitute yourself. That's why. And because you're seventeen and need help before your life really starts going wrong.'

Tears glistened in the corners of her eyes.

'Will I be punished?'

'That depends on what you've done. If you've done anything at all, that is. But to me you look like a young girl who needs help more than punishment. So what do you say? Yes or no?'

'Yes.'

He excused himself and went to the gents, informing her that she was free to go if she wanted. His aim was twofold: first, and most importantly, it meant he couldn't be accused at some later point of keeping her against her will, and secondly it gave her a chance to think. He didn't need a slash, so he splashed some water on his face,

41

dabbed himself with a couple of paper towels and counted to thirty. When he got back she was sitting where he'd left her, staring vaguely at the window. He sat down and went straight to the point:

'Jørgen Kramer Nielsen, Johannes Lindevej number twenty-seven, Hvidovre. Sunday, January the twenty-seventh, ten a.m.?'

Her reply was barely audible.

'It was the first time I was there on my own. Without Tobias, I mean. I was scared stiff.'

'Tobias Juul?'

'That's right. Until then, I'd only ever... tried it... at his place. He'd invite a friend of his round...'

She made air quotes on the word 'friend'.

'Or maybe two, but there were always two of us girls there. I had to let one of them get off with me, but I knew that. Afterwards, I got half the money and Tobias kept the other half for himself. I usually made a couple of thousand out of it, three if we were lucky. Sometimes he paid it in dope or coke, but he was always good with me and never tried to pull one over.'

That depended on the way you looked at it, Simonsen thought to himself. He went on in the same quiet tone:

'But with Jørgen Kramer Nielsen it was different?'

She nodded.

'He was paying six thousand and all I had to do was be there at home with him, watch TV, chat with him, eat... ordinary stuff, only with no clothes on. Then in the evening I could go home. That was it.'

'Is that what you did?'

'To begin with I wanted nothing to do with it. It sounded creepy, and he was old. But Tobias talked me into it and promised it was just a few photographs, nothing more. Jørgen wouldn't even touch me, and he kept all his clothes on, Tobias guaranteed he would. So eventually I gave in and went there.'

'Sunday the twenty-seventh of January, in the morning?'

'It sounds right.'

'Tell me what happened.'

'There's not much to tell. It didn't work out. He talked to me for a bit, only then he sent me away again. I was there less than half an hour.'

'Didn't he like you?'

'It wasn't his fault, really. He'd asked for someone over eighteen, but I was only sixteen at the time. Tobias told me to lie if he asked, so I did. I told him I was eighteen, in my second year at upper secondary, but he sussed me out straight away. Asked me about subjects and stuff, and I didn't know what to say, did I? So he sent me home. Not in any unpleasant way, he was quite nice, really. He gave me two thousand for my trouble and paid for a taxi on top.'

'Did he tell you why he wanted you to go around naked for him?'

'No, we never got round to it.'

'Did you get the impression Tobias Juul was procuring other girls for Jørgen Kramer Nielsen?'

'I think so. Otherwise he couldn't have known what he knew. But I'm not certain.'

'How did Tobias Juul and Jørgen Kramer Nielsen know each other, have you any idea?'

'Tobias once had a student job at the same post office where Jørgen worked as a postman. It's in Rødovre, I think. But that was a long time ago.'

It was true, so the girl was probably telling the truth. Simonsen stared into her eyes before speaking again.

'Jørgen Kramer Nielsen was arrested yesterday. We suspect him of carrying out at least seven rather brutal attacks on young girls.'

The blood drained from Maja's face. She went white as a sheet. He knew it was the sort of reaction that was impossible to fake. Once she'd digested the announcement, she said:

43

'I won't say he hurt me, because he didn't.'

Konrad Simonsen told her what had really happened then, explaining why he had needed to test her and apologising. Then he asked her another batch of questions, the answers to which left him none the wiser.

He wrapped up proceedings by praising her.

'Well done, Maja. Two more interviews, and that's it. If you're as truthful then, everything will be all right.'

'I'll do my best, but… can you stay here when the others come?'

'They're not coming here, you're coming with me to Police HQ. No need to be nervous, it's all going to be nice and relaxed. Perhaps we should get you something to eat on the way. And, yes, I'll be there, if you want.'

On their way to HQ Maja was silent, speaking only twice, the first time when they returned to the car with their brown paper bags from McDonald's.

'I really did think he shot all my classmates. I was convinced I saw him do it with my own eyes, mow them down like that. But it didn't happen, did it? I can't understand it.'

Simonsen believed her. He felt sure she had been in no doubt that she'd seen what she'd told them she had just after getting out of the classroom at Marmorgades Skole. Under extreme pressure the brain often creates its own versions of reality. He tried to explain it to her, but couldn't.

'Was that why you shot Robert? Because of what I said?'

'Absolutely not. We shot Robert Steen Hertz because there was no other way. It had nothing to do with you.'

He squinted at her and could tell she didn't believe him. She changed the subject.

'I'm sorry about what I called you in the pub.'

He dismissed it. He'd been called worse.

After they got in the car, Maja spoke again.

'There's something I forgot to say before.'

'Go on.'

'It's a bit... I don't know. Maybe I should wait.'

She blushed slightly, and he guessed:

'Until there's a woman you can speak to?'

'Yes. Well, no, it's all right, I suppose. When I went to Jørgen's, when he took my photo, it was important I was *hairy*. He didn't want me shaved, if you understand what I'm saying. We had to wait until... well, until I was.'

'Interesting,' said Simonsen, and meant it.

No one in Homicide was in any doubt that Maja Nørgaard was not the only girl Tobias Juul had run as a prostitute, nor were they under any illusion that she was the only girl Jørgen Kramer Nielsen had met. In that respect, the seemingly wanton attack on the postman in 1996 had perhaps not been entirely without motive after all.

Konrad Simonsen spotted the woman he was looking for on a bench at the far end of the children's playground, where she sat engrossed in a women's magazine, rocking a pram with her free hand. Now and then, she glanced across and smiled at a little girl lying flat on her stomach in the sandpit, energetically digging a hole with a toy spade.

Simonsen sat down on the bench next to her. The woman looked up for a second, then carried on reading. Simonsen searched his inside pocket for his ID, discovering to his annoyance that he must have left it behind. He introduced himself cautiously and explained:

'I'm afraid I've forgotten my badge.'

The woman folded her magazine and tossed it on to the rack under the pram, slid off her glasses and meticulously put them away in a case she took from her bag, before expelling a deep sigh and answering him.

'I've seen you on TV. This is about Tobias, I suppose?'

'Partly, yes.'

'Tobias Juul was the most despicable person I've ever met. It took me years to get over him. It still made me sad, though, when I saw he was dead. It's odd, having hated him so much.'

'When did you know him?'

'It's a long time ago now, more than ten years. I was seventeen when I moved in with him, and I'm twenty-nine now, so what's that… twelve years? Will my husband have to know about… back then? I'd rather he didn't.'

'I can give you a guarantee of discretion, nothing to worry about. You lived together, you and Tobias?'

'For two years, yes. Unofficially, though. I was still registered as living with my parents. How did you find me anyway?'

'I guessed. Your father attacked a postman on the fifth of March 1996.'

'Yes, Jørgen Nielsen, that poor man. It was terrible, and all my fault. He died six months ago, by the way. I still think about him sometimes.'

Simonsen informed her briefly of the circumstances and then held back, allowing her to tell the story in her own words. Her tale was in many respects the same as Maja Nørgaard's, apart from the fact that Jørgen Kramer Nielsen hadn't rejected her. She had visited him regularly for two years, always on the last Sunday of every other month, taking home four thousand kroner each time, until her father happened to get wind of what was going on.

'How did he find out?' Simonsen asked.

'A neighbour. An old gossip with eyes on stalks. She's dead, too, now.'

'And all you had to do was spend time with him, with no clothes on?'

'That was all there was to it. I could do what I wanted while I was there, and I soon got used to being naked. Tobias had me

46

doing all sorts of things elsewhere, but this was nothing. It was a bit cold at times, but that was the only uncomfortable thing about it.'

'Didn't he ever make a pass at you?'

'Never. And he wasn't ever dirty, either, though obviously it must have been sexual for him in some way.'

'Did you ever ask why? I mean, you must have got to know each other in some way.'

'We did, yes. He bought me presents, for my birthday and Christmas. He was sweet. But no, I never asked him what he got out of my being there. He did show me the loft, though, one of the last times I was there. I sort of worked it out then. I think I was a kind of surrogate for the girl up there, even if he never told me about her. The loft was his big secret and I had to promise never to tell anyone about it. I never did either, until now. But you'll know all about that, won't you?

Simonsen called the priest as soon as he left the playground, then ordered a taxi.

Forty-five minutes later he was at the house where Jørgen Kramer Nielsen had lived. The priest led him up the stairs and into the first-floor flat while he explained:

'It took us a while to find the trapdoor after your call. The man who lives here now gave me a hand, but he had to get off to work before you came. We were beginning to think there was no access, but then eventually we found it. Jørgen fitted it to look like an ordinary ceiling tile in the bathroom. I was the first to go up, and as soon as I saw what he'd done, I thought I'd better come back down again and wait until you got here.'

Entering the loft was an overwhelming experience. Konrad Simonsen had never seen anything like it and he felt oddly alien as he stepped cautiously into the room. After a couple of steps he halted, wondering quite ridiculously if he should remove his shoes, seeing himself as what he was: a timorous intruder, a voyeur, forcing his way into a dead man's soul.

The room was clad with mirrors. Small, rectangular bevelled mirrors, each no more than a handspan, meticulously covering all the surfaces: the long, sloping side walls of the roof, the two end walls and the floor. Below the ridge beam, the harsh illumination of fluorescent lighting was an endless reflection, avidly reproducing the figure of anyone who ventured inside. There were no windows or furniture.

But most captivating were the photographs. He counted them, as if in some way to hold his own. There were eighteen in total, all poster-sized enlargements, all exactly dimensioned, in width and height, so as to cover the same number of mirrors to the millimetre. The subject was the same, and yet each picture was unique. A lifelong variation over the same enthralling theme: shimmering mountain peaks beneath a cold, ice-blue sky, bathed in the brightest, eternally sparkling sunlight. And then the girl. Everywhere the girl. This was her room. Her pretty face was on every poster, merged to perfection with the sky, from where, as if according to mood, she could play hide-and-seek with her beholder. Now she was visibly smiling; now, by the slightest movement of his head, vanishing into the clouds, only to peep out again in one of her countless reflections.

Stepping closer he could see that each poster was made up of several photographs, but the transitions between them were so seamless he had to focus in order to see the joins, even at a distance of mere centimetres. Here, too, was the secret behind the girl's compelling gaze, that seen from other angles seemed to alternate so irresistibly with the cold rays of the sun: dozens of tiny holes pierced the paper, allowing the mirror behind to lend her eyes the quality of diamond dust sparkling in her pupils.

Konrad Simonsen closed his own and for a moment felt himself returned to a time long since past. Then he emerged once again into the present and spoke aloud.

'And who might you be? I wonder.'

CHAPTER 2

The discovery of the photographs in the loft was naturally of interest to Konrad Simonsen in his role as head of investigation on a case he too had gradually begun to think of as the *postman case*. But at the same time, the images of the girl had a positive personal effect on Simonsen in as much as she ousted another, that since his operation had tormented him more than he had been willing to acknowledge.

His daughter Anna Mia and the Countess had been with him as he stared at the screen and watched while the surgeon, whose name was Shears, widened Simonsen's obstructed coronary arteries. It was a film he did not wish to see repeated: an invasive body poking about inside his heart, steered by two foreign hands, the ultimate surrender of control. He sincerely hoped his next heart attack would be swift and without warning: bang, and then dead. It was a scenario much preferable to the intravascular meddlings of Dr Shears.

Some days later, the same physician again took Simonsen's life in his well-manicured hands, albeit verbally, taking his time to turn over every stone of his misfortune, eagerly supplemented by cues from the Countess and Anna Mia. Most of it was lost on

Simonsen, but the long, foreboding words stuck: *damage to the rear wall, balloon catheter, collapse of the coronary arteries, restricted blood circulation, chronic obstructive lung disease, diabetes diagnosis, drug dosage, period of convalescence.* He had hoped for some remote Latin terminology, that unfortunately was unforthcoming. Anna Mia wrote down the list of horrors, while the Countess discussed them with the doctor, nodding earnestly when he spoke, then bombarding him with new questions. Simonsen himself said nothing. He sat in a stupid wheelchair, in a dressing gown. Who could be rational in a dressing gown? Besides, he needed time for it all to sink in. If he even had more time.

As a farewell token he was presented with a highly illustrative colour photograph of his formerly fatally decrepit arteries, readily interpreted by his physician, whose biro pointed out to him what was living tissue and what was dead. The image appeared to show a poorly woven rag mat in shades of red and black, marred by numerous little blue flaws, treacherous calcium crystals patiently accumulating, until one day they were ready to shut down his life.

Ever since, the rag-mat image had regularly returned to haunt him and plunge him into the darkest of moods. It was particularly bad before sleep and he would have to contain his urge to go downstairs and speak to the Countess about it. He kept quiet – pathetic was the last thing he wanted to be, and what good did talk ever do? Now the problem had solved itself all of a sudden: he no longer slept with the rag mat foremost in his mind, but with the image of the girl in the postman's shrine of mirrors, wondering who she might be, and what she wanted him for. It was a definite improvement.

The investigation was in a state of limbo.

Jørgen Kramer Nielsen paying young girls to walk about his flat naked and his turning his loft into some weird hall of mirrors were sufficient grounds for Simonsen to put off handing in his routine report to the Deputy Commissioner. But what they had discovered was far from enough to justify a request for resources to conduct a full-scale investigation, one that included anyone besides Simonsen himself and Pauline Berg. There was still nothing to suggest that the postman's death was the result of a crime. Simonsen would have to wait for the forensics report and Kurt Melsing's take on the mobile photos showing the position of the body on the stairs before he reached a conclusion on that, and neither of them was even remotely on the horizon. The case was hardly a priority, which for Konrad Simonsen was an unfamiliar state of affairs he kept telling himself was a good thing. Nonetheless he found himself annoyed by it. He tried to give things a nudge in the right direction one day in Arne Pedersen's office, where they chatted for a few minutes about nothing very much until Simonsen casually said:

'By the way, do you think you could give Melsing a ring and get him to have a look at my postman? I'm stuck before I get an answer out of him.'

Arne Pedersen laughed in his face and refused point blank.

'Would you, in my position?'

Simonsen had gone away again, feeling restless and in a bit of a sulk. And, as if to make matters worse, he had bumped into the Countess in the corridor. He grumbled about it, without really intending to, and she recommended he take a couple of days' holiday, before hurrying off again.

Today's workload consisted of interviewing Hans Ulrik Gormsen, which took all of fifteen minutes and turned up less than zero, Gormsen's mobile having died a watery death in his toilet bowl since he'd used it to photograph the dead postman. Forensics would have to make do with the printouts they already had. Apart from that, Gormsen's statement matched the others Simonsen had taken in the case. But the man was unbearably annoying, with a superior, know-it-all attitude, so once it became clear he had nothing to add to the investigation, Simonsen thanked him half-heartedly and hoped never to see him again.

Afterwards, he called Pauline. He'd got her compiling a profile of Jørgen Kramer Nielsen and had left her to get on with it. She was far from done but obviously glad he'd called. Which was a relief, since he'd feared the opposite. He glanced at his wrist watch and noted that he wasn't due to be picked up for another two hours.

On the Saturday Simonsen went for his daily walk, this time with his daughter. Anna Mia was in buoyant mood. Both of them wore tracksuits and trainers. The September rain fell, warm and dusty, while the neighbourhood seemed to have gone into hibernation. A battered Chevrolet with four youngsters in it passed them slowly, breaking the listless silence with a series of whoops and toots on the horn. Anna Mia waved at them cheerfully and they returned the gesture before speeding up, the screech of tyres ruffling the listless afternoon.

'I like exercising with you. I've been looking forward to this,' said Simonsen's daughter.

Her high spirits were infectious: Simonsen smiled. He, too, had started to grow fond of his walks, if only because it was the one time of day he didn't miss smoking. Even when he slept he wanted a cigarette. At least, that's how it felt.

'It's nothing for you... you're young, fit and sensible.'

'Every little helps. Have you noticed how it gets easier?'

'Not really, no.'

'When you first started, you couldn't walk and talk at the same time. You're not snorting like a pig any more, either.'

She was right. He hadn't thought about it like that.

'Pigs don't snort. Horses snort, pigs grunt.'

'And heads of Homicide Departments.'

'Not this one.'

'Wait till we start jogging! It'll be great, I promise. Anyway, tell me how things are getting on at work. Are you glad to be back? Has the wicked witch given you a decent case to be getting on with?'

As a matter of routine he reminded her to speak respectfully of the Deputy Commissioner, then without enthusiasm told her about his postman case.

'A killing, wow! I thought she was going to ease you in gently. Has it been in the papers?'

'It happened more than six months ago, and he probably wasn't killed at all. That's what I've got to find out, if I can.'

'So now you're gathering evidence to have him dug up?'

'That's not quite how it works. Anyway, he was cremated.'

'It sounds like you've quite a job on your hands then. How are you going about it?'

'We're just trying to gain an overall picture at the moment.'

'Dad, who's Rita?'

Characteristically, she'd changed the subject quite without warning. Her mother had had the same habit, which he'd found highly annoying back then, but with Anna Mia it didn't bother him.

'Why do you ask, kid?'

'Can't you stop calling me that? If you must call me something, try my name.'

She was right. It was childish, and Anna Mia was no longer a child but in fact in her third year at police college, having previously studied for a legal degree at university, though she had not completed it. Now she was part of a trial scheme where candidates received time and support to study law alongside completing their police training. And besides that, she had a sensible approach to life. Too sensible, he sometimes thought.

'Oh, I am sorry,' he said. 'And why do you ask, little diddums?'

She ignored his teasing.

53

'Nathalie says you called her Rita when you woke up after the op.'

Anna Mia always called the Countess by her proper name. She was the only one he knew who did. He tried to evade the question with a non-committal grunt.

'I'm sure Nathalie's going to ask you herself at some point.'

'I don't doubt it.'

A bit later his daughter had another go:

'How come you never talk about yourself? I mean, really talk about yourself. Your feelings.'

'I feel like having a cigarette, and besides that I feel a loathing towards everything low-fat, free-range or organic.'

'Thanks for nothing! You're incorrigible.'

'Rubbish. You don't tell me about your sweethearts.'

He could have bitten his tongue off, but the damage was done. Exercise and thinking at the same time were clearly incompatible. Anna Mia responded like a spring suddenly released:

'You mean, you've got two on the go? Blimey, I never saw that coming.'

'Come off it, I'm not even sure I've got one, never mind two. Forty years ago I knew someone called Rita, and that's all there is to it. I can't remember anything other than that, and it doesn't mean a thing.'

It was lies, all of it. He had thought about her every single day since he woke up from the operation, as if a door had suddenly opened in his heart after being closed for an eternity. To begin with, he'd thought she would leave him again, but it was almost the opposite. And after seeing the girl in the postman's loft, thoughts of Rita had become even more prominent in his mind, as if the two women somehow fed off each other. Her face seemed newly clear in his memory: a smatter of freckles; her lively eyes and turned-up nose; her teeth, ever so slightly wonky. If he was lucky, he and Rita would again come together in his dreams.

His answer seemed momentarily to satisfy Anna Mia, only then she added matter-of-factly:

'If you can remember her name, you can remember more. She must have made quite an impression for you to wake up pining for her forty years on.'

He parried further questions by pleading a feeble memory, and eventually his daughter gave up in annoyance. He defended himself using the same argument as before:

'You don't talk about *your* sweethearts.'

They walked on for a while without speaking, until suddenly she said:

'I met this student teacher, Kim, in the winter holiday. Tall, great figure, nice little bum, very musical movements. We went skiing together at...'

He put his hands to his ears.

'I don't want to know about him.'

She raised her voice:

'Who said it was a him?'

'You could find yourself a shop dummy for all I care, I still don't want to know.'

His daily exercise was over, and Anna Mia turned the conversation back to work.

'That case of yours sounds boring. But what about the people in Homicide, were they glad to see you back?'

'I'm sorry if my work doesn't entertain you. When I meet this postman in the afterlife, I'll tell him his death was boring.'

'You shouldn't joke about things like that, Dad.'

Anna Mia halted, as did he, regretfully.

'It makes me really sad to think about someone dying like that.'

'I'm sorry, I wasn't thinking. I was just defending myself, that's all. It's hard sometimes. It feels like there was no transition. One minute I was lying there, struggling to come round. The next I'm here, needing all sorts of help. Everything's new and different now... I don't know how to explain it... I think I'd been expecting a break, only I never got one.'

'You must be glad of the help you're getting from your colleagues?'

'I am, yes. I'd never have got through it without them. It chokes me up, thinking about it sometimes. The only thing is, I can't show it. I never learned how.'

'I think you're getting there.'

'Easy enough for you to say. When I was your age I never needed help from anyone, ever.'

'Now you're mixing things up. You just need someone to love, that's all.'

'I've got someone to love.'

'Two, then.'

They held hands up the garden path of the Countess's mansion. The path was narrow, but stepping on the grass was forbidden. Not that he knew why, it just was. Simonsen and Anna Mia jostled for position like children playing. Eventually, she nipped in front, one step ahead, but without letting go of his hand.

On Tuesday Pauline briefed him on what she had dug up on Jørgen Kramer Nielsen. It wasn't much, and most probably a waste of time and effort. Simonsen found it hard to concentrate on her presentation, which wasn't particularly well structured. She went up to the whiteboard and wrote two words in her hand-writing, fussy and over-particular: *Mathematics* and *Photography*. She drew an oval around each, then said:

'I'm not going out to that storage facility again. It's scary.'

'You don't have to, then.'

She stood for a moment, staring into space. Simonsen wondered if he should say something, tell her he understood her reaction, comfort her or something. But he didn't need to: she picked up the thread herself.

Most of the books Jørgen Kramer Nielsen had left were about maths or related subjects. His many exercise books were filled with mathematical puzzles he'd solved, meticulously recorded in the old-fashioned way using a fountain pen and blotting paper. Mostly it was differential equations, probability calculus and analytic integrals. The exercise books were from the bookshop at the Butikstorv on Hvidovrevej, where the owner remembered him. The look of them changed from time to time for sales purposes, bringing the design up to date, and while the owner was reluctant to commit himself he reckoned the first of them dated back as far as the 1970s, if not before. He'd suggested Pauline get in touch with the manufacturer.

Besides the Hvidovre bookshop, she had been to the university and had shown the exercise books to a maths lecturer, who'd assessed Kramer Nielsen's work to be at about the same level as a capable undergraduate's. Clearly, he had felt no intellectual drive to expand his mathematical horizons, and over a span of almost forty years his abilities remained the same. His calculations were therefore best seen as a past-time, the equivalent of doing crosswords or solving jigsaw puzzles.

She ticked the *Mathematics* oval on the whiteboard. That was dealt with. Simonsen stifled a yawn, and she went on:

'Oh, I nearly forgot. Those Netto receipts with the figure on the back that I couldn't get a handle on. Remember them?'

'Of course I do, I'm not senile.'

She laughed, which felt like a release.

'So you say! Anyway, the figure turns out to be the length of the receipt in centimetres. Once a year he did a regression analysis of the total price of goods bought as on the receipts, and...'

She stopped, noticing the expression on Simonsen's face.

'It's not that interesting, is it?'

'No.'

She skipped it and moved on to her next point. The postman developed his own photos. He used to have a darkroom; she'd spoken to the fitter who'd installed it for him.

'It was nine years ago, when he moved up on to the first floor. Anyway, he was a regular customer at the photo shop on Hvidovrevej, just next door to the bookshop as it happens. The owner calls himself Photo-Mate.'

She told him how Photo-Mate and the postman used to talk regularly about photography and developing. She'd also drawn up a list of prices and dates relating to photo equipment Kramer Nielsen had purchased there in recent years. And then she ticked *Photography*, commenting half as a question, half as a statement of fact:

'That wasn't very good, I know.'

'No, it wasn't.'

'It's difficult when you're on your own.'

He agreed with her. Anyway, it was partly his fault, he ought to have given her a clear brief to work to. He just hadn't thought it necessary, though he didn't say as much. He looked at the whiteboard to see if he could squeeze any relevant information out of her uninspiring efforts. It wasn't easy. He asked her about the photography angle in respect to the girl and the landscapes in the loft, but Pauline it seemed hadn't any answers. Instead, he turned rather half-heartedly to her second point.

'Do you know when he graduated from upper secondary school?'

'No. Probably some time in the late sixties, I'd imagine.'

'What was his final mark in Maths? Any idea?'

'I'm afraid not. I didn't come across his exam certificate. I reckon he burned it.'

'Burned it? What on earth makes you think he'd do that?'

'We saw a film once in Social Studies... when *I* was in upper secondary, that is, and we were studying the sixties. There was one year when all the new graduates from the gymnasium schools burned their exam certificates on Kongens Nytorv in protest against something or other – the school system, Vietnam, or maybe to express their solidarity with the workers – what do I know? I've no idea what got into them. They were all stoned, I suppose. And they wouldn't wear the traditional student caps either.'

To his own surprise, Konrad Simonsen felt a twinge of annoyance at her negative views. What did she know about the sixties? She hadn't even been born then.

'See if you can find his exam certificate. Check out the Ministry of Education, or the National Archive. And what school did he go to? That shouldn't be too difficult to discover. I'd like a copy of his will, too.'

She jotted it all down, before asking:

'Is this just to give me something to do?'

'No, I've got this inkling...'

He let the words hang promisingly in the air, but in fact they weren't true. He had no inkling at all, and it *was* just to give her something to do, though strictly speaking that wasn't his responsibility. Nevertheless, Pauline refrained from further comment and instead asked if she could drive him home, much to his astonishment.

He accepted.

An hour later, as they went down to the car, she complained to him:

'I'd really like to have my own case. Like you, like everyone else.'

He made do with a nod and a grunt, though he could have said a whole lot more on the matter. Such as, the Homicide Department's cases were not handed out to please its employees, or that she had just displayed a complete lack of overview, which didn't exactly put her first in line to lead an investigation. Instead, he asked casually:

'How about a little detour and then a walk? There's something I want to see.'

She hesitated:

'It sounds good, only I'm not sure…'

'Roll on the day I can drive myself again.'

'Yeah, I understand that, it's just…'

Pauline stalled, willing to go along with his request as a friend, but clearly afraid of what the official consequences might be.

'You're not exactly following orders that much anyway at the moment, or so I've heard.'

'This is different.'

'Are you scared I'll drop dead?'

'Yes.'

He couldn't fault her honesty, at least.

'Listen, Pauline, it's not going to happen. Look at me. I haven't felt better in years.'

They both knew he was exaggerating.

'As long as it's no more than fifteen minutes then… and you're not to tell anyone. Not even the Countess. Especially not the Countess.'

'Scout's honour.'

Pauline followed his directions. They were lucky and found a parking spot. As they crossed Gothersgade she took him by the arm and didn't let go until they reached the other side. He let it pass without comment. They chatted as they walked along by the wrought-iron railings of the Kongens Have park.

'That's Rosenborg Castle, isn't it?'

She pointed back over her shoulder with her free hand, as though she could have meant just about any other structure.

'It is indeed.'

Then suddenly she said:

'You know I get panic attacks, don't you?'

'Yes. I don't imagine they're much fun, either.'

'No one can imagine anything who hasn't been through it themselves. It's terrible, but I've got these pills I always carry around with me. Truxal, 30 milligrams. When I take one of them I can sleep standing up after twenty minutes. The thing is, if I haven't got them on me I start panicking wondering if I'm going to panic, so I have to keep making sure about fifty times a day that I've got them on me. Literally.'

He guessed what she was angling for.

'And you want me to carry one of your pills around with me, just in case you need one when you're with me?'

'Would you?'

'Of course. I'll put one in my wallet, I've always got that on me.'

She handed him a little pellet of tinfoil.

'Can we just check before you put it away?'

He unfolded it carefully while she watched. The pill was black and it was there.

They carried on without talking for a bit, both finding it difficult to know where to start. Then Pauline asked:

'Where are we going anyway?'

They had just turned left down Kronprinsessegade and still had Kongens Have on their left-hand side.

'Nowhere, we're here now. Would you be kind enough to leave me on my own for a couple of minutes?'

Mystified, but asking no questions, she let go of his arm and Simonsen stepped up to the solid wrought-iron gate leading into the park. He gripped a bar of it gently in each hand and allowed his mind to drift.

Here it was that Rita had played guitar and sung for him one summer evening when it had seemed like they were the only two people in the entire city. She'd brought sandwiches and a rug, and he'd bought four bottles of beer. Her voice was enchanting, even if she couldn't play the guitar, and he'd been utterly besotted, on that evening especially. Her songs were always simple, melodious and in English:

Stop complaining, said the farmer,
who told you a calf to be?
Why don't you have wings to fly with,
Like the swallow so proud and free?

He tried to hum along, and she sang softly, so that he, too, might be heard. Afterwards, he cautiously asked what 'complaining' meant. She translated, but her overbearing smile hurt. She would soon graduate from the gymnasium, like all her friends, if they hadn't already begun to study at the university. They were better educated than he, all of them could look forward to greater opportunities in life, so why didn't they just stick in and study? It was beyond him.

And here it was that he and Rita had spoken for the last time too. He hadn't seen her since. They had kissed through the railings. He was in uniform and people stared: a policeman and a hippy kissing in public, far from done in those days. Her former friends sat on the other side, a little group of them, jeering and whistling. They were stoned, and she was too, he supposed, although she no longer had much to do with them. She had chosen another path, a political one, and had come to say goodbye to them. They had sat themselves down on the lawns only a few metres from the sign saying *Keep Off the Grass*, and there they had openly passed around their pipe. It was hopeless...

He tore himself away from his thoughts and went back to Pauline Berg, who again took him by the arm. He felt he should explain.
'It's a dream I've been having of late, something from the old days. It may sound odd, but it means something to me.'
'I don't think it's odd. Not in the slightest.'
'Thanks. It's nice to hear I'm normal.'

'Sometimes I dream in cartoons, or in black and white.'

'You should see a therapist.'

'I've got two, that should be enough.'

She gave him a shove with her hip. They laughed, and above them the sky was as cloudless and quite as tritely blue as it was meant to be on a late-summer afternoon in Kongens Have.

Two days later, the Centre of Forensic Services in Vanløse finally got round to Konrad Simonsen's case.

The abrasion on Jørgen Kramer Nielsen's hand was the primary topic when Simonsen eventually met Kurt Melsing in his office. The room itself was rather ordinary and could just as easily have belonged to Simonsen, but for the fact that the glass wall facing the centre's machine room, as it were, revealed what looked more like the kind of scene one might expect in a chemical laboratory than a venerable department of the National Police. Modern forensics was high-tech and demanded highly specialised knowledge and constant training. It was a standing joke among police officers that fingerprint experts were now called *dactyloscopists*, and how hard was that to get your tongue around? Despite the self-aggrandising new job titles, however, the help forensic science gave to police investigation could not be denied. It had increased tenfold over the last decade.

Without any superfluous chatter Kurt Melsing placed his guest in front of an oversized computer screen and hit the keys. Melsing was famously reliable in terms of the conclusions his department reached in any investigation, and quite as infamous for his total lack of communication skills. He began the briefing now by methodically displaying each of the photographs from Hans Ulrik Gormsen's mobile in turn, and for each image that appeared on the screen he stated a number. Like a caller in a bingo hall, only more systematic. At regular intervals he gazed fixedly in the direction of the glass wall. When at last he was done, having spent ten minutes telling Simonsen what he could have said in ten seconds, i.e. the unsurprising information that the hard-copy photos had now been digitalised, Melsing revealed the reason for his restlessness.

'I've got someone coming who'll help put you in the picture.'

Simonsen nodded and said nothing.

'I'm glad you're not dead,' Melsing added.

They both stared through the glass and waited.

At home in Søllerød later on, Simonsen mentioned Kurt Melsing's taciturn ways to the Countess. They were lying on the lawn, she with her head resting on his arm. It had gone numb, but he ignored the discomfort and told her about the interminable wait in Melsing's office.

'We just sat there, mute, until help arrived. It was barely five minutes, but it felt like an eternity.'

'Yes, he can be rather trying.'

'I like him, but he's a hard man to get along with. How he can head up a department of several hundred staff is beyond me. I mean, those forensics people are incisive and efficient while he... he can hardly utter his own name.'

'Now you're exaggerating.'

'What are you smiling about?'

'I can't say, you don't want us to talk about it yet.'

'Did Kurt come and see me when I was ill?'

'Yes.'

'Really?'

'Yes, really. You can't remember a thing, can you?'

'I remember going to work in the morning, and then I remember waking up in the hospital four days later. The rest is a black hole.'

'Most of the time you were asleep. Do you want me to tell you about it, or do you want to wait?'

'Maybe it's time.'

'We were at Poul Troulsen's leaving reception and you were standing holding a glass of wine and a sandwich. First you complained about pains in your chest and then, shortly afterwards, in your back. Then all of a sudden you started gasping for air, dropped your glass and sank to your knees. Later, the doctor said you'd had a massive myocardial infarction… or heart attack to the rest of us. You certainly created havoc at the reception, and I panicked, I'm afraid. Started to cry. Malte Borup too. Poul Troulsen even loosened his tie, and Arne Pedersen the same. You had everyone running around like hens. Everyone except Kurt Melsing. He upturned my handbag and found my mobile, then he climbed on to a table and shouted for everyone to shut up, in a booming voice that must have echoed all the way through HS. Then he called the emergency services, ordered an ambulance with coronary-care facilities and identified your symptoms as precisely as any doctor. In the meantime a Samaritan arrived and administered first aid.'

HS for Head Square, the Homicide Department's internal slang for Police HQ, so she was exaggerating, of course. The point she was making was obvious enough, though.

'Are you saying Kurt Melsing saved my life?'

'We'll never know for certain, but as soon as they got you in the ambulance they filled you full of anti-coagulants and something for the shock. It stabilised your condition.'

'And that was all down to Kurt Melsing?'

'Whose taciturnity would seem not to be a permanent affliction, which is my point here. He's even been eloquent in a number of other situations I can recall, though none quite as dramatic.'

Simonsen removed his arm and sat up, the Countess bumping her head on the ground as a result.

'Ouch, you could have warned me!'

'Sorry. I just feel embarrassed, that's all. I haven't even thanked him. He must think I'm the most ungrateful man in the world.'

'No, he doesn't. He knows full well you can't remember anything and that you've been wanting to wait a while before being put in the picture about what happened.'

'Well, that's something anyway. How does he know all that?' Simonsen lay down again.

'He phones regularly, to ask how you're getting on.'

'You never told me that.'

'You can't be put in the picture and left out at the same time! Where's your arm? And how did the meeting with him go, anyway? Did he give you anything significant?'

'He did, as it happens. And there's more to come, apparently.'

Once Melsing's spokesperson finally arrived, things got going. Melsing ran the computer and his young staff member did the vocals. Simonsen listened. They were a good double act.

'We've focused a lot on the abrasion on the back of the victim's right hand.'

Melsing clicked up an enlarged image on the screen.

'It was a good observation from your side, though at first we weren't really sure if it was going to be useful to us. We were wrong, though. As you know, mobile images are pretty limited in terms of quality, these ones especially so, having been scanned from printouts. Basically, that means we can't really zoom in on the hand in any way that's going to be profitable to us.'

'I'm with you. But information isn't created by enlargement, only made clearer, if it's there.'

'Exactly. But we've done something else instead that's almost as good. Using the matchbox as a reference, we can rotate and trans-pose objects in all three directions, then by a process called affine...'

Melsing interrupted gently.

'All the hands mapped together.'

He displayed the result.

Simonsen was impressed.

'Blimey.'

The mark on Jørgen Kramer Nielsen's hand was as clear as if it had been photographed from five centimetres away. Next to it, a close-up of the stair carpet had been inserted at a slightly distorted angle: smooth-faced sisal hemp with an easily recognisable granulated pattern. The weave of the carpet and the mark on the hand matched up, and Melsing's spokesman condensed the important points.

'This is irrefutable proof that the deceased had a fall down the stairs. Moreover, we're certain most of his body weight went down on that hand when he scraped it, otherwise it wouldn't have been as pronounced.'

Melsing interrupted again.

'It's not all good, though.'

His man elaborated:

'Unfortunately, we don't much care for the position of the body at the foot of the stairs. Or, more exactly, in our experience it sets off a lot of warning bells...'

This time it was Simonsen who cut him off.

'That's not very exact.'

Melsing smiled wryly, but his man wasn't thrown.

'No, of course not. What I mean is, experience has us wondering how Kramer Nielsen's body could end up in the position in which it was found, following a fall of not quite two running metres down a staircase with an approximate gradient of thirty degrees. Especially when he breaks his neck at the same time on his way down *and* manages to get his right arm under him and scrape the back of his hand against one of the steps. *And* in the direction of the knuckles rather than the other way round. If we knew what step he scraped himself on things would be a lot easier, but we haven't been able to work that out, seeing as the skin cells he must have left behind are all gone. Besides that, you've got to bear in mind that the most natural reaction of any living person in a fall is to put their hands out flat in front of them, to cushion the impact.'

'So Jørgen Kramer Nielsen could already have been dead when he hit the stairs?'

'Perhaps. But note that we're basing this on our experience, and that's not wholly scientific. Falling humans can react in all sorts of different ways, and this might be one of the more extreme examples we just haven't seen before and for that reason are unable to recognise.'

'In other words, you can't come to any solid conclusion?'

Both men smiled broadly. Kurt Melsing was the one to answer:

'Well, we might.'

'Go on.'

'Your intern's helping us. And you, too, you could say.'

'That needs explaining.'

Kurt Melsing clicked open an app and typed in some words before jabbing a finger towards the glass wall. Simonsen turned his head, and to his surprise saw Malte Borup stand up at the far end of the room and come towards them. Malte Borup was the Homicide Department's intern. He was supposed to be on holiday at the moment, but apparently had chosen to spend it here.

Malte came in, and Melsing's man addressed him.

'If you'd like to open the programme and prepare to demonstrate, I'll explain what it is you're working on.'

He turned to Konrad Simonsen and began talking before the young intern had a chance to respond.

'A couple of months ago we purchased some new software from the FBI. It's called a *Human Object Movement Simulator*, a bit of a tongue-twister, but a highly sophisticated and complex tool that can simulate human reactions to various stimuli in an astonishingly precise manner. It's the result of years of development work involving various branches of science, but first and foremost classical physics and physiology, and that's exactly what we need in this situation.'

He paused, presumably to breathe in, and Konrad Simonsen took advantage of the lull.

'But?'

'Correct, there is a *but*, and it's the time factor. The manual that comes with it runs to no less than eleven volumes, and we simply haven't had the time or resources yet to immerse ourselves in it. I'm off to Washington to receive instruction in October, but that's not much good to us at the moment in September. But then Malte offered to help, and I must say he's come a long way in a very short time indeed.'

'He's a good lad.'

'He certainly is. Now let's see how far he's got.'

Malte Borup had started up the software. A graphic depicting the staircase of Jørgen Kramer Nielsen's house appeared on the screen. Borup clicked the mouse and a dummy-like figure materialised at the top of the stairs. Melsing's man went on:

'It might not look like much, but the room and the dummy are correctly dimensioned, which has taken a lot of time to set up. The software can now allow the man to fall from any conceivable position, with or without human reactions underway. Moreover, we can simulate different kinds of external resistance the body might encounter before and during the fall. Make him fall forwards down the stairs, Malte.'

Malte Borup was transfixed.

'Er, I haven't got through all the manuals yet.'

'Never mind, all we want is the general impression.'

He clicked again, hesitantly this time. The dummy jumped into the air and smashed its head against the ceiling like a fly on speed.

'Like I said, I haven't got through all the manuals yet.'

Melsing wrapped things up:

'Later, Simon. Come back later, we'll give you a call.'

* * *

Later was a lot sooner than Simonsen had feared. Someone must have been putting in overtime. At any rate, three days later he was back at the Centre of Forensic Services and in his own car, the doctors finally having allowed him to drive again. Besides that, there was another little triumph that for the time being he was keeping to himself: he had run. Twenty metres, thirty perhaps, that same morning, between two cracked flagstones meticulously selected to be his starting and finishing lines, a brief and rather seamless change of pace during his walk. Slow and poorly co-ordinated, and yet unmistakably running. It had felt absolutely marvellous.

It was the forensic technician from the previous meeting who received him. Neither Malte Borup nor Kurt Melsing seemed to be around. Simonsen had been hoping for a clear-cut conclusion, which indeed was forthcoming, though not quite the way he had envisaged.

Melsing's man laid it out for him.

'We've tried endless variations, but the only thing we can make fit is this.'

He started up the software. The dummy's point of departure was still the top of the stairs, only this time it wasn't alone. Another dummy grabbed it from behind, crooking its arm around the first one's neck and breaking it with a single twist. The effect was amazingly lifelike. The dead figure was then shoved backwards down the stairs, falling limply like a sack of potatoes. On its way down it scraped its hand in a brief slow-motion sequence before landing seven stairs down in the position familiar to Simonsen from Hans Ulrik Gormsen's photos.

They watched the animation three times before Simonsen rather solemnly asked:

'Are you absolutely certain about this?'

'Ninety-nine per cent.'

'Why not a hundred?'

'In the version you've just seen, the victim receives a pretty hard shove down the stairs. What we don't understand is why his assailant didn't just let go if Kramer Nielsen was dead. But it doesn't matter how we do this, the victim has to be lifeless, has to have had his neck broken first and has to fall backwards for us to get him to land in the position in the photos. As well as, like I said, to be given a good shove after the neck has been broken. Unfortunately, all these things can only come together if...'

He allowed his words to hang in the air, and Konrad Simonsen completed the sentence:

'... if Jørgen Kramer Nielsen was murdered, outside his own door.'

CHAPTER 3

Jørgen Kramer Nielsen's death was upgraded to a murder investigation. Konrad Simonsen informed the Deputy Commissioner who was less than over the moon though unable to do anything else but hope for a swift turnaround, even if she did have the sense not to say so out loud. Murder cases weren't going to be solved any quicker by hurrying the head of investigation, that much had long since become plain to her. And yet Simonsen was tactless enough to suggest the opposite when he demanded from Arne Pedersen that he should allocate the necessary resources.

'I need at least five detectives for three days, including the Countess or yourself. It's imperative we establish some kind of insight into the victim's life as soon as possible. Not necessarily in detail to begin with, just the bare bones. But Pauline and I can't do that on our own, it'll take far too long. And afterwards I want at least a couple of men at my disposal, as and when they're needed.'

Arne Pedersen was sweating and looked flustered. Simonsen went on:

'She's got the Legal Affairs Committee breathing down her neck, but maybe I should ask her to call you instead of playing piggy in the middle.'

The reference to the Deputy Commissioner did the trick: Simonsen got what he was asking for.

Their intensified efforts paid off and a fuller picture of the murdered postman began to emerge.

Jørgen Kramer Nielsen had attended his local comprehensive, moving on to upper secondary at the Brøndbyøster Gymnasium, both schools situated in Hvidovre. Following his graduation from the gymnasium in the summer of 1969, he found employment at the post office on Julius Framlev Allé, now called simply Framlev Post Office, where his father was postmaster. In the spring of 1972, both his parents and his younger sister died in a plane crash in Mallorca. They were his only family. Kramer Nielsen inherited the family home, living there until the day he died. His life could only be described as quiet, seemingly solitary, and his workmates at the post office seemed barely to have known him.

Konrad Simonsen sent his officers out into the surrounding area, to neighbours and shopkeepers, and results were indeed forthcoming, though hardly earth-shattering. Jørgen Kramer Nielsen ate out every Saturday without fail, always at the same restaurant, even sticking to the same choice from the menu: steak and chips with Béarnaise sauce, the establishment's most expensive dish at 135 kroner. Konrad Simonsen sighed on receiving this piece of information, though without bothering to note it down. Moreover, Kramer Nielsen was a regularly borrower of library books, his selections unwavering: maths, travel books – though only on Norway, Sweden or Finland, science and biographies of famous scientists. The Countess, who had investigated this part of the profile, added:

'He had a nickname, *Ninety-nine point four Nielsen.*'

'Meaning?'

'Ninety-nine point four is the library classification number for biographies. It's supposed to be funny.'

'Hilarious. Anything else?'

There wasn't.

Then there were the victim's financial affairs. On this matter, Pauline Berg was able to add one detail, albeit a minute one: Jørgen Kramer Nielsen stuck to using an ATM card and paid his bills in person at his bank.

'Is that it?' Simonsen said with obvious disappointment.

She flicked vigorously through her notes.

'He made an agreement to tithe two per cent of his income when he converted to Catholicism. It's usual, and tax-deductible, too, though not counted as taxation officially, since religious communities other than Church of Denmark don't have the same standing in the eyes of the Inland Revenue.'

'When did he convert?'

'No idea.'

'What about his will? Did you find out anything there?'

'Yes, he made it back in nineteen ninety-nine, wanting the rest of what he made on the sale of the house, which is to say about a million and a half kroner, donated to a British charity called Missing Children. They're based in London, but they've got branches in all the major cities over there. You can check their website. His personal belongings weren't bequeathed, though, so technically they belong to the state.'

73

'Where did he get that idea, Missing Children?'

'We don't know. The solicitor who drew up the will can't remember the case at all. Why should he?'

Konrad Simonsen gave her a new job to do.

'Check up on holidays. Where did he go? He must have done something with himself besides working and sitting at home on his own. The girls, too. Find out if there were any more of them. His loft and those girls are the only things we've got that give him a bit of light and shade.'

'They make him creepy, if you ask me.'

'Which could be why someone killed him.'

She went off, just as he was about to probe some more.

Summer went on, and it was hot. An area of high pressure had parked itself over the country and the weather people said it would be staying put for a few days, at least.

Konrad Simonsen lay stretched out on a sofa in the Countess's living room. It had just gone eight in the evening, but the heat of the day persisted. He had dumped his jacket and shirt and was wearing only an undershirt and short pants of thin cotton. The air conditioning was on full whack. And yet he was sweating. He glanced at the time on the antique grandfather clock that stood against the far wall and whose eternal ticking had driven him mad the first few weeks after he had moved in. Now he seldom noticed it. For a brief moment he thought he might have a nap, but it was too late in the day, he might not be able to sleep later on if he did. Instead, he immersed himself in a Sudoku on the back page of the day's paper, but found his mind began to wander as soon he got stuck.

He felt at home here with the Countess, he couldn't deny that fact, and it had been weeks since he'd been back to his own flat in Valby, apart from picking up his mail twice a week. He wasn't sure if it was a good thing or not. Both of them avoided the issue of a more permanent arrangement involving an official change of address, and actively making a decision about it seemed to become superfluous as time went by. The previous week he'd received his own set of keys. Before that he'd used the back-door key that hung in its secret place in the outhouse. It wasn't the best of arrangements insofar as he'd had to go to back and forth with it every time he came or went. The Countess had given him his own complete set one morning before they went to work, casually, with a comment about its being the most practical solution, as though he were a plumber needing access to do a job while she was out. No more was said. She had also divulged the password to her online banking, so she wouldn't be the only one able to pay the bills. That was practical, too.

He stared into space. At what point could you say two people were living together? When they shared the same postal address? Slept in the same bed? Pooled their finances? Or was it enough just to… live together, like they were doing?

The Countess was late, it was almost nine o'clock by the time she finally got back. He tried to shake off his annoyance, not wanting to be unreasonable. He, more than anyone, knew how domestic arrangements crumbled in the face of work.

'Hi, Simon, sorry I'm late. The meeting dragged on.'

'Fair enough. You should have called, though.'

They kissed, rather more ritually than usual.

'Sorry. Have you made anything to eat?'

'Leek flan. Cold, now.'

'Cold leek flan is just what I need.'

She was hard to be annoyed with, and he was glad to see her, despite that flan having cost him two hours in the kitchen. He couldn't understand the recipe and had to phone his daughter twice, though she hadn't been much help. He didn't know anyone else to ask.

They ate, and the Countess complimented his cooking. Feeling proud of himself, he told her about his day's exercise.

'I ran two hundred metres, at least. Or just short, I suppose.'

'That's brilliant, Simon. You'll make an athlete yet. What about your postman, how's he getting along?'

He'd been hoping she would ask, but at the same time had decided he wouldn't mention it of his own accord. It was one of the disadvantages of having lost his status as department head: the Countess and Arne Pedersen no longer converged on him naturally to discuss his investigation. They had other, more important things to be getting on with, and he had to ask if he wanted their opinions. Usually, Pauline was the only person he had to talk to, and she'd been away today for an appointment with her psychiatrist. Another appointment.

'I was at the post office again, but it's the same old song. Jørgen Kramer Nielsen lived a very quiet and exceptionally regular life, as you know. I thought about the way that priest at Kasper Planck's funeral condensed his life into two minutes. It really made me sad.'

Kasper Planck had been Konrad Simonsen's boss in the Homicide Department, and his friend. Simonsen went on:

'A long and vibrant life reduced to a few objective statements by someone he never knew, even if it did happen to be a priest. I found it almost offensive. But in Kramer Nielsen's case I think anyone would have a hard job filling two minutes.'

'Tell me about it.'

'Do you really want to hear? Are you sure you wouldn't rather wind down?'

'I'm winding down, and I want to hear.'

He loved her for that. He'd slipped his notebook into his back pocket in readiness. He took it out, flicked through the pages and began to fill her in.

'I've spoken to close on two dozen of his former workmates and all of them concur: *A loner. Reliable, but dull. Never joined in when we went out. Kept himself to himself. No real friends at work.*

76

Never a sick day. Never glad. Quiet. Polite. Never stuck out. Hardly said a word unless spoken to. Went straight home after work, no matter what. Never had an opinion about anything. The guy worked there nearly forty years, but he might as well never have been there.'

'What about elsewhere? Clubs, associations, hobbies, that sort of thing?'

'I haven't got that far yet, but we do know mathematics was a hobby. Bear in mind that I'm surrounded by sticklers, however well-meaning, who make sure I go home after only four hours on the job. I'm sure they've got a stopwatch somewhere.'

She smiled without comment, and he went on.

'Tomorrow I'm going to see a retired postman. None of the current people has been there anything like as long as Kramer Nielsen was. Then on Monday, Tuesday as well maybe, I'm going to go through his stuff. Something has to turn up, surely? He must have done something with his life. Arne's said he'll give me a hand, though I don't know how he's got the time with you all so run off your feet.'

The sarcasm was obvious, but she chose to ignore it.

'It's Arne's job to involve himself in your investigation. But I do agree with you that Kramer Nielsen must have done something else with himself besides just sitting around at home. It's against human nature otherwise.'

'He didn't watch TV. He didn't even have one, or a computer. Pauline's found that out already. He didn't have a car, either.'

'Perhaps it was a good thing, him being so anonymous.'

'How do you mean? So far I can't imagine why anyone would be bothered to bump him off.'

'Because it made no difference if he was alive or dead?'

'Not morally, or legally, of course. But in practice, yes. Like I said, I've still got a long way to go before any fuller picture emerges. Why do you say it was good that he was so anonymous? If not inconsequential.'

'It makes the other things stand out more clearly.'

'That's true. You're thinking about the girls and his loft?'

'No, more about that plane crash. Losing your entire family when you're only twenty must impact rather heavily on the rest of your life. Especially if he was, well, predisposed to certain things. There were no crisis counsellors in the seventies. I imagine he was pretty much left to his own devices.'

'That's why I want to talk to someone who knew him back then. But there's something else, too, that makes him stand out, if you like. He was a Catholic, and there aren't many of them about in this country.'

'What about his priest, have you spoken to him?'

'Not yet, but I will. Kramer Nielsen paid a tithe to the Catholic community, and is laid to rest in the Catholic cemetery at the Sankt Nikolaj Kirke in Hvidovre, so his faith must have been important to him.'

'Do you think it's got anything to do with his downstairs neighbour? Kramer Nielsen sold the house to him after all. Have you looked into that?'

Simonsen shook his head apologetically.

'Like I said, there's a limit to how much I can do in four hours a day.'

'You could ask Arne to free up some resources for you again. After all, it's a murder inquiry now.'

It had already happened, but he only made use of them when there was no other way. But then, a few more officers were a good thing to have in hand, which was why he'd asked Pedersen in the first place. Perversely perhaps he found that he was beginning to enjoy his rather modest investigation, perhaps for the very reason that it was tucked away out of the spotlight compared to the rest of the department's activities. He hoped it would stay that way; there was no reason to involve more people in it than absolutely necessary. His next moves were lined up: first the postman's workmates, then his stuff, then after that the priest. Once he'd got that far, he might want to bring in more resources, then again he might not. He was keeping an open mind.

'I've got Pauline,' he said.

'Yes, you have.'

The Countess sounded curt, jealous even. Now and then, she could be quite possessive, and it was something he hadn't seen in her before he'd moved in. He knew too that she occasionally stalked her ex-husband and his new family. Not personally, but using a private detective. Sometimes covertly, other times in the open, with a camera in public places. Simonsen only found out by chance and had not spoken to her about it yet. Strictly speaking, it wasn't his business.

She went to the kitchen to put the kettle on. When she came back her voice was normal again.

'The truth is you're liking this little case of yours no one else is interested in, aren't you, Simon?'

'I've certainly become curious about it. Tell me, have you ever smoked cannabis?'

He relished bringing her off course. It didn't happen that much.

'Cannabis? Why are you asking me that all of a sudden?'

'Because your eyelids were getting heavy just before and I thought the question might wake you up a bit. Usually, I'm the one who's falling asleep. And because I'd like to know.'

'I don't get the chance to nap two hours a day, do I? Not like some people.'

'No, I'm lucky. But what about the cannabis?'

'Yes, I've tried it. Years ago now, though.'

'What was it like?'

'Fun, to begin with, then stupefying. Come on, why are you asking?'

'I'd like to try some.'

It didn't sink in at first. She asked again:

'Try what?'

'Cannabis, I just said. I'd like to smoke a joint, a spliff, what-ever they call it.'

The Countess got to her feet, put her hands on her hips and rubbished the proposal well and truly.

'Konrad Simonsen, you are not going to smoke, ever again, under any circumstances, whether it be cannabis, tobacco, beech leaves, or whatever. You can have a cup of tea instead.'

He hadn't thought of it like that, and stopped her on her way into the kitchen.

'It wasn't for the sake of smoking, Countess. There's other ways, I do know that much. I want to know what cannabis is like, that's all.'

She seemed to soften a little.

'And how were you thinking of getting hold of some? Just ambling over to Narcotics, perhaps, and asking if they've got any surplus? For private consumption, of course.'

'I was hoping you'd know how to go about it.'

'Do I look like a drug dealer? Is that what you're saying, so elegantly?'

'Now you mention it, I've been having my suspicions about you.'

She paused and looked at him closely.

'You're not joking, are you?'

'No, I'm not. I'd like to try, just the once.'

'Well, let's start with some tea, shall we? Then we'll have to see what the future holds in store.'

He followed her into the kitchen, where he made himself useful getting the cups out and said no more about it.

The next day confirmed the Countess's assumption that Jørgen Kramer Nielsen's life had taken a marked downturn when his parents and sister were killed. A picture of this began to emerge at a care home on the outskirts of Køge.

Simonsen introduced himself and explained why he was there and that he had found the name of the man he was visiting in the post office's old personnel files. The old man glared. Simonsen smiled accommodatingly and found himself thinking the interview was doomed. The man smelled rather offensively. Fortunately, however, there was nothing wrong with his memory.

'Jørgen was lively young lad when he started. That'd be in the early seventies. His dad was postmaster in those days.'

'The summer of 'sixty-nine.'

'That sounds right.'

'Why did he want to join the postal service? He went to the gymnasium school, you'd have thought there were other opportunities?'

'He wasn't intending on staying, it was only supposed to be temporary. He was saving up to go round the world. I remember very clearly his dad wasn't too keen on the idea. He wanted him to carry on with his studies, university and what have you. But there was no stopping Jørgen, he never talked about anything else but that trip of his, all the exotic places he wanted to go. Most of us were sick of hearing about it. We might have been a bit envious, too. We hadn't the opportunities he had. Our wages were for rent and keeping up the family. He didn't have any of that to think about.'

'And then there was that plane crash?'

'That's right. He wasn't as full of himself afterwards.'

'It sounds like you think he had it coming. Didn't you like him much?'

The old man tossed his head and his eyes grew moist. Simonsen wanted to find him a hankie, and to draw his chair back a bit, but he never got the chance. The old man came back at him sourly:

'That's my business, not yours.'

'Absolutely, of course. How did he react to the plane crash?'

'Changed him completely. Broke him apart, it did. Never the same again.'

'Can you elaborate on that?'

'From the day they told him, he went about like a ghost. It was like he stopped living, only without being able to die.'

The man proceeded to echo the chorus of other witnesses who had talked about Jørgen Kramer Nielsen's social reticence. The old man recalled a handful of episodes, a couple of which Simonsen had already heard before. Others, however, were new to him, albeit uninteresting insofar as they merely corroborated what he had heard elsewhere.

After a few more questions, he thanked the man and said his goodbyes, glad to get out in the fresh air again, even if it was suffocatingly hot. He had got what he wanted, though he hadn't cared for the old man one bit, a feeling that had obviously been mutual. The interview, however, had made it all worthwhile. Jørgen Kramer Nielsen's life seemed finally to be taking shape.

Following his visit to the care home, Simonsen drove back to Police HQ in Copenhagen, even though it was hardly half an hour before he was due to go home again. He found Pauline Berg in his little annexe, stretched out on the sofa reading a newspaper. She spent more time on that sofa than in her own office, often when he wasn't even there himself, which seemed to annoy everyone else but him. Comment had been passed, in the canteen and elsewhere. He ought to get himself a padlock, it was said, to stop people swanning in and out. No one said it in as many words, but *people* meant Pauline Berg. Until now he hadn't paid much attention. It was his office, after all, not theirs, and he was perfectly capable of drawing a line if he didn't want company. He didn't need his colleagues to point it out for him. He poked his head round the door and said hello, but then went to his desk and switched on his computer. She came in before he'd logged on.

'I've got something on his holidays,' she told him.

'Who, Kramer Nielsen?'

'Yes, who else? Package holidays weren't for him, I think we can be sure of that, but then I struck really lucky with DSB at Hvidovre Station. The train lady, or clerk I suppose she is, said she recognised him when I showed her his picture. He used to buy a return to Esbjerg once a year, always the same dates, from Copenhagen Central on the nineteenth of June and back again from Esbjerg two days later.'

'Was he connected in any way to the railways?'

'Not that I know of. It was almost in desperation I tried them. I thought if he didn't fly, then he'd have to go by train. Like I said, it was just luck, really.'

'Because the clerk knew him?'

'Recognised him, that's all.'

'Was he a regular customer besides that?'

'Only once a year, as far as she knew.'

'I've come across some good witnesses in my time, but that's ridiculous. How on earth could she remember one customer who came in once a year?'

'That's what I mean. But she remembers him because he wouldn't queue like other people. That was what first drew him to her attention. He kept going to the back of the line, like he didn't want anyone standing behind him. She'd never known anyone do that before. Then, as it happened, he came in again the year after, on her shift, the same behaviour as the first time. She thinks it must have been the summers of nineteen ninety-six and -seven. She sold him tickets a number of times after that, though not every year, it depended on whether she was at work that day or not. But then I checked with the post office and the postmaster told me Kramer Nielsen was very flexible with his holidays, and his shifts generally, but always asked for a certain week off in June, and that checks with the week including the nineteenth to the twenty-first. There was never any problem with that from his employers' side.'

'Why wouldn't he queue up?'

'Who knows? Maybe he was just shy. The train lady thinks he didn't want anyone else to know where he was going. But that's with *thinks* underlined.'

'What did he do in Esbjerg?'

Pauline shook her head, she'd no idea. Simonsen conscientiously praised her, but it didn't seem to make any impression. He never quite knew how she was going to react. Sometimes she seemed pleased with the recognition, at times extremely so, and sometimes she was indifferent to it. Today it was the latter.

'Did you make sure to give that cow a bollocking?' she suddenly asked.

The 'cow' was the nervous female officer who had appropriated Jørgen Kramer Nielsen's mobile phone, though she had not done so with ill intent, and certainly not to steal it. On her way up the stairs to the postman's body she'd been directly behind Hans Ulrik Gormsen and seen how he almost stepped on it without noticing. She'd picked it up and held it in her hand for some time while her colleague photographed the body and kept repeating how *obvious* it was that they were dealing with a killing, while all the while he argued with the priest. At some point she'd absent-mindedly put the phone in her pocket and, as things turned out, forgotten all about it until the next day back at Glostrup Politistation. There, she'd bagged it as evidence, but instead of allotting it a catalogue code she'd scribbled down her mistake in a few words and then put the bag in the drawer of her desk. Subsequently, she'd explained the matter to her superior in an e-mail and asked what to do. She never received an answer, and Jørgen Kramer Nielsen's mobile stayed put in the drawer.

Months later, when she was called into Konrad Simonsen's office, her oversight suddenly turned into a liability, for which reason she'd tried to conceal the facts. She'd done the same when Pauline interviewed her, forcing herself to lie for fear of the consequences should the truth emerge. But at the suspicion this raised against her she grew increasingly restless and irritable, realising the bind she'd got herself into and at the same time genuinely not wishing to hold back evidence in a murder inquiry. Eventually, her husband managed to drag it out of her, and after mulling the matter over he put himself in touch with Pauline Berg. He it was, too, who subsequently drove over to Police HQ and handed in the phone.

Pauline wagged her finger angrily in front of Simonsen's face. 'I've wasted a lot of time on that cretin.'

Simonsen agreed, albeit in more conciliatory terms that he hoped would rub off. To his surprise it worked.

'I know I ought to calm down… it's just…'

And all of a sudden there were tears in Pauline's eyes and he saw that she was clenching her jaw to hold them back. She managed to control herself and said tonelessly:

'Go on, I'm all right.'

'Where did she find the phone? Do we know?'

'On the landing where the body was, up against the wall on the right. It was lying face down and the cover's pretty much the same colour as the carpet, as you know, so…'

'And you're certain about that?'

'No, but it's what the husband told me. She never said anything herself, the stupid little…'

Simonsen thought for a second before telling her what to do next.

'Get hold of your stupid little friend and take her back to the house in Hvidovre. I want her to identify exactly where she found that phone. I'll have a word with her chief constable once I get a minute.'

Pauline Berg's expression left him in no doubt how little she believed that would ever happen.

By now it was mid-September, with the usual forecasts of rain and wind that nonetheless had amounted to nothing. The warmth of summer continued and on the global scene major upheavals were occurring. International money markets were nose-diving and new words crept into everyday language: *sub-prime mortgages*, *collateralised debt obligations* and *hedge funds*. Nothing ordinary people needed to bother about, and yet it affected them anyway. All of a sudden the country was plunged into financial crisis. Banks had to be bailed out and the welfare state was under pressure. There wouldn't be enough money to go round in future, they were saying.

A stiflingly hot morning at Express Move's storage facility in Hvidovre added new pieces to the jigsaw that was Jørgen Kramer Nielsen, though not many and certainly none that revealed even a shadow of a perpetrator.

Konrad Simonsen and Arne Pedersen worked together, the Acting Head of Homicide helping out his actual boss. But while the case had now been officially categorised as a murder inquiry, Simonsen had the feeling Pedersen had come out to Hvidovre more to assess how he was feeling than to help him rummage through Kramer Nielsen's belongings. However, he refrained from mentioning it, so as not to embarrass both of them. Besides, he needed a hand with this, it was dreary work, and with his head pounding and sweat seeping from every pore in his body as they toiled in the unbearably unventilated storage room, there was a genuine risk of overlooking some important detail. Especially when they didn't know what they were looking for.

The storage firm had been kind enough to set up a work surface for them, a thick slab of chipboard the size of a table-tennis table, resting on solid trestles. Here they could stand and sift through

Kramer Nielsen's life. Now and then, the manager brought them tea and coffee, or cold soft drinks. On day two, a Tuesday that seemed even more sweltering than the day before, the man had even provided them with an extension lead and a fan that turned slowly from side to side and provided at least some measure of relief.

Arne Pedersen stood examining a camera in his hand.

'A Leica M4. State of the art in the late sixties. It must have cost a fortune back then… still does, I shouldn't wonder. A real collector's item, and look at the gear to go with it.'

Simonsen glanced up from the papers he was immersed in, but felt none the wiser.

'What? I don't know a thing about photography.'

'This is an enlarger. If I'm not mistaken, it's from the same period as the camera. And here we've got telephoto lenses, tripods, projectors, as well as developing trays, timers, tongs, developer, light box, photographic paper… everything you need to set up your own darkroom. He developed his photos the old-fashioned way. Nowadays it's all digital, done by computer.'

'I know all that. We haven't found any photos, though. Apart from the ones in his loft, of course. No negatives either, for that matter. I suppose they'll turn up.'

'No doubt. Only about a million boxes to go now.'

'Don't remind me.'

A bit later, Pedersen returned to the subject.

'A darkroom requires running water and therefore a drain. It can't be that hard to find out if he had one. Whoever cleared his flat should know. Maybe the local photo shop, too.'

'There used to be a darkroom, Pauline's already established that. It's his photos and negatives we haven't found.'

Pedersen received the information as if it didn't surprise him, then said:

'I can give you a couple of officers. Can't expect you to clear this up on your own.'

Simonsen thought he sounded like an echo of the Countess, who likewise wanted to burden him with personnel, though for the moment he didn't need any. He replied the way he'd become accustomed to:

'I've got Pauline.'

He glanced up as he mentioned her name and noted the look of annoyance on Arne Pedersen's face. Not that it surprised him, for it was clear that their working relationship was rather strained at the moment. Which obviously was down to Pauline's often provocative way of going about things. But there was more to Pauline than that, and he wasn't sure Arne Pedersen realised it. Simonsen had on several occasions now seen his young colleague emerge from the toilets or his own TV room red-eyed after she had clearly been crying, and at least once she'd suddenly gone home in a taxi, presumably following an anxiety attack and one of her black pills. Pedersen probed cautiously:

'How's she getting on anyway? Are you working all right together?'

'Fine.'

The rebuff was unambiguous, but Pedersen, now his relationship with Pauline was in the past, persisted.

'Her behaviour's unacceptable, and it's getting worse.'

'I've got no issues with her.'

Simonsen carried on working without batting an eyelid.

'Did you know that when she's afraid of being on her own at night, she picks up men in hotels or bars?'

'No, I didn't, and I wish you hadn't told me.'

Simonsen raised his voice slightly and gave his former subordinate a firm look.

The subsequent pause dragged out. Pedersen clearly felt uncomfortable. Eventually, he picked up the conversation again, a bit flustered, and indicated Simonsen's pile of documents.

'Didn't our man have a passport or a driving licence? Or any other form of ID with a picture on it?'

'No passport, no driving licence. And unless we turn up something now no other photo ID either.'

'He's starting to annoy me. How can anyone go through life so alone? It's almost a sin.'

'Appearances can be deceiving. Who knows? His whole life might unfold before our eyes once we open the next box.'

'I've always envied your optimism, Simon. But I'm beginning to have my doubts.'

'Wait a minute...'

A fleeting thought had formed in Simonsen's mind, something important he was unable to pin down. A feeling of things coming together, though the essence of it had evaporated. He tried to rewind:

'Can you just say again what you just said?'

'I've always envied your optimism. Was that it?'

He concentrated, but the moment was gone. Reluctantly, he abandoned the notion, hoping it would come to him again a bit later. It often did, if you didn't force it.

'Just a passing thought, that's all. It's gone now. Anyway, I think the plane crash set him back, brought him to a standstill.'

'What plane crash?'

Pedersen clearly couldn't be accused of poring over the reports he had received on the case, but Simonsen curbed his irritation and patiently laid the matter out for him.

Some thirty boxes later, the two men were just about done for the day. The fruits of their labours had not been impressive. Searching through the deceased postman's effects and in particular sifting through his many personal papers and documents, most of which seemed merely to reflect his mathematical pastime, had failed to take them any further, and was more interesting for what they *hadn't* found: photos and negatives.

Simonsen tried to convince himself he had not perspired in vain. Some small pieces of information had been gleaned, and in the greater scheme of things could easily prove useful. Or so he hoped.

The normally good rapport between them had long since been re-established, and neither of them mentioned that moment of dissent about Pauline. Moreover, the fact that Simonsen had exceeded his daily quota of four hours by a long way was allowed to pass without comment. Neither man was enthusiastic about pressing on with the remaining boxes the next day.

Simonsen bent down to investigate one final box. Apparently it was full of books, rather more in number than a removal man's back ought to be burdened with according to the health and safety rules, but since the firm had packed the boxes themselves, that would be their own lookout. He lugged the box on to the table, opened it and froze.

'How stupid we are.'

Arne Pedersen looked up.

'What?'

'What's usually inside a camera?'

They found the Leica again and could see it had taken four pictures.

'If it's going to take Forensics a fortnight to get these developed, I'd prefer to go to our friend Photo-Mate with it,' Simonsen said.

Arne Pedersen promised to see what he could do.

Detective Superintendent Konrad Simonsen made his debut as a cannabis user one Tuesday afternoon on a lawn in Søllerød, and the experiment was hardly an unequivocal success. He had been expecting more from it and was rather disappointed. The Countess's three hash cakes, whose origins she steadfastly refused to divulge to him, tasted of nothing in particular and failed dismally to kick in. The Countess herself did not wish to take part in the festivities and so he had sat down in the garden to await getting stoned, albeit with a sneaking suspicion that the cakes had never been anywhere near cannabis and were instead the result of wholly lawful and quite unextraordinary activities at the local bakery. He felt this was borne out by the astounding speed with which his partner had produced them.

After a while he began to grumble. He would go to the baker's, he declared, and ask them why there was no cannabis in their muffins. *You can't pull the wool over my eyes*, he would tell them. To their faces, right there in the shop. He imagined the assistant's reaction and giggled. Or perhaps he might simply say, *Muffins!* Loudly and with authority. *Muffins! Muffins!* And allow her to infer the rest. What's more, he'd caught them selling yesterday's papers. He would bring one home so the Countess could see for herself. He laughed and laughed again until he was compelled to wipe the tears from his eyes with the back of his hand. The other customers would be on his side. Yesterday's news, the cheek of it! *Am I right, or am I right? Hands up!*

His convulsions of merriment forced him to lie back, flat out on the grass, and after a bit he settled into a more mellow mood, gazing up at the Countess's shrubbery, whose plants from such an unfamiliar angle seemed toweringly tall, adorned with a pretty, synthetic sheen of yellow and green cellophane. A bit later the lawn began to ripple pleasantly beneath him and he imagined himself to be in a canoe, lazily drifting downstream on some exotic river. The fuchsias in the background became tangerine trees on the banks, and when he put his tongue out, the gentle breeze that wafted across the waters tasted of the sweetest marmalade.

Nothing more was forthcoming. He had hoped for a girl in the sky with diamonds, had even felt entitled to her, but she never materialised. Instead he fell asleep.

* * *

There was a change in the weather, an area of low pressure from the east, and temperatures in Copenhagen became bearable again. The first leaves yellowed on the trees and windcheaters began to appear. In the Homicide Department, Konrad Simonsen finally discovered what it was Jørgen Kramer Nielsen had photographed. The film in the postman's camera had been developed, and he and Pauline Berg showed the results to Arne Pedersen, who took his time considering the first of the four prints in order to seem interested. It was a nice picture, albeit rather dull. A low sun above a spectacular landscape of rugged rocks, its rays reflected in the leaden waters of a fjord. Daytime, frozen for all eternity. Arne Pedersen glanced at the three others, whose theme was the same, albeit with different subjects. He checked the time at the corner of his computer screen, before trying to find something appropriate to say.

'I think I saw something like that the other day. In the... aren't they from...'

'One of the illustrated nature books Kramer Nielsen had taken out on Norway. They're still among his effects out in Express Move's storage facility, gathering dust and a hefty fine.'

'*Pictures of Lofoten?*'

'Couldn't be more wrong. *Lofoten in Pictures.*'

'So he took photos of photos?'

'Exactly, and very expertly, too.'

'Why would he do that?'

'For his loft, I think.'

Arne Pedersen's expression suggested he thought there had to be more of an explanation than that. Pauline Berg, sounding surprisingly friendly, explained:

'He combined the images with photos of the dead girl and made posters out of them for the loft. He must have some negatives of her somewhere, we just haven't come across them yet.'

Simonsen looked at Pauline in astonishment.

'What makes you say she's dead?'

'It's obvious, isn't it? Or is it just me?'

Arne Pedersen said nothing. Simonsen, on the other hand, discovered to his surprise that he agreed with her.

CHAPTER 4

The first time they slept together was predictable, and cautiously investigative.

Afterwards, neither of them felt the urge to talk about what words could so easily damage, and besides there was little to add.

The Countess sat up in bed and bundled a pillow behind her back. Spontaneously, she pulled the duvet up over her breasts, then ran her fingers through her hair a few times by way of rearrangement.

It was Sunday and already mid-morning.

Simonsen felt a craving for a cigarette, more so than for a long time. A walk would be a good substitute, or rather a run as he was justified in calling it since he now jogged at least a third of his route. Sleep was a second alternative, if hardly realistic. He wondered if from today he would be sleeping where he now lay, in the Countess's bed, rather than in his own upstairs. Perhaps she even expected him to. He realised that telling her he actually preferred to sleep in his own would not be easy. It didn't occur to him that she might feel the same way. He removed his hand, that had been resting on her knee. It was sticky and warm, and he wiped it discreetly on the duvet without her noticing. Then he folded his hands behind his head, looked up into her face and asked:

'Have you ever been deployed to a demonstration?'

'A violent one, you mean? I've been called out to peaceful ones lots of times.'

'Yes, a violent one. A big one, the kind that gets out of hand, so eventually you can't think about anything but your own safety.'

'No, not really. They used to keep female officers well out of that sort of thing when I was young. Not that anyone ever said as much. Besides, all the big demos were before my time, the ones that really gathered the crowds. You must have seen your share, though?'

She was right.

When he was a young constable back in the late sixties and early seventies, there had been protests all the time. Or that's how he remembered it, anyway. Demos for better wages and working conditions, equal rights for women. Demos against nuclear power one day, and ballistic missiles or Denmark's Common Market membership the next. Not to mention the student demos targeting whoever happened to be Minister of Education at the time, regardless of which party he belonged to and what policies he was implementing. Or she, of course – as if it made any difference. Then there were the protests in support of everything under the sun: anti-apartheid in South Africa, the Palestinian cause, the oppressed masses of Central America, Copenhagen's free town of Christiania, and probably a whole lot more besides that he had since forgotten. It had not been uncommon for a Copenhagen demo to attract upwards of 50,000 people, mainly young. It was a hallmark of the times and the phenomenon was by no means confined to Denmark. Throughout the Western world the picture had been the same, and often a lot worse, with protesters or police officers killed in the fray. The Deutsche Oper in West Berlin in 1967, the May 1968 protests in Paris, Kent State University, Ohio, 1970.

He picked up on the Countess's opener with enthusiasm. Yes, he had been at many of the big demos.

'The Vietnam protests were the worst. The IMF summit was bad, too. I was really scared at that one. My legs wouldn't stop shaking, literally, and I was afraid my colleagues were going to notice, but they were probably just as terrified as I was. I just didn't think so at the time, standing there in the front line with my helmet on, and my shield and baton in my hands, like some soldier in a war I didn't understand. It was horrendous.'

'But part of the job.'

She'd meant it to be supportive, he realised that from the tone of her voice. Nevertheless, the harshness of his reaction surprised him.

'Police work was a choice. I could have gone back on it, resigned from the force and got myself another job. No one forced me to join up. It's no excuse.'

Her hand found its way to the back of his head, and she stroked him where once there had been hair.

'Are you looking for one? An excuse, I mean.'

He ignored her question and went on sombrely:

'*Pig, rozzer, plod, fascist, scum, bastard…* some of the things they used to shout after me.'

'Not everyone, surely.'

The protesters did, though, and how he hated them. Their long hair, their placards and banners, their eloquence and the way they stuck together… he hated them all. But more than anything he hated their studied lack of respect, the way they disdainfully turned their backs on everything he believed in, everything his parents had worked for all their lives, the old values dying off one by one while they jeered and gloated. No, he'd almost forgotten: what he really hated most was their daring... their dedication to the cause and their daring.

'The protesters weren't scared. They had a cause to fight for, and they had each other.'

There was no longer resentment in his voice, only puzzlement. The Countess sensed the ambiguity.

'And you could never be a part of it because you had a job to do, guarding the established order, is that it?'

'I was a guard, yes. In front of the US Embassy, looking out on a foaming sea of rage, an open target because of the errors of others. It wasn't me showering little kids with napalm and dropping *bombies* on the villages.'

And then there were the ubiquitous red flags. Sometimes just a simple rag on a stick, sometimes the fine standards of the trade union branches, but always red. He was no supporter of US involvement in Vietnam, but no matter how the spoiled hippies of the world looked at it, the United States was a democracy and the Soviet Union was not. The youth of the Eastern bloc weren't protesting, or certainly not against the ruling establishment, the oh-so-marvellous Communist state made sure of that. But the pamphlets, flyers and folders the protesters handed out showed images of Vietnamese children caught up in the horrors of war, while photos of Soviet tanks rolling into Prague to crush the Spring Uprising there were seldom, if ever, disseminated. Besides, the very foundation of the freedom enjoyed by these young people had been paid for in American lives and dollars only twenty-five years before during World War II, but none of them ever stopped to think about that. He went on:

'The Christmas bombings of Hanoi... I remember the Swedish Prime Minister joining the rallies against them, and I actually agreed with him. *You cannot save a village by wiping it out, by burning fields, by destroying houses, by locking up or killing those who live there.* His words rang true, though the Americans didn't care to hear them. Vietnam was horrendous, but I couldn't see why that had to be taken out on Danish police officers, and still don't to this day. What are you smirking about?'

He sat up, and she kissed him on the cheek.

'Nothing, it doesn't matter.'

'No, tell me.'

'The Christmas bombings of Hanoi took place in 1972, Olof Palme's protest was in 1968, and he was Minister of Education at the time. He didn't become prime minister until the year after, but it's true, his criticisms did anger Washington. President Johnson called his ambassador home from Sweden.'

Sometimes Simonsen just couldn't be doing with all this knowledge of hers. Besides, she'd probably still been in kindergarten at the time. But that didn't stop her, she was such a know-all about everything, it got on his nerves. Unwittingly, the Countess contradicted him.

'What are *bombies*, anyway? I've never heard of them before.'

He shook his head in annoyance.

'It's stupid of me, talking about all this now. Who needs it?'

'No, it's all right, Simon.'

She held his gaze.

'Really, it's all right.'

His heart attack had well and truly stirred up the stew inside his head, he had sensed it for quite some time. But why must he start thinking about such unpleasantness now? It would have been a hell of a lot more fitting if he'd showed her some attention, gone out of his way to be nice to her, that kind of thing. They still had breakfast to share, too. Then all of a sudden it struck him why he had begun to dwell on such uncomfortable recollections. He smiled to himself and said:

'I don't know why I go on about all these things, it's decades ago now and it doesn't matter anyway. This all started after my operation.'

'You don't always have to explain.'

Maybe she was right, she often was. He went on, softly now:

'There are two expressions from back then that I absolutely despise. One is *bombies*, which is what the Vietnamese called the Americans' anti-personnel cluster bombs. They were about the size of a tennis ball and looked like a child's toy.'

'How awful.'

'Awful doesn't go near enough. The second expression is *crowd control*.'

As a young officer he had been sent back to school. Or rather, he had been sent on a course, but it was the same thing. *Crowd control* was a shiny new concept, and the English designation made it sound so appealing in the classroom. The police had to learn how to manage large assemblies of people, but what did their fine theories help once you were standing there with a tiny strip of no-man's-land in front of you, three backward paces off getting crushed to death against the iron railings of the Embassy. In the fray, *crowd control* was a simple matter of survival, a fact of which the powers that be were only too aware of and even complicit in. Only he hadn't realised until much later. *Crowd control...*

He snorted in disgust.

'They should have called it *generation control* instead. Then we'd have known what we were up against.'

He pulled the duvet aside and got up.

'Weren't you a part of your own generation? I mean, you were allowed to be there, too.'

'The sixties weren't about inclusivity. Tolerance was a thing the people with the correct opinions demanded rather than practised. Shall we shower?'

The Countess considered the offer with surprise at first, and then laughed.

'Yes, why not? But tell me about your demo first.'

He sounded almost wistful.

'It got me smoking. And I could really do with a cigarette now.'

'You mean, you smoked on duty?'

'What do you think? Of course I didn't! But afterwards…'

'Go on.'

'Later, later. I've got what feels like the entire Catholic Church to tackle tomorrow. Now that's what I'd call a sizeable opponent. Too much for a bunch of long-haired dropouts, at any rate. Maybe you can offer me some support, erudite as you are? You read books for fun, and I haven't even prepared yet.'

'Only if you stop staring at me like that.'

She bagged the best place under the shower before he caught up with her.

The priest welcomed Konrad Simonsen on the patio, where a table was set for tea. His host did the pouring. Simonsen allowed his gaze to wander over the tidy little garden, wondering at the same time whether the breeze that rustled in the corkscrew willow opposite them would be too much background noise on his Dictaphone. He made himself comfortable and looked the priest in the eye. In any other circumstances this visit might have been pleasant, but the other man's forthright announcement immediately laid down boundaries.

'I should say right away that we may have a conflict of interests here. As I'm sure you know, Jørgen Kramer Nielsen was a member of our parish, and as such I, his priest, have received information I am not at liberty to divulge.'

It was straight talking at any rate. Simonsen frowned and maintained his dissatisfied expression, though the priest subsequently endeavoured to modify his words by assuring his visitor he wished to do everything else in his power to aid the police in their investigation.

'Should I be unable to give you an answer, you must know that it certainly isn't because I'm trying to obstruct you.'

He smiled apologetically and appeared calmly steadfast in a way that indicated to Simonsen it wasn't worth arguing.

'Well, if there's nothing I can do about it, I'll just have to make do.'

The priest's proviso was hardly surprising. Simonsen had reckoned on certain constraints, though he had been hoping the religious argument wouldn't be raised until much later in proceedings. As things stood, it was more like the introit. He tried to win himself a bit of time.

'Are you really prevented from divulging anything, even after the man's death? I would have thought confessional privilege was only valid with respect to the living.'

'It makes no difference.'

Simonsen fell silent and considered how to proceed. The priest waited with no sign of impatience, and with accommodating body language, made an effort to ensure the pause need not be embarrassing. Could a body seated two metres away be accommodating? The priest's could. The man invited openness, albeit without offering it himself. It was remarkably well done, Simonsen thought, before eventually carrying on.

'You realise, of course, that any reticence you might have as to passing on important information about a crime may be against the law?'

'I'm aware of that, yes.'

The other man remained unruffled, and Konrad Simonsen elected for a different approach. If he was lucky, his new strategy would pay off and provide him with answers to some of his most pressing questions. Indirect answers, perhaps, but better than nothing, and certainly worth a shot.

'Can you tell me more about Confession?'

The priest showed no surprise at this change of tack.

'What do you want to know? It's a subject I could spend hours on, but I imagine that's not what you have in mind.'

'Some other time, perhaps. I'd like to know what I can ask you and what I can't. You've chalked up the court, so it's only fair you run through the rules for me, too.'

'You can ask whatever you like. The rules I abide by don't apply to you.'

'I realise that. Let me put it another way: I won't try to hide the fact that I'm unused to this situation, to say the least. Of course, lots of witnesses refuse to co-operate and hold back information, so it's not that. The unusual thing here is that I'm accepting your terms, mainly because I don't think I would come out on top in any confrontation between us. But tell me instead, in theory as it were, in what specific circumstances you as a priest would be bound by professional secrecy.'

The priest smiled smugly at his question, before proceeding to elaborate with great passion on the confession of sin, the repentance that went with it and was so crucial, and then forgiveness and the *sacramental absolution* by which the faithful received divine mercy for their sins.

'Confession can occur in a number of ways. One of which, the one I'm sure you're thinking about now, is in the confessional box, in personal conversation with an appointed priest.'

'Such as yourself, for instance.'

'I am approved to carry out that function, yes. Partly because I've been ordained, and partly by canonical jurisdiction.'

'And what you hear in that connection is protected by rules of professional privilege?'

'Complete confidentiality, *under seal of Confession*.'

He poured them some more tea. Simonsen thanked him politely as he concentrated his thoughts. It was all about timing. Timing and luck. He switched to a more casual tone.

'Next question: would you mind if I use a Dictaphone for what we have to talk about now?'

'Not at all, go ahead.'

'I'm glad you're willing to make my job that bit easier, but I'm afraid I have to do a little soundcheck here to eliminate background noise.'

He indicated the willow tree; the priest nodded his understanding. Simonsen switched on the Dictaphone, asking somewhat absently:

'Tell me, to whom do *you* confess when the need arises? I'm assuming you can't absolve yourself of your sins?'

'Not like that, no. I go to my bishop.'

'Further up the ladder, is that it?'

'That's the normal practice, yes.'

Simonsen was still fiddling with his recalcitrant Dictaphone.

'How often do Catholics confess? I mean, I know that depends on the sins, if you can put it like that, but how common is Confession exactly? On average. How about yourself, for instance? Have you been to your bishop during the last six months, say?'

The priest laughed. You couldn't look at it in terms of averages, it seemed, and yet he endeavoured to provide an honest answer, pleased with the interest shown in his faith.

'Actually, I haven't at all, not for some years. But then we priests are expected to set a good example, aren't we, even though it doesn't always work out that way.'

Simonsen glanced up and noted the man's expression. The patient smile seemed genuine enough, as genuine as good old truth.

The priest looked up into the willow tree. There was no doubt that he had now realised what had occurred. Twenty seconds too late. Simonsen put the Dictaphone back in his case. It had been purely for the sake of distraction and was now superfluous. He considered the priest's mournful expression and realised that he felt ashamed. It was odd. He had manipulated witnesses in worse ways than this, and yet he felt stricken by remorse. Three months ago it wouldn't have bothered him in the slightest. He tried to convince himself his subterfuge had been justified, even in the priest's best interests. It was of the utmost concern that he be eliminated as a suspect, and surely he could see that as Kramer Nielsen's downstairs neighbour and his landlord he was a prime candidate as likely perpetrator. Either on his own or in collusion. His holiday, for a start, had all the marks of his wanting to give himself an alibi. And then there was his being bound by the doctrine of priest-penitent privilege, that very conveniently excused him from having to answer questions from the police. There was absolutely no reason for Simonsen to feel embarrassed. And yet he did.

At last the priest spoke.

'Was that really necessary?'

'It's my job. I was eliminating you from our enquiries.'

'You subverted a coming together of two people. You could just as easily have asked me straight.'

Simonsen tried to be thick-skinned. *A coming together of two people*... how unctuous could it get? And those wounded, puppy-dog eyes. *Read it and weep*, this was a murder inquiry and priests weren't above the law.

His excuses to himself didn't really cut any ice. The priest's words had hit home.

'Perhaps we should call it a day?' Simonsen suggested.

'I think that would be a good idea.'

'I hope I can persuade you to come by Police HQ at some point. We still have a lot to talk about, regardless.'

'Indeed, we hardly got started, did we? I'll come, of course. Call me and we'll fix a time.'

'I'm sorry it had to be like this.'

It was a hasty parting. Simonsen wanted to get home, and the priest had work to do.

That same evening, Arne Pedersen came round to play chess and had hardly taken off his coat before he was asking about Simonsen's interview with the priest. He led his guest into the kitchen where they could sit undisturbed. He had already laid out the board, set up all the pieces and put the game clock on the table next to it. He took a beer from the fridge for Pedersen and poured himself a cup of tea.

'The priest had nothing to do with the killing.'

He gave Pedersen an account of their conversation without entering into detail, then summed up:

'He never knew what was coming. Not in the build-up, not even when I got to the crux of it, whether he had confessed recently. He hadn't. He didn't even realise I was watching him while he answered. I'm certain of it. He didn't kill Jørgen Kramer Nielsen, and he doesn't know who did either. I'd be willing to stake my life on it.'

'Without reservation? No humility about your own fallibility?'

Konrad Simonsen had never for a moment imagined he could always tell when someone wasn't telling the truth. Certain people were such proficient liars they could pull the wool over anyone's eyes, certainly his. But sometimes, in specific situations, he could unambiguously determine whether someone was telling the truth. Or rather, whether they believed what they were saying to be the truth, regardless of whether it actually was or not; that was another matter. And the interview with the priest had belonged to the truthful category.

Arne Pedersen congratulated him.

'Not bad at all, outsmarting a guy like him in the field of rhetoric.'

Simonsen didn't look at it like that at all. The priest's defence mechanisms were tuned in to the matter of his professional secrecy, not to his own self, and why should they have been? From his angle there was no reason for him to be on his guard. He hadn't done anything wrong. But then, no one could know that beforehand. *A coming together of two people...* Simonsen hadn't behaved unethically at all, not in the slightest. Nevertheless, he would prefer to forget about the interview altogether. He answered Pedersen with a grunt that could have meant just about anything.

Pedersen went on:

'As I understand it, they're trained scholastically for years on end at their seminaries, right down to the smallest verb.'

'Well, yes, if you want to reduce the Catholic Church to the sort of obscure cult that brainwashes its representatives. But that's hardly the case. This man attended Saint Michael Pastoral Centre in Dublin for seven years and got through with flying colours in a host of recognised subjects, whatever academic standards you might care to apply. Prayer and learning off by heart wouldn't have got him very far there.'

'You're very well informed about him. Been cribbing, have we?'

'As a matter of fact, yes.'

'He must have realised he was the most obvious suspect. And yet he refuses to answer your questions. What does he think... that priests have automatic immunity in murder cases?'

'Not at all. And anyway, it wasn't like that. To my mind he's a very decent man. I don't think the thought even occurred to him that someone might suspect him of a crime, certainly not murder. I don't believe he thinks like that.'

'To the pure, all things are pure.'

'Something like that.'

'Are you finished with him, then?'

'No, nothing like. I'm picking it up with him again at HS. Along with the Countess or Pauline, I think. I'll let you know.'

Arne Pedersen thanked him and asked:

'Any idea when you're going to get back on the job? As head, I mean. I'm assuming you don't want to be hanging about.'

Simonsen didn't know, it was up to his doctor. And the Countess. She'd be wanting her own say in the matter, no doubt about that. He dismissed the question and jabbed a finger at the chessboard.

Konrad Simonsen and Arne Pedersen's chess games had evolved into a somewhat one-sided affair. When Simonsen's former boss Kasper Planck had been alive, the two of them had played together for a number of years to their mutual enjoyment, not least because they were a good match for each other. After Planck's death, Arne Pedersen had taken his place as Simonsen's chess partner. The first times they played, Simonsen had come out on top, but that seemed like a long time ago now. These days, Arne Pedersen won just about every game, and easily, too. He had a talent, it was as simple as that, though he hardly showed much interest in the game at all. To him, their evenings were all about getting together informally and having a good time. His opponent looked at it rather differently.

Simonsen pondered what looked like his final predicament.

'I can't do much about this, can I?' he said eventually, with some small hope of a miracle.

'Doesn't look like it.'

They shook hands politely, a ritual they took pains to uphold after the final game.

'Don't you get bored by this?' Simonsen asked. 'I mean, I'm not much of a challenge for you, am I?'

'No, it doesn't bore me at all. I look forward to our chess nights. I hope you're not thinking of knocking it on the head just because I win a few more than you?'

Simonsen echoed the words with disdain:

'Win a few more than me? You *always* win.'

'All right, so I always win. Or nearly always. We played a draw last time, in case you'd forgotten.'

'That was the time before last, and you were so exhausted you were falling asleep.'

Arne Pedersen set the pieces out and they ran though the game again, Pedersen explaining to Simonsen where he'd gone wrong.

It had been an enjoyable evening, and it had done both of them good. For a bit the Countess came in and sat with them without ruining the mood. Simonsen's heart surgery had brought the Countess and Pedersen rather closer. Not so long ago they'd hardly been able to work together.

It was past midnight by the time Pedersen went home. Before getting to his feet there was something he wanted to say, now he had them where he wanted them, as he put it. He reached up to fiddle with the knot of his tie, only to realise he wasn't wearing one. His other hand repeated the movement automatically, with the same result. Simonsen and the Countess exchanged glances, recognising the gesture all too well.

'You'd make a lousy poker player, Arne,' Simonsen said. 'What's up? Spit it out.'

'Nothing, as such. I was going to tell you in the morning, but the thing is she came down to my office, out of the blue, without an appointment or anything. I think she's keeping an eye on me, trying to catch me out and stuff. She just sat there with that cold look in her eyes...'

Simonsen cut him off.

'Wait a minute.'

Pedersen fell silent. Simonsen had to get him started again:

'I'm assuming *she* is our boss.'

'You can say what you want, but she's got it in for me.'

The Countess stood up and put a hand on his shoulder.

'Listen. The truth of the matter is you're doing brilliantly as head of department, better than anyone expected, including me. And I'm sure the Deputy Commissioner is very pleased with what you're doing. If she isn't, she's got to be stupid.'

'She's not stupid, just malicious, that's all. But that's my problem, not yours. Anyway, the thing is, she told me that you, Simon, are now in charge of your own hours. But we're supposed to make sure you don't rush things. She was adamant about that bit. And you're still not to take on any executive function, which I'm really sorry about, even if I do understand why.'

Konrad Simonsen and the Countess had to stop themselves from laughing. It was three days since they'd been told Arne Pedersen's piece of news after the Countess had phoned the Deputy Commissioner herself, albeit with Simonsen's knowledge and consent.

They showed their guest out and shut the front door behind him.

'You'll have to think of something, Simon,' the Countess said. 'He's scared of her. I had no idea it was that bad.'

'No, it's not the best scenario, is it?'

'Not the best scenario? It's pure paranoia, that's what it is. We can't have two people going around the department seeing ghosts wherever they look.'

'You mean Pauline?'

'Who else?'

She was right, of course. Pauline, who else? He promised to think about it.

As Head of the Homicide Department, Konrad Simonsen was accustomed to any number of people approaching him requesting an appointment. There'd been e-mails, letters, phone calls, and not infrequently people turning up at Police HQ in person, to demand he give up his time to them on the spot. The vast majority of these petitions were filtered away by lower-ranking staff and never reached him, and only in a very few cases did he become directly involved. When that occurred he would generally tend to find a younger officer to sit in, who could take care of the matter on his behalf.

These approaches from the general public fell roughly into four categories. The first consisted of mentally unstable individuals wishing to share with him what were obviously figments of their imagination. A TV host staring at them during a programme, for instance, and planning to kill them. Then there were the well-meaning amateurs who were convinced that by their genius and logical thinking they had solved some closed or ongoing case, usually a murder. Then came the pathological liars, people who would do anything to be interviewed by the police and who made up stories with the same intention, most often in the form of false confessions. Finally, there was a fourth category, without doubt the worst of them all: family and friends unable to come to terms with the fact that a loved one was dead, and who imagined it must be as a result of crime. These traumatised individuals were often exceptionally persistent in their endeavours to capture the time of a senior crime investigator, and if they succeeded they were almost impossible to get rid of again.

The two people waiting for Konrad Simonsen outside Police HQ when he came in for work on Tuesday morning belonged to this latter category. The duty officer at the desk managed to warn him over his mobile before he got there, and he was able to use another entrance in order to avoid them.

On entering his office he found a stack of papers on his desk, meticulously placed by the keyboard of his computer, allowing him no chance of not seeing them. On top was a yellow Post-it note informing him that the material had been sent in earlier by the two people waiting for him outside the main entrance.

He flicked through the papers casually. The first contained a printout of three long e-mails, all addressed to Simonsen himself, but filtered out before reaching his mailbox. Each had been politely answered by a sergeant whose name he didn't recognise, and these replies, more or less identically worded, stated that Københavns Politi regrettably were unable to pursue the matter, the sergeant referring them instead to the Nordsjællands Politi and concluding rather laconically that Detective Superintendent Konrad Simonsen was *therefore unable to offer any personal appointment to discuss the matter.* Which was correct.

The remainder of the documents consisted of a Xeroxed autopsy report. Simonsen paused upon seeing the name of the deceased. *Juli Denissen.* Somewhere, a bell rang. About a year before, Juli Denissen had been a witness and had provided valuable information in connection with Pauline Berg's abduction. Later, when it was all over, Simonsen and the Countess had found themselves in Hundested on another matter. On their way home they'd stopped by the woman's address in Frederiksværk and had given her the Countess's mobile phone. Juli's old one had been broken and Simonsen, who had been surprisingly taken with the young woman on meeting her, thought she deserved a new one. After that, he had neither seen nor heard of her and had long since forgotten all about her.

Distracted, he rolled the documents until they were a tight cylinder in his hand, and wondered for a brief moment if he should dump them in his wastepaper basket, only then to glance out of the window at the dense, grey autumn sky. It was not the sort of day on which to stand outside and wait for a person for hours on end, which they undoubtedly would do, and probably the day after as well, if they followed the norm. Instead of discarding the roll of papers he went out into the corridor, determined to offload the matter on to the first lower-ranking investigator he ran into.

Unfortunately, it was Pauline Berg.

Most of Konrad Simonsen's work this dismal autumn Tuesday consisted of reading the reports of investigators who had been out knocking on doors in Hvidovre trying to turn up something on Jørgen Kramer Nielsen. But apart from a couple of notes he wanted to pursue, his endeavours provided him with little else but the feeling of being slightly better informed than previously. After lunch he met the Deputy Commissioner, a meeting that went well, it seemed, his boss apparently delighted by the idea he put forward. But just as he was about to leave, she stopped him.

'While you're here, Simon, I got this e-mail about an hour ago and I want you to have a look at it. I was going to forward it, but now you're here you might as well read it.'

She turned her computer screen and allowed him to see. It was from the National Police Commissioner and was presumably to be taken as a formal reminder to make sure that the various police districts' fields of jurisdiction continued to be respected. Simonsen wasn't sure he understood, which was hardly surprising since he never did know how to interpret e-mails from the country's highest-ranking police officer, the head of the Rigspolitiet. Nor was he the only one.

'What's it got to do with me?'

The Deputy Commissioner placed her elbows on her desk and put the tips of her fingers together, resting her chin on her index fingers.

'Nothing, as such. But it sounds like Arne Pedersen might have too much on his plate. Can you sort it out for him?'

'Sort what out? Now you're making as little sense as our number one.'

'Call the chief constable in Frederikssund, preferably before you go home today. It's better he gets the story from you. It's only second- or third-hand to me.'

It was a request that ought to have set off alarm bells, but it didn't. Back in his office, Simonsen decided the phone call to Nordsjælland's chief constable could wait until tomorrow. And then he went home.

That evening he and the Countess had visitors again.

Malte Borup, the Countess's favourite intern, and his girl-friend Anita Dahlgren were invited to dinner, and it was all much more enjoyable than Konrad Simonsen could have dared to hope. The Countess had hired a chef to prepare some low-fat cuisine. Simonsen was used to her indulging in such extravagances now and then, and while the chef's physical stature in no way adver-tised the benefits of his slimming recipes, it was money well spent. The dinner was no less than excellent: a selection of fine cheeses on toasted bread, tournedos with rice and peppers, and a home-made blackcurrant sorbet with whole berries to round things off.

Simonsen ate heartily without feeling any pangs of conscience. After the feast, the two women disappeared and Simonsen was left on his own with Malte, who enthused incomprehensibly about the virtues of the HOMS app, the software he had spent the greater part of his summer holidays familiarising himself with, and which it seemed provided them with unparalleled opportunities and was destined to become a powerful tool in future investigations.

Later on, they all played Ludo together. It was no holds barred, only victory mattered. Each had their own way of playing: the Countess tried to establish fleeting alliances, Simonsen stuck to probability calculus and Malte cheated, even after getting caught. He carried on regardless, rules for him apparently being little more than loose guidelines. Anita won. She had decided to be lucky, and it was a strategy that trounced all opposition twice on the trot.

The Countess drove the young guests home. When she got back, Simonsen had tidied up and flopped down on the sofa, where he sat staring emptily into space. He had lined up the Ludo tokens in a row on the coffee table in front of him, a couple of centimetres from the edge. She sat down next to him.

'Are you killing off your troops for losing? If you are, we're going to be a token short.'

He ignored her comment.

'There we were, lined up to defend the Embassy, while our superiors were light years away in their cosy riot vans. But they'd taught us well. Get stuck in, that was what they said.'

'Those protesters weren't exactly sweetness and light.'

'No, but these days we try to stem any violence in advance. Back then, they sent us out to fight.'

'I remember hearing about petrol bombs and potatoes with razor blades in them.'

'That was the IMF confrontation, and it was an exaggeration. This was anti-Vietnam. And yes, sweetness and light were in short supply. The protesters were terrifying and despicable. *Ho, Ho, Ho Chi Minh! Ho, Ho, Ho Chi Minh!* That was the chant, from tens of thousands of people. That's why I can't stand football. The game itself and the cheering is OK, but I can't take the aggressive, co-ordinated chants of the fans.'

'That's a shame, Simon. One of these days I'll show you something really beautiful. But go on.'

'Most of all I was afraid of any kind of wave action in the crowd. We'd have been trampled to death as easily as anything. What the high-ups called our "opponents" were far stronger than us, they just didn't know it. Nor did our crowd-control instructor. The hatred he preached, you wouldn't believe. I wish I'd spoken out, but like everyone else I stuck my head in the sand and let the anger towards the hippies and the Provos flow... the red rabble... they were going to get a good hiding like they deserved. Fear and anger make a dangerous cocktail, especially for a big, strong lad like I was in those days… with a truncheon in his hand.'

The Countess agreed cautiously, though she found it hard to follow him.

'*Der Staat ist auf dem rechten Auge blind.* The state is blind in its right eye. Only the youth of the day were just as blind in their left. No wonder it went wrong.'

'I suppose so.'

He stared into thin air for a moment, immersed in thought. Then he spoke quietly.

'And then came the girl. Handing out roses. Smiling and unfazed, as if it were the most natural thing in the world to go from one policeman in riot gear to the next, offering a rose, while hatred and anger were boiling over in our midst. Of course, none of us accepted, but still she went down the whole line. When she got to me she dropped her flowers. Maybe they were knocked out of her hand, maybe she was pushed, I can't remember. But whatever happened, the flowers lay there on the ground between me and my mate, just behind us. A matter of centimetres perhaps, but enough. When she bent down to pick them up, she broke the line and I hit her, as hard as I could, on her shoulder. After she sank down I kicked her in the side. She was seventeen years old, a fragile seventeen-year-old girl, a student who wanted to give me a rose.'

'Oh, Simon…'

'Oh, Simon, indeed. After that, all hell broke loose and the fighting started, just like we'd been waiting for. The next day, I was commended for being ruthless.'

They sat for a while and allowed silence to descend. The Countess leaned closer and whispered:

'You've been wanting to get that out for a long time.'

'There's never been anyone to tell, and I don't think I would have been able to before. But it's like this sort of… talk… is easier for me now.'

'This sort of talk is what's called having feelings.'

'All right, feelings then. But it's easier for me since we got together, and especially after...'

'After you seduced me?'

The comment broke his melancholy.

'After I what? That's pure falsification of history! Anyway, it wasn't what I was going to say.'

'Fibber.'

'Not a bit.'

'Yes, you are, you're a fibber, admit it! Full of fibs!'

'OK, so I'm a fibber, now button it. I want you to hear this good idea of mine regarding Arne. This priest who shared the house with our victim is bringing his bishop along with him to our interview on Thursday, so I've thought of something that might kill two birds with one stone. Do you want to hear?'

'If you're quick.'

The Countess found Konrad Simonsen's idea to be both reasonable and original. This was praise indeed, coming from her: the Countess seldom uttered a superlative.

Arne Pedersen, however, had his reservations when Simonsen gave him it in outline in Simonsen's office on the Wednesday morning.

'Have you gone daft? It's out of the question. Not under any circumstances. A categorical no.'

Simonsen held up his hands in a defensive gesture.

'Just calm down a bit. Allow it to sink in first.'

'Nothing's going to sink in here. What a ridiculous idea! What possible use would she be? She's a legal person, and Deputy Commissioner on top of that. She hasn't a clue about questioning. Besides, she hasn't time for that sort of thing, and thank God for it!'

'She'll make the time. In fact, she's looking forward to it. What's more, she knows she's got to keep quiet and speak only when you give her the nod.'

Arne Pedersen got up from his chair and paced the width of Simonsen's office. The glimmer of hope in his face was quickly extinguished:

'You're taking the piss, Simon. All very funny, I admit, but it's got to be a joke, surely?'

'I mentioned it to her yesterday afternoon, and she said I was to say hello and congratulate you on such a good idea. She's delighted to play her part.'

'This is worse than bad. Have you something for your nerves that I can borrow?'

'I'm on all sorts, but nothing like that.'

'Booze then. Anything alcoholic?'

'Bad idea. You don't want her suspecting you of drinking on the job while you're putting her in the picture ready for tomorrow. Which you'll be doing between three-thirty and four o'clock this afternoon. I've booked it into your diary so you won't forget.'

'Help! That's all I can say. Help.'

'I knew you'd come round.'

They worked purposefully together for the next three hours. Arne Pedersen was particularly sharp today. The fact that he would soon be relaying the results to the Deputy Commissioner was the perfect intellectual catalyst. After a number of fruitful discussions they agreed on five main questions to which they hoped they would receive answers during the course of the following day's interview with the priest and his bishop, whose presence the priest had insisted on.

Arne Pedersen typed out the five points, printed them out and, with the sheet of paper in his hand, demanded they go through it all again one more time. Simonsen, who by now was feeling somewhat fatigued by all their hard work, reluctantly agreed.

'The first point has to do with what kind of relationship there was between the priest and Kramer Nielsen. What did he know about him besides whatever it was they talked about in the confessional?'

'Right. The cohabitation angle. Everything that doesn't come under the privilege of the confessional.'

'The next step is to uncover Kramer Nielsen's religious life as best we can under the circumstances. A lot of it's going to be privileged information, but we want to know why he converted, and in particular whether he had any sort of relationship going on with anyone from the Catholic community, as well as who was there when they buried him.'

'Cremated. Kramer Nielsen was cremated.'

'Whatever. So, who was at the funeral? Focus with regard to any friends or acquaintances… Hey, hang on a minute, Simon.'

'I'm hanging on.'

'What's the difference between getting buried and cremated? In terms of the ritual, I mean.'

'In the first instance the body's lowered into the ground, in the other it's driven away for cremation.'

'What happens if there are no family or friends? You can't ask a corpse, can you, do you want to be buried or cremated?'

'Buried is the default, I think.'

'Jørgen Kramer Nielsen was cremated.'

Konrad Simonsen mulled this over before responding. Eventually, he replied, cautiously:

'I see what you're getting at. In Kramer Nielsen's case, the Catholic Church stepped in and took over the duties of burial from the state. I've no idea if there are any other standards that might apply in that case. There could have been a stipulation in Kramer Nielsen's will, of course.'

'Which Pauline unearthed six months *after* cremation had taken place. I think we can dismiss that possibility. And if there was some departure from normal procedure, then someone must have known it was the wish of the deceased. They could only have known if they'd spoken to that person about Kramer Nielsen's death. The most obvious candidate would be the priest.'

'Interesting. I can do the groundwork for you tomorrow morning, then hopefully you'll have a really good question to put to him. But let's get back to these five points, because I'm knackered.'

It wasn't entirely true, but Simonsen felt Arne Pedersen could very well keep on going over every detail until his briefing meeting with the Deputy Commissioner, and Simonsen couldn't be bothered.

'The third area is Jørgen Kramer Nielsen's Confessions. What were they about? Does the priest know things we ought to know too? Is Jørgen Kramer Nielsen's religious affiliation in any way linked to his killing? These all being matters where I can expect to encounter unco-operative witnesses.'

'Basically, we want to know whether the priest thinks if, with his help, we'd be able to clear this killing up if it were possible for him to share information divulged to him during Confession.'

Arne Pedersen summed up their thinking so far.

The main thrust of the interview was going to consist of hypotheses, negation and indirect correlations, and as interviewer he would need to draw the right conclusions as quickly as possible in respect of a *no* and a *no comment*. Hesitation, a look or any other sign of uncertainty between the two witnesses would give him the information he needed, whatever they actually said. Moreover, the pace at which he proceeded would be crucial. It would be all about timing rather than the third degree.

Simonsen approved Pedersen's appraisal, thinking to himself that in fact the purpose of this exercise was more to do with Pedersen's presentation of their groundwork to the Deputy Commissioner than the actual interview itself. Pedersen repeated:

'Swift, seamless logic. That's the key.'

'Good. Let's take the last item.'

The last item was Kramer Nielsen's relationship to the girl in the loft, including who she was, why he was so obsessed by her, and so on. Though that all depended on whether the priest even knew about the girl, which was what they had to uncover first.

'The most important question of all being: who is she?' said Pedersen.

'Or rather *was*. I've been thinking a great deal about this, and I'm inclined to go along with Pauline's hunch and assume she's dead. That loft's a mausoleum. If you can clear up the main issue of whether she's dead or alive for certain, we'll have come a long way. Oh, and while we're at it, Kurt Melsing says you'll have a photo of her tomorrow morning first thing. The technicians have done a composite from the posters in the loft. Right, that's it, we're finished here. Any more and you're just waving to the crowds, Arne. You've got it all off pat, and I want something to eat.'

'Wait a minute. What about... what about her?'

Meaning the Deputy Commissioner, that much was obvious. Arne Pedersen began going through the possibilities: what if *she* said this, what if *she* asked about that or, worse, what if it turned out *she* thought that *he*...

Simonsen stopped him in his tracks.

'Knock it off, Arne. You're as prepared as can be, and besides, she'll spend most of the time telling you she doesn't mean to interfere.'

'How come?'

'You can work that one out, surely?'

'You didn't tell her I was scared of her, did you? You didn't!'

'You are, though, aren't you?'

'Yes, but... but that doesn't... what did she say?'

'She was very sorry to hear it, as indeed she ought to be. There's no point in your going about like a bag of nerves. You can die from that.'

CHAPTER 5

Autumn was setting in. The Boston ivy on the Homicide Department facing Niels Brocks Gade changed colour, the summer's weary green all gradually replaced by cheerful yellow and orange hues that lent the gentle morning drizzle a golden appearance. Soon they would turn again, into bright reds, and when they did the summer half of the year would be definitively over according to Konrad Simonsen's calendar. He raised his head and looked out over the roof. Pale grey clouds, barely discernible against the blue-white sky, drifted east like smoke wafting from a chimney.

He had clocked in earlier than usual so as to come in with the Countess. She was run off her feet and needed a long day at work so she wouldn't get home too late. He thought to himself that she probably wouldn't get back until evening anyway, and truth be told it was a bit daft coming in together in separate cars, but it had been his own idea that they leave home at the same time, so...

His train of thought came to a halt when he discovered the note. She had stuck it to the TV screen in his annexe with Sellotape, and as soon as he set eyes on it he knew it was from her. No one but Pauline Berg would leave a message for him there, if only because she was the only person familiar with his new habit of starting the day by zapping through the news on Teletext before getting on with his work.

He tore the note from the screen and shook his head in annoyance at the small but no less visible area of sticky tape that was left behind. Couldn't she have stuck it somewhere else instead? He read her words with puzzlement. Pauline couldn't come in to HS today because she had gone to Frederikssund to pursue the Juli case. That was it, apart from the signing off which he found slightly inappropriate: *Lots of love, Pauline.* Whether she had left the note for him when she went home the day before, or whether she had come in early and then gone again, he had no idea. He addressed the note with a frown: *the Juli case?* And then at last his brain joined the dots and he put a clenched fist to his brow.

'Oh, God, tell me she hasn't.'

A long conversation with the chief constable in Frederikssund told him she had.

The chief constable seemed reasonable enough, and once Simonsen as far as he was able had given him some background on Pauline Berg's behaviour, the man calmed down and showed himself to be rather co-operative. He could quite understand the problem from Simonsen's point of view, but it wasn't on, having an errant crime investigator running about on his patch, poking her nose into a case that wasn't even a case, and which without a shadow of a doubt was nothing but a natural, albeit tragic, death. Simonsen could do little else but agree with the man: it wasn't on at all. He promised to call back later in the day and assured the chief constable he would do everything in his power to rein in his runaway subordinate.

As soon as he'd uttered the words Simonsen realised he might be promising more than he was able to deliver. It was a concern confirmed only moments later when he called Pauline's mobile, only to be put through to her answering service. He left a message telling her to get back to HS right away and without further ado, and wondered at the same time whether the Countess's unauthorised contacts in telecommunications might be able to trace the phone so he would at least know where the hell Pauline was. But then he took a deep breath and tried to relax, telling himself it would be overkill. Then, after thinking again, he decided to see if he might have a quick word with the National Commissioner.

The secretary at the National Police Commissioner's office was adamant once she heard what it was Simonsen wanted.

'Not today, Simon. Not even for a minute, not unless it's absolutely vital.'

He knew her well: a friendly, efficient woman who without exception treated everyone with respect.

'I can't say that it is, I'm afraid,' he said with a sigh.

She swivelled on her chair and looked him in the eye.

'Is it about Pauline Berg?'

He wasn't at all surprised that she was so well informed, and confirmed this.

'I've heard she's gone off on her own, but if it's about disciplinary sanctions I can't help you. I wouldn't even book you in for another day. If she's not breaking the law, or doing anything that might bring herself or others into danger, then no one can touch her. And there are no buts.'

This, too, came as no surprise to Simonsen. He knew the game only too well. But it left him with a problem, and she could help him with that.

Her response was affected, coquettish almost: what could *she* possibly do?

He told her as much as he knew. In her own mind, Pauline Berg now had the case she desperately wanted: her own. Apart from the fact that there *was* no case, though unfortunately there did seem to be some parallels with his own, which presumably had encouraged Pauline to snatch at this one.

'Your dead postman?'

'My dead postman, yes. But the woman from the Frederikssund police district wasn't murdered, and besides that I'm sure it's bad enough for her family as it is without them being dragged through a superfluous and unauthorised criminal investigation...'

He gave it the works, though within reason, realising she wouldn't buy it if he came on too strong.

'And you don't think Pauline Berg will come to heel if you ask her?' she asked.

'I doubt it. A lot of the time she does what she wants, and it looks like she can get away with it, too.'

'Yes, it looks like it. Tell me what I can do.'

Konrad Simonsen nodded towards the Commissioner's closed door.

'Get him to transfer the matter of the woman's death to me. Then I'll see if I can shut it all down nice and gently.'

'How do you imagine I can transfer a case that doesn't exist?'

'I don't know, but it's the sort of thing you're good at, if you want to be. All it takes is a few keystrokes, surely?'

'And what do you suppose Nordsjællands Politi will have to say about that? They'll think we're idiots.'

'I'll drive up to Frederikssund tomorrow morning and explain it to the chief constable there in person.'

She thought about it for a moment. Her previous reservations about its feasibility evaporated. Eventually, she gave in.

'OK, Simon, you win. You'll have it in writing from him by tomorrow at the latest.'

Simonsen was irritable after this poor start to his day. He holed up in his office for a couple of hours, isolating himself from his surroundings with two reports from Interpol he had been meaning to read for a long time, without giving the postman case a thought. At intervals he called Pauline's mobile, though each time unsuccessfully.

His mood improved considerably, however, when the interview with the priest and his bishop evolved into the most perfect piece of police work he had been party to in years.

Shortly before their ecclesiastical guests arrived, he went to Arne Pedersen's office and found its occupant looking rather surprisingly unruffled. A few minutes later they were joined by a relaxed and smiling Deputy Commissioner dressed in bright yellow like an Easter chick, albeit regrettably an Easter chick with a mobile phone, and hardly had she entered the room before it began to ring. Konrad Simonsen and Arne Pedersen exchanged glances. Superiors who were present and yet half the time absent because of their *very important* phone calls were all too familiar to them both. But they were doing her a disservice: what the two men thought to be bad manners turned out to be sensible groundwork. The call was a short one. The Deputy Commissioner hung up and briefed them.

'Just as I thought. That was the duty desk. Our guests are on their way and it looks like we should prepare ourselves for a display of ecclesiastical ceremony. But two can play at that game. I'll be back in five minutes. No need to worry, the duty sergeant will keep them busy in the meantime. Let's give them the reception they deserve.'

And with that she was gone.

'What on earth was all that about?' asked Arne Pedersen.

'Dress, I reckon. Can't be too sure, though. In five minutes all will be revealed. Are you nervous?'

'I could have throttled you yesterday. Now I could give you a kiss.'

'I'll settle for something in between, if you don't mind. But remember, don't force things. You're too impatient by half sometimes.'

When the Deputy Commissioner eventually returned she was in full uniform. The effect was that much more impressive, given the slightness of her frame: she was impeccably clad, with a display of badges of rank and insignia that would make even an untrained eye blink. Simonsen and Pedersen, far from untrained, both rose to their feet immediately. The symbolism was demonstrative: from the decorated shoulder straps to the cap under her arm, gold-braided foliage of oak luxuriating about the crown of the realm, all speaking its own unambiguous language of power.

'Right, are we ready to receive our guests, Arne?' she asked, buoyantly. 'They're on their way up now. It's not exactly the first time in the history of our country that the crown and the cross have clashed. But I'm rather interested to see which of us will come out on top today.'

She held the door open for Arne Pedersen, who swiftly stepped out into the corridor ahead of her.

Konrad Simonsen lingered a moment in the office until he heard the door of the interview room close. He hurried into an adjoining room, where a two-way mirror allowed him to follow events as they unfolded.

The bishop, a man in his mid-forties with a fleshy, open face and a steady gaze, was in full choir dress. His cassock was of fuchsia silk that hung in folds about his large frame, and on his head was a matching zucchetto that, besides complementing the rest of his ecclesiastical garb, hid an encroaching bald patch that Simonsen noted when the man found himself compelled momentarily to lift the little skullcap in order to scratch his head. Most imposing of all, however, was the pectoral cross, a crucifix with corpus that hung from a thick gold chain around his neck. That, and the man's unflappable calm.

The Deputy Commissioner asked them to be seated, offering coffee, tea or mineral water before affably introducing herself and

Arne Pedersen. That done, she placed her uniform cap on the table in front of her and commenced the interview, thanking them with professional courtesy for coming and guaranteeing full respect for their religious sensibilities. Simonsen noted how she addressed the bishop almost exclusively, while Arne Pedersen focused intently on the priest. Moreover, she managed to imbue her words about co-operation and mutual respect with such sincerity as to raise her introduction far above the usual platitudes.

The bishop was by no means unmoved, and his first utterance, about wishing to help the police in their enquiries as far as it lay within their means to do so, certainly seemed genuine enough. Then, just as everyone thought the Deputy Commissioner would now hand over the stage to the main players, she began to talk about her holiday in Rome last spring. The bishop listened with interest, and before anyone could say *time-wasting*, the two superiors were chatting away about the Colosseum, the Spanish Steps and narrow, ochre-coloured streets, while their respective subordinates looked impatiently at the ceiling then at each other. Simonsen rested his head in his hands and swore it was the last time he would ever involve a jurist in a police interview.

Not until what seemed like twenty minutes later, when the Deputy Commissioner had filled them in on her grandchildren and the bishop had told her about his ordainment, both had waxed lyrical on the Sistine Chapel, and their involuntary audience had yawned, one surreptitiously, the other quite unabashedly, did Konrad Simonsen realise this was all collusion. From where he was sitting he saw how Arne Pedersen discreetly patted his boss on the thigh, of all places, underneath the table. It went without saying that no one on the force, and certainly not Arne Pedersen, was invested with the authority to fondle the Deputy Commissioner's thigh, and Konrad Simonsen's hitherto wearied demeanour was at once transformed into a broad and appreciative smile. The holiday recollections and exchange of personal chit-chat had all run according to a hidden agenda. Their small talk had in part undoubtedly established new group relations between chief and chief, minion and minion, just as it had served to erode the defence mechanisms the priest almost certainly had set on red alert from the outset. Being ready and bored at the same time is not a feasible combination.

The Deputy Commissioner rounded off with a few pleasantly uttered words, and then Arne Pedersen dropped a bombshell:

'Whose decision was it for Jørgen Kramer Nielsen to be cremated?'

His tone was sharp, offended almost, and he was addressing the bishop. The Deputy Commissioner, who had otherwise now leaned back into the role of expectant onlooker, interrupted in puzzled tones:

'Cremated?'

She made it sound like he'd been stuffed and put on display, but was quick to beat a retreat.

'I'm sorry, don't mind me. Please go on.'

Arne Pedersen paused. Long enough for the first real question for the priest to be put to him by the bishop.

'Yes, who decided that?'

The priest hesitated, and again Pedersen's timing was impeccable. He cleared the table and dealt the cards anew.

'Perhaps that's the wrong place to start. Let's get back to that later.'

He looked at the priest.

'I'd like you in your own words to tell us as much about Jørgen Kramer Nielsen as you are able, in view of your being sworn to uphold the doctrine of confidentiality between priest and penitent.'

The priest was forthcoming. He had little to tell them that they were unaware of beforehand, but the picture they had of Kramer Nielsen being a loner was supported. As two people living in the same house, they got along together on friendly, polite terms, though their relationship went no further than that, and yet Konrad Simonsen was able to find answers to some of the questions he and Arne Pedersen had posed the day before. Most of them negative. For instance, as far as the priest knew, the postman enjoyed no further associations with anyone from his parish; the priest knew nothing about any plane crash; and the only person he recalled having paid a call on his upstairs neighbour had been a plumber. Apart from that, he had very occasionally got the impression there were two people in the upstairs flat, although… well, he wasn't sure, by any means. One matter, however, was perhaps of interest. It concerned the deceased's conversion to Catholicism. Arne Pedersen interrupted, sounding eager:

'We'd like to hear about that.'

'It was something Jørgen had been thinking about for a long time, certainly way before I knew him. I think what decided it for him in the end was my wanting to buy his house. There were others who were interested, too, and I'm sure I would have lost out had it been down to money alone. Not that he gave the place away, far from it, but then I'm sure you've already looked into that.'

Arne Pedersen confirmed:

'Yes, we have, and it was all above board. With property prices at the time it wasn't even that cheap.'

Konrad Simonsen smiled. Arne Pedersen was making it up.

'But there were others who bid more than I was able to. All the interested parties were invited in turn to a short interview that took place at the post office, as it happens. Jørgen wanted to make sure he wasn't going to end up sharing the house with someone he didn't care for. As soon as he realised I was a priest, a Catholic priest, that is, he told me all about his wish to convert. I promised to help him as much as I could, naturally, if he felt the way he did, and at the same time I made it clear to him that the offer stood regardless of who he decided to sell the house to. I do think it was instrumental in his eventual choice, though.'

'Do you know why he decided to move into the upstairs flat? Or why he wanted to sell at all?'

'I do, yes. He told me he didn't want to look after the garden any more.'

'It's not so big.'

'No, but that's what he said, and he sold up because his tenant on the first floor moved into sheltered accommodation. That was what did it.'

Simonsen thought it fitted well with Kramer Nielsen having set up his mirrored loft nine years ago, if that's what all the window spray was for on his receipts from Netto. But some of the posters of the girl probably dated from a considerable time before.

Arne Pedersen pressed on.

'So converting was something Jørgen Kramer Nielsen had been considering for a long time?'

'Yes, a very long time indeed.'

'Why?'

'I can't answer that.'

'Because you don't know?'

'I can't answer that.'

Both servants of the Lord shook their heads with regret, and Simonsen noted that *can't answer that* in the second instance obviously meant *no*. Pedersen rounded off the first act with a short summary, and the priest confirmed its accuracy. Again, Pedersen gave the Deputy Commissioner an unseen nudge under the table, then went on:

'That was the more general stuff. Now...'

The Deputy Commissioner cut in:

'Wait a minute, you said you were going to tell us who decided Kramer Nielsen was to be cremated.'

Once again, it was the bishop she addressed. Konrad Simonsen was enjoying the way things were developing. What began with a question about who had decided on cremation was now presented as a promise of an answer with the man under fire being the bishop, who knew nothing about the matter.

'That's right, I did. Why did we choose cremation, exactly?'

The priest replied, after a moment's thought:

'The decision was mine. It was Jørgen Kramer Nielsen's wish to be cremated.'

There was a heavy pause, before the bishop asked:

'Is that what he told you?'

The priest was not happy about the situation and answered reluctantly.

'No, not directly, but it was my clear impression. He was afraid… afraid of darkness.'

Hardly had the words passed his lips before Arne Pedersen slapped a photograph down on the table in front of him.

'Did it have something to do with the girl in this photo?'

'Yes, but I'm afraid that's all I can say.'

'Do you know her?'

'No.'

'Not even her name?'

'No.'

The questions came like a volley of shots, Pedersen's eyes fixing the priest's.

'Do you know anything about her?'

'I can't answer that.'

'If you knew nothing about her, would you be able to tell me that?'

'Then there'd be nothing to say.'

'But you'd be able to answer me on that?'

'Yes.'

'If I ask you if she's dead, are you going to answer me?'

'I'd like to, but I can't.'

'Is she dead?'

The door opened and a red-haired intern from the Deputy Commissioner's office came in with a tray of mineral waters. Without words, but with a friendly smile worthy of any waiter, she swapped the bottles for empties and withdrew again. Not even Konrad Simonsen reflected on the matter. Procedures were always bent a bit when bosses were taking part. Arne Pedersen repeated the question from before the interruption:

'Is she dead?'

'I can't answer that.'

The Deputy Commissioner's timing was impressive. A split second before the bishop could cut in she turned to Arne Pedersen.

'There's something wrong here.'

The bishop concurred.

'Yes, it would seem there is.'

The priest grasped the pause eagerly, though was clearly unaware of what was going on. Certainly he seemed oblivious to Arne Pedersen's presence.

'What's the problem?' he asked the bishop.

'The problem just left the room.'

He nodded towards the door through which the intern had just gone out. The Deputy Commissioner delivered a cutting rebuke of her subordinate:

'You must get a grip, Arne. This is embarrassing.'

Arne Pedersen flicked calmly through his folder, leaving the photograph of the intern in plain sight in front of the priest. Then, apologetically, he said to no one in particular:

'Sorry about that. Our red-haired friend would be three or four years older than the other girl would have been.'

The priest studied the photo for the first time, and his sad eyes seemed almost to be staring inwards when Arne Pedersen finally picked it up and replaced it with one of a good-looking young girl that Kurt Melsing's department had extracted from the clouds.

'Perhaps this one's dead, then?'

The bishop shook his head pointedly.

'This is getting too complicated for me. I think you've had your answer. I'm afraid we can add no more.'

Arne Pedersen let the issue lie, skipping instead somewhat absently through a few loose ends concerning the landing where the deceased was discovered, before declaring the interview over. All that remained was for the Deputy Commissioner to thank them for their co-operation, a matter she dealt with quite as elegantly as she had introduced them. On their way out she apologised once more:

'I really am sorry about the mix-up with those photos. Perhaps we might return to the issue once we've made more headway?'

Arne Pedersen blushed appropriately like a schoolboy. The bishop, however, was quick to play down the matter, content that the interview had gone off in an atmosphere of mutual co-operation.

'These things happen. And we'd like to help as much as we can, of course.'

'Excellent, and thank you for a most pleasant chat. I do hope we've shown tact as to your faith, though I must admit I'm still not sure what you're allowed to divulge and what you're not.'

The priest commented with a tight-lipped smile:

'I should get my own photos sorted out one of these days.'

Konrad Simonsen was painting that afternoon, a job he enjoyed and had got stuck into as soon as he came home.

The Countess had let him borrow a wing of her annexe as a makeshift gallery for Jørgen Kramer Nielsen's posters. His excuse for hanging them at home was poor: they ought to be viewed properly, he contended, in decent suroundings, after the psychologists, behavioural scientists and photo buffs had been asked to give their takes on what the images might mean. No one bought the explanation, but nor did anyone feel much like delving into the real reason, so the upshot was that the posters ended up in Søllerød after first having passed through Kurt Melsing's lab in Vanløse. Now they were leaning up against a wall, waiting to be hung in their newly decorated room. Some tradesmen had cleared the place and carried out a few minor repairs, but Simonsen had insisted on doing the painting himself and he had just got started on the third wall when the Countess came home and found him hard at work. She stood for a while in the doorway watching him. The radio played a decades' old song as he methodically swept the roller up and down the surface in front of him. Now and again he stepped back to consider the results of his efforts. When eventually he realised she was there he switched the radio off.

'Are you spying on me?'

'You know I am. How did Arne's interview go?'

He told her all about it, standing with the paint roller in his hand.

'They'll have been proud of themselves, then?'

'I'll say. You should have seen them. Striding along the corridor arm in arm like a pair of lovesick teenagers, soaking up the applause and boasting their heads off.'

'And you were the audience?'

'Yes, and I can tell you it got a bit tiresome after their eighth curtain call. But credit where credit's due, they were the perfect double act and I got all sorts of useful information out of it.'

'Sounds brilliant.'

'The priest simply assumed it was the girl from the loft on the photo he was shown, and answered accordingly. So there's no doubt now that he knew about her before.'

'Right, I get you. And I take it Arne's not scared of our Deputy Commissioner any more.'

'Scared? He called her by her first name – *Gurli*, he said – and was hugging her like she was a cuddly toy.'

'I'd like to have been there for that.'

'It's all on video. They were so pleased with themselves they forgot to turn the camera off. It wasn't my interview, so I let them get on with it. Wait till you see it, you'll have a laugh.'

'It sounds like something that'll turn up in the entertainment slot at the Christmas do. Anyway, I actually came to ask what time you wanted dinner. And to see how the decorating was coming on, of course.'

The Countess looked around the room.

'It's a bit... gaudy. Why the primary colours?'

'Don't you like it? It's not finished yet.'

She came up to him, but stopped short. Turning one room in the annexe into a rainbow was fine by her, but she didn't want her new cardigan suffering the same psychedelic fate.

'Are you having a good time?'

'I am, actually. Very good.'

'Have you been for your run?'

'Of course. Before long I won't have to walk it at all any more.'

'I'm proud of you, Simon. But there's something we need to talk about.'

He stiffened. Such words from a woman's mouth were seldom encouraging.

'What's that?'

She told him.

Their colleagues had been talking, though of course only when Simonsen himself had been out of earshot. And Pauline Berg as

134

well, since no one really knew where they were with her these days and largely avoided her for the same reason. What if their Head of Homicide was taking them in the wrong direction? Apparently, he'd decided that the postman's murder was to be cleared up by uncovering the man's past. But what if it had been random? A break-in gone wrong? A couple of maladjusted kids who reckoned he had money stashed away? The Countess filled him in on this cautiously.

'And there's any number of other possible scenarios. But you're looking back into Kramer Nielsen's past, and only back.'

His reply was infuriatingly evasive.

'I'm fixing a hole where the rain gets in, filling cracks I should have mended a long time ago.'

'Your own?'

He put the roller down in the tray and elaborated on the case.

'It doesn't really matter that much if I'm right or wrong. It may be a blind alley, and it may not. Remember, no one in the world showed the slightest interest in Jørgen Kramer Nielsen while he was alive. Now I am, after he's dead. And as for myself, I'm spending time on a lot of things that weren't important to me before. As it turned out, reality and circumstances conspired to give me the chance all of a sudden. Where it's going to take me I don't know. But as long as I've got you and Anna Mia, I'm pretty sure I can't go wrong.'

The Countess laughed, a bright, disarming sound, and threw caution to the wind with respect to her cardigan. The paint was surely water-based anyway and could be washed out if need be. And if it couldn't, then she would have an excuse to go into town and buy a new one. Two, even.

'That's sweet of you. I was afraid you couldn't keep the two areas separate.'

'Of course I can. I just don't want to, that's all.'

The Countess stroked his shoulder, then stepped back and looked at him.

'I hear you're having trouble with Pauline.'

It was true, but he'd decided to put the issue off until tomorrow. Besides, he wasn't as worked up about it any more. On the one hand, Pauline was only doing what he would have done himself, if he'd cared to look at Juli's death like that. On the other, it was completely unrelated to his current inquiry. In either case it would have to wait. He just couldn't be bothered to think about her at the moment.

The Countess accepted his explanation. It was reasonable enough. And it was important he didn't do too much at once. She indicated the posters at the far end of the room.

'What about her?'

He turned and looked at them.

'There's no need for me to be jealous, I hear,' added the Countess.

'How do you mean? I didn't even know her. Anyway, to all intents and purposes Arne got the priest to confirm that she was dead. That loft is her memorial.'

'And now you're making her a new one?'

There was a pause before Simonsen replied, and when he did he tried to make it sound casual, jokey even. It didn't work.

'She's used to light.'

'What about Rita? Was she used to light, too?'

The name pulsed in the air between them. She had guessed, but then it had only been a matter of time. He didn't know what to say, so he said nothing.

'The girl with the flowers, the one you hit on that demo. You met her again, didn't you?'

'Yes.'

'And her name was Rita?'

'Yes, but it's my story and I won't tell it until I'm ready. Right now I want to get this painting done.'

To his mind it sounded reasonable, but the Countess ignored him.

'Is she still alive?'

'I don't know, I suppose so. But if you imagine I'm viewing the girl in the posters as a substitute for Rita, you'd be wrong. Is that what you're thinking?'

'It's what I'm afraid of.'

He went over to the posters and tried to make contact with the face in the clouds on the one facing out.

'She was prettier than Rita.'

'Prettier than most, I'd say.'

'Am I declared of sound mind?'

'Yes, you are. And your reward is broccoli, cauliflower and tomatoes in half an hour.

'What would I have got if I wasn't?'

'Broccoli, cauliflower and tomatoes in an hour.'

He had met Rita again two days after the demo. At the time he was living in a flat in Brønshøj, and when the doorbell rang he was in the middle of washing the dishes from the day before. He remembered it vividly. A long, aggressive ring on the bell. He opened the door and two young girls were standing there. Neither would say how they had found his name and address, and to begin with they wouldn't tell him their names either. They had come for the sole purpose of showing him what he had done. Even now, thirty-five years on, he recalled his embarrassment and shame when Rita without warning pulled her blouse over her head so that he could see her bruises. In those days, bras were out. Fortunately so, too, were the majority of his neighbours, but when he heard a door being shut on the floor above, followed by footsteps on the stairs, the only thing he felt he could do was to drag the girls inside and close his own door. Lewdness on the staircase was not the kind of thing that was tolerated in the social housing blocks of the Danish welfare state, and certainly not if you happened to be a police officer and were supposed to be safe-guarding society against the subversive activities, moral as well as political, of the younger generation.

It took him a while to make his uninvited guests understand that he had struck out because he had been scared. At first, they thought he was lying. The pigs were fascists with secret orders from the government to beat up as many protesters as they could. *Draw your truncheons and lay into them!* Could he not remember the shrill voice coming from the loudhailer, while people were being clubbed and the blood was beginning to flow? He stuck to his guns since the truth was he hated demos, as did nearly all his colleagues. And standing there in the police line, before he hit her... well, he couldn't recall ever being so frightened in his life. Or rather, he could, because all he had to do was think back to the demo before that.

Eventually, they believed him, though without letting him off the hook quite so easily. *What about the people of Chile? Weren't they frightened, too? Weren't they scared of Augusto Pinochet's henchmen after the CIA had overturned and murdered President Salvador Allende?* Or was it some other issue they had harangued him about? He wasn't quite sure now. Rita always had some oppressed people or other to hold up in front of her while she waved her fist. Maybe it was the Palestinians who had been frightened. Yes, that sounded likely. They argued again, but even they could see that no matter how oppressed the people of Palestine happened to be, it still didn't make him any less scared on the streets of Østerbro. It ended up with them grudgingly accepting his explanation, and he apologised to Rita. He was really sorry, and his words were genuine.

And that was that, or so he thought. Surely they would leave him alone then? But instead of saying goodbye they started nosing around in his flat. Without inhibition, as though it were the most natural thing in the world to rummage around in another person's belongings. Rita went into the bedroom and inspected his wardrobe. He followed her, feverishly hiding away the night's underwear that had yet to find its way into the laundry basket. Her friend called out from the kitchen. *Where does he keep the salt?* She was hungry and had put some rice on to boil. He helped her, until called from the living room. Rita had put on his police uniform. It was several sizes too big and swallowed her up, but it didn't seem to bother her one bit.

She stood outside on the balcony, informing passers-by on the street below that they were under arrest. He tried to pull her back in, but she resisted and kept tight hold of the railing. People were jeering at him, and he smiled forcedly, apologising to his next-door neighbour who had appeared on his own balcony, and then the rice boiled over. Her friend blocked his way back to the kitchen. *Is that really you when you were little? How cute!* She'd found his family album. He turned down the gas and managed to save the rice, while Rita was busy auctioning off his police cap to the cluster of people who had gathered below. *It's all going to Cats' Protection. Who'll bid twenty kroner for this fine item? Cats' Protection. Twenty kroner I'm bid. Who'll give me twenty-five? How about you, man in the tie, you look like you can afford it? Twenty-five kroner?*

The girls were impossible to keep in check, and so he gave up.

When evening came, they drank tea and watched television. In colour! The TV was his pride and joy, even if Rita did call it a *proletarian gogglebox*, slapping him playfully on the back as the film started. It was an Arena with a 21-inch screen in a swish teak cabinet, with a crisp sound that reached into the kitchen without the slightest distortion. He'd bought it on hire-purchase a couple of years before so that he could watch the Americans landing on the moon. Man's first steps on an alien celestial body, an image he felt certain he would remember, even when he grew into an old man. Live transmission, and in colour! But Neil Armstrong's 'small step for man, a giant leap for mankind', was not the image he remembered best from that time. That was a quite different one entirely, and, ironically it was in black and white.

The Countess interrupted his thoughts.

'You've got yellow paint in your hair, Simon. You'll have to have a bath before you go to bed, I don't want my bedroom painted, if you don't mind.'

He promised to do as she said, noting that now it was *her* bedroom all of a sudden. At other times it was *theirs* – when the bed linen needed changing, for instance.

'You're miles away, what are you thinking about?'

They had sat down on the sofa after dinner, she with a book, he with the day's paper, though he couldn't be bothered to read it.

'A picture I remember.'

It was of a man on a step, taken from the side. His head with its receding hairline; his folded hands contrasting to his long, black coat and shiny, polished shoes. The man was kneeling. Behind him photographers could be seen, the front of a crowd, a single soldier with epaulettes and cap. All eyes were focused on the man on the step, albeit from a respectful distance, as if they already knew that this spontaneous moment was historic. Further back you could make out the housing, the dismal grey blocks that had been thrown up in no time in this city whose every building was new. The image of the West German chancellor kneeling before Warsaw's Ghetto memorial went around the world, and Willy Brandt was the only politician he and Rita ever jointly respected. And millions along with them. West Germany had a chancellor who brought together rather than divided, no mean feat in the days of leftist rebellion. The following year, the man on the step was awarded the Nobel Peace Prize, and seldom had it been more deserved.

The Countess spoke.

'What picture's that?'

'A picture of a statesman, the greatest of his time.'

She guessed the name, of course. It wasn't difficult. Simonsen went and had his bath.

As soon as the alarm went off and Konrad Simonsen opened his eyes, he thought to himself that he would much rather stay in bed than get up and start the day that lay ahead of him. His humour was little improved when it turned out he still couldn't get in touch with Pauline and was instead put through to the answering service he was already sick and tired of. He sulked at breakfast, and the Countess left him alone. She knew by now how to spot the telltale signs of his changing moods and was able to navigate around them to the extent that suited her. This morning she was out of the door long before him, and he barely had the chance to kiss her goodbye before she was gone. He cleared the breakfast things, spent fifteen minutes half-heartedly skimming through the day's paper, then drove to Frederikssund.

The chief constable turned out to be a pleasant and sensible man, who received Simonsen at the duty desk since his office was being done up. They sat down in a corner where they could talk undisturbed, and the chief constable put him in the picture about the death that Pauline Berg had seemingly decided to treat as a murder investigation.

A twenty-four-year-old woman, Juli Denissen of Frederiksværk, had been found dead on 10 July at Melby Overdrev, a former military training area out towards the Kattegat between Asserbo and Hundested. The place was now a conservation area, part of the National Park that had been dubbed Royal Nordsjælland. The circumstances surrounding the discovery of the body were particularly poignant: the persistent crying of the woman's two-year-old had been heard by a forestry worker. The death was singular, not only because of the woman's young age, but also because it had occurred in such a deserted spot. For that reason it had been investigated thoroughly by Nordsjællands Politi, who nonetheless had been unable to unearth anything untoward. The autopsy report concluded quite unequivocally and without reservation that death had been due to a massive cerebral haemorrhage, for which reason the death was classed as occurring from natural causes and duly closed. Juli Denissen had been cremated from Kregme Kirke on Saturday 2 August.

'That's the short version,' said the chief constable. 'I'm skipping the fine detail, of course, but there's a couple of case folders you can take with you, if you want to delve into it.'

Konrad Simonsen shook his head emphatically.

'No, thanks, I'd rather not. I've no doubt at all it's like you say, natural causes.'

'Glad to hear it. However, the National Commissioner has transferred everything concerning the woman's death to you. There was an e-mail yesterday, but you'll know all about that already. I hope we're not going to have to allocate resources to this again, because if you ask me it would be a waste of time.'

Simonsen assured the chief constable there would be no such expectation. And the transfer was purely so that Nordsjællands Politi could refer to him should anyone start... stirring things up. He couldn't find a better expression, and the chief constable picked up on it straight away:

'Stirring things up, indeed. The only person stirring things up here is your own detective sergeant, Pauline Berg.'

'Yes, I'm afraid so. Tell me what she's been getting up to.'

'Well, not much really, besides what we talked about on the phone yesterday. And of course it's no skin off my nose now it's all been handed over to you.'

'I'd like you to endorse the two folders you mentioned with a signed note to the effect that they can only be lent out if sanctioned by you or me.'

'No problem. Are you having trouble getting in touch with her?'

'Trouble isn't the word.' He held up his hand to stem any protest. 'All right, I know it's a bit unorthodox, but like I say, her situation isn't normal.'

'Is it PTSD?'

Post-traumatic Stress Disorder. The thought had occurred to Simonsen, too. Pauline Berg's behaviour at work at times verged on self-destructive. She forced herself and those around her into situations that could only end with her... it was hard to put into words exactly... being put in her place, passed over or sometimes even ignored. He was aware that this followed the recognised pattern of events before some people caused themselves physical harm. Both kinds of behaviour were in order to dull the trauma they had suffered. But Simonsen was no therapist and refused to hang psychiatric labels on others. He replied frankly:

'I don't know. Sometimes she appears unbalanced, at other times her work is just as good as before she was abducted. Of course, we hope she's going to stabilise at some point. However, it seems like she views this young woman's death as a chance to investigate a case that's hers and hers alone. And there's another aspect to it, too. When Pauline was banged up in that bunker, the dead woman came to us with vital information that saved Pauline from dying. I think she has merged the two things in her mind and convinced herself she owes it to the woman to proceed with an investigation. Unfortunately, there's not much doubt that at the moment she's consciously avoiding not only me, but her other superiors, too.'

The chief constable was understanding of Pauline Berg's situation, familiar with all that had happened, like most of the country's police force. He gave Simonsen something to go on.

'She'll be out at Melby Overdrev this afternoon. They're showing her where the woman died.'

'Who? Not your people, surely?'

'Denissen's kin. Her stepfather and sister.'

'How come you know?'

'The sister's husband called us yesterday. He's frustrated by his wife's… let's call it *dedication*, and wanted to know why we'd reopened the case. Actually, she's not even Juli Denissen's real sister, that's just what she calls herself.'

The chief constable showed him a map and indicated the place where Juli had been found. Simonsen thanked him. They chatted for a few minutes about other things, people they both knew, the new police reform.

They shook hands, and as Simonsen was about to leave, the chief constable asked:

'Is it true you knew her? The young woman who died, I mean?'

Simonsen answered hesitantly:

'No, I didn't know her at all.'

Konrad Simonsen struggled with his satnav to calibrate the chief constable's directions to the place where Juli Denissen had died. He failed, and wondered for a moment if he should drive back and request a more exact explanation, but decided instead to stop off in Frederiksværk, where he found his way without difficulty to the local arts centre that also housed the tourist information office. He ate a reasonably good low-cal burger with a bowl of dreary salad and was given a little folder, in the middle of which was a map of the area he wanted to see. The woman behind the desk marked his route in biro.

He drove with one eye on the map and turned off the main road shortly after Asserbo. There he followed a poorly kept forest track, taking care to avoid the worst potholes. After ten minutes the track opened out and ended in a large parking area. He pulled in at the far end, almost at the beach, where he stood for a moment and took his bearings. The area was enclosed by big, whitewashed stones, with a row of wind-battered saplings of what looked like oak in the middle. There were two cars besides his own. Rain was spitting. Not much, but enough to make him take his umbrella from the boot even if he didn't put it up.

He climbed a dune. It was steep and he clutched at tufts of lyme grass to steady himself. At the summit he looked out over the sea that lay green and tumultuous before him, waves topped with foam that rose up and vanished again, filling his field of vision as far as the horizon where sea and sky merged into one. To his left, the coastline curved away, a smooth arc that ran out into a point. In the distance it curved back again, the details blurred but for the red-tiled roofs of a cluster of houses he could just pick out somewhere near what must be Hundested. The wind rushed in his ears. Turning his head towards it made it sound like canvas flapping, the noise drowning out even the roaring breakers that crashed on to the shore below.

He stood there for a while, taking it in, before descending again and walking north, cutting across the grassland that lay between the dunes and the woods, extending as far as the eye could see. Here he was sheltered from the wind, but then the rain came and he put up his umbrella. The path he followed dwindled in places to little more than a trampled-down ribbon. It led him to a signpost: a yellow circle with a broken black bomb issuing its stylised shrapnel in an arching red explosion. Graphically, it was poor, but the message was unequivocal. The area had belonged to the military and been used for training purposes; anyone walking here did so at their own risk. He carried on through the gently undulating landscape with its tight blanket of heather interspersed with clusters of low, stunted flowers cowering in the sand. He looked around and saw nothing but nature. Now and then he stopped and stared left towards the woods, to see if anyone had perhaps sought shelter from the rain there. The treeline comprised mainly old shore pine, whose red-speckled bark and oddly twisted trunks resembled a coloured illustration in one of his boyhood adventure books, alluring, and yet eerie and intimidating at the same time. He saw no other people.

After walking for another ten minutes or so, from the top of a rise he caught sight of two figures further ahead. He adjusted his course and went towards them. As he approached he could see that one of them was Pauline Berg. He slowed down and cautioned himself to deal with the situation calmly. There was nothing to be gained by getting worked up.

The two women were soaked. Neither was dressed for the weather. He greeted Pauline as if nothing were untoward, introducing himself then to the woman who accompanied her. They shook hands and she responded by telling him her name.

Linette Krontoft was a fair-haired, corpulent woman in her twenties with attentive blue eyes and a doleful smile he assumed was attributable to the circumstances. Konrad Simonsen noted her exceptionally white and regular teeth, and it crossed his mind, too, that she would benefit from a hunger strike or two. Moreover, that he hadn't the slightest wish they should meet in this way. And yet here he was.

'Where was she found?' he asked quietly.

Linette Krontoft pointed to the bottom of the dip in front of them. He gave the two women his umbrella, their need being greater than his own, then sidestepped his way down the incline and stood for a moment considering the surroundings, scanning the landscape for 360 degrees before peering down at the sandy earth, which he poked at with the toe of his shoe. He scrabbled his way up again. His eyes met Pauline's and he thought to himself that her defiant gaze did not bode well. Linette Krontoft broke the silence.

'You're not here to help us. You're here to prevent Pauline from doing her job, aren't you?'

He said nothing, his eyes darting from woman to woman. He wished he had a cigarette. He considered his words carefully before he replied.

'You two have a choice. Do you want to hear what it is?'

They agreed with obvious reluctance. Pauline seemed almost hostile.

'You can carry on with these investigations off your own bat and behind my back. If you do, there'll be no support, no co-operation from anywhere within the police force, and all the people who provided assistance here on the tenth of July when Juli Denissen's body was discovered will receive a letter, signed by me, instructing them to ignore you if they are approached.

'The alternative is that the three of us, unofficially and privately, get in touch with a highly competent pathologist I know. But I may as well tell you straight off, it could be some time before we get an appointment, and in the meantime you must do nothing. If, after studying the autopsy report, this pathologist of ours should express even the slightest doubt that Juli Denissen died a natural death, I promise you I shall have the case reopened officially. If, on the other hand, he should consider Juli Denissen's death was indeed attributable to natural causes, then I must have your promise to let the matter drop and leave her in peace.'

Pauline Berg asked:

'Would this pathologist be Professor Arthur Elvang?'

These were the first words she had uttered since Simonsen had joined them. He turned to face her. Yes, it was Elvang he had in mind.

'I'm going back to my car now,' he added. 'I'll wait there for fifteen minutes. If you two reach an agreement before that, then we can talk more about it. If not, you call me tonight, Pauline.'

He walked off without waiting for their reaction. They could keep the umbrella.

He had to wait until evening for his answer. Pauline called. She and the group had discussed his proposal and decided to accept, though with the proviso that they be permitted to complete their photographing of Juli's flat before the place was cleared. The *group*, indeed. Not to mention the overly familiar *Juli* without using any surname. What on earth had got into her? He shook his head while simultaneously recognising that she had reached the sensible decision finally. And then, suddenly, as he cautiously asked if she might be coming in to work on Monday, Pauline began to cry.

She was incompetent, she said, she knew that herself. She was of no use to anyone for anything. There was no end to her self-reproach. He had no idea what to say, and how he got through the next half-hour was a mystery to him. But when at last she rang off, sobbing and apologising profusely for just about everything under the sun, he poured himself a brandy for the first time in months and knocked it back in one without the slightest feeling of guilt. After that he turned off his phone, switched on the TV and fell asleep.

The Countess woke him up an hour later when she got home, noting immediately that he'd had a drink. She ticked him off for it: his health wasn't up to it, when would he realise? And with that, the day ended as annoyingly as it had begun.

He slept on his own, in his room upstairs.

Summer, extended by the heatwave at the beginning of the month, was now definitely gone. The weather was changeable; it was windy and the mornings arrived with a chill. Konrad Simonsen once again had to make an effort to go for his runs. He had just begun to enjoy them, but running in a headwind and bad weather wasn't fun at all.

The investigation into the death of Jørgen Kramer Nielsen was at a standstill. He called in Arne Pedersen and the Countess for a status meeting in order to breathe some much-needed life into the case.

They met in Arne Pedersen's office. It was Wednesday 1 October, mid-morning.

Simonsen kicked off by summing up their progress since the last time they'd gathered. It wasn't encouraging.

A fragment of the photo paper from each of the eighteen posters had been sent off to Germany for chemical analysis, and a comparison of paper brands from various periods would later give them an estimate as to when the posters had been created.

'I'd especially like to pinpoint the first one, but it may be a while before we're given any sort of answer. So the only definite progress as far as that goes is that we've now positively established it's neither his younger sister nor his mother as a young woman.'

His audience of two loyally echoed his words: *Neither his younger sister nor his mother.* So that was that out of the way. It was obvious they both had other matters to which they would rather be attending, despite their making an effort to pass appropriate comments.

'Besides that, and on request, I've spent some time mapping break-ins in the area.'

There was nothing to indicate the killing might be related to a burglary or a robbery gone wrong. Moreover, the situation of the house was such that a burglar or anyone wanting to carry out a robbery in the home would surely choose another, more accessible property, one set much further back from the street than Kramer Nielsen's was.

Not a burglary, not a robbery. What were they supposed to say? The Countess made a half-hearted comment, Pedersen glanced at his watch and Simonsen carried on down his little list of items.

'What bothers me most is that I can't find the negatives. The original photos of the girl. They must have been somewhere in his possessions, but there's no sign of them. One theory could be that whoever killed him took them with them. They're gone, anyway. We've been through the post office, his flat, all his stuff. Not once but four times now, without turning up anything at all... as you know.'

He had set up three teams of two. Experienced officers, and meticulous. People who didn't moan when he got them rummaging for the fourth time in search of the negatives none of them any longer believed to exist. Fortunately, the young couple who had moved into Jørgen Kramer Nielsen's former flat were co-operative and had left a key for the policemen to use while the occupiers were out at work.

Unfortunately, the team charged with searching the flat had got the idea of bringing in a dog to help them. The male tenant had called Konrad Simonsen as soon as he got home that night: his wife was seriously allergic to dog hair, it seemed, and the couple had to be put up in a hotel at the department's expense until the place was cleaned. As if to add insult to injury the man had furthermore reported another... irregularity.

Konrad Simonsen had called in the two officers for a dressing-down, a procedure he commenced in all seriousness before eventually concluding:

'The poor woman's coughing and sneezing and can hardly breathe, all because two plods managed to poison her in her own home. I will admit, however, the idea wasn't bad. A film-tracer dog... why not? Whose is it anyway?'

One of the men indicated that it was his. At present, it was still under training and doing rather well. Despite the situation, it was clear he was proud of the animal.

'I gave him the scent of a roll of negatives and then some prints, and then we went all along the skirting boards, doors, ceiling, window sills... everywhere we'd turned up blanks.'

'Is your dog horny?'

'No, why?'

'I'd say it is. Because the truth of the matter is it found something, didn't it? You see, my very reliable source can't understand how a certain cardboard box containing private photographs has been all messed up. *Very* private photographs, as it happens. I had to explain to him that we didn't take fingerprints to clear up matters of that nature. Which is true, of course, and also rather fortunate, seeing as how your dog seems to have been so horny it couldn't keep its paws off.'

Neither of the officers responded: both of them stared at the floor and had very red ears indeed.

'Not a hair. Not one single, invisible little dog hair from that randy hound of yours, understood? I want that place hoovered and cleaned as if your careers depended on it. Now, get going the pair of you.'

'Did they get rid of all the hairs?' the Countess asked.

'I think so. It would have been a very costly affair if they hadn't.'

'But the idea was all right. The dog, I mean. Have you tried it out at the post office or in the storage facility with Kramer Nielsen's effects?'

'I've thought about it and left a message on the dog handler's answerphone. He's on holiday this week, so I should hear back from him no later than Wednesday, I reckon.'

'I wouldn't bank on it,' said Arne Pedersen drily.

Simonsen went on with his discouraging briefing as if he hadn't heard.

'The last thing's the matter of the posters, which at the moment are adorning the walls in Søllerød.'

The Countess cut in:

'Your gallery.'

Arne Pedersen laughed, though not derisively. Simonsen ignored him nevertheless and informed them that experts in

151

various fields had now been out to study the posters of their girl in the clouds: professional photo technicians and a behavioural psychologist who waffled on without saying anything at all.

'Let me guess. Clarification would mean getting in a host of others just like him?'

The Countess was pretty much spot on.

Simonsen admitted:

'So basically my gallery, as you call it, has been a failure.'

'What about your parapsychologist? Didn't you get her in on it?' asked Pedersen.

It was the worst-kept secret in Homicide that Konrad Simonsen now and again made discreet use of a clairvoyant in his investigations, a fact that on occasion had led to some rather surprising conclusions, while at others it had proved utterly worthless.

'She's been in hospital with a broken hip, but maybe I can persuade her to stop by if she's finished her rehab.'

His exclusive audience concurred: it wouldn't do any harm, at least. He clapped his hands together, feigning optimism.

'Well, that's it. Does either of you have any bright ideas as to how we might proceed?'

No startlingly original thoughts were forthcoming. The silence was oppressive. Arne Pedersen was the first to give up:

'Perhaps we can think about it, Simon?'

The next day, Pauline Berg came up with something new to go on in the case of Jørgen Kramer Nielsen. It wasn't earth-shattering by any means, but by then Simonsen was glad of anything he could get. She was sitting in his office when he arrived on the Thursday morning and announced proudly that she'd got a present for him, even if it wasn't gift-wrapped.

Following her unfortunate outing to Nordsjælland the week before, she had turned up for work on the Monday as if nothing had happened, and neither of them had mentioned the episode at all. She had returned the documents he had given her without comment and now they languished in the bottom drawer of Simonsen's desk, waiting for him to pull himself together and get in touch with Professor Arthur Elvang and ask him to read the autopsy report, just as he had promised her on the grasslands of Melby Overdrev almost a week ago. She hadn't pressed the matter, in fact hadn't even enquired about it yet, but he was well aware that she wasn't going to forget about it and that he would soon have to get things squared with the professor.

Contrary to what he'd expected, she had seemed happier this past week than he had seen her in a long time. She was almost back to being the old Pauline, from before the abduction. She was more sociable, too, he found, and not only towards him.

He looked at his present.

'Jørgen Kramer Nielsen's final exam certificate from his upper secondary. So it turned up, after all. Where did you find it?'

'It used to hang on the wall in his dad's office at the post office, until they got a new postmaster. That's why it's framed. Two of the old postmen remembered it hanging next to King Frederik the Ninth, and probably about six months or so with Queen Margrethe as well, after her father died, I imagine, until the plane crash. We found it in the post office's basement.'

'So his dad was proud, then.'

'He was. In fact, he was the first person at the post office whose offspring had graduated from the gymnasium, so it was something to boast about in those days. But have a look at this.'

She handed him a small pile of papers.

'This is correspondence between Tom Kramer Nielsen and the Ministry of Education in nineteen sixty-nine, and you may as well pat me on the head now because you wouldn't believe how many phone calls it's taken to get hold of these copies. Of all the foot-dragging institutions in this country, government ministries are the worst. Most other places they at least get their finger out as long as you say *murder inquiry* and *urgent,* but with central administration it seems to have the opposite effect.'

'They can be a bit reluctant at times. So, yes, a pat on the head.'

She put him in the picture.

Jørgen Kramer Nielsen hadn't turned up for his final exam, oral maths. The reason seemed rather unclear, given that his father appeared to change his story during the course of the correspondence, but according to the rules his son could not officially graduate, having first to resit the exam at a later date. And yet Jørgen Kramer Nielsen hadn't attended the resit either.

'Why not?' Simonsen asked.

'I'm not sure, but his dad kicked up a fuss and wanted to know why they couldn't just give him a fail in oral maths, because that would have meant he graduated with the rest of his class. His other grades were more than sufficient to make up for a zero in the one subject. So they correspond back and forth a few times. Only the ministry sticks to its guns and goes by the book.'

'But he passed eventually?'

'Yes. That's this country for you, isn't it? You see, one of Tom Kramer Nielsen's old army friends from the days of national service had gone on to make a career for himself in just the right place. He'd become chairman of the association of folk high schools, and old mates scratch each other's backs, don't they? So, hey presto, Jørgen Kramer Nielsen graduates. Take the certificate out of the frame and look at the signature on the back.'

Simonsen did as she said.

'You've certainly been digging into your modern history. Who told you all this anyway?' he said as he fumbled to remove the certificate.

'The folk high-school chairman himself. Still bright as a button and nearly a hundred. He went on for two hours. It was

154

all very pleasant, quite fascinating actually. So what do you make of the signature?'

'Well, I never. Old *Evil Helge* himself.'

'Why do you call him that? Is there something I'm missing?'

'It was a sorely unjust nickname. Helge Larsen was a very competent Minister of Education who became the butt of public criticism for the entire youth rebellion back in the day. His job put him on the front line. No politician could ever achieve any kind of popularity in that position then. These are very good grades Kramer Nielsen got, aren't they?'

'They are. And look at written maths, and physics for that matter, too.'

'And yet he never took oral maths or carried on into higher education. I wonder why.'

'Don't ask me. But I was wrong about when they burned their exam certificates. It was the year after, in 1970. On the square of Kongens Nytorv.'

Pauline paused for a moment, then added pensively:

'I'd like to have been around in those days. It must have been really exciting.'

Konrad Simonsen shook his head.

'Not for me, it wasn't. I had a job to do. And besides, I never went on to upper secondary.'

The next piece of input that brought the case forward, to view it positively, came the week after from an unexpected quarter and, for Konrad Simonsen, at an equally unexpected time. He had taken Monday and Tuesday off as holiday and spent them developing his repertoire of exercise. In poor weather he could hardly drag himself outside for his daily jog, and in a couple of months the pavements would most likely be covered in snow and ice, which would make running his usual route tantamount to idiocy. Consequently, he'd purchased an exercise bike that he set up in his gallery. And on the Monday morning, as he was working up a sweat for the second time on this new contraption, his unknown poster girl watching him with a twinkle in her eye, he was interrupted by a visitor.

Klavs Arnold was from Esbjerg. He was a big man in his late thirties, thick-limbed and full-chested. There weren't many superfluous grams of fat on him, and it was a good bet that he seldom had anyone fronting up to him at his local drinking establishment. His clothes were practical and worn. He had taken off his solid leather boots, which wouldn't have been out of place in an army barracks, and left them outside the door before knocking and entering.

'Excuse me, are you Konrad Simonsen, from Homicide in Copenhagen?'

Simonsen wound down his cadence as he studied the man, who had to lower his head slightly to get through the doorway.

'Who wants to know?'

'Sorry, I should have introduced myself. Klavs Arnold, detective sergeant from Esbjerg.'

He shook Simonsen's hand, or rather his entire forearm, then twisted the bike's resistance dial.

'That's too much for you, you shouldn't be on more than three to start with. Beginner, yeah?'

Simonsen admitted rather curtly that this was true, only to realise that the man was right. He stopped pedalling, but remained in the saddle.

'And you'd be an expert, then?'

'I wouldn't say that, but I do a few shifts at the local gym every now and then to make ends meet.'

He handed Simonsen his towel.

'I won't keep you long. Me and the wife are in the city looking for a place to live. We're moving over this autumn. I thought I'd look you up while I was here, see if you could help me clear up a problem that's been bothering me this last month. I went in to Police HQ and your wife, I think it was, sent me out here.'

'And what kind of problem would that be?'

'Well, it's like this. You people asked me to find out where this person stays… the one who goes to Esbjerg once a year… if I could. But the only thing I've had to go on is a name. So far it's turned up a blank, so I sent an e-mail and phoned to get some more info. The man's age, a photo, whatever. Only no one was getting back to me. Eventually I got an e-mail with some likely arrival and departure times.'

He paused, before continuing:

'Obviously, Esbjerg's nowhere near the size of Copenhagen, but… well, it's not on.'

Simonsen could see how unreasonable it was.

'Who was the officer you were in touch with?' he asked with trepidation.

'I can't tell you, can I? Some of the lads say you can get a bit narky if the mood takes you, and I'm not here to get anyone into trouble, just to ask for some help, that's all.'

'So you won't tell me?'

'Nope.'

'What if I order you to?'

'You can't. I'm on holiday, and so are you.'

Simonsen looked at the man's torso. It wasn't easy to see, even to a trained eye:

'But you're carrying a firearm?'

The Jutlander nodded:

'Yeah.'

'What for?'

'I received threats, back in the spring. The family, too. I don't like to think about it, but… since then I've protected myself. And we've invested in a gun safe at home, so everything's by the book.

157

But don't think I'm some cowboy, because I'm not. That's not what it's about.'

The man smoothed the bulge of his jacket where his shoulder holster was.

'Do you want a beer or something?' Simonsen asked.

He ran through the case for Arnold and found it depressingly quick to get to the end. Annoyingly, Arnold stressed the point:

'It's not much, is it? Mind if I have a look at these posters?'

He walked slowly round the room without speaking. Simonsen followed him and felt like a custodian. At the end of the tour, the Jutlander asked:

'Which is the first?'

Simonsen pointed:

'We think it's one of those two.'

They went over and stood studying them both. Again, Arnold was silent, but after a while he spoke.

'It's hard to tell with the naked eye, but a photo technician would probably be able to say.'

'Say what?'

'He might well have taken the first one himself rather than from a book, the way you said. On a trip. And that'll be where he met her. Unless she was with him from the outset. Maybe it's the *Hurtigruten*, the boat from Bergen to Tromsø. Didn't you say he was saving up so he could travel?'

Simonsen was impressed and said so. But he needn't have bothered. Praise cut no ice with Arnold.

'Who decorated this room? Was it you? It's nice. My kids'd love it.'

'Thanks. Everyone else thinks it's dreadful. How many have you got?'

'Five. But the last two are twins. Couldn't be helped.'

He laughed engagingly.

'What makes you want to move to Copenhagen? Change of air?'

'No, the wife's got herself a new job, so me and the kids have to tag along. It was hard for me to get sorted out with something. No one wanted a redneck like me. Someone did eventually, though.'

'Where's that, then?'

'Helsinge. Between...'

'I know where Helsinge is. What does your wife do?'

'New member of parliament. I was hoping it'd never happen. She was only a substitute, but then her member went and got ill and had to pack it in.'

'How long are you staying in Copenhagen?'

'I'm off back tonight. Going to work in the morning.'

'No, you're not. I want you to come in to my office. I'll square it with your chief constable.'

'What for?'

'Because there are some people I want you to talk to.'

CHAPTER 6

Restaurant Sult on Vognmagergade in the heart of Copenhagen was a bright and pleasant place with a cheerful atmosphere and plenty of room between the tables. So thought Konrad Simonsen, who had arrived at the appointed time, albeit resigned to the thought that his partner's shopping spree would hold her up for some while yet. He was right. He had ordered tea and sat down at a table by the window, absently stirring a teaspoon in his cup, though he took neither sugar nor milk. It was his lunch break and he was feeling guilty. First two days off that he hadn't felt entitled to after his long period of sick leave, and now a break that could easily last an hour and a half if the Countess didn't get a move on.

His morning had been mixed. On the minus side, it looked like it would be some time before they could get a dog in on a search of Jørgen Kramer Nielson's effects. Simonsen still hadn't found the negatives he was so convinced had to be there somewhere, but the dog had gone down with a cold. Or at least, that's what its owner had said when Simonsen had spoken to him earlier in the day. Most probably it wasn't true, revenge for the bollocking he'd given the officer in question the week before. But what could he do about it? Order the animal to the vet on suspicion of shirking? They could get another dog in, of course, but there was a backlog in the booking system. The advantage of the one that had now taken ill was that it wasn't yet fully trained. As such, it wasn't a part of any roster and he shouldn't have to wait. And yet here he was, waiting anyway. Perhaps until a month of Sundays came round. It was frustrating, to say the least. He had put Pauline Berg on to the matter and was hoping she'd be able to talk some sense into the dog handler so he could get his charge back on its paws again as soon as possible.

Klavs Arnold had been a more positive help. Simonsen had got the Jutlander's sojourn in the capital extended by two days, having spoken to his chief constable over in Esbjerg. Arnold was permitted a day off to traipse about and explore the city on his own. Which was much needed, insofar as the man seemed hardly able to find his way from one corner of Rådhuspladsen to another. Today, Simonsen had introduced him to selected colleagues in Homicide, and this had gone off well. Arnold and Arne Pedersen had taken an instant liking to each other, which pleased Simonsen no end. He had been worried about a clash of testosterone and territorial markings, but they had put his concerns to shame. Pedersen had even taken the time to show Arnold around Police HQ and had not displayed the slightest reticence in deploying a detective constable to go back with him to Esbjerg so that he wouldn't be on his own trying to find out where Kramer Nielsen had stayed on his annual trip. This was a job made all the more feasible when Arnold at long last was given a photo of the deceased postman to help him in his enquiries. Simonsen had himself taken on the task of picking out a suitable officer, though as yet he had done nothing about it. On the other hand, Pauline Berg's reaction to the new man from Jutland had been swift: *a redneck nonentity* was her appraisal. The thought occurred to him that he might send her off to Esbjerg with Arnold, but... well, it probably wasn't that good an idea, on second thoughts.

He felt a hand on his shoulder and for a brief second thought it was the Countess.

'Do you think you could stop doing that? It's rather annoying, to say the least.'

The man from the next table jabbed a finger towards Simonsen's tea and it took a second for him to realise the man meant the teaspoon he was still stirring in his cup.

He apologised and put the spoon down, then looked at his watch, despite the presence of a large clock on the end wall. At the same moment there was a tap on the window next to him. He turned his head to see the Countess standing outside, burdened like a bag-lady. At the top end of the scale, naturally.

They deposited her parcels on the floor, tucking them out of the way under the table before ordering lunch.

'I'm thinking of giving our friend from Jutland a job,' he said. 'Or rather, I'm thinking of getting Arne to give him a job. What do you reckon?'

'Sounds all right to me. Is he good?'

'According to his chief constable, yes. His idea about the first of those landscapes being taken in real life was good.'

'But wrong?'

'So it seems, unfortunately. Melsing had already looked at it, don't ask me how. But there was nothing wrong with the idea, at least.'

'No, but still a bit flimsy, perhaps, as a reason for taking him on.'

'I've asked for his HR file. I should have it tomorrow. I've a feeling he'll fit in, and that's just about all it boils down to. There'd be a trial period, of course, so we can see how he gets on.'

The Countess agreed, both about the trial period and the Jutlander seeming to fit in.

After they'd finished their lunch, Simonsen was allowed to see the yield from the Countess's autumn shop-amok. Not bothering wasn't an option. One garment after another was produced from its carrier bag, unfolded, commented upon and put back again. It took some time: her credit card must have been glowing. Simonsen made an effort, but after a while found it hard to vary his reactions. There were no more superlatives left in him, and he floundered. If he didn't immediately extol the virtues of one jumper, he was invited to compare it to a previous one: *Do you like it better than the purple one with the stripes?* When, truth be told, he'd already forgotten all about the purple one with the stripes. But if she realised that, it would only be produced once again to refresh his memory. *Which do you like best?* Moreover, *They're both nice* didn't count as a valid reply. Potentially, it was endless, and yet it stopped.

There was only one parcel left and it wasn't from a clothes shop. The Countess removed something from its carrier and placed it proudly on the table in front of him. It was a camera. More specifically, it was a Nikon F6 single-lens reflex camera, so the packaging informed him. Despite this, he asked:

'What's that?'

'Anna Mia's birthday present. Don't you remember we talked about getting her a camera? It's what she wants.'

It was true, he remembered now. He stared mistrustfully at the box.

'I was thinking we could give it to her in time for that trip of hers to Bornholm. It's next week, isn't it?'

'Yes, I think so. It's a bit of an expensive birthday present, though.'

Her gesture indicated it didn't matter. Unsurprisingly, for money was never an issue for the Countess. Most of it she had inherited from her father, who in her own words had accumulated a fortune by means of lawful swindling: buying flats, doing them up on the cheap and selling them on at a profit. On his death she had become wealthy at a relatively advanced age and was still rather at odds with the idea, which meant that every now and then she would throw her money about, though without ever making so much as a dent in her account. Sometimes, however, he felt her extravagance to be over the top. Like now, for instance.

'If I'm going to give my daughter a birthday present, I want to know how much it cost,' he said sullenly. 'And besides that, I'd like to pay half.'

She tossed her head slightly and presented him with the amount:

'Fourteen thousand kroner, plus four thousand for a long lens that's coming tomorrow.'

No sooner had she uttered the words than they both knew they had a problem. They sat and stared at each other, considering their next move. Simonsen spoke first, categorically:

'No way. You can take it back.'

'Take it back? You mean you don't want to spend nine thousand kroner on your own daughter?'

He felt derided and retorted harshly:

'Of course I do. But in our family we don't give each other things as expensive as that. Besides, it would be humiliating for her mother and stepbrother. What are their five-hundred-kroner presents going to look like next to eighteen thousand?'

'You could tell them you were compensating for not having given her anything when she was confirmed. And since when did you start caring about what Anna Mia's mother feels?'

He felt himself blush and snapped at her:

'I'm perfectly capable of upholding a decent relationship with my ex-wife. I don't need to be for ever consciously winding her up.'

'What's that supposed to mean? Go on, what's that supposed to mean?' the Countess hissed back.

'You know perfectly well what it means.'

She gathered her carrier bags together in a huff, her movements angry and abrupt, before striding out of the premises with a straight back and her nose in the air. The box containing the camera was still on the table in front of him.

An hour later Simonsen arrived back at Police HQ with the camera under his arm. He was still in a foul mood, albeit prepared to discuss the matter more calmly with her. He went straight to her office, only to find it empty. In the corridor he ran into Arne Pedersen.

'Hi, Simon. Good idea of yours, sending the Countess to Esbjerg.'

His jaw dropped. Pedersen noticed the picture on the box under his arm.

'Wow, a Nikon F6. Mind if I have a look?'

He handed it over.

'There you go. Give it back to the Countess, it's hers.'

In his office he found Pauline Berg lounging on the sofa in his annexe reading a report. She looked cheerful.

'You took your time. Now, listen to this. I've set up a time with that dog handler: tomorrow morning at ten out at Express Move's facility in Hvidovre.'

Simonsen pointed a finger at her.

'Get out of my office!'

She stared at him, then burst out laughing and said something about how reassuring it was that he could act like a tosser as well. When the door slammed behind her he flopped down on the now vacated sofa with the distinct feeling that everything was falling apart.

The weather had gone cold, the mornings were bitter and in the Countess's garden the climbing rose by the garage was scattered with meticulously spun cobwebs glistening with tiny droplets of dew in the faint early rays of sun, prompting Simonsen to pause and relish the sight for a few seconds.

The country's economy, too, had chilled. No one was spending: you knew what you'd got, but not what you were going to get. There was a feeling of impending crisis and the National Police Commissioner invited the whole force to take part in an inspirational conference at the Øksnehallen in Copenhagen, with live video hook-ups to the eleven other police districts in the country for those unlucky enough not to be able to take part in person. Austerity measures, cutbacks, service reductions were to be viewed as a challenge, a springboard for new creative processes to flourish, a unique opportunity to think anew. In the Homicide Department, the week's discussion topic was finding the best excuse for not coming in.

Konrad Simonsen missed the Countess. They'd had a long talk on the phone the evening before, and both of them had apologised. Nevertheless, she thought it would be healthy for them to spend a few days apart. He declared himself in agreement, but waking up on his own in the morning he found it hard to see any benefit. He took a quick shower and hurried his way through breakfast. Hardly more than an hour after waking he pulled into Express Move's facility in Hvidovre, still drowsy, yet pleased to be getting started on the day's work. It would take his mind off her.

In the storage hall he met up with a disgruntled and somewhat taciturn dog handler and his happy charge, a playful Labrador that had yet to leave puppyhood fully behind. Four men with bulging biceps, dressed in blue overalls, were in the process of lugging Kramer Nielsen's furniture out of its storage place. They worked efficiently with few words and were almost done. It crossed Simonsen's mind that Arne Pedersen would be receiving Express Move's bill, but decided that wasn't his problem. Shortly afterwards, Pauline Berg arrived. She patted the dog and turned on the charm with the dog handler, all the while eating yoghurt from a little plastic beaker in her hand. She seemed to be in an excellent mood.

The dog was given a roll of film to sniff at and then put to work. It weaved its way in and out between the various items with its tail wagging, then stopped abruptly at an empty bookcase at which it began to scratch frantically. The dog handler praised and patted it, and uttered his first voluntary words of the day:

'He's found something.'

The three officers searched the bookcase. It was teak with a backboard and six movable shelves. They investigated every square centimetre. They tipped the bookcase over and examined the bottom, but nothing was forthcoming. The dog had lain down, its tail occasionally thumping the floor as it watched its owner's every move. They pulled the shelves out and looked them over carefully, again without result. Simonsen sent the dog a frown. After fifteen minutes they gave up on the bookcase and the dog handler issued a command to the Labrador, which promptly sprang into action. It pounced forward and did a little dance with its front paws on one of the shelves that had been put aside on the floor. The dog handler spoke again:

'He's found something.'

Simonsen and Pauline Berg examined the shelf again. The dog handler asked them:

'Can you see anything?'

Simonsen replied drily:

'Yes, a laminated teak shelf, sixty by thirty centimetres, I'd say. Twelve, maybe fourteen mill thick. Ends grooved to fit the shelf hangers.'

'Anything else?'

'Yeah. One surface scratched by a dog,' Pauline rejoined, though the sarcasm seemed to be lost on the man.

'There's something about that shelf.'

'There's nothing about that shelf.'

'Try hiding it among the others, but keep your eyes on it.'

He drew the dog away and they both turned round so they couldn't see. Knowing not to underestimate the intelligence of the animal, Simonsen shuffled the shelves thoroughly. Pauline had given up on the project.

'No cheating, mind,' she called out to the dog handler.

'We won't.'

Simonsen was ready and the dog received its command. It ran straight to the correct shelf and scratched the other side as well. Simonsen was quick to react:

'He's found something.'

He examined the shelf again, only to shake his head. Now he'd given up, too. He handed the shelf to the dog handler, who turned out to know rather more about wooden shelving than Simonsen did.

'It's not laminated. There's two layers of three-millimetre teak veneer on the outside and four-millimetre chipboard in the middle, so you can hollow the chipboard with the teeth of a saw if you've got the patience. It's softer than the veneer, so the saw'll find its own way. Nice little hiding place once you've done it. It's been seen before.'

He produced his mobile phone from his inside pocket.

'Are you phoning for a new dog?' Pauline asked in earnest.

The man said nothing, but shone the phone's torch into the groove at one end of the shelf.

'There's a crack there, I reckon. Maybe he made a plug from another piece of chipboard, to put in and cover the hole. Have you got anything pointed, something that'll bend? A paper clip or a bit of wire?'

Simonsen had to go off down to the far end of the storage hall where there was a small office behind a glass wall. The place was empty. He took a handful of paper clips from the magnetic holder on the desk. Returning, he handed them to the dog handler, who straightened one out and shaped a little hook from it. The remainder he tossed on to the floor. He gave his mobile phone to Pauline who shone the torch for him as he inserted the makeshift tool into the groove and began to fiddle about with great concentration and immediate result: he removed a thin wafer of chipboard, took the torch from Pauline's hand and peered into the hiding place.

'There's an envelope in there.'

Simonsen beamed.

'We'll leave it for the technicians and stop here. But let me say, you and your dog have done a tremendous job, even if I was a bit sceptical at first.'

As they left, the dog received a treat and Simonsen thought his owner deserved one, too. He patted him on the back a couple of times instead.

Konrad Simonsen had to wait four long days before receiving confirmation that a sorely needed breakthrough had finally been made in his investigation. He spent the time tying up a loose end that had been bothering him for quite a while.

The retired postman he had visited at the care home had lied to him. Young kids in 1969 didn't save up to travel the world. At best, they made themselves a packed lunch and took off. But more importantly, Jørgen Kramer Nielsen didn't have a passport, a fact that didn't tie in very well with his supposed wanderlust. That thought had occurred to Simonsen the first time he and Arne Pedersen had gone through Kramer Nielsen's personal effects, but had quickly slipped from his mind. Much later, one morning while he was taking a shower, he suddenly remembered it. The brain was a peculiar organ. Subsequently, he deployed an officer to check up on the old man, and the pieces had all fallen nicely into place.

Back at the care home he confronted the misleading witness.

'You lied to me last time I was here. You told me Jørgen Kramer Nielsen saved his money up to go round the world. That wasn't true.'

The man hid conveniently behind his advanced years.

'I don't remember that.'

'You also told me he was a lively, outgoing lad until his family died in that plane crash. That wasn't true, either.'

'It's ages since you were here. I can hardly remember us talking.'

'And now you're lying again. There's nothing wrong with your memory.'

'How would you know? Anyone can remember wrong.'

'Are you fond of the police?'

The old man's miserable face grimaced more deeply. He didn't answer the question, but shook his head in annoyance.

'You applied to join the force often enough in your younger days,' Simonsen observed.

'I wasn't tall enough. It wasn't fair.'

'Is that why you led me a dance? Or did you have something against the postmaster? Maybe you didn't care for his son either?'

'I don't care for anyone much.'

That, at least, seemed true enough, Simonsen thought. He pulled two cartons of cigarettes out of his briefcase. He had been trying to think of a way to motivate the old man. Cigarettes were the only thing he could come up with.

'They say without a pension scheme and money in the bank it can be hard making ends meet once you're retired. The manager told me this was your brand.'

He put the cartons down on the table.

'The truth, and nothing but.'

The old man stared greedily at them and abandoned his grudge.

'Jørgen was strange from the day he started, and I didn't like his dad one bit either. A big head, always boasting about one thing or another. His son never did any harm, though. Then again, he never did any good. He was just there, that's all.'

'The song's familiar.'

'Everyone found him odd, even his dad, as long as that lasted. Odd, but harmless.'

'And all that about him wanting to travel, that wasn't true, right?'

'I don't think he could have got it together. He wasn't like the rest of them.'

'Who?'

'The youngsters they took on in those days. I couldn't stand the sight of them, me. All that long hair, and filthy dirty, no respect for anything. Oh, they could tear things down, no bother, but that was it. And all familiar we were supposed to be all of a sudden. No more "sir" and "madam". It was like a clearance sale, everything had to go. A good hiding's what they should have had.'

'And you'd have given them one, is that it?'

'Too bloody right I would, but you couldn't, could you? Society bent over backwards for them. That filthy pornography getting legalised. No one was there to stand up for morals, not to mention good old-fashioned decency. It came crashing down like a house of cards, all in the name of tolerance. And then their so-called flower power turned into red terrorism, didn't it? Drug addiction, noise instead of music, women's libbers letting it all hang out on those stupid island camps of theirs, while the rest of us were grafting to foot the bill...'

Simonsen interrupted.

'All right, I get the picture. Let's try and stick to the point, shall we? The postmaster, was he the tolerant type, as you put it?'

'Not when I started working there, he wasn't. It was more like inspection in the mornings to see if you'd washed your ears out. But ten years later, the youngsters were walking in and out of his office without even knocking. Oh, he kept up with the times all right.'

'What about his son? Was he long-haired and filthy dirty, too?'

The old man paused for thought. It was obvious he was doing his best to deserve his cigarettes.

'Long-haired, no. Jørgen had a crew cut, I remember that. Filthy, most likely. They all were.'

'Was Jørgen odd as a child, too?'

'No idea. I never saw him until they took him on.'

'Is there anything else you can tell me about him?'

The old man thought about it.

'Do I still get the cigarettes?'

'They're yours.'

'In that case, no, there isn't. Or maybe just one thing. He always had to have his holiday in June. Certain days, I can't remember which. Then he'd go off on some boat trip for a week. Don't ask me where.'

171

'Is that what he said? That he was going on a boat trip?'

'Not in so many words. It was more the way he was tanned when he got back. Under the chin, for instance. It's the reflection of the sun off the water.'

'Interesting. Anything else?'

'No.'

Konrad Simonsen got to his feet

'Before I go, was it the police or the postmaster that made you lie the first time?'

'The police are useless. I was only two centimetres short.'

'Short of what? A free pass to beat up some hippies?'

'It'd have been my pleasure. Two bloody centimetres!'

'Nine, actually. And besides, your school marks weren't good enough, so don't kid yourself I'm swallowing that boat-trip story. You avoid eye contact when you're lying. Page one in the big police textbook.'

The man grimaced and Simonsen left.

On his way back, he tried in vain to shake off the old man's bitterness, but memories that had been tucked away for years suddenly came flooding back. *Flower power turned into red terrorism.* In a way, the man was right, though other Western countries had been much harder hit by it than Denmark. But the intentions were there, certainly, among the chosen few, the vanguard, the spearhead of the revolution, or whatever they chose to call themselves. The short-haired hippies. That was his terms for those of Rita's friends for whom flowers, pot and music were no longer enough. What they wanted was a revolution, and riding on the crest of the wave of a society in turmoil, with Chairman Mao's Little Red Book in their back pocket, increasing numbers of young people became radicalised. Or more exactly: increasing numbers of young people from an academic middle-class background, who studied at the universities of Copenhagen or Aarhus.

Democracy was thrown out with the bathwater, and the magnificent dictatorship of the proletariat was just around the corner... only the corner was a long way off, and in the meantime the flowers withered.

The posters on Rita's wall were taken down and replaced. She lived in a basement room in her mother's house in well-to-do Gentofte until moving into student halls. Pictures of her rock idols gave way to propaganda posters for guerilla groups around the world. She explained to Simonsen about mobilising against the bourgeoisie and the fascist state, sounding like she was reading aloud from the phone book. Her guitar had been given away, her songs making way for books he didn't understand and which she read without pleasure.

One day in June he biked up to the Louisiana Museum of Modern Art at Humlebæk in Nordsjælland. He bought a poster of Picasso's 'Guernica' there, a symbol of the horrors of the Spanish Civil War. On his way home, he was caught by a shower and the poster in its cardboard tube got wet. It couldn't be helped, and he could hardly afford a new one. Besides, he'd already got as far as Vedbæk and didn't fancy going all the way back. A couple of days later he gave the poster to Rita as a birthday present. She was glad and put it up on her door, in the place of honour. And there it remained for a fortnight, wrinkled from the rain and all the more interesting for it. But then one day it was gone, replaced by Leila Khaled, the becoming Palestinian hijacker with her keffiyeh and her AK-47, and loving eyes gazing down upon an infant child in a cradle. Rita explained to him that Cubism was degenerate middle-class art that sneered at the working-class revolution, and moreover that the Louisiana Museum that had printed the poster was owned and run by a capitalist Nazi.

'So when the revolution comes the museum will be torn down, is that it?' he'd said snidely. 'Funny, because the place was teeming with ordinary people.'

She had an answer to that, too: the people had been tricked, deceived by bourgeois ideology and brainwashed by a capitalist press. It was the ultimate last resort, an all-purpose claim to wipe the board every time people failed to fit in with their new theories.

They made love.

He suspected it was compensation for her having thrown his birthday present out. Afterwards, as she lay with her head resting against his chest, he ventured a new take on the matter.

'There's something I don't understand, Rita. Why would a Nazi museum director put on an exhibition of Kandinsky and Klee? They were banned by the Nazis, weren't they? Amazing how cunning the Nazis are getting these days.'

She told him it was called *repressive tolerance*. He stroked her hair and cautiously suggested she take more interest in Kandinsky and Klee, and rather less in Marcuse and Habermas. She got out of bed and stood there. What would he know about that? The policeman with his elementary schooling?

Later that month she graduated from the gymnasium school.

Dark thoughts from his past kept niggling away at Simonsen until he parked the car in the garage at Søllerød and realised that he hadn't even meant to drive home. This had happened to him a couple of times before in his life, but never over such a long distance. He found it frightening. Not least because he'd been completely lost in recollections and was could not recall a single thing about the journey he'd just made. He sat for a while in the car, unable to decide whether to go back or not. He ended up getting changed and going for his run, determined to beat his own record, for which reason he overreached himself and clocked his poorest time for weeks. After that, he had something to eat and then headed in to the Teilum Building at the Rigshospitalet in Copenhagen, wondering what might be in store for him.

Professor Arthur Elvang had at long last retired from his position in Copenhagen University's Department of Forensic Medicine and as such was now Emeritus Professor and entitled to come and go as he pleased. The staff informed Konrad Simonsen that the old man hadn't made much use of the privilege, a fact bemoaned by all, insofar as Elvang was still regarded as one of the best pathologists in the country. His retirement was bad news for Konrad Simonsen, too, since it meant his only way of meeting the man now was to visit him at home. He drove up to Klampenborg, north of the city, feeling somewhat nervous as to how he might be received. He had heard that Arthur Elvang was by no means always the most affable of persons. Indeed, truth be told, he could be positively unpleasant.

He found the professor's residence without difficulty on a residential street off Klampenborgvej not far from the Dyrehaven, and after sitting in the car for a few minutes to muster the courage went up to the front door and rang the bell. It took a while before someone answered and Arthur Elvang's emaciated features and skinny frame appeared in front of him. The initial words of politeness Simonsen had prepared remained stuck in his throat as the professor peered at him through the thick lenses of spectacles that Simonsen reckoned must have had a lens power capable of correcting blindness.

'What do you want?'

Simonsen sighed with relief. He had been afraid the old man would slam the door in his face. Now at least there was contact. He did his best to explain, while Arthur Elvang listened with his head tilted to one side, thin-lipped and sceptical. When he was finished the old man barked out a command:

'Tell me again!'

Simonsen repeated his words, well aware now of how weak it all sounded. The professor was of the same opinion.

'What rot! I haven't heard such poppycock since Sunday school. Come with me!'

175

Arthur Elvang stepped out of the door and walked around the side of the house. Simonsen followed him. In an outhouse the old man handed him a garden rake and relieved him of the folder he had been holding in his hand. Elvang poked a crooked finger towards the lawn. It was covered in leaves from the chestnut tree over by the fence that divided the garden from the adjacent property.

'You can shift some leaves for me while I consider the matter. I don't work for nothing.'

It took Simonsen an hour to get finished. The professor needed only five minutes. They met on the patio.

'If you're thirsty there's water in the tap. Get it yourself, in the kitchen.'

Simonsen declined. He preferred to hear Elvang's conclusion on Juli Denissen's autopsy report. And yet he was made to wait. The professor grunted:

'I hear your new woman's left you now.'

Blushing slightly, Simonsen refuted this. *The Countess was on a job in Esbjerg, there was no more to it than that.* He wondered where on earth the man got his information from, but then put the thought from his mind and went straight to the point.

'So what's your first conclusion? About the report?'

'My first conclusion is the same as my final conclusion, which in turn is the only conclusion. I thought you wanted to wait? Said something about bringing two women with you to hear my conclusion. Wasn't that what you were waffling on about before?'

'Yes, but I'd like to know your verdict beforehand.'

'My verdict is that the young woman's death was caused by cerebral haemorrhage. That's bleeding in the brain, to you. It's all there in black and white, man. Any first-year medical student could have told you that.'

* * *

Ten minutes later, Konrad Simonsen was strolling on familiar paths in the woodland expanses of the Dyrehaven, thinking about what a first-year student of the Royal Danish Academy of Fine Arts, School of Architecture had to tell him in 1972. They had walked there together, though with a void between them. He remembered it vividly, even the date: 2 November.

Rita was wearing her Afghan coat, a full-length sheepskin worn with the smooth side facing out. It was edged with gaudy embroidered borders of red and yellow flowers, a garment that looked like the factory had never got round to finishing it. The coat of the honest, hard-working Afghan peasant... bought for a small fortune in the Janus clothes store on Larsbjørnsstræde in the centre of Copenhagen, but it was the symbolic value that mattered. He loved to see Rita wearing that coat, though it often made him laugh, too. It could only be done up at the front by means of hooks, so if the weather was cold she froze. Most likely in solidarity with the honest, hard-working peasants, but nonetheless impractical in November.

They had biked out to the Dyrehaven at Rita's suggestion: there was something she wanted to talk to him about, she'd said. He could tell by her tone on the phone that it was serious, and he had tried to prepare himself in the event that she was going to break off their relationship. Maybe it was for the best. The past year had been hard on them: there were so many things that set them apart from each other. Often he loathed and loved her at the same time; likewise the company she kept. He felt clear dissociation from her one minute and sullen envy the next, at least with respect to the people she used to know. He didn't envy her new political friends at all.

Rita was by that time enrolled in the School of Architecture, where she immersed herself in Marxist economics and Leninist theory. There were no free rides to the revolution, even for the elite. She'd moved into a room at the Grønjordskollegium student

177

halls in Amager, on the seventh floor with a view out across the grasslands of the Amager Fælled and inland towards the city's towers and steeples. He had helped her decorate and move in. And he had built her shelving system, fitting the elements together until it took up the whole of one wall. It was quick, easy and ugly to look at. But she had lots of books. He'd glanced at some of the titles after putting them in place and found himself wondering who was actually going to be designing Danish housing of the future, since students of architecture apparently weren't learning the slightest thing about it.

Nineteen seventy-two was a year of momentous world events. He and Rita disagreed about most of them, especially the Munich massacre. During the Olympic Games that summer eleven Israeli athletes were murdered by a Palestinian terrorist group, Black September. The world was in shock, and Simonsen with it. It was a cowardly and horrendous attack. Following a day of mourning the Games continued. But the joy was gone from the contest. He turned off the TV, and for once he didn't mince his words. *Congratulations, Rita. Your friends have won a great victory. Eleven defenceless athletes. I hope you're proud.*

Rita clenched her fists and flew off the handle: she didn't give a damn about Munich. As long as the comrades banged up in Stammheim Prison were being tortured in isolation while the world looked the other way, she wasn't going to get herself worked up about a few dead athletes. She stomped off in a rage. *The comrades banged up in Stammheim* – Andreas Baader, Ulrike Meinhof, Gudrun Ensslin and Jan-Carl Raspe, murderers all four. As far as Simonsen was concerned they could rot away in their isolation. Later, he got hold of a *Fahndungsplakat* from a colleague in the border police at Kruså. It wasn't hard, the posters were all over the place, in every public institution in West Germany. Twenty black-and-white portrait photos of young people, high-contrast. The headline was unequivocal: *Terroristen.* With a thick black felt-tip he crossed out the faces of those dead or captured. He put the poster up on the door outside her room without her noticing. It remained there for a day and a night. When eventually Rita discovered it she could hardly catch her breath for rage, but he denied all knowledge: *Who, him? Of course not. It must have been one of the other students. Maybe there were still one or two who didn't agree with her opinions. Had she considered the possibility?*

Then, on 2 October, she and the radical left she idolised received an emphatic kick in the teeth. Denmark voted to join the Common Market by an overwhelming majority. They were at Simonsen's place, watching the count on television. He openly gloated, but she didn't react as he was expecting. The defeat wasn't that important to her. Six months before, she'd been involved in the People's Movement against the EC, *Folkebevægelsen mod EF*, but now she couldn't seem to care less. And it wasn't because her side had lost, it was something else, more chilling. That evening he felt for the first time that something wasn't right. He was afraid.

The oak tree beneath which they had sat was still there. He recognised it among a thousand others. He sat down. Again. And almost felt she was at his side. Perhaps the reason he had loved Rita, in spite of everything, was that she always managed to surprise him. To do things he could never quite predict, or say things when he was least expecting it. She was impossible to pin a label on. Just as he thought he knew her, he didn't. And that day thirty-five years ago was no exception. She'd leaned her head against his shoulder. It was the first time they had touched in what seemed like an age. He was thinking it was over between them. And then she said quietly:

'Konrad, I'm pregnant.'

A hundred thoughts passed through his mind in an instant. Marriage, responsibility, money. The prospect was overwhelming. A child. He was going to be a father.

'I'm not sure if it's yours. I think so, but... I don't know.'

He couldn't remember what he'd said in reply. Or if he'd spoken at all. But her next sentence had stayed with him:

'I don't want it. The time isn't right. Not yet.'

He protested, albeit half-heartedly. But Rita ignored him.

'Put your arms around me.'

He held her as requested. It was less than a year until Denmark introduced free abortion.

The house in Søllerød was big when he was on his own. He missed the Countess, that was it, there was no point in denying it. Certainly not to himself.

He spent the Saturday on the postman case, mainly to kill time doing something worthwhile. He reread a couple of reports he'd taken home with him and spent most of the afternoon going through Jørgen Kramer Nielsen's supermarket receipts to see if he could turn anything up besides what Pauline Berg had found. He couldn't. Then he wrote an e-mail to the priest after considering for a moment whether he should pay him a visit. For no other reason than that he felt like it: the man had made an impression on him, a good impression at that. In the end he couldn't be bothered and wrote to him instead, asking directly if, in his work, the priest had ever come across the British charity Missing Children, to which Kramer Nielsen had bequeathed so much money. An hour later he received a reply in the form of a link to the organisation's website, accompanied by a polite *Best wishes*. He'd visited the site before, so it wasn't much use. Still, it had been worth a try.

Later in the day something happened that made him happy. The doorbell rang, rather cautiously, he thought. He went to the door and there was Maja Nørgaard with a sheepish smile on her face and a lavish bouquet of flowers in her hand. He hadn't seen her since the day he'd interviewed her in the bar near Enghave

Station over a month ago. She was looking well, her eyes bright and attentive, the way a girl ought to look at that age.

Her thanks were awkwardly delivered: she shook his hand and made a mess of the words that had clearly been practised beforehand. But there was no mistaking her genuine gratitude: she had got a grip on her life now, stuck to soft drinks during the week and would be keeping away from drugs until she was a hundred. Her mother, a therapist and a social worker had all helped her. Konrad Simonsen sat down on his front step. He didn't want to invite her in, it seemed wrong somehow. On the other hand he didn't want to turn her away either if she wanted to talk. She sat down next to him and spoke hesitantly, as though searching for some bigger picture:

'It's weird. All through school they tell you not to bully and not to leave others out. But it's only now that I understand how right that is. I could have been nicer to Robert... we all could. He was in love with me, and there was nothing wrong with that. I should have looked beyond the surface instead of thinking about how fat he was. I should have talked to him, told him I actually liked him. I could easily have done that without... without...'

She ground to a halt, eventually adding, 'I'm sure it would have meant a lot to him.'

Konrad Simonsen replied softly:

'I'm sure it would, Maja. But what happened wasn't your fault. That's important to remember, too.'

She smiled uncertainly. He told her about other people he knew whose lives had gone wrong, without anyone being to blame. She listened gratefully, and he elaborated to make his stories fit the bill a bit better. Eventually, he got to his feet, and Maja did likewise.

'The therapist says the same as you, that it's not my fault.'

'It isn't, you'll see.'

He thanked her again for the flowers and she edged away, only then to submit to an urge and spontaneously run back to hug him. They stood there for a moment before she let go and ran back down the garden path to a waiting car, waving as she went. Happy.

On the Sunday, Anna Mia came by unannounced. They'd agreed to have dinner together the next day and Simonsen had promised to take her to a restaurant in town, so her visit came as a surprise, though he was no less pleased on that account. He sat in the kitchen while she ravenously plundered the fridge. Making herself a sandwich, she asked:

'If you've bought my present, can I have it now instead of having to go about the town with it tomorrow?'

This wasn't good. He'd forgotten all about her birthday after his argument with the Countess. Moreover, she read his look of surprise like lightning.

'Don't tell me you've forgotten my birthday, Dad.'

It was a minefield. There'd been so many birthdays in her life when all she'd wanted was a present from him. It didn't matter what it was – just something. Tears welled in her eyes and she put the knife down. There was nothing for it but to tell the truth.

She wiped her eyes and pulled herself together. Rather too quickly, he thought.

'Where is it then, this camera?' she asked, trying to sound casual. 'I'd like to see it, at least.'

He had put it in the garden room together with the long lens that had been delivered a couple of days before. Twenty seconds after he told her, the boxes were in front of him on the table. She got the camera out.

'Wow, this is nice.'

He finished making the sandwich for her while she admired the Nikon. They talked about it. Maybe she could pay half herself, if that was all right, bit by bit over a few months. He wouldn't hear of it and went off to get scissors, sticky tape and wrapping paper, realising it was all a foregone conclusion.

'Are you sure you can afford it, Dad?'

Of course he could. He earned a decent salary, but after moving in with the Countess it was as though he was continually comparing his finances to hers, and in that game he was always going to come out the loser. Nonetheless, at the moment he was spending rather less than he earned, partly because the Countess did most of the shopping herself and refused to keep tabs. It was a waste of time, she insisted. But he told none of this to Anna Mia, making do with the bare bones:

'Yes.'

They wrapped her present together. In Christmas wrapping paper, the only sort he could find.

'What about your mum, though?' he asked.

Before, when he'd told her, she could see the problem and had partially agreed with him that the present from him and the Countess would overshadow everything else she was likely to get. But then all of a sudden the solution was right in front of them.

'I'll just take the lens with me.'

Of course. How hard did it have to be?

When Simonsen went into work on the Monday morning there was an envelope from the lab waiting for him on his desk. Feeling expectant, he opened it and emptied out the contents in front of him. Photographs, just as he'd hoped: twelve black-and-white prints that looked like holiday snaps. He examined them closely, lingering on one in particular. All showed a group of young people in various everyday situations, as far as he could see, taken in and around the type of wooden house that city dwellers liked to take in the country or by the sea for the summer months. In all twelve he recognised the girl from the posters, and in six of them she was on her own. Besides these prints the envelope contained a smaller packet of negatives, cut out individually so that they could be pressed flat together. He picked one out at random and noted that it was the same image as one of the prints and that the number of negatives matched up.

The most surprising, and immediately informative, item was the front page of a newspaper. It was folded once down the middle. He opened it and smoothed it out carefully, scanning the details: *Jyllands-Posten*, second section, page one, Sunday 17 February 1974. The smiling image of a girl dominated the article, headlined *What Price Rebellion?* The caption below the photo gave the girl a name: *Lucy Selma Davison left her home in Liverpool in May 1969 and was last seen in Harwich on 14 June the same year.* Simonsen spoke the name quietly out loud:

'Lucy Selma Davison.'

For a minute he sat and stared at the girl's portrait. She could hardly have been more than fourteen or fifteen when it was taken. Seventeen at most, certainly no older than that. Her face was softly rounded about a delicate, slightly pointed nose that displayed a slight smattering of freckles across its bridge. Her eyes hinted at an impish smile, bashful perhaps, or provocative, he wasn't sure. Her long, dark-blonde hair was pulled back behind her ears and held in place by two hair slides, one on each side. Her straight fringe reached almost to her eyebrows. She wore no make-up: none was necessary.

Cautiously, as though committing some unlawful deed, he allowed his fingertips to pass across her image as he whispered:

'You were beautiful, Lucy. Beautiful.'

He folded up the article again and tried to think of what he knew about Liverpool. It was next to nothing. The *Titanic* was registered in Liverpool, and the Beatles, of course, were from Liverpool. Neither of these things were of any relevance, it seemed. *Liverpool, May 1969*. What happened in Liverpool in May 1969? It was a blank to him, as good a place to start as any.

All of sudden it suited Simonsen fine that the Countess had put off her return from Jutland until Wednesday. It gave him more leeway with regard to his work, and now suddenly he had lots to be getting on with. He told her about his discovery when they spoke on the phone and they agreed it made it all the more imperative that they were able to map Jørgen Kramer Nielsen's movements during his annual holiday trip. It was an investigation she and Klavs Arnold were working hard on, though as yet they'd made little headway.

Only after he'd hung up did the thought occur to Simonsen that he'd forgotten to tell her the issue of Anna Mia's birthday present had now been settled. He shook his head at himself: *settled* was just a euphemism for the resounding defeat he had suffered. And then it struck him: he'd better cancel his dinner appointment with his daughter that evening. He wouldn't have time now. He was lucky. She didn't answer her phone and he could make do with leaving a message. After which he got started on the job at hand.

On Tuesday Pauline Berg appeared in his office mid-morning, looking cheerful and bright. He was glad to see her. It meant he could bring her up to date on the inroads he'd been making into the postman case. Besides, he'd been growing rather fond of her occasionally challenging demeanour and anarchistic behaviour. As long as it didn't get out of hand.

'Hi, Pauline. I hope you can spare me some time. There's a few things we need to talk about, and one thing in particular I need your help with.'

She sat down, eyes scanning his office with suspicion. The bulletin boards were covered with photos, a big pile of dusty suspension files had been dumped on a table and the whiteboard was a scribble of diagrams.

'The Countess has been trying to get in touch with you. How come you don't answer your phone?' Pauline demanded.

'I've been out of range in a basement most of the day, but I'll tell you about that later. First of all: how good's your English?'

'Good. Arne called me as well, he couldn't get in touch with you either. And neither could your daughter. She tried to call you last night. She thought you were supposed to be having dinner.'

'I cancelled.'

Pauline gave him a reproachful look and waited for him to go on.

'OK, it was a bit late by the time I got home, but listen: I want you to phone England later today. My English isn't good enough for phone calls, too much gets past me. I don't know where I want you to start just yet, I haven't had time to think about it. I need to find someone fairly high up you can use as your point of entry. Someone here must have a personal acquaintance over there... maybe one of our superiors. But I'll sort that out later, like I said.'

'What am I supposed to find out about?'

'Anything you can about a seventeen-year-old girl who went missing in 1969. She was from a place called Fairfield in Liverpool, and her name was Lucy.'

'Is she the girl on your posters?'

'Yes, and I've made further headway there. The girl's full name was Lucy Davison, and there was some contact with Jørgen Kramer Nielsen before she disappeared.'

'Is she dead?'

'I think so, but we've no way of knowing for sure yet. That's why I want you to be a bit careful when you make that call to England. I don't want her family building up false hopes. Her parents could still be alive now.'

'So more exactly, you want to know what?'

The most important thing was to make sure Lucy Davison hadn't turned up again in Liverpool safe and sound, or that her fate hadn't been happily resolved in some other way. He had been unable to find anything at all about her in the archives, despite having picked his way through metres of shelves with files on missing children and youngsters in 1969 and a couple of years following. He continued:

'I've got twelve photos of her, or rather photos in which she appears. All taken by Jørgen Kramer Nielsen. I'm gradually working towards establishing the time frame. Tomorrow, I'm off to the National Archive to look at exam lists and external examiners' reports. Would you believe those things are kept for posterity? To be honest, though, I'm not in much doubt as to the dates.'

'Kramer Nielsen's holidays every year in June?'

'Exactly. Ninety-nine per cent certain.'

'You've made a lot of progress, well done.'

'It's been hard graft, but if all goes well I should be able to present some pretty solid leads by tomorrow. You've seen I've called a meeting, I take it? The Countess should be home by then, too, and Arne can make it as well.'

'What are those boxes over there?'

'Exam papers. Advanced level school-leaving exams in Danish. Anno nineteen sixty-nine, Class Three Y of Brøndbyøster Gymnasium. Plus end-of-term papers, same year. The first lot I photocopied at the National Archive, the latter set is from the school's own basement, and the two green boxes are the school magazine, years sixty-seven to -nine. They call it the *Dispatch*.'

'And you reckon you're going to get it all read by tomorrow?'

'Skimmed. Most of it's going to be of no use to us, obviously.'

'Would you excuse me a minute, Simon? There's something I need to sort out. I'll be back in fifteen minutes.'

Fifteen minutes turned out to be right, only it wasn't Pauline Berg who came back. Simonsen didn't notice the Deputy Commissioner until she'd sat down in front of him.

'Simon. Working late these days, I notice.'

'Oh, hello. What can I do for you?'

'It's more what I can do for you, as a matter for fact. I hear you've got a problem with your English. I ran into Pauline Berg, you see, and she mentioned some information from England. Liverpool, to be precise.'

Simonsen pricked up his ears.

'My English isn't good enough, I'm afraid, and we need a decent introduction, preferably to someone high up the ladder who can open doors.'

'In which case, I'd probably be the right person, though my English isn't much better than yours. But I did attend a conference once in Liverpool, so at least I've heard the local accent. I didn't understand it very well, though. Let's just hope they're feeling kind when I give them a call.'

'Would you? It'd be a great help. Are you sure you've got time?'

'Things have been a bit slow this week in the corridors of power. We've got the big convening of the force at the Øksnehallen coming up, but we're all ready for that. And I won't hide the fact that I'm rather excited about this case of yours after having played my own little part the other day.'

'Excellent! Then I'll draw up a list of questions we'd like some answers to. You'll have it on your desk by tomorrow morning.'

'That's where I beg to differ, Simon. First you tell me all about this young girl you're so interested in, and then you go home and pack.'

'Pack? What on earth for... where am I going? I've called a meeting tomorrow, it's important.'

'Not any more it isn't. It's rescheduled for next week. Amazing what they can do downstairs in IT as soon as something urgent comes up, isn't it?'

'Urgent? Sorry, I'm not with you.'

He was being dispatched to an Interpol conference or seminar, she wasn't quite sure which. At any rate, the Deputy Commissioner had just discovered that the Copenhagen Police had been allocated three places and not two, as she had thought. It was important they fly the flag on such occasions, even if they did involve a lot of wasted time. It was fortunate that he was available or she'd have had no idea who to send. Her orders were given in a tone that was friendly, but firm:

'You fly out tomorrow at twelve-thirty. Make sure you're at the airport two hours before your flight.'

'Where am I going?'

'Nesebar in Bulgaria. It's on the Black Sea. Very cultural, and they've got health spas, too, if you need to wind down after the morning's talks.'

'What's the theme?'

There were many themes, and all of them important. International collaboration, transnational teamwork, virtual-experience exchange groups... all of considerable relevance, not least for Denmark with its official proviso as to police and judicial co-operation in the EU. But he didn't quite get the connection: what had Interpol to do with the EU? She spelled it out for him: it was all about personal networks, the ABC of international co-operation, and in particular establishing personal contacts within the major EU countries. Her enthusiasm was infectious and he listened with interest.

'I'll make sure you receive the programme. The secretaries upstairs are making all the arrangements for you.'

Simonsen glanced at his bulletin boards and the Deputy Commissioner followed his gaze.

'That'll have to wait a week, Simon. You know how significant international relations are, and how much importance we in the executive attach to them. Besides, Bulgaria's new to the EU,

189

which makes it all the more crucial we're represented. *Interpol is our backbone.* Isn't that what you say?'

'But it's all a bit sudden... and with my own case... very well, yes, I suppose it can wait a week.'

'I'm sure Pauline Berg would drive you to the airport tomorrow. You can brief her on the way, then she and the others will prepare for your meeting in a week's time.'

'All right, if that's what you want.'

'Thank you, Simon, I'm pleased. In the meantime I'll do my best to get hold of the information you want from England. You scratch my back, and what have you.'

Her ear-to-ear smile raised his spirits.

'Now, tell me about this girl of yours.'

He started by removing one of the photos from the bulletin board and placing it in front of her. Then he found the newspaper article. The Deputy Commissioner studied the photo.

'What a pretty girl. Has she got a name?'

He ran through the facts they'd got and then summarised the article for her.

The angle, as hinted at in the headline, was a broadside against youth rebellion and all its negative ramifications, focusing in particular on the many teenagers who left their homes to seek out a new life in the city. Copenhagen's so-called free state of Christiania was mentioned several times.

'The main gist is clearly to add to pressure being exerted on the new government to clear Christiania, which to the journalist's mind is little more than a drug den. They might not be that explicit, but you get the idea, I'm sure.'

'Oh, I'm with you. Call in the bulldozers, Prime Minister.'

She was right. That was certainly what the paper had been angling for. But for Simonsen it was the human interest story that grabbed his attention. Then, as now, it was the human angle that sold copies, not the statistics about missing youngsters, though it seemed there were many in those years. The poor souls, who paid the price for society's relentless progress and sank to the bottom, casualties of drugs and prostitution, were of little interest either. But a devastated elderly couple from a decent working-class home in Liverpool, touring around Danish and Swedish towns every summer in search of their missing daughter, was something that tugged at the heartstrings in the small homes of Jutland.

'Lucy's parents, you mean?'

'George and Margaret Davison. They scrimped and saved from their pay packets all year so they could afford the trip every summer to hand out flyers and put up posters appealing for information about their daughter. They were Catholics, or maybe still *are* Catholics. I don't yet know if they're alive.'

'Things are starting to come together, aren't they, Simon?'

'Perhaps. We'll have to wait and see. At any rate, the Davisons have been forced to accept the fact that their daughter is most likely dead, and now I'm certain all they want is to get her home so she can be buried in consecrated earth.'

'Those poor people.'

'Indeed. They wanted to see the back of flower power, free love and macrobiotics as fast as possible, I'm sure. Listen to this.'

He put on his glasses and read from the newspaper:

'"*One Wednesday we found a short farewell note. It was the worst morning of our lives. She was gone. Our little girl, run away.*" *Tears run down Mr Davison's cheeks, but he does nothing to wipe them away. He sits, powerless in his grief. Mrs Davison carries on where her husband left off.* "*What did we do that was wrong? We gave her everything money could buy, everything we could afford. Why would she treat us so thoughtlessly? How could she do this to us?*" *The question remains in the air. Who can answer them?*

'And so on and so forth… *damaging influence of subversive elements…* then there's a bit that isn't of much interest… hang on a minute, there's more here.

'"We know that two days later she went off with a young man from our local car dealer's. He drove her to Harwich where she was going to sneak on board the ferry to Denmark, and we think that somehow she succeeded." Mrs Davison nods. "She was a bright and cheerful girl, anyone would have helped her. She was no bother as a child, but then last year she got into bad company." Then *Jyllands-Posten* makes of that what it will, as I'm sure you can imagine. And there's the last bit of factual stuff.'

He ran a finger down the page and quickly found what he was looking for:

'"We got a postcard from Sweden. The postmark was Orsa, the twenty-second of June nineteen sixty-nine. Then later her tent and rucksack were found near Lycksele, a little town high up in Sweden. But that wasn't until the beginning of April nineteen seventy. The tent had been put up in a forest." Once more Mrs Davison picks up from her husband as he breaks down in tears and apologises for losing control. "The Swedish police took the matter very seriously indeed. They started an investigation right away and searched throughout the forest. There were all sorts of people out looking: police, volunteers and soldiers from the Swedish army [Ed. note: the Hemvärnet, or Swedish Reserve], but they didn't find anything. Later, the police said Lucy hadn't been in Sweden at all, somebody else had put her tent up and sent the postcard to make it look like she had. The Danish police didn't want anything to do with it. We've tried so many times, as has our priest, too. But all in vain. That's why we're hoping it'll help if Lucy's picture gets in the papers."'

Simonsen put the article down.

'There's something I don't understand,' said the Deputy Commissioner. 'How can anyone send a postcard and make it look like it's from her? It can't be that difficult, surely, to find out if she wrote it herself or not?'

'No, that struck me, too. It's one of the questions you'll need to ask the English police, if they even know anything about the case. I'm thinking it'd be fine if to begin with we don't inform her family that we may have something new. They've suffered enough as it is.'

'I agree entirely. What about the Swedish police? It sounds like they'll have a file on her too. Have you been in touch with them?'

'They've promised to send me a copy of the final report as quickly as they can.'

'Do you want me to lean on them a bit while I'm at it?'

'No need, they're usually efficient, even if our colleague over there in the Rikskriminalpolisen did point out to me that we already received the report once, in late seventy-two. Where it got to, and what we did about it at the time, is something I've not been able to find out, so the article is probably right: we did nothing.'

'And you don't think she ever got to Sweden, do you?'

'I think Lucy Davison was killed sometime between the fifteenth and the nineteenth of June in a summer house over on the west coast of Jutland, and buried in some out-of-the-way place by Jørgen Kramer Nielsen and five of his mates from Class Three Y, Brøndbyøster Gymnasium. What's more, I think Jørgen Kramer Nielsen paid for that misdeed with his life.'

CHAPTER 7

As the plane took off from Copenhagen's Kastrup Airport Simonsen thought about Lucy, gazing at the passing clouds as if in search of her image. After a while he put all thoughts of the case aside. The Deputy Commissioner was right: others were quite capable of keeping things together while he was away, and moreover he had meticulously instructed Pauline Berg during the course of the morning. Shortly afterwards he fell asleep, waking again only when the stewardess placed a gentle hand on his shoulder with a reminder for him to fasten his safety belt as the plane prepared for landing.

Only once during the conference did he receive word about the case. It was in a lunch break and he was relaxing in the hotel's giant jacuzzi after the morning's exertions, flanked by an Argentinian and a Korean. He'd put his mobile down on the edge of the pool behind him in case the Countess happened to call. When it vibrated he couldn't reach it, but one of the ubiquitous staff was swiftly at hand, dashing forward and holding out the phone in time for him to answer. Unfortunately, there seemed to be no connection. He said his name into the receiver a couple of times in forlorn expectation before giving up with a sigh. The Argentinian at his side uttered something incomprehensible and pointed at his phone. Simonsen made to hand it to him, only for the man to shake his head, a gesture that was accompanied by further pronouncements in Spanish. The Korean translated for him without opening his eyes:

'You got text. No phone call. Text.'

Simonsen loathed text messaging and had forbidden his staff from ever communicating with him in such a childish manner. Even Anna Mia respected his stance, though she found it silly. With some difficulty he managed to open the message. It was from Pauline Berg:

Hi Simon. Hope you're enjoying the 'conference' :) Arne and I are at the big crisis meeting. Totally meaningless, be glad you're away. Report in from Swedes. Lucy D was never there. Do you want more info now? Loads of time here.

He replied with a *yes* that took him several minutes to type and send. Thirty seconds later a second text came in:

The Swedes conducted perfect investigation in 1969. Tent put up in depths of forest. No one wld ever spend night there. Too far from road and habitation. No sign of normal activity in tent. Only unrolled sleeping bag, rucksack still packed. More in a bit...

He waited, unsure as to whether he needed to reply. Shortly afterwards, her next text arrived:

Twelve brand new Swedish 10-kronor notes in her wallet. Traced to bank in Copenhagen! No Swedish coins. No fprints on notes. Not even her own! Technology re prints on paper new at time though.

This time he simply waited, and another thirty seconds passed as he'd anticipated.

Postcard pic from Esbjerg. Written by her but sent with Swdsh stamp from Orsa. Nothing about arriving Sweden, only that she was heading to Nth Cape to see midnight sun. Stamp (commemorative, Vasa warship) sold only by block. Rest of block not found among effects.

Simonsen smiled at the Argentinian who was unashamedly following his correspondence, though what he might be gleaning from it was another matter entirely.

Forgot to say UK sending orgnl postcd plus othr stuff to Gurli (Arne called her that not me) :) More indicatns Lucy D never got to Swdn. But signature on report most compelling. You'll nvr believe it! Guess!

He swore under his breath and fumbled his way through a *No*. A moment later he found himself staring at the name of

Scandinavia's most famous crime investigator, a police officer whose reputation extended throughout the world. The Argentinian was quick to acknowledge the fact, jabbing a finger at Simonsen's display and slapping the flat of his other hand against the water in delight:

'*Es mi hero grande. Un hombre fantastico.*'

The Korean opened an eye, and Simonsen commented with pride:

'I just received a message from a legend.'

The man nodded almost imperceptibly and closed his eye again.

'Lucky you.'

The jaunty voice of the stewardess informed the passengers over the tannoy that the plane would be landing at Kastrup Airport in approximately thirty minutes. The weather in Copenhagen was chilly and windy, the temperature around twelve degrees Celsius.

Konrad Simonsen dozed, but the announcement, along with a few jolts of turbulence, made him stir. He rubbed his eyes and looked out of the window. Below lay a thick, grey blanket of cloud, obliterating all sight of land. He was feeling well, and pleasantly at ease. He hadn't given the postman case much thought at all in Bulgaria. Rita neither, for that matter: his flashbacks seemed to have abated, a fact he rather regretted. After all, they had been through a lot together, good times as well as bad, in an age with which he had been at odds. Then and now. *Chilly and windy*, wasn't that what the stewardess had said? No weather for a girl in an Afghan coat.

A cold wind blew through the streets of Copenhagen and whistled in the gateway. Rita was freezing. She stood up against the wall, teeth chattering. Konrad Simonsen glanced at the door leading to the back stairs, its green paintwork in flakes. A messenger boy was lugging fuel up to the top floor, a hectolitre of coke per sack, one at a time slung across his shoulders. The boy was skinny, the weight of his burden unsteadying him as he stepped through the gateway towards the stairs. His delivery bike was parked outside. He still had two sacks to go.

Simonsen and Rita weren't due to knock on the door for another fifteen minutes. At eleven o'clock precisely, not a minute sooner or later. He had spoken to the woman on the phone and she'd been quite clear about that. *The woman.* The backstreet abortionist. They'd spoken for less than half a minute, and yet Konrad Simonsen disliked her intensely. Her Danish had been poor, interspersed with words he hadn't understood. Perhaps that was the source of his animosity. Yes, that was probably it.

Finding the money had been easy. He'd been prepared to sell his TV, to dig into his savings and, if needs be, to approach the bank about a loan. He was on a regular income and could see no obvious hindrance. But none of these options proved necessary. Without her knowledge, three of Rita's student friends from the School of Architecture had collected the money for her, at the halls where she lived as well as in the school itself. Solidarity was no empty word in such circles, and in less than a week they'd reached the amount she needed. Most of those who chipped in had no idea who Rita was. Nor had the collectors gone into any detail as to the reason for the collection; it had been enough for them to say that one of their comrades was in dire straits. And yet the hat had seldom been passed round in vain: who was going to miss ten kroner, anyway? The four thousand an illegal abortion cost was soon raised.

Konrad Simonsen and Rita went through the door and up the back stairs, she in front, he bringing up the rear, his mind full of horror stories about dirty knitting needles, syringes injecting soap solutions into the womb, the use of large doses of potentially lethal quinine. Rita knocked. Three times, followed by a pause, then three times again. The performing of an illegal abortion was punishable by law, carrying a term of up to eight years' imprisonment. It was not a matter to be taken lightly.

The woman who opened the door and led them though the narrow kitchen into the living room fully lived up to Konrad Simonsen's prejudices: middle-aged, small and plump, with Slavic features and a look of avarice in her dark, almost black eyes. They sat down and the woman demanded payment. Rita handed her an envelope which she tore open greedily, counting the notes twice. As she did so, Simonsen studied her grubby nails. He turned his head and looked at Rita. Her face was pale. Resolutely, he stood up, snatched the money from the woman's hands and dragged Rita away from the place.

They adjourned to a cafeteria to discuss the situation. They could give the child up for adoption if she – they – didn't want to keep it. She refused, rejecting any other suggestion than abortion. He promised to make enquiries for another abortionist, though he had no idea how to proceed. Backstreet abortionists didn't exactly advertise in the phone book. Connections were required, and he had none. But before long the issue had resolved itself.

A couple of days later – at least, that's how he remembered it, though it might easily have been a week or more – he was called out to a gassing. November and December was peak season for suicides, one of the most popular methods being to turn on the gas and simply lie down in the kitchen to await the end. It was an effective, albeit devilish way of shuffling off the mortal coil. If the neighbours didn't smell gas in time, a single spark could turn a whole building into an inferno. He'd seen it happen twice and heard of many more instances besides. In this case, as in most, the suspicions of a downstairs neighbour had thankfully been aroused. The flats on the same stairway and those adjacent were evacuated and the fire brigade had gone in. Windows and doors were opened, those that stuck were smashed.

Konrad Simonsen sat on the top step outside the main door, half sheltered from the wind. The police had been called as a matter of routine and he was expected to keep the peace while the firemen did their bit, and later, when the ambulance crew carried the dead body out, to hold nosy onlookers at bay. But there was no one there to disturb the peace, no one to be held at bay. So he had sought shelter from the cold while waiting impatiently until the firemen finished and he could get back to the station and warm himself up with a cup of hot coffee.

A person approached and Simonsen looked up at him. The man was in his early forties, with sharply defined features, an intelligent look in his eyes and an air of authority that prompted Konrad Simonsen to get to his feet. For a brief moment, the man considered him without concealing the fact that he didn't care for what he saw. Then he reached his hand into the inside pocket of his sheepskin and produced his police badge, holding it briefly in the air for Simonsen to see before putting it back in his pocket and rebuttoning his coat.

'Make sure you and your girl are ready tomorrow at yours. I'll pick you up around midday.'

He held up his hand, the palm facing Simonsen:

'No questions.'

And with that he left. Konrad Simonsen trotted after him, astonished.

'What about the money? We've only got four thousand kroner. Where are you going to take us anyway? I need to know. And how did you know we...'

The man stood still and cut him off.

'To a hospital, of course. And it's free. I saw you go up to that quack. We're watching her in connection with something bigger. The rest doesn't concern you. Now get back to work before I report you for dereliction of duty. And while we're at it, don't let me catch you sitting down on the job again. We're police, not an OAP club.'

The man kept his word. At twelve the next day he pulled up outside Konrad Simonsen's place in his Opel Record. He said a polite hello to Rita and nodded curtly to Simonsen before ushering them both on to the back seat. He remained silent as he drove. They headed south along the Gammel Køge Landevej to Køge, eventually arriving at the hospital there. He drove slowly past A&E, turning off by some bike sheds before following a narrow lane barely wide enough for a vehicle to pass, and then parking on a lawn in front of a low building. He sounded the horn once before turning round and instructing Rita in a kind voice:

'You're bleeding, rather considerably, and irregularly.'

Rita interrupted:

'But I'm not...'

'No, like I said, it's irregular. In a minute, a woman will come out and collect you. She's my sister and she's a consultant here in the Gynaecological Department. She'll give you a D&C, outpatient. We'll be waiting here again at ten o'clock. Understood?'

Rita understood, and thanked him. The man added:

'My sister doesn't care for present-day informalities. Address her as *Doctor*.'

Five minutes later Rita was duly collected and Konrad Simonsen was left alone with the man, whose friendliness at once evaporated.

'Haven't you ever heard of a condom, you bloody idiot?' he growled.

It was the first bollocking he ever received from Kasper Planck. But far from the last.

Subsequently, Rita gave back the money that had been collected, which presented the students with something of a problem. Who was to have it? After prolonged debate, the field was narrowed down to two options: an organisation that supported the military junta in Greece, and one that was active in the struggle against Francisco Franco's oppressive fascist regime in Spain. Meetings were held, in groups and larger assemblies, and the matter was still the subject of heated discussion in the halls of residence after the

Christmas break. Eventually, the junta won out. Konrad Simonsen's suggestion, the Mother's Aid organisation, fell on deaf ears.

In the arrivals hall at Kastrup, Simonsen was met by the Countess. It had been almost a fortnight since they'd last seen each other, and their reunion was warm indeed. She gave him a big kiss for the little figurine he'd brought home for her, and another for the bunch of flowers that had greeted her when she got back from Esbjerg. Simonsen sent a kind and grateful thought to Maja Nørgaard and willingly took the credit for her gift.

'Arne, Pauline and Klavs are all ready back at HS if you want to have a meeting today,' said the Countess. 'But tomorrow's fine if you're tired after the journey.'

He wasn't tired at all. In fact, he hadn't felt so relaxed in years. At least, that's how it seemed. She smiled.

'Right, let's get going then. There've been quite a few developments in that case of yours while you've been away.'

Simonsen sat, tanned and full of expectation, flanked by the Countess and Pauline Berg, as Arne Pedersen conducted the meeting in his own office. At the rear of the room, Malte Borup ran Pedersen's computer.

Pedersen himself appeared nervous, and Simonsen was surprised by the fact. Arne had run countless meetings like this and had steered any number of briefings during ongoing investigations. Moreover, with the exception of Klavs Arnold, all five of his audience were long-time colleagues, and Arnold himself was affable enough. Perhaps Pauline Berg was playing up again. He hadn't had the chance to ask the Countess about her on their way in to Police HQ.

'First, let me say welcome back, Simon. I hope you had a pleasant and fruitful time down there.'

Simonsen replied briefly: the trip had been beneficial indeed. At the same time, he noted that Pedersen had difficulty looking him in the eye. Simonsen's puzzlement mounted as Pedersen spent far too long assuring him that he categorically was not in the process of taking over the investigation into Jørgen Kramer Nielsen's killing. Certainly not, on the contrary! All they'd done while Simonsen had been away was to collate the information he'd already gathered with some new findings that had come up in the meantime. He felt compelled to stress the fact, which he then did, several times, waffling his way through the same rubbish almost from the beginning again. Fortunately, Klavs Arnold interrupted. The man from Jutland turned to Simonsen and explained:

'It's still your investigation, but we need to stoke it up a bit. The way things are, we're looking at a double murder inquiry, so the expectation is that you'll involve the rest of us and seek other resources at your disposal, too. That's from upstairs to Arne, and quite reasonable, too, if you ask me.'

Arne Pedersen confirmed this was indeed the case, albeit rather more diplomatically. He looked at Simonsen and after a slight pause received the answer everyone was hoping for.

'That's fine by me, as long as I'm still in charge. I'm not having you vetoing me, Arne. And if you want to be in on the investigation, I'm your boss and not the other way round.'

It was quickly agreed, and Pedersen's nerves evaporated just as swiftly.

'We've borrowed Klavs Arnold for a while. There's the Esbjerg link, and he's the expert there. Moreover, as you can see, I've had some new equipment installed. A smartboard, to be exact, computer screen and whiteboard all in one. Like the one in the big conference room, only not quite as advanced. Malte's running it for us today, I've not had time to familiarise myself with it yet.'

A collective snigger went up as Malte clicked a photo of himself on to the screen the instant Pedersen mentioned his name. The mood became more serious when it was replaced by one of Lucy Davison.

Lucy Selma Davison was born on 20 April 1952 in Liverpool. Her father George was now retired from his job as a fitter, her mother Margaret had worked as a waitress. There were two other children, Lucy's younger brother and sister. The girl had left home on 28 May 1969, leaving a brief, uninformative note. Following the recent approach from Copenhagen, Merseyside Police had resumed enquiries into her disappearance, albeit discreetly and without the knowledge of her kin. Lucy Davison had not returned home in the intervening period, and police believed there was nothing else to suggest that anyone in the UK had heard from her in the forty years or so that had passed since her disappearance.

Arne Pedersen went on:

'We know nothing about why she might have wanted to run away, but a reasonable guess would be that she was gripped by the general urge of young people at the time to liberate themselves from the constraints of traditional norms and values. She lived in the suburbs and came from a Catholic home, and I'm sure a city that produced the Beatles had more to offer.'

All they knew for certain was that Lucy Davison had been in Harwich on 14 June 1969. Most probably she arrived in Esbjerg on 16 or 17 June. According to her postcard, she was heading to northern Norway *to see the midnight sun*. In Esbjerg she made contact with six pupils from Class Three Y of the Brøndbyøster Gymnasium who had got together in a summer house to revise for the last subject of their final exams, oral maths, scheduled for Friday 20 June.

Arne Pedersen took a gulp of water and the Countess interjected for Simonsen's benefit:

'We call them the Gang of Six.'

He nodded, though he didn't care for the name, finding it vaguely accusatory and therefore liable to lead them towards the wrong conclusions. Pedersen continued:

'Our theory is that Lucy Davison died in that summer house and that our Gang of Six concealed the body. Two of them then drove to Lycksele in Sweden, which is in the Västerbotten region, about a thousand kilometres from Malmö as the crow flies. Some way outside the town they put up her tent in the forest. Before they got to Lycksele, however, about halfway there, they stopped off in Orsa and sent her postcard. There are three things in particular that we still haven't a clue about. How did she die? What happened to her body? And where is this summer house? Any questions?'

He looked at Konrad Simonsen, who had a couple, at least.

'Are her parents still alive?'

'Yes.'

'I assume we know the identities of all the members of this Gang of Six?'

'We do. I'll get to that in just a minute.'

'What about the other pupils in Three Y? Do we know where they are today?'

'We haven't looked into that. What do you want them for?'

To everyone's astonishment, Klavs Arnold interrupted:

'He's right, you know. We've only got one shot at those bastards.'

'I'm not with you,' said Pauline Berg.

The Countess butted in:

'If we don't get a really good idea about this Gang of Six, what they were like in their school days, then we won't have a chance when it comes to assessing their stories once we interview them as adults. Now I see why I spent hours going through their useless essays as well as the school magazine from nineteen sixty-seven to sixty-nine while you were relaxing in mud baths by the Black Sea, Simon. You might have told me.'

He begged to differ.

'How did I know you were reading their essays? I'm not a mind reader. Did you come up with anything?'

Within a second everyone was talking at once and Arne Pedersen sat there like an idiot, not knowing whether he should involve himself in the debate, wait until it was over or ask for quiet. Malte Borup solved the issue on his behalf. A silent-movie speech caption appeared on the screen: *Shut up and listen to Arne.* It was ambulance siren, however, that cut most effectively through the babble. Everyone fell silent at once, and Pauline Berg put her hands to her ears.

Pedersen sent Malte a look of gratitude before he carried on as though nothing had happened:

'I'll put a couple of men on the rest of the class, Simon. OK?'

'OK, but data only. No contact. We'll do that ourselves.'

'Fine. Let's move on to the photos.'

There seemed little doubt that Jørgen Kramer Nielsen had taken these himself. He appeared only in one, a group photo most likely taken with a self-timing release. Moreover, the negatives had been found in his possession. In contrast to the postman, Lucy Davison appeared in all twelve photos, though conceivably there had been others from which she was absent and which Kramer Nielsen had discarded. It was a reasonable assumption, and supported by the technical evidence indicating that he had taken images of her face from the twelve photos he'd retained in order to produce his posters. And yet they could in no way be certain that all those involved had been captured on Kramer Nielsen's film, that the Gang of Six was not a Gang of Seven or maybe even more. Conceivably, another member might well have avoided being photographed, for whatever reason, perhaps because he or she didn't like having their picture taken, or because Jørgen Kramer Nielsen had omitted to photograph them, regardless of whether Lucy Davison was in the frame or not. But it didn't seem likely, even if they couldn't eliminate the possibility entirely.

Arne Pedersen gulped down another mouthful of water, and this time his audience refrained from interrupting. He cleared his throat.

'The photographs tell us a number of things, not least the identities of our Gang of Six. We already have a small amount of knowledge about them, and more information will be coming in. We know Jørgen Kramer Nielsen, of course, and then there's this guy here, though we needn't waste much time on him.'

Malte Borup changed the image on the screen. A spotty-faced kid with big ears and a daft grin on his face appeared instead.

'His name is Mouritz Malmborg.'

Pauline Berg sniggered, apparently without reason. Pedersen looked at her in surprise.

'What's funny, Pauline?'

'Sorry. It's just… Mouritz Malmborg… the name and the way he looks. The poor lad never stood a chance, did he?'

She sniggered again.

She was right. Mouritz Malmborg's time on earth was short and he died in 1973 after crashing his moped. At the time, he was a biology student at Aarhus University. Arne Pedersen suggested they set him aside and focus on those who were still alive.

The image on the screen changed again. This time a girl appeared, plump and dull-looking.

'She's got a bit of meat on her, hasn't she?' Pauline commented.

No one said anything, though the Countess grimaced and flashed her a look of annoyance.

Hanne Brummersted had graduated from medical school in 1977 and gone on to do her doctoral dissertation in 1982 on the subject of chromosomal defects. At present she was a consultant in the Department of Clinical Genetics at Herlev Hospital, resident in Roskilde and divorced. She'd had her children late, two girls now fifteen and eighteen. The police had nothing on file about her and her financial situation seemed to be sound.

Next, please, Malte. Another girl, this one with somewhat irregular features and sporting a pair of imperious horn-rimmed glasses. Arne Pedersen consulted his notes.

'Helena Brage Hansen. No further education, as far as we know. A Norwegian citizen these days, living in Hammerfest. Unmarried, with various jobs, a tourist guide in the summer season. Financial standing as yet unknown, and we're unsure if she's known to police up there either. We've asked them to get a move on with that. Last one now, Malte, if you don't mind.'

This time, two images appeared. A boy with a pleasant face and a bright smile, displaying white teeth. Next to him a girl, pale and sickly-looking.

'I've put them together because they're married. They weren't at the time, of course. His name is Jesper Mikkelsen, and she's Pia Muus...'

Pauline Berg snorted disdainfully, but by now Pedersen had had enough.

'That'll do, Pauline. It may well be she hasn't got your looks, but if that bothers you, you can keep it to herself.'

Pauline mockingly gave him the finger and asked a question as if nothing had happened:

'What's that he's got on his face?'

'A birthmark. Or stork bite, as they say.'

'Must have been a big stork.'

'Do you mind if I go on?'

'Be my guest.'

Pia Muus was now Pia Mikkelsen, and the couple lived in Aalborg. After graduating from the gymnasium school, both had begun studies at Aalborg University, though neither had completed them: they both read Sociology, dropping out after three terms. For a considerable number of years they ran a record shop, Used Records, in the town centre, specialising in LPs from the sixties and seventies. The shop had long since closed down, but their online sales were still a huge success, giving them a turnover of almost four million kroner in the previous tax year. They had no children, and the business meant their financial situation was more than healthy. Police had been called out to domestic disturbances at the couple's house on several occasions over the years, though neither party had ever gone so far as to press charges, and the reports in each instance stated that it had been a case of six of one, half a dozen of the other. Moreover, there were vague indications of involvement in Aalborg's drugs and porn circles. On this matter, though, Aalborg Politi couldn't make up their minds, as they readily admitted, and the fact was the couple had never been charged with anything at all.

Arne Pedersen put down his notes on the table.

'That was our Gang of Six for you in brief. Any comments?'

Klavs Arnold stuck a finger in the air, in stark contrast to his usual way of going about these things. He even waited until Arne Pedersen indicated it was his turn:

'Klavs?'

'Yeah, I'm a bit scared of Malte's ambulance siren, but what was that about the porn scene in Aalborg? Are we talking brothels, film, what?'

'Films. All perfectly legal, though. Both of them seem to have an interest in rather young girls. Young and vulnerable. But Aalborg have nothing concrete, so it's all just speculation as it stands.'

Simonsen got to his feet.

'Listen here a minute. Malte, have you got a shot with all six of them at once, including the two who are dead, but without Lucy Davison?'

Malte Borup shook his head.

208

'Can you do us one on your own computer? It doesn't matter if it's a composite.'

The intern nodded this time, and got up and left the room.

While he was away Simonsen stood there staring into space and the others kept quiet so as not to disturb his train of thought. Apart from Klavs Arnold, who at one point muttered an *of course* to himself, no one said a word. After a few minutes Malte Borup came back and clicked the photo on to the screen. Simonsen sat down again.

'Pauline, would you tell us what springs to mind, looking at these people?'

She answered hesitantly:

'Well, six ordinary kids, gymnasium types...'

Simonsen cut her off abruptly.

'That's not what I mean. Tell us what you think, your gut feeling. Don't try to be politically correct about it.'

She blushed slightly. Arne Pedersen was one thing, she could cope with him no trouble. But Simonsen was another matter entirely. She followed his instruction.

'OK, I know I'm bitchy now, but they're not exactly lookers any of them, are they? See for yourself. I'm sorry, but they seem like a bunch of losers to me. If that's all the sixties could come up with, I'm glad I wasn't born until...'

Simonsen interrupted again:

'Thanks, Pauline, you've made my point.'

'Which is?'

The Countess provided a tentative interpretation.

'Which is that we're dealing with a group of outsiders, and I can support that with some information about Jesper Mikkelsen. The school magazine has this list of nicknames of those graduating from the third year, in which he's dubbed *Yes, yes, yes, yes, Jesper*. Apparently, he had a dreadful stutter when he was young.'

Simonsen concluded:

'We need to know how tight they were. Were they a group or not? And we need to know before we talk to them, if at all possible.'

'OK, we'll slog our guts out, day and night.'

Which was Klavs Arnold's way of saying he thought Simonsen was asking a lot of them..

They took a ten-minute break to get coffee, go to the bathroom or just stretch their legs. Pauline Berg collared Simonsen in the corridor.

'I know you've just got back, but aren't you going to do anything about that meeting you promised us with Arthur Elvang? The group are getting a bit impatient. I am, too, for that matter.'

The group! He'd been hoping that no longer existed. He replied almost with animosity:

'And how many people would there be in this group of yours?'

'There are five of us.'

'I see. Well, you can tell the group that you'll be informed of a date later this week. But the group will not be meeting Elvang. It'll be you and your friend from Melby Overdrev only – and no one else.'

The Countess took over and led the meeting, though remaining seated in her chair as she outlined what had been uncovered with respect to the summer house.

She and Klavs Arnold had been through Esbjerg and its surrounding areas with a fine-toothed comb in search of where Jørgen Kramer Nielsen had stayed on his annual three-day visit in the summer holidays. Eventually, after days of hard graft without a result, they'd found the place. Kramer Nielsen had lodged at the same hostel, the Nørballe Vandrehjem, every year without fail. The first time was as far back as 1980, though no one at the place had any idea what he'd been doing in the area. True to form, he kept himself to himself. And yet he did always rent a bike, and the Countess thought it likely he visited Lucy Davison's grave. However, none of the town's florists seemed to know him. If he took flowers with him, he must have picked them himself. They'd also made efforts to find out if Kramer Nielsen met with any of the others from the Gang of Six on his annual trip. Without wishing to put her head on the block, the Countess felt that he had not. Or most certainly not all at once. She turned to Klavs Arnold.

'Would you like to say something about the house?'

'No, you go on. Your accent's so charming.'

'Well, in that case I will, but there's not a lot more to say really.'

Knowing that Kramer Nielsen had rented a bike during his stays at the hostel, they had considered a radius of about fifteen kilometres to be about right. Unfortunately, the area contained hundreds of summer houses, and since the information they had been able to glean from the photos was so sparse, the police had a mammoth task ahead of them if they were to check each one individually. Moreover, the photos showed no visible landmarks of any kind, meaning a cursory check would be insufficient and closer investigation would be required. And as if that wasn't enough, the last forty-odd years had changed the face of Esbjerg's summer house areas considerably. All in all, it was going to take a huge effort and an equally huge amount of resources to go from house to house. The Countess went on:

'We can't tell from the vegetation on the photos whether the place is on the coast or further inland, so our best bet is to check whether anyone connected with the Gang of Six owned a summer house in the Esbjerg area. That work is being done as I speak. Another avenue is to have Klavs do the rounds of builders, DIY centres, that sort of thing, and get them to have a look at the sections of the house visible on the photos and see if they can tell us anything from a professional perspective.'

Simonsen interrupted with a question:

'If we find a likely place, can we make a definitive match using those photos?'

Klavs Arnold replied:

'Definitely.'

'So the house-to-house can get us a result as long as people are doing their jobs properly?'

'I'd say so, yes. It'll take time, though, and you can't put just anyone on a job like that. Besides, like the Countess says, it's going to cost a bomb. Aside from that, it's a possibility. A distinct possibility.'

'Could you head up that kind of effort?'

'Yeah.'

'Do it.'

'I will, as long as you take any flak from on high.'

'Of course, no problem. As Arne said at the beginning, we may be dealing with a double murder here, and in that case it's no use penny-pinching. What would the press say if they got word?'

Arne Pedersen spluttered a few half-hearted words about budget and resources.

Pauline Berg silenced him.

'You've got to admit, Simon's right, Arne. The tabloids would tear Gurli apart. Imagine the headlines.'

Pedersen capitulated and slid back into the role of running the meeting. The screen now showed a grainy blow-up of a man beaming a broad smile at the camera. His age was hard to gauge.

'They had a visitor. This guy features on two of our photos and as you can see he's got Down's syndrome. We reckon he's some-where between twenty-five and thirty-five. We don't know if he's significant for us in any way, whether he was on holiday or local. If he was local he might be able to help us narrow things down with respect to location. There's also a chance he may have been part of the group, on the trip with the others, but we don't think that's likely, partly because of the way he's dressed. At the moment we've got nothing more on him.'

Simonsen cut in:

'While I remember, let me just say that Kramer Nielsen must have had his hair cut shortly after he got back to Copenhagen, before he got taken on at his dad's post office. It probably means nothing, but bear that in mind.'

Pedersen followed up.

'Let me kick something in here as well, before we go on to the last and most interesting of these photos. We're assuming Jørgen Kramer Nielsen and Hanne Brummersted were the ones who took Lucy Davison's effects over to Sweden, since both of them missed their final exam. Hanne Brummersted did a resit, Kramer Nielsen didn't, as we already know. Moreover, she was the only one of the six who'd passed her driving test.'

The Countess had a question:

'How long do we think they were in Sweden? Lycksele's quite a way.'

'At least three days, more likely four, unless she drove at night as well or he took over the wheel despite not having a licence. Hanne Brummersted's parents had a car, we know that, but we don't know if she borrowed it. They could have rented one. She was eighteen by then. Anything else?'

There wasn't.

'Then let's move on to our final photo, which we assume was taken with a self-timer. Have a good look at it and see what you make of it.'

Seven teenagers appeared on the screen, standing in a line, outdoors, their arms around each other's shoulders. All were in various stages of undress. Jørgen Kramer Nielsen was far left, Lucy Davison to the right. The three young men were completely naked apart from sandals or shoes. Hanne Brummersted, too, was naked, standing at an awkward angle, twisted away from the camera, one hand covering her genitals. The two other girls were in their pants. Lucy Davison was naked under her Afghan coat, hamming it up for the picture. The others were looking down at the ground. The weather was as disheartening as the photo itself.

It was the Countess who broke the silence.

'Well, you don't need a degree in psychology to see that none of them cared for this. Poor kids, they're so embarrassed, all apart from Lucy Davison. What's that the guys have got written across their stomachs?'

'*No revision.* It's red paint, we think. And look at Lucy Davison's index finger.'

'I don't blame them for being so shy. I would be, too,' said Pauline Berg.

Klavs Arnold came back at her in his Jutland drawl:

'That's beside the point. The thing is, would you do it?'

'Not likely, and not in front of a camera.'

'But they did.'

Simonsen cut in:

'They ran into a little hippie girl from the big, wide world who welcomed them to the sixties. Did she pay for that with her life? I wonder. Jealousy? Sex games gone wrong? Drugs?' he mused in a low voice.

'Mushrooms… maybe they were on magic mushrooms. It was all the rage in those days,' Pauline Berg persisted.

Klavs Arnold brought her back to earth.

'They'd have been a bit short on mushrooms in June. Even in those days.'

Now the Countess spoke:

'I can see there might have been some tension there, and our Gang of Six might well have been marginalised in respect of their classmates, which wouldn't have helped the situation with Lucy. It's an interesting angle, and we need to investigate it further, but before we go off half-cock, I have to say I just can't see six young kids colluding to kill one of their friends like that. If one of them didn't do it on their own, then two, maybe, by some quirk, at most. Six just doesn't seem realistic. I've read their essays. They might not have been too fortunate in terms of their looks, but on the whole we're dealing with normal young-sters here. I can't see them ganging up to kill someone, and if one of them did kill her by accident, the others would never have covered it up. Not once they got home again and thought about it. Something else must have happened. Something we haven't thought of yet.'

Her reservations triggered nods all round.

Simonsen realised they were all looking at him to pull things together, Pedersen included. He stood up and indicated they were done, at the same time outlining what they were to investi-gate next.

'We need to find out as much as possible about this Gang of Six. We've got too little to go on yet, if we're to confront them in person.'

This, too, won widespread support, whereupon Malte Borup conjured forth a finale, this time in the shape of a video clip: Napoleon out of Disney's *Aristocats*, repeating himself in a never-ending loop, that he is the leader, and only he can say when it is the end.

Only when the Countess gestured for Malte to wrap it up did he cease the clip and make himself scarce.

After the meeting, Simonsen drove home to Søllerød to unpack. When it was done and he'd got the washing machine started, he went for his run, only to discover he felt heavier than usual. The good food in Bulgaria had left its toll, though no more so than a couple of days' exercise would undo. The weather was grey and damp, ideal in fact as he didn't get over-heated while jogging and nor did he feel cold while walking. A car slowed down alongside him and he gave it a casual glance.

It was a blue Jaguar and he assumed it was going to turn up the driveway of the house was passing. Only when it continued to follow him did he look again and realise he knew the driver.

Helmer Hammer was a man in his mid-forties, an executive of the Administrative Division of the Prime Minister's Office, a position that placed him securely within the upper echelons of government power. He was also a man capable of concealing his intentions whenever necessary. The car drew to a halt and the passenger window slid down.

'Jump in. I've only got half an hour before I have to be back at work. Welcome home, by the way.'

Perplexed, Simonsen climbed into the car. Helmer Hammer explained:

'I've come to see this gallery of yours everyone's talking about, and to give you a piece of information.'

Helmer Hammer wandered slowly around Simonsen's exhibition, allowing himself time to study each poster. When he was finished he asked about the girl. Simonsen told him as much as he knew.

'Her name's Lucy Davison. She was from the UK. We're assuming she's dead.'

Hammer nodded sadly, as if he'd been expecting him to say just that. After a moment, he spoke.

'I've got this friend, a solicitor in the city, one of the big boys in his field. We play squash together once a week. Last week he told me he'd been contacted by some British *officialis*. A judge of the ecclesiastical court of some Catholic diocese, if I'm correctly informed. Someone high up, at any rate.'

Simonsen grunted and pricked up his ears.

'Anyway, this *officialis* requested that my friend get in touch with the official receiver at the Glostrup probate court and put in a bid for your posters. What's more, he was to make sure that if anyone else bid more, the receiver would contact my friend before selling them off. My friend's been invested with the authority of the British diocese to spend a considerable amount of money if necessary to secure them. A rather surprising amount, as a matter of fact.'

'You mean the Vatican wants my... Jørgen Kramer Nielsen's... posters?'

'The Vatican? No, I shouldn't think so. But someone in the Catholic Church does.'

'Who? And why?'

'No idea.'

'Can't you ask? I'd like to know.'

'I don't think I can. The Catholic Church isn't an organisation that's open to scrutiny. Besides, I don't want to. It could cause all sorts of problems if *I* were to start poking about in matters like that.'

Simonsen accepted the rebuff and asked instead:

'How much are they prepared to pay?'

'Not much unless they have to. Were you thinking of keeping hold of them?'

Simonsen replied frankly:

'Yes. One, at least, but preferably the lot.'

'I quite understand. They're beguiling, aren't they?'

'You didn't answer my question: how much are they willing to bid?'

'Five hundred kroner per poster. Eight thousand five hundred for all seventeen.'

'Eighteen. There's eighteen of them. So that's nine thousand kroner... quite reasonable, I'd say.'

'They are, as I said, prepared to go somewhat higher if need be. But don't tell me I can't count, Simon. There are seventeen in all, and that's what I'll be telling my friend. He asked me to find out how many there were. He doesn't know, you see.'

After Helmer Hammer had gone, Simonsen did a quick tour of his own, staring at each poster in turn and thinking to himself how fortunate staging this little exhibition had turned out to be. Quite apart from the personal pleasure he derived from it – a pleasure he played down and perhaps underestimated, if he were to be frank. Now, though, it had provided him with a tangible piece of information that was by no means uninteresting. He decided to call the priest at a suitable opportunity and, in strictest confidence, ask him what might be going on. He might even invite him up to Søllerød. He still had Madame, of course, his clairvoyant consultant, so all in all it was far too soon to write off his posters as a failure. Or rather, Jørgen Kramer Nielsen's posters. Simonsen reminded himself that unfortunately he had only borrowed them. Naturally, they belonged to Kramer Nielsen's estate. He cast a wry smile towards the door through which Helmer Hammer had left. Only borrowed... all seventeen of them.

For the rest of the week Simonsen's investigation made little headway. The autumn again turned damp and dismal as police officers methodically sifted through the area surrounding Nørballe Vandrehjem, comparing summer houses with images photo-copied from Kramer Nielsen's photographs. It was a slow and meticulous business, and one that produced nothing in the way of results. Klavs Arnold insisted on a second pass, and then another.

The paper type on which Kramer Nielsen's posters had been printed was determined with painstaking German rigour. The first work showing Lucy Davison's image had been created around 1973, a result that had required a very considerable amount of work, all of which now seemed of little consequence. The same was true of a report from Kurt Melsing that concluded, partly on the basis of the cement used to put up the mirrors in the postman's loft, that the shrine had been erected somewhere round 2000. This was another unastonishing fact that Simonsen, with a shrug, archived in what was now a rather bulging case folder.

Homicide were also hard at work collating information about the Gang of Six. When did they get together? Was there a formal or informal leader? Did they meet up with any regularity? If so, what was the agenda? These were just a few of the many questions that needed answering to provide them with an impression of these young people's lives since 1969.

Simonsen interviewed their peers from Class Three Y of the Brøndbyøster Gymnasium, working outward in an increasing radius from the capital, though without turning up anything that seemed to be of use. It was a long time ago; all he heard were reminiscences of no worth and utterly without relevance to the six in their spotlight. His last interview had been in Ringsted, his next would be in Nykøbing Falster. If he kept on, he'd end up in Detroit and Wellington, which financially was hardly on the cards, double murder or no. Instead, he had to struggle his way through a couple of days on the job with an annoying throat infection and a feeling that the investigation was getting nowhere fast. Eventually, on Monday 27 October, he got in the car and drove to Nykøbing Falster.

The woman who opened the door looked to be around sixty, vocal and angry. No sooner had he introduced himself than he was showered with invective. Swear words were the usual currency here, it seemed.

'You can stop right now before you get started. Take your stupid badge and shove it! And if you haven't got a warrant, you can sod off. It's ten years since he got out, and still you keep coming round bothering him at all hours of the day and night. Clear off!'

Her hands were planted on her hips, forming a defiant obstacle he would do well not to underestimate. A man's voice called out from inside the house:

'Who is it?'

'It's the police.'

'Tell them it wasn't me.'

'I've told him to get lost, but he's a bit thick, this one. He's still here.'

The man stepped into the hall. Simonsen recounted events to the Countess when he got back.

'As I first clapped my eyes on him I thought they were playing tricks on me. But it was him right enough. There he was, the old charmer, charismatic as ever. Pelle Olsen himself. Pelle the Pretender, King of Elmegade.'

'Oh, I remember. I liked him.'

'Everyone liked Pelle, even the people he conned. One of the truly great rip-off artists. They said he could charm the money out of any man's pockets, and the knickers off any woman.'

'He owes me three hundred kroner, come to think of it.'

'He must have made an exception in your case.'

Simonsen received a dig in the ribs in return for his jibe.

'Is he retired now?'

'Not quite. If you promise not to hit me, I'll tell you. Right, so he invited me in…'

The mood had quickly turned convivial. Rent-a-gob from the doorstep had morphed into a hospitable hostess with an engaging smile and kindly air. She made lunch while the two men talked about the old days. Simonsen broke all the rules and had a glass of aquavit with his roll-mop herring. Pelle Olsen held forth.

'I know what you're going to think, but I'm a certified hypnotist these days. Completely on the level. It cost me three years of hard graft, and that for someone with natural talent. You don't believe me, do you?'

Simonsen grinned:

'Of course I do. That's the problem, though, isn't it? Everyone always believes you.'

Olsen's wife came to his aid. Without the slightest hint of aggression, she explained what their business consisted of.

'We work with smoking cessation problems, phobias – as long as they're not serious – and a bit of transcendental. The transcendentals want to get in touch with their past lives and we give them a sound file of what they tell us while they're in the trance. No more nor less than that. Anything remotely smelling of healing we leave well alone. We're not interested in conning people who are having a bad time of it. You can believe us or not, but that's the truth.'

This time Simonsen was more convinced.

'It's the way you always were, Pelle. That's why we liked you. It was the fat wallets you emptied, never the workman's.'

'It's a matter of morals, isn't it? Do you want to hear about the call-girl scam we worked on two high-court judges? Eighty-four or -five I think it was. You never did get wind of it.'

It took a while before Simonsen was able to get round to why he was there. Olsen's wife was by no means unwilling to help, but like her classmates her recollections were romanticised and imprecise.

'It was all happening in those days, wasn't it? I was in the first year of the gymnasium in nineteen sixty-seven, the summer of love, and *Sergeant Pepper*, the ultimate LP. In 1968, my second year, it was the student riots in Paris, and in 1969 when we graduated it was the man on the moon and Woodstock. The timing couldn't have been better, brilliant it was, from start to finish. But then, you'd have been there yourself, wouldn't you?'

'I was indeed.'

'You've got to admit, it was the best of times.'

'Maybe. I don't know really. Personally, I'm a bit ambivalent. When someone like yourself says *Paris 1968*, I immediately think *Prague Spring*. On the other hand, when people moan about *pot heads* and *dropouts*, I say *peace and love* and *counterculture*. The truth is, I'm at odds with myself.'

Pelle Olsen was immediately on hand.

'Get yourself on the couch, we'll get you sorted in no time.'

'I think I'll give it a miss, if you don't mind.'

'I thought you might say that. I'm not going to pretend to be academic, but one thing I do know is that making money was easy back then. I used to traipse along behind the parrot man and his pram on the pedestrianised street, do you remember him?'

'Sigvaldi. He sold a book of children's stories, written by children themselves.'

'That's the fella. And I sold beaded bracelets I got for next to nothing in a toy shop in Østerbro, calling them Tibetan handicraft from Lhassakya, the highest-situated monastery in the Himalayas. Trickle-down effect, you could say. Sigvaldi sold his books and I sold my bracelets. People were so unsuspecting in those days. It was like everyone was finding their feet in the new age and no one knew yet what was all right and what was rubbish. I even had a guitar and a wig. I'd go round the student hangouts. I sounded like hell, but they'd be chucking money at me.'

He played air guitar and sang along in a voice that sounded like a pair of squealing brakes:

'Mum and dad were working-cl-a-a-s...'

The Countess smiled as Simonsen related the story, mostly because he found it so amusing himself.

'Did she remember anything at all, his wife?'

'Nothing. When it came to concrete facts she was as blank as all the others I've spoken to. None of the names of our Gang of Six even rang a bell, and the photos didn't help either.'

'Another flop then. I think you might as well give up on that little project, Simon.'

'Not just yet. I actually drove down there on another matter, but then I thought I might as well take a chance and see if she was in while I was there. As it happens, she was. After that I went on to Rødby.'

'What for?'

'I'll tell you that later. Just listen for a minute. At Rødby police station I borrowed a computer and looked up Pelle's website, out of interest while I was waiting. Then I got thinking about what he'd said about finding myself, so on the way back I stopped by again.'

'You're not going to tell me you were hypnotised, are you?'

'You must be joking. But I thought his wife might give it a go.'

Pelle Olsen had given the suggestion some thought before replying:

'It won't be cheap. That kind of hypnosis requires the utmost preparation, and of course there's no guarantee she'll remember anything, so you may be wasting your money.'

'I was hoping for a discount.'

'Of course, Simonsen. Old friends and all that. I can't go under four thousand, though, that'd be unprofessional. Or two and a half cash in hand? No, wait a minute, that's not on in your case, I suppose?'

'Sounds reasonable, but only if you chuck in a jar of those ginseng tablets for nicotine cravings. I stopped smoking not that long ago and I could do with a bit of certified organic homeopathic support. Isn't that what it says on your website?'

'On the other hand, Simonsen, I'll tell you what. I'm so pleased to see you, and you were always so fair in our dealings with each other, let's say...'

Pelle studied his guest.

'A thousand kroner?' Simonsen ventured, then stared at the ceiling, holding his ground.

'All right, gratis then. How does that sound?'

'That's very decent of you.'

'Not at all. Friends are friends. How about Wednesday afternoon? That'll give me time to talk the wife round.'

At the police station in Rødby, Konrad Simonsen had overstepped a psychological line he was far from certain he ought to have crossed.

It was to do with Rita's name. For more than two years of his youth they had been a couple. It had been a period of ups and downs, and at times their relationship had seemed all but over. It didn't worry him unduly that he had thought so much about her since his operation, occasionally even finding himself daydreaming about her. It had been nice. Or rather, it was nice, and without strings. However, one matter in particular made sure she remained a memory, a voice from his youth, rather than a part of his life again: he could remember only her first name, no matter how hard he racked his brains.

He made no effort to conceal the fact that his errand was private, and yet the duty sergeant of the Rødby Politi ushered him past the counter and into an office.

'I'll just need to check your ID again, if that's all right? And what was it you wanted to do?'

Simonsen pulled out his badge.

'It's a personal thing. Nothing that requires preferential treatment.'

'No problem. What is it you're looking for?'

'A woman. I've only got a first name... *Rita*. The surname's a common-or-garden *something*-sen. Jensen, Nielsen, Hansen, Petersen, something like that. And she had a funny middle name I've forgotten, too. She was arrested for attempted cash smuggling in November or December nineteen seventy-two.'

'That's a while since.'

'I'm afraid so. I'm only interested in her name, though. I'm not bothered about the case itself.'

'You might just be very lucky indeed. We had two students in last year sorting out our archives. Maybe no one else would give them a job, what do I know? Anyway, they definitely got stuck into all the prehistoric stuff. It's downstairs in the old basement. I'm not sure, though...'

'I've got three bottles of good claret with me, if that'll help.'

The sergeant returned after only ten minutes.

'Easy as pie. *Rita Metz Andersen.* The intelligence boys at PET stuck their noses in, but the case was dropped.'

The priest came to Søllerød on the Tuesday. It was mid-morning and the sun was out. The day was pleasant: blue skies and a gentle wind playfully tossing the withered leaves that lay here and there in heaps on the residential streets of Konrad Simonsen's jogging route. He had walked the whole way, ambling in the manner of an elderly gentleman, more than once dragging his feet through the accumulated drifts as he had done as a child. It could hardly be called exercise, but the walk put him in more cheerful mood, and by all accounts that was the sort of thing that prolonged a life such as his. Back home he managed to carry a small, square garden table and a couple of chairs over to his gallery and to fetch his chess set before the priest knocked at the door. The man had biked all the way from Hvidovre and his cheeks bore a healthy flush. They greeted each other and Simonsen was genuinely glad to see him, and told him so. It was mutual, the priest said. The simple truth of the matter was the two men liked each other. The priest took off his jacket and dumped it on Simonsen's exercise bike.

'I'm rather intrigued as to what you might have in store for me today, I must admit. You had me completely outmanoeuvred last time.'

The words were spoken quite without bitterness, and Simonsen replied in the same friendly tone:

'There'll be no tricks today, I assure you. Like I said on the phone, I thought you might like to have a proper look at Jørgen Kramer Nielsen's posters. And besides that I've got a couple of questions for you about them. But then I suppose you'd gathered as much?'

'Indeed. It'll be good to have a closer look. I didn't care to venture further into Jørgen's loft when I found it, so I've only seen them from a distance. I will admit, though, that I did stare for quite some time when we first discovered the place, with my head poking through the trapdoor.'

He jabbed a finger at the table in the middle of the room.

'A chess player, I see. You people must have run a check on me. It's been a while since I played.'

'Second place in the UK university championships in nineteen eighty-five. Not exactly the kind of achievement that comes from sheer luck. That's why I've invited Arne Pedersen over, the detective who interviewed you at Police HQ. He's a lot better at the game than me. However, he seems to be running a bit late, so you may have to make do with yours truly. Unless you'd prefer to look at the posters first?'

The priest sat down and they tossed a coin for white or black. The priest drew white.

'I didn't bring a clock. I thought we might chat while we played,' Simonsen said.

'Fine by me.'

They began, and the opening moves allowed little time for conversation. As Simonsen had anticipated, the priest was a far superior player, despite Simonsen's highly defensive and exceptionally cautious strategy. After a dozen or so moves, at which point he was already staring defeat in the eye, he turned to the topic at hand.

'I hear the church would like to buy the posters. I take it that was your idea?'

The priest moved a pawn before replying:

'Yes, it was.'

'May I ask why?'

'I'll tell you as soon as they've been released and we've secured the purchase.'

'Why not now? Won't they let you?'

Simonsen responded at once to the priest's move, the priest himself countering swiftly, then answering Simonsen's question in a gentle tone.

'I could, but I think it best to wait.'

'An *officialis*. You're well connected.'

'It would seem so, yes. But the man's position as *officialis* has nothing to do with the case. That's something else entirely.'

'You do know the posters won't be released until my investigation has been completed? That may take some time.'

'We're patient people. We don't mind waiting.'

Arne Pedersen entered the room. He greeted them and apologised for being late, saying his car wouldn't start. He studied the game for a moment, then placed a hand on Simonsen's shoulder.

'You're in a spot of bother, Simon.'

They made a few more moves before Simonsen had no option but to capitulate and offer his hand in congratulation.

The three men made a leisurely round of the gallery, studying each poster in turn, none of them saying a word to begin with. The priest was meticulous, standing for a long time in front of each image, considering it from every angle. The process took a while, but they were in no hurry. At the fourth poster, Arne Pedersen suddenly spoke, his voice a challenge:

'D four.'

The priest replied instantly:

'D five.'

Pedersen was equally swift:

'Knight to C three.'

Simonsen stepped back. He was way out of his league now: blindfold chess was quite beyond his reach.

The game was over even before they reached the final poster, Pedersen coming out on top. The priest congratulated him without resentment. Simonsen, however, gloated, though was careful not to show it. Pedersen himself seemed unruffled.

They adjourned to the living room for tea or coffee. The priest told them about his social work, and Simonsen and Arne Pedersen waxed lyrical about the Greenland ice cap where they had been together on a case the year before. It was all very pleasant, not least because the two policemen skilfully avoided all mention of their current investigation.

After the priest had gone, Pedersen admitted:

'He let me win. I'm pretty certain. Don't you think?'

Simonsen shook his head.

'I wouldn't have a clue. I couldn't keep up.'

'At the end I had my knight pawn against his rook. He could have got my knight with a straightforward check, but what he did was to go for the pawn and ran straight into a simple fork. Do you want me to show you?'

Simonsen did indeed. They ran through the game and agreed that the priest almost certainly must have lost on purpose. Pedersen was perplexed.

'Why would he do that?'

'He didn't want to win two games on the trot. I think it's just the way he is,' said Simonsen.

'Funny kind of guy, if you ask me.'

'A very pleasant one, in my opinion. But certainly not a man to be underestimated.'

If the priest was a funny kind of guy, as Arne Pedersen maintained, Konrad Simonsen's next visitor to the gallery was even funnier. He had talked his clairvoyant consultant, Madame, into coming up to Søllerød. Normally, he went to see her at her place in Høje Taastrup, always bringing her some item pertaining to the case at hand: a piece of clothing, perhaps, or the victim's wristwatch. This time, however, it was out of the question, since he had nothing at all in his possession that had belonged to Lucy Davison.

He allowed Pauline Berg to see how Madame worked; she had been rather insistent on the point and eventually he had given in to her pestering. She arrived just as Arne Pedersen was leaving. Simonsen noted hat she barely said hello to the man, mustering only a muttered *Hi*, whereas Simonsen himself was accorded hugs and a big smile to boot. He followed Pedersen back up the path to the gate, asking, as soon as Pauline was out of earshot:

'Have you two fallen out again?'

Pedersen hesitated.

'I wouldn't say fallen out, exactly. It's just that every time she doesn't get her way she sulks. I've grown immune to it.'

'What didn't you let her do?'

'She wanted your occult lady to help her in that little project of hers, that Juli Denissen thing. I'm hard pressed as it is to finance your little foibles, and I'll be damned if I'm going to fund Pauline's as well. Especially when there isn't the semblance of a case.'

He was right. How to enter Madame's services in the books was always going to be an issue. Not even Simonsen himself cared much for having it written down in black and white that the Homicide Department was spending good taxpayers' money on spiritualism. He had fiddled a bit with the categories so as not to make Madame's fee too obvious, and now Arne Pedersen would have to do likewise. However, it was not a subject Simonsen cared to broach. Instead, he said:

'Odd get-up she's wearing today as well. Sometimes she outdoes even our Deputy Commissioner.'

Pauline Berg was in a matching grey jacket and skirt that would have suited an elderly accountant. Perhaps in order to compensate for her old-fashioned appearance she had flung a cheap and garish scarf around her neck. Pedersen asked in surprise:

'What's wrong with Gurli's dress sense? The woman's got style, if you ask me.'

Ten minutes later, Madame arrived in a Mercedes van that had been converted to carry a wheelchair. The driver was her husband, Stephan Stemme, and Konrad Simonsen didn't care for him. Not many people did, if anyone at all.

From the living-room window, Simonsen and Pauline Berg watched as Stemme got out of the vehicle and gazed towards the house.

'I hope he's not thinking of coming in. We'd better go out and get her.'

Outside, Stemme offered his hand in greeting and furnished them with an explanation: his wife had suffered a complicated fracture of the hip and the joint had furthermore become infected after the operation. Now she was unable to walk until the antibiotics had done their job and she'd been back to the hospital for a check-up. The van had been hired for the day and the cost added to the invoice, which he duly handed to Simonsen in an envelope. He went to the rear of the vehicle, opened the doors and manoeuvred a ramp into position with a remote control. With some difficulty he clambered up and wheeled his wife out on to the ramp, carefully secured the wheelchair, then lowered her down, delivering her directly to Simonsen.

He wheeled her into the gallery, he and Pauline having carried her up the steps of the garden path in the wheelchair. The Countess's property was built on a slope and the annexe was elevated above the main house, so steps were unavoidable.

Madame was a somewhat wizened woman with a toneless voice and a pair of piercing grey eyes that seemed to stare right into whoever she was looking at. Much to Simonsen's relief, her husband stayed outside in the van. As they'd received her the man had gripped Pauline Berg by the arm and rudely demanded coffee. Pauline had hissed back at him that he could take his grubby hands off her, and as for coffee he could make his own when he got home. Taken aback, he'd immediately beaten a retreat to the van. Madame had failed to react to the scene. Perhaps she was used to it.

Like the other visitors to his gallery, she allowed herself plenty of time. Simonsen and Berg stepped back so as not to disturb her concentration and waited patiently. She reacted to the very first poster. The spirits had apparently made themselves known to her, and she tossed her head in annoyance.

'Who's that screaming kid? I can hardly hear myself think!'

For a moment she covered her ears. Then suddenly she gripped the spokes of one of her wheels, spinning herself round and pointing an accusatory finger at Pauline Berg.

'Get rid of that scarf at once. Get it away, now!'

Pauline scurried out of the room without protest. When she had gone, Madame turned to Simonsen.

'Where is the eighteenth picture?'

Simonsen ventured a lie.

'In my bedroom. I'm examining it and having it framed. Do you want me to get it?'

'A lie! You're stealing it. Only don't.'

When Pauline Berg returned, minus her scarf, Madame carried on studying the images on the walls. After a while she spoke.

'The girl's name is Lucy. She was from England and now she's dead. It's a long time ago, many years. She came to Denmark on the back of a motorcycle. And a boat, a ferry. Esbjerg.'

Simonsen confirmed this and Madame went on:

'She's pleased the church is buying her pictures and she's looking forward to new surroundings, but she thinks it's all right about the one that's missing.'

'What do you mean, the one that's missing?' asked Pauline Berg.

Madame was seemingly still annoyed with her for having tried to con her way to assistance by wearing a scarf that had belonged to Juli Denissen. She barked at Simonsen:

'Tell her to be quiet, Konrad.'

Simonsen gave Pauline a look and hoped she would get the message. Then he turned back to Madame.

'Why does the Catholic Church want to buy her pictures? Does she know?'

Some moments passed before Madame answered. Her eyelids fluttered, then eventually she spoke.

'It's seldom I see them so clearly. How pretty she is. But she's being coy. *Wouldn't you like to know?* is what she says. And with a smile, too.'

Simonsen felt a warmth consume him such as he hadn't felt in years, and he blushed as Madame went on with the same gravity in her voice:

'The young women seem to be swarming over you at the moment, Konrad. But perhaps you're overlooking the most important of them. It will prove fatal.'

After this rather nebulous warning she leaned forward and passed her hand over the poster in front of her and spoke again, searchingly this time.

'Lucy is buried in black sand. Black Danish sand. Yes, that's what she's saying… black sand. She was killed in her tent.'

She paused and stared into space, continuing only after a while.

'It wasn't her own tent. She'd borrowed it from her friend. Her friend on the motorbike.'

'Was she killed by her friend?' Simonsen asked.

But Madame wasn't listening. Instead, she spoke softly:

'She was raped... or, rather... I think she was raped. I'm not quite sure. Attacked, certainly. Sexually abused. But what a mess. Two dead girls and this screaming child as well.'

She wheeled herself back a metre and sat there like some general watching a parade, with remote interest.

'Listen to the Christian man you don't like, Konrad. Promise me that.'

'All right. But how did she die?'

'I don't know. I sense a sudden fear. Panic. Dreadful.'

It was the sounds Pauline Berg made that caused Simonsen to spin towards her. She had stiffened in mid-movement and stood there white as a ghost, gurgling as if she were about to vomit. Her wide eyes stared without seeing him, her hands clutching her throat as though she were grappling an assailant. She reached out to him in desperation, pitifully almost. He shouted out: *'What's wrong?'* Then: *'Pauline, what's the matter? Say something. Do you need an ambulance?'* But Pauline failed to respond.

Madame reassured him.

'No point in your panicking. Calm down, she won't die.'

It helped him to know that. And yet it was clear to him that Madame's seance had to be abandoned immediately. Mercifully, she was in agreement. Pauline needed attention, that much was obvious. He wheeled Madame out of the room, manhandling the wheelchair down the steps in the path and delivering her to her husband before dashing back to the gallery, where he found Pauline sitting huddled up against a wall, knees drawn to her chin, shoulders tightly raised, her whole body twisted into an unnatural knot of tension. Droplets of perspiration glistened on her brow and upper lip. She didn't respond to his questions. He placed a protective hand on her shoulder, only for her to shuffle away from him as if he were burning hot. He wondered again if he should call an ambulance, but decided to give her the tranquilliser he kept for her in his wallet. He left her for a moment to fetch some water, then almost forced her to swallow the pill. After a while there was some contact again. He could tell from her eyes that she was coming round from her panic and asked cautiously:

'Is the medicine working?'

She shook her head.

'What should I do?'

It was simple: she wanted to go home. But he was *not* to call a doctor, she was adamant about it. Instead, she wanted him to stay with her. She gripped his hand insistently.

'You mustn't go. I can't be on my own. You've got to promise.'

He promised not to leave her. It was all he could do. Even though, as far as he could tell, she needed a psychiatrist, or perhaps ought even to be admitted to hospital. But what was he to do when she expressly told him not to call for medical assistance?

In the car on the way she gradually succumbed to exhaustion and her anxiety seemed little by little to fade. In the lift up to her flat she leaned her head against his shoulder, and outside her door she handed him the keys. Her legs buckled and he had to support her as he unlocked the door.

It was the first time he had seen where she lived. The flat was neat, meticulously so, and made him think of a library. He would have expected her to be more untidy. The view from the living-room window was dismal: two concrete blocks of flats the same as the one she lived in, next to the S-train line somewhere between Rødovre and Brøndbyøster, as far as he could make out. He led her into the bedroom, helped her off with her shoes and put her to bed. Again, she made him promise not to go, a snivelling plea and yet unequivocal, and again he promised to stay. She drifted into sleep almost as soon as her head touched the pillow, while he sat at her side on the edge of the bed. In the living room he picked up an armchair and lugged it into the bedroom. He sat down and once more took her hand, then after a while turned on a small TV set on the dresser at the end of the bed, muting the sound, though she would hardly wake up even if he were to let off fireworks.

At one point the Countess rang. They were supposed to be going out to see a film together but now they would have to put it off until some other day. She offered advice: he was to remember to put Pauline on her side, that was important. Then two equally sensible-sounding instructions he failed to take in fully. Besides that, she had little to say apart from suggesting she come and take over, an offer he rejected.

He listened for a long time to the sound of Pauline's steady breathing while thinking about what Madame had told him. Not about the investigation – he would hold off on that until the morning – but more her comment about young women swarming over him. That, and the fact that he had overlooked the most important one of all. His mind ran through a list of candidates: Lucy, Rita, Anna Mia. Maja Nørgaard perhaps, or Pauline Berg? He glanced at her huddled figure as she lay in the dim light. Who was he overlooking? He racked his brains. The most important of them all. Who was that?

The evening was long, the night even longer.

The hypnosis session displayed a side of Pelle Olsen that Simonsen had never seen before. Olsen had toned down the light-hearted banter of Monday in favour of a more professional demeanour. His wife sat down in an armchair and within minutes was guided into a state of mental relaxation Simonsen could best describe as semi-sleep. Olsen then led her gently back to her time at the gymnasium school as though the forty-odd years that had passed since then were little more than a wink of the eye.

'Where are you now?'

'In the classroom. We've got maths with Kite.'

'What class are you in?'

'Two Y. The coolest class in the school.'

'What day is it?'

'Thursday the fourteenth of March nineteen sixty-eight.'

Pelle Olsen turned to Simonsen and spoke softly.

'I'm going to chat with her for a while about what she's experiencing. You can ask questions afterwards, but do it through me. Is that all right?'

Simonsen confirmed with a nod, sceptical as to whether or not he was being taken for a ride.

'Can you ask her if there are any animals in the class? Pets, I mean.'

If Olsen felt he was being tested, it didn't show.

'Are there any animals in the classroom?'

'No, Uffe's ill, so Silver isn't here.'

Simonsen was satisfied, and Olsen went on.

'Kite, is that your teacher?'

'Henderson, the principal. We call him Mr Kite because of his hobby. He's a champion kite-flyer. That's why those Japanese are here. He's a big name in Japan.'

She giggled like a teenager.

'It might even be true, for all we know. He goes on about it sometimes, but apart from that he's nice enough. They say he's a hard examiner, but I don't believe it. They say that about everyone. The third years, I mean. To put the wind up us.'

'Tell me about the Japanese.'

'They're not here today, they're off on a trip to Elsinore. Kite's organised their whole stay. They go to some kind of circus school in Japan where they have acrobatics as well as ordinary lessons

like us. There's seven of them, six boys and a girl, and they're staying with some of us while they're here. We like them, even if
their English is really poor and they're hard to talk to. On
Saturday we're putting on a show with them for anyone who
wants to come.'

An expectant smile appeared on her face.

'Are you looking forward to that?'

'It's going to be great. You should see them! They jump about
on trampolines and juggle with flaming torches at the same time,
and you'd think there was no such thing as gravity. It's all to
honour Kite, so he and his family are going to be on the front
row. We're performing, too, at least some of us are. Dancing "Les
Lanciers", but only three of the tours: "La Victoria", "Les
Moulinets" and "Les Lanciers" itself.'

'Will you be dancing?'

She giggled again.

'Of course, my horse!'

'What does that mean?'

'It's just something we say, too much sometimes. You get sick
of it. It's because of our English teacher. He takes us for music, as
well. He says it all the time: *Of course, my horse.* We just started
copying him. At one point we actually started calling him Horse,
but it never caught on, so now we just call him by his first name,
Henry. Not all the teachers let us do that, but Henry's not that
old. He has us for dance practice, "Les Lanciers", and on Saturday
he's going to be doing a Viennese waltz with his wife. They go to
ballroom dancing, competitively. They're on after us.'

Pelle Olsen gave Simonsen a nod.

'Ask her if she can see Jørgen.'

She gave an indifferent shrug and replied before her husband
spoke.

'Jørgen Kramer Nielsen. What's there to say? He's just there,
that's all. He's one of the Hearts.'

'The Hearts? What's that? Are you one of them, too?'

She snorted disdainfully.

'The Lonely Hearts Club. That's too corny, so we just call them the Hearts instead. Helena's the one who got them together. Jørgen, Jesper, Hanne, Pia, and two or three more from the other classes. Mouritz is one, when he's here. Mouritz Nitwit, we call him.'

'What do they do, the Hearts?'

'Nothing, they just stick together. I think they wish they were like the rest of us, only we couldn't be bothered with them.'

'Why not?'

There was a pause before she replied.

'Helena's weird, nobody likes her. She's going to America for three weeks because she won some stupid competition the American Embassy ran. We write *USA OUT* on her desk and pick on her because her friends took a hiding from the Viet Cong in the Tet New Year Offensive. Holy Helena. I can't stand her! We call her the Virgin Helena, too, and she goes really red in the face, because it's true. She's ugly, and all dried-up. She's not stupid, though, I'll give her that.'

'What about the other Hearts?'

She ignored the question and carried on, rather more hectically than before, and her husband gestured to Simonsen to indicate he would now take over again.

'She's got her own problem page with all sorts of smarmy stuff about the kids of today, and her hair's always in a bowl cut. She wears a bra, too, but her boobs are like a pair of egg-cups. In PE once we hid her bra, but she had a spare in her bag!'

'Can you tell us about the others?'

Again, she failed to answer the question. Simonsen sensed something wasn't quite right. Her voice had become too hurried. With a thumb and index finger, Pelle Olsen indicated there wasn't much time left.

'Her dad came to the school play in a uniform with all sorts of medals and what have you. It was so embarrassing, we all cringed. Even my parents were better, even if they are pissed half the time. Then, when we were onstage...'

Olsen interrupted, shaking her gently to wake her. She sat there for a moment, as if in a daze, then spoke.

'That was horrible, Pelle. That last bit. I don't like it. I told you I wouldn't.'

'You're all right, love, I'm here.'

'I'm not doing it again. We knew what would happen.'

Olsen put his arms around her and waved his guest away. Simonsen took his leave. In the car, he wrote down some notes, and on the way home he couldn't make up his mind if he was happy or sad.

CHAPTER 8

The autumn had so far been unpleasant. Unemployment had risen, the property market had collapsed and the price of basic foodstuffs had plunged millions of people all over the world into poverty. Watching the news was a form of torment.

The Countess turned off the TV in the living room in Søllerød and went out into the kitchen to make her partner some iced tea. She'd seen a recipe in a lifestyle magazine: quince tea, organic elderflower cordial, freshly squeezed lemon and orange juice. She measured out the amounts, filling three tall glasses and topping them off with sliced strawberries and a scattering of blueberries for effect. Three long, silvery straws and she was good to go.

In the garden room, Konrad Simonsen was in difficulty. Again.

He rocked his head slowly from side to side as he struggled to find an escape. He was down to two pawns with no way of defending his rook line. An imaginative, highly incisive attack on his king had ripped apart his position and left him with a lost endgame. He pondered his limited options once again, finding the situation to be utterly without hope. Eventually he leaned back in his chair.

'I do love chess. It's as if one's inner thoughts join up with the external world and unite in this *love* of the game. I don't mind calling it that,' he said, rather seriously.

Arne Pedersen laughed as Simonsen continued to wax lyrical.

'It makes me think of people who hide behind a wall of illusion, never glimpsing the truth before it's far too late. We must share here in life. Share with others. Make sure everyone wins and everyone loses. Unless we do, we're never going to find peace in our minds. That's what chess is about. That's the very essence of it.'

The Countess came in with her tray and put it down next to the board.

'What on earth are you waffling about now?' she asked him.

Pedersen explained:

'He's trying to talk his way to a draw, but he'll have to do better than that.'

'If you want to find peace with yourself, it's no use winning the world if you lose your soul. Do you want that to happen, Arne? No, I think not…'

'All right, I can't take it any more. You've got your draw. I won a free game last time I was here, this can be the payback.'

They shook hands and Simonsen quickly packed the game away, then found himself staring in disbelief at the drinks on the Countess's tray.

'What's this? Mud with strawberries?'

'Cold quince tea. It's good and healthy.'

'I was afraid you'd say that. I don't even know what quince is.'

Pedersen took a sip, while Simonsen watched inquisitively. The Countess picked up her own glass.

'This is really delicious,' said Pedersen. 'Try it, Simon. You don't know what you're missing.'

'Is there any precedent here? I mean, have people like us ever before imbibed this quince, whatever it may be?'

Despite his words he took a sip, and then another. Arne was right, it was actually rather good. He glanced at the Countess and noted her prompt. He took another sip, put down his glass and turned to Arne Pedersen.

'I was at the hospital yesterday, Arne. They say if all goes well I can be back in charge after Christmas, or at least start taking over again.'

'Oh, that's great news. I'm happy you're feeling up to it again.'

'It doesn't have to be like that, though.'

'How do you mean?'

Simonsen had discussed the matter at length with the Countess and given it a great deal of thought on his own. The conclusion was that he actually wouldn't mind at all if Arne Pedersen carried on heading up the department. Naturally, it was a decision that had its drawbacks as well as its benefits. The loss of prestige, in particular, was a bit hard to swallow, but on the other hand it would relieve him of a great deal of work he had never cared for at all. Budgets, HR management, representation and the National Police Commissioner's e-mails, at the very least. And this was why he and the Countess had invited Pedersen round in the first place, the chess game in this instance merely providing the pretext.

'I've decided I like things the way they are at the moment, so if you want you can carry on in charge, provided we can get the go-ahead from upstairs, of course, but that shouldn't be too much of a problem.'

Arne Pedersen fell silent. Simonsen and the Countess gave him room to think. Eventually, he spoke.

'I won't pretend I'm not flattered, because I am. Are you sure?'

'We're sure. Both of us.'

Again, Pedersen hesitated.

'To be honest, I do feel I've got the measure of the job now, but all in all I'm going to pass. It's too early, I'd rather wait until you retire. Which, if you don't mind my saying so, isn't that far off.'

That was it. Pedersen's mind was made up and there was nothing more to be said.

Simonsen picked up the thread:

'I'm packing it in as soon as I get to sixty-four, no reason for that to be kept a secret. I was twenty-five when I started at HS, moved on to Homicide when that was set up, at which time I was thirty-six, and then took charge when I was forty-nine.'

Pedersen looked relieved. His decision had been far from easy and he had been sorely tempted.

'I had no idea you were into numerology. Let's say I ascend the throne once you step down, if they'll have me. That sounds a lot better to me. Truth is, I'm enjoying myself the most while working for you on that postman case. Those are the good days at the moment. I'm actually looking forward to our meeting tomorrow, which is a bit weird. Three months ago that would have been a day like any other, but now I'm almost excited about it. What that tells me is it'd do me good to wait a few years before heading up anything at all.'

The Countess finished her iced tea and put the glass down on the tray next to Simonsen's. He'd finished his a while ago.

'Now that we're talking shop, Arne,' she said, 'how do you feel about Klavs Arnold? And just so you know, Simon and I have been talking about him, and we're both in agreement.'

'You mean, if we should take him on?'

'Yes. What do you think?'

Pedersen squinted at Simonsen.

'And not just take him on but bring him into the inner circle, is that what you mean?'

'That's the idea, yes.'

'I think it's a good one. No two ways about it. He'll have to learn Danish, though.'

'Well, there are certain issues about his dialect, I'll admit.'

The Countess interrupted:

'Listen to you, whatever happened to diversity? Anyway, you're OK with it, Arne, is that right?'

'He's easy to get along with, methodical and industrious, intelligent and not overly afraid of authority. So, yes, I'm positive. I'm not sure what Pauline thinks, though. Does she even have a say?'

Simonsen was rather abrupt in his reply.

'Yes, she has a say. As big a say as the rest of us. No more, no less. That's how it is. I was thinking she and someone else could go over to Esbjerg soon, just a quick trip there and back to see how Klavs is getting on looking for that summer house. It won't help things there, but just to show him and everyone else who's on that job that we take the matter seriously...'

'We're with you, Simon. Sending the right signals and all that. I'll go over,' offered the Countess. 'I'm sure Arne hasn't got time. Besides, it's been a while since I spoke to Pauline on my own. But if Klavs is doing a proper job, as everything would seem to indicate, I think we should let him know we're done with his trial period.'

Simonsen agreed, it sounded reasonable enough. And then he asked:

'Have you got any more of that quince juice?'

The next morning the Countess and Simonsen had an early breakfast. The evening before, the Countess had hastily arranged her trip to Esbjerg with Pauline, and if they were going to get over there and back the same day she needed an early start.

She sat leafing through yesterday's paper: it was still too early for today's to have come. Simonsen himself was preoccupied with breakfast and casually asked about Pauline. Did the Countess have to go into town and pick her up first? It was mostly for the sake of conversation and to display some sort of interest. Yes, she did, as a matter of fact. She sounded hostile when she replied, and folded the paper and put it down.

'When you were in Rødby, it was to look up Rita's name that you couldn't remember, wasn't it? It's Rita Metz Andersen, in case you didn't find out.'

He admitted it was true, though without comprehending what exactly was happening here. Only in the pause that followed did he realise she knew things she couldn't possibly know unless...

'Have you been checking up on me behind my back? How come you know Rita's surname?'

The Countess persisted in what he now felt was an ominous inquisition.

'You're thinking of looking her up, I know you are. What's all this about.'

Contemptuously, she tossed a printed folder down in front of him. He picked it up and stared at it with puzzlement. Then he remembered. It was the folder he'd been given at the tourist office in Frederiksværk when he'd been on his way from Frederikssund to Melby Overdrev to meet Pauline Berg. In the middle was a map he'd used to find his way. He'd stuffed the folder away in the glove compartment and would have thrown it out next time he cleaned the car. Now there it was, staring him in the face, an accusation.

'"Songs for a Grandmother", page three.'

There'd been nothing wrong yesterday, she'd been sweetness and light, cooked dinner and made that lovely tea, and now all of a sudden... he failed to understand women sometimes and had no idea at all why she'd chucked this folder at him. He ignored it and instead tried to talk some sense into her. She simply had to trust him if their relationship was going to work. She *had* to – he savoured the words and felt oddly adult. What's more, he didn't want to know where she'd got her information on him. Or on Rita, for that matter. He loved the Countess, he loved living with her and he quite understood how it felt to be afraid of losing someone. He didn't mention in as many words her once having lost a child, speaking instead more indirectly about her *history*, her *background*. He understood all too well, she would have to take his word for it about that, but... His words ran on in a loop, repeated with increasing intensity and frustrated gesticulations.

The Countess waited until he was finished, then spoke serenely, melodically, almost with tenderness, as if he were the one with the problem.

'Yes, you're right. We both know.'

What it was they both knew was not elaborated upon, nor did he ask, and after a brief pause she concluded:

'You can do as you please. Suit yourself.'

With that, she got to her feet, drank the rest of her tea standing and kissed him goodbye as if nothing had happened. The front door shut behind her with rather more of a slam than usual, he thought.

And there he sat, with a cup of tepid tea and a feeling of not being able to count to four.

Later, on his way in to Police HQ, he plugged in the satnav, regardless of the fact that he could find his way there in his sleep.

The tinny female voice drilled into his ears. *Right turn ahead.* Bossy, authoritative, in command. *In six hundred metres, turn left.* He burst out: 'Shut your mouth, woman!' It felt good to be so vulgar. 'Shut it now, I don't want to know.' He savoured being loutish for a few kilometres until eventually tiring of it. He muted the satnav and forced his thoughts back in time. He could decide for himself who and what to think about. Or meet up with.

'Why don't we just go to Vordingborg?'

He remembered the question so vividly. It was a Sunday, a dismal early morning on the seventh floor of the Grønjordskollegium student halls in April 1973. He'd thought Rita was asleep. Or at least, he had striven not to make a sound as he got out of bed to put on his clothes. There was no reason to wake her. He had to go to work and wanted to stop by his own flat first and had therefore set the alarm for five o'clock, only to wake up before it went off. He'd just got his socks on when he lay back next to her again, relishing her warmth for a moment, however brief.

'For May the first, you mean?'

She did.

Her suggestion came as a surprise. He asked her again, to make sure. The previous evening they had talked about what to do on the day. Not an argument, but a joint consideration of the matter, which in itself was new. The year before, he hadn't been invited. The first of May, International Workers' Day, was usually celebrated with a demo in the Fælledparken together with Rita's friends, not him. But this year was different. Her enthusiasm for demonstrating had fallen off dramatically. Maybe they could sit and enjoy a beer, just the two of them, somewhere in the centre of Copenhagen, away from the demonstrators.

But now she didn't even fancy that. She wanted to go to Vordingborg.

It was an odd time for them, the six months or so that passed between her terminated pregnancy at the hospital in Køge and her emigrating and his losing touch with her. In some respects it was all bad, or rather: it felt frightening. In others they seemed to pull closer together. Their ideological differences weren't as divisive as before. They seldom argued, and when they did it rarely seemed to be about politics. His barbed comments and questions no longer found their mark:

'Rita, what's actually going to happen to me when the revolution comes?'

A year previously he would have been lucky to have escaped a bullet through his brain in exchange for being put in a rehabilitation camp. At that time his questions could trigger lengthy dialogues in which Rita was wholly unaware that he was having a dig at her.

'How long does that kind of rehabilitation actually take?'

It varied, and she was unable to provide him with any exact answer.

'I'd like you to be in charge of it, if that'd be possible?'

She doubted it, but could not entirely rule out the possibility.

Humour wasn't on the cards for the serious subjugators of capitalism.

But if he asked her now, all she would say would be that she had no idea, seeming listless and without any apparent enthusiasm for her revolution. As if she could hardly be bothered thinking about it.

They'd found a little bolt-hole close to Vordingborg, eleven kilometres outside the town, halfway out on the slender tongue of land called Knudshoved Odde, in a commune whose members had chipped together to buy up a former smallholding. He and Rita – and anyone else, for that matter – were free to come and go as they pleased. To begin with, Rita had known one of the people who lived there, but even though he had since moved out

247

they kept coming back and were accepted as friends of the household. Konrad Simonsen loved the place. It was a hippie refuge that remained stuck in time, an anarchistic shanty without any structure, without a plan, and yet undeniably pleasant. New arrivals deposited whatever money they could spare in the communal kitty, a battered old coffee tin kept on the shelf above the dining table. The tin had the Cirkel logo on it, an African woman in profile. And if you had nothing to spare, that was all right, too. Anyone had the right to eat whatever was in the fridge whenever they happened to be hungry, and in the morning to put on a pair of clean socks from the communal sock basket in which it was impossible ever to find two that were alike, not to mention the same size.

Next door to the place lived the co-op manager and the district midwife, a couple in their forties who held each other's hand when they went for a walk and called each other embarrassing pet names. Their place was a former farmhouse fully renovated from cellar to chimney stack. He was a cheerful, happy-go-lucky sort who almost daily brought the young people of the commune perfectly good food just past its sell-by date. Good neighbourliness was what it was all about, and it was a shame for things to go to waste, he would say as he dumped his crates in the kitchen with a thunderous laugh and poorly concealed expectations of a cup of tea. She was rather more reserved, a woman of strong limbs and a peculiar kindliness that often took people by surprise. Only when the hippies, as she consistently called them, sunbathed in the nude in the commune's front garden did she take offence, marching up the driveway with long, unco-ordinated strides. What kind of behaviour was that, naked bodies lounging around in full view, when Arnold had to whitewash the house? They could at least go round the back.

Konrad Simonsen loved that couple. He could sit for hours staring across at their marvellous property while Rita lay beside him reading. He would imagine Rita and himself living like that. Peace and quiet, in lovely surroundings. She could get a job teaching at the Vordingborg Gymnasium, work her way up into something secure. And he could be... well, a policeman, that was good enough, surely? What else could he do? They would have three children, three happy kids, one after another, running bare-foot about the place and spreading joy with their laughter. In time he might learn to sail and they could have a little boat and visit the islands of the Smålandshavet at weekends.

Rita looked up from her book.

'What are you thinking about, Konrad? You're gawping.'

He told her. She let out a sigh.

'Yes, that'd be nice. It really would.'

She sighed again, perhaps wiped away a tear she thought he hadn't seen, and tried to regain her composure.

If the weather was good they went for long walks along the spit. Here they spent what might have been their best times together, ambling slowly through the hilly moraine landscape with its low-lying outwash plains. They saw ospreys and red kites, and heard the croak of the fire-bellied toad in the wetlands as the hawthorn blossomed all around. Copenhagen was far, far away.

Unlike Konrad Simonsen, who was full of energy, Arne Pedersen was bleary-eyed when the two men met in Pedersen's office. The Homicide Department's temporary head had been up balancing the books half the night and kicked off proceedings in somewhat manic mood.

'Right, let's get to work, Simon.'

Hardly had the words left his lips before Malte Borup barged in, heaving to regain his breath and apologising at the same time.

'Oh, I didn't mean to interrupt, only you said it was urgent.'

Pedersen reached up to fidget with the knot of his tie and replied in a resigned tone:

'I'd been hoping you'd make it before Simon got here.'

'Sorry. I've been as quick as I could. The thing was I had to do the dishes first or else Anita will go ballistic when she gets home. I promised, you see.'

'All right. So now both of you can see how I've made a mess of this bloody smartboard…'

Arne got to his feet and removed the cloth he had hung over the board.

'I used an ordinary felt-pen and it won't rub off.'

Simonsen gazed at it with interest, There were three bullet points:

- Problem page = correspondence column / where?
- Father's uniform, what sort?
- Simon flying off at a tangent?

He recognised the first two as his own from the report he had drawn up a couple of days before.

Pedersen continued to bemoan his own ineptitude.

'I've tried everything I could get my hands on, but nothing works.'

'Everything you could get your hands on? What would that be? Water?' Simonsen enquired snidely.

'And washing-up liquid. All right, I know meths probably does the job, and I'm sorry, Malte, I just thought it was urgent. I take it you didn't have time to buy Coca-Cola?'

'You're right, I didn't.'

'Do it now, and get hold of some meths while you're at it. When Simon and I are finished you can clean the board and show him that clip you found of Mouritz Malmborg, are you with me?'

Malte went off and Pedersen speeded up.

'You weren't supposed to see that last point, obviously, but done is done, so let's pick up on that once we've talked about one and two. I've read your notes about the hypnosis in Nykøbing Falster, and Helena Brage Hansen having her own, quote, "problem page", which I'm sure you've realised, too. Besides that, her father wore a uniform, according to what transpired during your seance. We don't know what kind of uniform, and I'm pretty sure it's not that relevant either, but I did come up with one thing that might be. Helena Brage Hansen has an older brother, and I know you're thinking we don't want her to know we're checking up on her, but… well, you know him, as it happens. It's Finn B. Hansen.'

'One and the same?'

'Senior deputy judge of the court at Næstved, yes. Of course, I've no idea how he gets on with his sister, but I'm guessing he wouldn't let on to her if we asked him a few questions. On the other hand, he might not tell us anything. That's a different matter.'

Simonsen agreed.

'It's worth a try. Do you want to come with me?'

'I'd like to, but I'm pressed for time. If you want me with you we need to get this out of the way sharpish.'

'Right you are. What's this about me flying off at a tangent?'

Pedersen explained frankly. It had long since been confirmed that the six students involved had all been on the periphery with respect to the rest of their class.

'At the moment it seems like no detail is too small. A parent in uniform and a problem page. Why don't you just bring the surviving gang members in for an interview?'

'What if none of them can remember anything? Collective memory loss. What do we do then?'

'We do as we always do in that situation, we play them off against each other. Find the cracks in their stories, niggle away until they start caving in, threaten them, fool them, lure them into a trap. The way we do, and do well.'

'When did you last investigate a crime that took place forty years ago?'

251

Pedersen hesitated for a second, but stood his ground.

Maybe Simonsen had a point in that respect, and that was what in the first instance had prompted them to uncover all they could by way of background. But they'd done that now, more or less. Some would say more.

'There comes a point where you have to say: all right, we've got the overview, this is as good as it gets. But you're still picking away. And what's worse, you've got no way of knowing the murder of Jørgen Kramer Nielsen has anything at all to do with Lucy Davison going missing. That's supposition, and not even well founded. Get them in for interview instead of dallying about in the sixties, or all of a sudden you'll look up and it'll be time to retire.'

Simonsen acquiesced without argument. He'd already heard the same advice from the Countess, albeit phrased rather more elegantly.

'All right, let's go to Næstved and see Finn B. Hansen. I'll try to set up an appointment with him today. After that we'll confront the lot of them, unless something earth-shattering turns up in the meantime. Agreed?'

'Agreed, as long as I'm deciding what's earth-shattering,' Arne insisted.

'Done. Let me pop back and check my e-mail. Call me once you've got your smartboard sorted so I can watch that film.'

When Simonsen saw the clip he had to admit the interviewer was not without charm. Behind the long-haired exterior and the wire-framed glasses a subtle wit sparkled, and it was hard not to be carried along by it, despite the fact that the man in question was making the two teenagers he had selected to be his victims suffer quite without mercy. In front of him stood Mouritz Malmborg and a girl whose identity as yet remained unknown. The interviewer's introduction was deadpan:

'We on children's TV are often accused of not caring about the ordinary kids of today, only for hippies, potheads, peace activists and other dregs of society. So today we've come here to Hvidovre Station in the capital's hinterland, and lo and behold... what have we here but two absolutely ordinary kids of today. One absolutely ordinary boy and one absolutely ordinary girl. And the most ordinary of them would seem to be you. What's your name?'

'Susanne.'

'OK, Susanne. And you can run all the way round the station building in a very short time, and twice around the station building in a bit longer. Is that right?'

'Er, yeah.'

'And your dream is one day to be as good as all those women athletes from East Germany. Is the reason they're so much faster than you... because the East German state, unlike Denmark, makes sure its young people get the very best training facilities and a healthy social upbringing? Or is it because the running tracks in East Germany are shorter?'

'I don't know... are the tracks shorter in other countries?'

'All right, so there we have it. What about you, Mouritz? What's your name?'

'Mouritz.'

'I thought it might be. Now, you're a jablin thrower, right? How about showing the viewers how to throw a jablin? No, hang on. Pretend you've got a jablin in your hand and now you're going to throw it.'

Mouritz Malmborg did as he was instructed. It looked like he was hammering nails into a ceiling.

'A bit faster, we've got to get these jablins away, you know.'

He increased his speed and was left to repeat the movement for a while before the interviewer eventually moved on:

'Thank you, Mouritz. Well done, that was very, very ordinary indeed. Susanne, would you like to gave Mouritz a round of applause while I say something to the viewers?'

The girl clapped and the interviewer wrapped things up.

Simonsen was impressed, and said so to Malte Borup.

'Nice work, Malte. You turned up one of public broadcasting's genuine red hirelings, as they said in the day. When's it from?'

'Tenth of April nineteen sixty-nine. It came up on Google. Is it any use?'

'Definitely, thanks a lot.'

'Why was he so unpleasant? He knew perfectly well it's called a *javelin*. And making them look stupid like that... it was cruel.'

'I don't know why. Perhaps he *was* cruel, or maybe he was doing it just because he could. Times were different then, Malte.'

It was Simonsen's standard comment whenever he wanted to close a discussion about the past: *times were different then*. And it was true enough, but when *weren't* they different? In this instance, however, his evasion didn't work. Malte Borup pondered for a second, still unable to get his head round it, in spite of times being different.

'Was it funny then? Picking on people, I mean?'

What was Simonsen to say to that? In a way it was. It was hard to explain.

In the car on the way to Næstved, Arne Pedersen buried his nose in a stack of spreadsheets and statements of accounts, poring his way through them with the aid of a pocket calculator and a biro. Occasionally he expelled a sigh, but said nothing. Simonsen, too, immersed himself in thought, transporting himself back into the past as he had done that morning. In his mind he lingered on his final meeting with Rita. She had disappeared for days on end. He had no idea where she went, and often her leaving came as a surprise to him. On her return she would refuse to answer his many questions, and it took a long time for him to discover that she was working as a courier, running cash from Denmark to Germany or France, money collected in Scandinavia with the aim of supporting Palestinian liberation. He never found out for certain which organisation had recruited her. Most likely it was the PFLP, the Popular Front for the Liberation of Palestine, though he had no clear indication, then or now. There were so many different groups and so many gullible idealists willing to do the dirty work, who at the end of the day had no idea at all who they were working for. Rita was a tiny pawn in a very big game that was becoming increasingly nasty. Hijackings, killings and kidnappings were the order of the day. The use of terror was accelerating, but the reactions to it were often equally violent: Mossad, the Israeli security agency, tracked down and liquidated the perpetrators of the Olympic Games massacre in Munich, one by one.

In the spring of 1973, Rita was away for almost two weeks. When she got back she looked tanned yet depressed. As usual, she wouldn't say what she'd been doing. It couldn't go on, and they paused their relationship, as they had done several times before, only to pick things up again after a short time. The crux of the matter, so they thought, was that they couldn't do without each other.

But then came the shock: staring him in the face in black and white, revealing to him just how far gone she was. As he remembered it, they were at a workers' festival in the Fælledparken, an event that had drawn tens of thousands, a perfectly orchestrated display of organisational talent and logistics. But maybe he was mistaken, perhaps the festival came later, and now he came to think about it he was unsure as to the time of year, too. But whatever, he had been put on duty to keep the peace at some event or other organised by the Danish communists. It was a cushy job. Regardless of his disdain for the party, he had to admit they kept their cadres in order. The communists were never any trouble: never a jeer was issued in his direction, the police were mostly ignored and he'd even on occasion been offered a cup of coffee.

He'd been approached by two men, middle-aged activists of the easy-going kind. They'd sat down on a bench by a table, in a tent, as he recalled. The tablecloth was the only thing he remembered vividly, red and white checks, as in the cheaper restaurants of the capital. The men had placed two almost identical photographs in front of him. Both showed Rita climbing the steps to board a plane. She carried crutches, and one of her legs was in plaster. The plane was an El Al flight to Tel Aviv.

The men had been friendly, though neither wished to reveal where the photos came from or how they knew about his connection to Rita. Their gentle advice to him was to get his girlfriend out of the mess she'd landed herself in. He never found out if the two men had been sent by the party – if they were even communists at all – or whether they'd approached him off their own bat as a matter of simple decency.

For two days and nights he pored over the problem. And then he went to PET, police intelligence. PET's headquarters was at that time on the first floor of the Bellahøj Politistation. He was interviewed by three colleagues. They took down his explanations and enquired in detail about his relationship with Rita. He was given a list of further questions to think about and answer to the best of his ability. Before leaving, he paradoxically received the same piece of advice the communists had issued. *Get her out of this mess and do it now.* Those were their parting words. Afterwards, he adjourned to a bar and felt miserable. The interview with PET had been unpleasant and he felt like a traitor: he'd betrayed Rita, no matter how many times he told himself he'd done the only thing he could have done and that it was right. Presumably, they were no longer in a relationship at all.

Senior Deputy Judge Finn B. Hansen had for a number of years been in charge of Department 14 of the High Court of Western Denmark with responsibility for preparing all civil cases to be tried by the court. Some ten years ago he had been moved down the ladder to the district court at Næstved, having completed an enforced sabbatical of six months on account of a somewhat far-reaching drink problem. Subsequently he had managed to get a grip on himself, but his career had suffered irreparably and he had been compelled to accept the fact that he would never rise to the echelons of magistrate.

He was a corpulent man with thin white hair and a fleshy face. He welcomed Simonsen and Pedersen and ushered them to the two Bauhaus chairs that had been drawn up in front of his desk. Simonsen hesitated. He found the furniture aesthetically pleasing, but was always reluctant actually to sit down on such an item, and whenever he did so it was always with a measure of scepticism as to the spindly steel tubing and the two missing legs.

'So, what can I do for you gentlemen? I was intrigued to hear from you, I must admit.'

Simonsen threw caution to the wind and sat down before explaining why they had come. Many years ago, Hansen's younger sister had spent some days revising for exams over on the west coast together with some classmates from her gymnasium. There they had been visited by a young English girl who had later disappeared. He showed the man a couple of photos, though not the one in which the youngsters were partially naked.

Hansen's expression turned from cheery to reticent. He studied the photos for some time, though all they required was a glance.

'And you think this English girl is dead, am I right?' he eventually asked.

The inference was reasonable: after all, they were from Homicide. Simonsen confirmed the suspicion that Lucy Davison most likely was dead. Finn B. Hansen nodded solemnly before responding:

'It's a long time ago. I'm sorry, can I get you anything? Tea, coffee, water?'

257

It was obvious the deputy judge needed time to digest the matter. Pedersen declined on behalf of them both, whereupon he explained as tactfully as possible Hansen's sister's possible involvement in the case, before briefly outlining the killing of Jørgen Kramer Nielsen. As soon as he was finished, Simonsen took over.

'We fully understand if you don't want to help us. I'm not sure how I'd react in the situation myself. Nevertheless, we'd like you to know that regardless of whatever you may decide to do, no record of this will ever be made, neither publically nor internally within the department. That said, we would indeed be very grateful if you were to refrain from informing your sister that we have spoken.'

Hansen shook his white head vigorously. It looked more like a shudder. After a moment's pause he spoke again.

'Two people died?'

'Hardly any doubt.'

'And worst case is my sister being charged with murder?'

'Worst case, yes. But it's not particularly on the cards as regards Esbjerg. We don't consider first-degree murder to be at all likely in that case, and anything else would be time-barred by now as you'd know better than anyone. As for the postman, it seems clear that...'

'Helena could never have broken anyone's neck. You know she lives in the north of Norway, I take it?'

'We're aware of that, yes.'

'Do you think I could have a minute to think this over? Perhaps you could go for a little walk or something?'

Hansen got to his feet, indicating they didn't have much choice in the matter.

'No need to worry I'll get in touch with her, because I won't,' he assured them as he showed them out.

They left the office and Pedersen returned to his accounts. The advantage of being overworked was always having something to do while waiting for something else to arrive. Simonsen chose to amble up and down the corridors of the courts building. The place was relatively new and the red-brick walls were lined with paintings, presumably at the instigation of the staff art society. The canvasses were hard to get a handle on and moreover rather dull.

Half an hour later Finn B. Hansen had come to a decision.

'I'd like to help you if I can. At the end of the day it would be the best thing for Helena. At least, I hope so. What would you like to know?'

Pedersen kicked off.

'Your father appeared in uniform at Brøndbyøster Gymnasium at one point, so we've been led to believe. Does that ring a bell, or would it be completely out of the question?'

'No, he may well have done. He was top dog, field master general or whatever, in the Scouts. Don't ask me what group it was, all I remember is he seemed to wear that uniform continually for a while. He was quite unabashed by it. The arguments we had in those days! I was studying law at university and my father went ballistic when we boycotted lectures and occupied the offices, not to mention the time we smoked pot on the stairs of the main building.'

Simonsen delivered a discreet kick to Pedersen's shin, preempting his colleague's interruption. Having already abandoned himself to recollections of the sixties as seen from class Three Y of Brøndbyøster Gymnasium, he was well aware that most who'd been around then had partaken of one substance or another at some point. It made fact a rather fluid concept, events being inclined to shift back and forth in recollection, one year or two, to accord with this or another reminiscence, and often suitably modified to fit the bill.

'Basically, I think the uniform was his reaction to the times. Today I consider that to be rather courageous. But at the time I thought he was a fool.'

259

'Was your sister in the Scouting movement?'

Hansen thought for a while before answering.

'I don't recall her being involved, but she may well have been. She and I were very different. Perhaps because of being boy and girl, but also because I rebelled against my parents while she rebelled against me. Had she been older than me it might have been the other way round. It's often such slight differences in circumstance that dictate where you end up, isn't it?'

'But you can't definitely say if she was?'

'I'm afraid not. She was my younger sister, so I wasn't that interested in the things that occupied her or who she hung around with.'

'While she was at the gymnasium she edited a problem page. Could that have been something to do with Scouting?'

'It could, certainly. I've got some stuff of my parents'... documents, papers... I'm sure I'd be able to find out what branch of the movement my father was involved in. You could take it from there.'

'We'd be grateful if you would. What happened to your sister after school?'

'She became ill with psychiatric problems. Whether it was following on from the gymnasium or later, I don't recall, but certainly around about that time. It took quite some years before she began to function reasonably again, if one can put it like that. Thinking back, what I remember most about her then is how ill she was. She was in and out of hospital all the time, and of course it took its toll on the family, though especially on my mother and father. And Helena herself, naturally.'

Again he paused and they waited patiently. Simonsen found himself wondering. Until now their enquiries in to Helena Brage Hansen's background had given them no indication at all that there had been mental health issues. He would have to chase that up himself.

Finn B. Hansen continued:

'I know what you're dying to ask, but I've no idea at all if her psychiatric problems can be linked to anything that happened in Esbjerg. Your guess is as good as mine, I'm afraid. All I can say is that her condition stabilised with time, I think probably due to advances in drug treatment. The psychiatrists found her a pill that could keep the demons at bay. In the eighties she lived in a farming commune. I went to see her there a couple of times, though it was quite a hike to Bornholm. Then when our parents died – that'd be, what, nineteen eighty-four and eighty-six – we inherited quite a sum of money. She spent hers relocating to Norway and establishing herself there. First in Bergen, then all the way up north in Hammerfest. She works as a nature warden and tourist guide there. At some point she became a Norwegian citizen, I don't recall when exactly.'

'And there's no family there, no children?'

'None. I believe she sees someone, though.'

'Are you in touch with her at all?'

'Not much. We e-mail once in a while, but months can easily go by.'

'So you don't get together much?'

'She did come to my sixtieth birthday, and my youngest son went to stay with her when he was in Lapland a couple of years ago. If I remember, I'll give her a call at Christmas, but that's about it really.'

Neither Simonsen nor Pedersen had anything more to ask, apart from one thing that potentially might make a difference to their inquiry. The agreement between them had been that the one Hansen hit it off best with during the interview was to give it a go. There was no doubt this was Simonsen's call.

'As I'm sure you understand, we're going to need to have a word with your sister. If that interview could take place in Denmark it would be in the best interests of all parties. We

261

wouldn't be able to go to Norway and question a citizen without the involvement of the Norwegian police. But you'll be fully aware of that, of course.'

'I'll see what I can do. When were you thinking of?'

'We'll give you a call. It'll probably be a week or two yet. We're starting off by interviewing her classmates. It might not even be necessary to talk to Helena.'

'Let's hope that's the case.'

The two policemen had only just left the court building when Konrad Simonsen halted and stood there like a pillar of salt. Pedersen was immediately alarmed.

'What's wrong? Are you feeling ill?'

'No, just slow on the uptake, that's all. Come on, we've got to go back in.'

Finn B. Hansen accepted the interruption gracefully as they came barging back into his office.

'We forgot something,' said Simonsen, slightly out of breath. 'The Scout group your father was with. Would they have had a hut or a cabin in the Esbjerg area, for summer camps and the like?'

'Yes, the Vesterhavsgården. A children's holiday camp. I remember the sea there, and that we went to stay sometimes when we were kids, but I honestly can't remember if it was Esbjerg, or Blokhus, or somewhere else.'

Simonsen thanked him. Hansen shrank visibly as he realised how significant the information might be, and then added gently:

'I'm afraid, as I recall, the grounds were rather extensive.'

The Vesterhavsgården turned out to be exactly right, though the place was now owned by Esbjerg's local authority and had since been renamed. Looking at Jørgen Kramer Nielsen's photos no one could tell one way or the other if their Gang of Six had been staying at a holiday camp or not. Officers investigating in the area had been instructed to look for a summer house. The holiday camp was therefore duly passed by, until Simonsen called Klavs Arnold.

The photos matched. Arnold took some pictures on the spot and e-mailed one to Simonsen right away. There was no doubt about it: the same wooden cladding on the outside walls; the corner of the building and the slope in the background, exactly as they'd been forty years before. The end of the bargeboard was carved in the shape of a dragon's head, presumably with a sheath knife, and the monster had been there in 1969, too, albeit rather grainy in Kramer Nielsen's black-and-white images. Moreover, the man with Down's had been traced. He had lived on the neighbouring farm until his death in 1991, but older people in the area remembered Daft Troels well – a harmless, happy soul, now sadly long-since gone. The only fly in the ointment was that Senior Deputy Judge Finn B. Hansen had in no way overestimated the extent of the grounds: thirty hectares, at least, of broken landscape comprising grass, scrub, heather, pine, fir and impenetrable thickets of brambles.

Konrad Simonsen and Pauline Berg zoomed in on the area on Google Earth. It wasn't the most encouraging sight for anyone wanting to find a body there.

Pauline shook her head.

'No way we can dig through all that without some idea of where she might be. They could have buried her anywhere, the place is surrounded by spruce plantations.'

'I shouldn't think they'll have lugged her around more than absolutely necessary,' said Simonsen.

'Maybe not, but if we don't know where they got rid of her she could be ten metres from the front door and we still wouldn't have a chance.'

'You're right. At the moment we haven't got a look in.'

'Isn't there some kind of scanner we can use that can find bones and stuff? I'm sure I heard something about that not long ago. Like a metal detector, only for bodies. Hasn't Kurt Melsing got one?'

'It would be almost impossible after such a long time.'

'What a pain. How are we going to go about it, then?'

'We're going to read.'

He had laid his hands on three volumes of *Scouting Youth* spanning 1967 to 1969. They were on his desk. Helena Brage Hansen had edited the problem page, and Konrad Simonsen thought the magazines would give them a window on her personality.

Pauline grudgingly indulged him. She didn't feel much like ploughing through forty-year-old Scouting mags, but for once she did as she was asked.

Only later did Simonsen realise he'd got his young colleague started on an impossible job. It was a realisation that came to him when, after an hour and a half of reading, she suddenly said:

'I'm not sure I understand what I'm looking for.'

He looked up from his own magazine.

'What you need to do is look at the advice Helena gives her readers and on that basis form an impression of what she's like as a person. What kind of opinions has she, what does she believe in, what are her morals, visions and dreams? That sort of thing. As far as I can see she often uses herself as a point of reference in her replies.'

'She was young, too.'

'True. And?'

'I think it's weird her giving all this advice. Usually agony aunts are older, aren't they? She's a good writer, though.'

'She wanted to be a journalist.'

'How do you know?'

'From the reply I just read. The same one you read ten minutes ago.'

Pauline rubbed her eyes.

'I don't think I'm very good at this. Can't you give me an example?'

'Like what?'

'Something you've found yourself that's important.'

Simonsen looked at his notepad and flicked through the pages.

'All right, how's this? She's replying to a girl who can't find a boyfriend and feels left out by the others in her class. "*Stay true to yourself. It can be hard, I know that. But it's not worth being admitted to any group if the price of entry is to stop being the person you are. That price is too high, even if sometimes you might be tempted.*"'

'Yeah, all right. But what's so special about that?'

He put it aside and moved on to another example.

'This one's to a boy who's been admonished by his Scoutmaster for saying he's against the war in Vietnam.'

'Nobody likes war.'

'He means the USA's involvement in Vietnam. Listen to what she tells him. "*You're entitled to your opinion. It's your right, and you should tell that to your Scoutmaster. But think about this, too: North Korea is a dictatorship, South Vietnam is a dictatorship, China is a dictatorship, the Soviet Union is a dictatorship. Saying so may not be popular, but it's the case nevertheless. Try imagining that the USA was a dictatorship, too. That may be difficult, but try as hard as you can and then tell me how that would affect life in Denmark. It doesn't take much courage to spit on a fortress when you know it'll remain standing.*"'

'Sounds reasonable enough to me. Don't you agree with her?'

'My opinion, whatever it might be, is irrelevant. The point is what her classmates thought about her.'

'How am I supposed to know that? The only ones who write to her are in Scouting.'

'She was certainly making waves.'

Pauline looked thoughtful and Simonsen concluded he had finally steered her mind on to the right track, an assumption he was shortly afterwards compelled to revise when she spoke again.

'I think I might know what you mean now. She ought to have made more of an effort with her appearance. She couldn't help the way she looked, of course, I know that, but she ought to have done herself up some more, sold herself a bit better. It needn't cost much. But then maybe it was the times... I wouldn't know about that, would I?'

'Just forget about it, Pauline, it doesn't matter.'

'What about the others? How come you're so interested in Helena?'

'Because she's the only one we know anything about, and because informally, at least, she seems to have been their leader, if you like.'

'They being the Lonely Hearts Club?'

'Yes.'

'Where did they get that stupid name anyway?'

Simonsen gave up and let her go.

But not entirely. As Pauline gathered together her magazines and sorted them into chronological order, he asked:

'What about Klavs Arnold? Does he need doing up as well?'

He'd been meaning to ask her for a while – not about the man's appearance, but about him joining them on a permanent basis. This seemed as good a time as any. Yet when her answer came he kicked himself for not having asked before.

'The Countess and I will take care of that once you give him the job.'

'How do you know I'm giving him a job? Did the Countess tell you? Or Arne?'

'No, but that's been the idea all along, hasn't it? You are going to take him on, aren't you?'

266

'Yes, I am. And very soon, if he'll agree.'

On Saturday morning Konrad Simonsen and the Countess went shopping in the Lyngby Storcenter precinct. The Countess wasn't holding back. Her approach to supermarkets was unstructured and governed by impulse: she picked from the shelves whatever took her fancy on her way round the store, albeit with an expression that was supposed to make it look like every selection was a carefully considered choice. This had fooled Simonsen to begin with, but now he saw straight through her. Occasionally he fished an item from the trolley and replaced it on the shelf without its seeming to bother her unduly. Sometimes he would do it without telling her, while at others his action was accompanied by a brief explanation: *The cupboard's full of coffee, what do we need another three packets for?* She would shrug and move on. Having passed through the checkout they trundled their trolley into the lift, then to the Countess's car parked in the underground car park. Here at their leisure they could transfer their shopping into carrier bags before dumping them in the boot. While they were doing so, the Countess said:

'I know I was unfair about that folder from Frederiksværk and accusing you about your trip to Rødby. I didn't mean it. I'm sorry.'

He grunted a reply and she elaborated the way she did, the way with which he had now become familiar. And yet he sensed she had given more thought to the matter this time: she still hadn't fully come to terms with her own divorce, though it had been nearly five years ago now. Naturally, she was no longer in love with the man, not at all, but she was still jealous of his family life, his children. Sometimes she could hardly go about in public without fearing she was going to bump into them and – worst of all – see them strolling with their pram. She readily admitted to being overstrung, and probably mean-spirited, too, but nevertheless it was the way she felt.

He understood, he told her. He did after all know the background, though he never mentioned it to her. The matter was taboo. A long time ago she had lost a child, her only one. That was all he knew, but it was more than enough. Now the shadow of her dead child fell upon their relationship and what was he to do? Nothing, apart from hope it would pass in time. He spoke again, in a voice he considered firm:

'How did you know I'd been to the police station in Rødby and asked about Rita?'

She smiled wryly.

'I worked that out when you were in the bath on Thursday morning and I heard a message on our landline from a sergeant in the Rødby Politi. Apparently, he'd informed you PET had been involved when Rita Metz Andersen was arrested for smuggling cash in nineteen seventy-two, but that wasn't right. PET didn't come in until a couple of months later. Something like that, anyway. You can listen to the message yourself.'

It was an explanation that relieved him somewhat. He'd been afraid of something more sinister. The rest of it they could work out, he felt sure.

'I'd be glad if you could look her up and get it over and done with as soon as possible, Simon,' said the Countess once they were in the car.

He was in no doubt she was talking about Rita. He promised nothing, nodding pensively in a way that could have been taken to mean just about anything.

As they got closer to home, the tension between them eased. They exchanged small, insignificant comments about the traffic and the weather.

'By the way,' she said, 'I've been invited out to the theatre tomorrow. Goethe's *Faust*. It's the Deutsches Theater, they're the guest company at the Royal.'

Simonsen sensed problems, though not quite as prickly as those of half an hour before.

'Not me. It says in my calendar I'm staying in that night.'

'Relax, I wasn't asking you. I'm going with Stella.'

'Who's Stella? I don't think you've mentioned a Stella.'

'Stella is a very punchy woman. Mother of five – six, if you include Klavs. Upcoming member of the Parliamentary Cultural Affairs Committee. Apparently they get free tickets. Her husband's probably just as anti-arts as you, so the ticket was offered to me.'

'I see. What party does she stand for?'

'No idea, never asked. I'm not bothered one way or the other.'

'I don't suppose it matters that much. Are you going to go?'

'Of course I am. I like Stella.'

'Now you mention Klavs, how did he get on organising that search for the summer house? Was it competent?'

'Very, and he was glad we went over, too. Even if Pauline was a bit moody, not to say mute.'

'So your view is he's professionally capable? And I don't mean just yesterday, but previously as well, when the two of you were working together.'

'He's excellent to work with, no question. We had a bit of a misunderstanding to begin with, though. He had to get used to the idea that working together means working both ways. Even with women. Once he got that straight, we had no trouble.'

'That sounds a bit defensive to me. Is that the best you can say about him?'

'He's good. Methodical and creative. Is that any better?'

'Much.'

'One thing did impress me, I don't think I've told you yet. The first time I was over there I had that touched-up photo of Jørgen Kramer Nielsen with me. It wasn't like it was poorly done or anything. It was hard to see he was dead, but his eyes were funny, a bit creepy almost.'

'The photo technician had to add in a pair of open eyes. On top of his eyelids, I mean.'

'Right, and it was OK, too, in a strictly anatomical way, but in practice it made our job a bit more difficult. All the potential witnesses we asked to look at the photo all looked away again just as quickly. Most probably weren't even aware they were doing it. But Klavs noticed, so second time around he'd had this drawing done that we used instead. That was what made the hostel manager at the Nørballe Vandrehjem recognise him, which she hadn't the first time we asked. Anyway, no more talking shop today, Simon. I really can't be bothered.'

'All right. I'll give Klavs a call and ask him if he wants to come over to HS this evening if he can.'

'This evening? Can't it wait? And surely you can talk to him on the phone without dragging him out there?'

'Yes, it could wait, and yes, we could do it over the phone, of course we could. Only I don't want to do it like that. You can come in with me if you want.'

She accepted grudgingly, and being in the mood to do it he called Klavs Arnold right away. Disagreeing with her wasn't easy today.

Not even when the opportunity arose a couple of hours later. He was hoovering the car and she'd sat down on a folding chair outside with a book. He turned off the hoover and the Countess instantly took her chance to speak.

'Since you're going to be looking this Rita up...'

He cut her off:

'I told you, I'm not sure I want to.'

'And I've told you, you might as well get it out of your system.'

'She might not even be in Denmark. In fact, I've a feeling she isn't.'

270

'Why not?'

'She went to America. It was a dream of hers to go to San Francisco.'

'And get away from Denmark?'

'That as well.'

He had confronted Rita with what he knew about her having gone to Israel. With an apparently broken leg. And he had been ruthless. Hijackings in which innocent people were slaughtered simply because they were Jews or Americans, on account of politics in the Middle East over which they had absolutely no control – was that the kind of despicable business she was involved in? She could cry all she liked, it cut no ice with him. Did she really want to be responsible for the death of innocent individuals, random passengers on an aeroplane who'd never done her or anyone else any harm whatsoever? He had hit her, too. The flat of his hand against the back of her skull while she sat with her head in her hands weeping. Not once, but several times, and hard. He demanded answers. Eventually, she gave him a few. She had no idea who she was working for. There were two men, one a Dane, the other foreign – Syrian, she thought. They met up at various cafés where they told her what to do. On the trip to Israel she was to observe airport security measures. It was important for them to know if her 'broken' leg would be checked.

He pressed her for information, firing questions at her, scribbling down her answers without caring what she might think of him. Eventually he had no more to ask and she stopped crying, sitting there as though paralysed, staring into space with empty eyes. Then suddenly she spoke:

'You can't get out again. That's not the way it works.'

He couldn't remember what he said in reply, nor did he recall his response when a moment later she added:

'Let's get away from it all, Konrad. We can go to America and start again. They won't find me there.'

The next day he called PET and phoned in his report. They thanked him for the information, but wanted more. He turned them down.

The emotionless voice of the Countess plucked him back into the present.

'I think she came back.'

He emptied the car ashtray into a plastic bag. The cigarette ends were from the time when he still smoked.

'Don't tell me you've done a search.'

'Relax, I haven't. Anyway, you make it sound so hard. It could be all you need to do is look her up in the phone book.'

'Perhaps, but I'm not sure I want to. What makes you think she might still be in Denmark?'

'She had no brothers or sisters, is that right?'

'Yes. And?'

'Did you ever actually look at that folder you brought back with you from Frederiksværk ?'

He shook his head. He had tossed it away in annoyance and never given it a thought. She went and got it and opened it in front of him.

'I think her grandchild's playing tomorrow afternoon in the Gjethuset there. The music schools are giving their annual concert and on the bill there's a Teresa Metz Andersen with "Songs for a Grandmother", three interpretations of songs by Joan Baez. The grandmother might very well be your Rita.'

Konrad Simonsen stared at the page, then said very slowly, almost lingering over every word:

'Yes, I suppose it might.'

Klavs Arnold's appointment was made official on the Saturday afternoon. Simonsen had talked the man from Jutland into stopping by Police HQ on the pretext of wanting to discuss strategy on the search of the holiday-camp grounds. Arnold's strategy, fully in keeping with where he was from, was simply to get on with it, but Simonsen the Copenhagener was insistent. They met at eight, as that was as early as Arnold could make it. Arne Pedersen had protested about going in to work on a Saturday evening for something that could just as well have been dealt with during normal working hours after the weekend. Simonsen, though, was adamant. He might well have called them in on impulse, but he wasn't forcing anyone to attend. He just felt they needed to get Arnold's appointment settled as soon as possible. *Felt*. A new word in his vocabulary, perhaps, but that's how it was, and his colleagues would just have to take it or leave it.

Pauline Berg arrived all dressed up to go out and looked amazing. Apparently, she had an appointment straight afterwards, though what kind of appointment and with whom she wouldn't say. It was good to see her like that again, outgoing and bubbling over with enthusiasm, however long it lasted.

It was dark before Arnold arrived. The days had grown shorter and the depressing blanket of heavy grey cloud that had lingered over the city for a week did the rest.

When the man they were all waiting for finally arrived, Simonsen went directly to the issue at hand. Klavs Arnold had hardly sat down before Simonsen put it to him straight:

'What would you say to joining us here permanently rather than going to Helsinge?'

They all thought he'd been waiting to be asked. Only when Arnold's jaw dropped and he sat gaping for a moment, visibly gobsmacked, did they realise he hadn't. Unless he was a born actor.

'Seriously?'

Pauline Berg replied promptly:

'No, it's just something we say to everyone, and we're only here because we couldn't think of anything else to do on a Saturday night.'

She mellowed again when Arnold faced up to her and responded to her barbs with a compliment.

'You're looking gorgeous tonight. Who's the lucky bloke?'

'Oh, thanks. Just someone I know.'

'Well, he's very fortunate. And yes, I'd very much like to carry on here, if you'll have me.'

After that, there wasn't much more to say. Arne Pedersen and Pauline Berg battled to be the first one out of the door, and the Countess, too, quickly made her excuses: she had a couple of things to do while she was here. Simonsen waited for her. It struck him that when, or if, Arne Pedersen was to head up the department at some later stage, the inner circle he himself favoured would no longer exist. After a minute, Pauline came back.

'I didn't actually say before because of all sorts of other stuff in my head but I'm really glad you're going to be with us, Klavs. Very glad indeed.'

And then she left again.

The two men exchanged glances without saying a word, before Simonsen spoke.

'How long are you staying in town?'

'Until tomorrow. I thought we were going to be talking strategy about that search, even if there isn't much to talk about.'

'Because we won't find her?'

'I've only been out there for an hour. The wife's got so much on at the moment, and I've got to help out with the kids. One of the girls was off colour yesterday and I had to stay home half the day. Never done that before.'

'What do you think?'

'What I think is, we don't stand a chance without knowing where to look.'

'That's twice in a very short space of time someone's said that to me. I'm going back with you to Esbjerg tomorrow. I need to see the place for myself.'

CHAPTER 9

The venue for the concert was a delight. The Gjethuset in Frederiksværk looked a treat in the pale autumnal sun that Sunday afternoon. Originally, the three-winged building had been an ordnance foundry, and the concert hall of today was an intriguing blend of raw eighteenth-century factory floor and modern arts venue with acoustics that were no less than fabulous.

Konrad Simonsen and Klavs Arnold had made the trip together. Once the concert was over they were heading off to Esbjerg, which would give them all day Monday to study the grounds of the Vesterhavsgården camp. They hung about in the car outside the concert hall and watched people as they arrived.

'Are you sure you don't want to come in?' Simonsen asked for about the third time.

But Klavs Arnold didn't. As a father of five, three of whom were of school age, he had long since grown averse to performing children, shunning everything in the way of school plays, nativity scenes, kids' circuses, or just plain music and song. Simonsen felt guilty about making him wait.

'What are you going to do in the meantime?'

Arnold laughed.

'Off you go, Simon. See you in a couple of hours.'

The concert had attracted a good-sized audience, the venue was packed, mostly with parents coming to see their musical offspring. Even as he made his way towards the doors, Simonsen had realised he would be more than fortunate to see Rita in all the crowds if indeed she were there at all, and if he would recognise her if he did bump into her. Whatever the circumstances, he had resolved not to go looking for her. Small steps, one at a time. If he didn't see her here today, the chance would surely come again somewhere else.

He found his seat, far back to the left of the stage, and felt comfortably anonymous in the throng.

The programme was introduced by the mayor of Halsnæs Kommune, Helge Friis. He was a balding man in his fifties with an unforced, casual manner, as though he was well used to appearing on stage, and an assurance in his voice that immediately put Simonsen at his ease. He'd been expecting the usual stiff and under-rehearsed official welcome. The mayor waxed lyrical about the building, the foundry in which generations of workers had grafted forging cannons and guns, today a place of culture, community and music, a language understood by all.

The well-thought-out speech met with resounding applause, an enthusiastic and genuine response from an audience who clearly weren't clapping just because they were supposed to. Simonsen joined in; the man deserved it. With the scene suitably set, the concert could begin.

The running order had Teresa Metz Andersen appearing second with her 'Songs for a Grandmother'. Simonsen was almost catapulted back into his seat when she stepped on to the stage, a reaction so violent and unexpected that for the first time in months he worried about his heart. To begin with he even had to look away. Whether it was his memory adapting to the sight of her or whether she really did resemble her grandmother to an astonishing extent was hard for him to say, but the likeness between Rita of the early 1970s and the girl onstage now was unnerving.

Not until well into her first song did Simonsen regain sufficient composure to listen. She sang in a clear, ringing soprano, accompanying herself on the twelve-stringed acoustic guitar, an instrument she played with great skill. 'Sweet Sir Galahad' once again climbed in through the window of Joan Baez's younger sister, this time in an excellent, albeit rather frail, interpretation that met with deservedly enthusiastic applause from her audience. According to the programme, her following two songs would also be Joan Baez, though this proved to be a slight misrepresentation. Nevertheless, her next song sent Simonsen on a journey back into his past. Teresa Metz Andersen dreamed of Joe Hill; Simonsen dreamed of Rita. The young girl's version of the judicial murder of the workers' rights activist was skilful and accomplished. But also bloodless and tame, a far cry altogether from her grandmother's. And then, abruptly, the memories came flooding back, as they had done so many times before in the past months.

In 1972 he and Rita had braved the cold of February and biked up to the Reprise Teatret in Holte to see a double bill of Bo Widerberg films. First up was *Ådalen 31* about the Swedish workers' strike in the communities of Sandviken and Utansjö in the Ådalen district in 1931, a conflict that ended tragically with the deaths of five workers when Swedish troops opened fire on a demonstration. Already in the interval between the two films they had argued, Rita conveniently leapfrogging the forty intervening years to claim brashly that such an incident could easily occur in the Denmark of their day. Subjugation of the Danish trade unions by the military was a scenario for which they had to be prepared. For his part Simonsen had found the film quite excellent, though hardly topical. He reminded her that representatives of the Danish trade unions regularly met and co-ordinated with the government and were hardly likely to be shot, even in the event of a general election tipping the balance of power in the opposite direction. They bought four grilled sausages with bread, ketchup and mustard, of which she devoured three. *Because he was so stupid.* He protested. *Would starving make him any more intelligent?* She finished chewing and gave him a kiss in reply. He found this preferable to the sausage.

After the second film, however, it all went wrong. Widerberg's *Joe Hill* was a gripping portrayal of the Swedish-American union agitator, syndicalist, social critic and satirical songwriter, executed in Utah in 1915 following a politically motivated show trial. When it was over, Rita's blood was boiling. It was as if she wanted them to disagree, to direct her indignation at a tangible target: him. Simonsen was annoyed with her. She and her left-wing friends had no monopoly on justice, and he had no desire whatsoever to defend judicial murder. What's more he felt in no way responsible for Joe Hill's execution, regardless of whether he was a policeman or not.

And so they had been at each other's throats all the way home, and in Sorgenfri she had seized the opportunity to let the air out of his front tyre, mean-spiritedly exploiting his need to stop and answer a minor call of nature. When they continued on their way, she cycled slowly, dawdling on the opposite bike path, singing the words of 'Joe Hill' to him as he trudged along, wheeling his own bike:

> *I dreamed I saw Joe Hill last night,*
> *alive as you and me.*
> *Says I: 'But Joe, you're ten years dead.'*
> *'I never died,' said he,*
> *'I never died,' said he.*

Rita's arrestingly beautiful voice cut through the winter night and he would gladly have arrested her for disturbing the peace if only he had been able to keep up with her. An angry voice demanded quiet from a window, prompting her only to sing even louder. It had begun to snow. She biked off, leaving him to walk the rest of the way on his own, furious with her for her senseless vandalism and yet missing her dreadfully. At the same time he envied her social conscience, though he would never admit the fact. Then suddenly she reappeared. As he passed through Lyngby a snowball struck him in the back of the neck. She was hiding in a bus shelter and had decided to feel sorry for him. He was an unenlightened pig who couldn't help being deluded. He could come back to her place, seeing as how it was so cold out.

They wheeled their bikes together, hand in hand, little clouds of frosty breath illuminated by the street lamps, and forgot all about the cold. When they got to Klampenborg they free-wheeled down the long hill on Rita's bike, he in the saddle, she seated on the pannier rack, while he steered his own bike along-side them with his free hand, hoping none of his colleagues was patrolling in the area. It had to go wrong, and it did. They had almost reached the bottom when the rear wheel skidded out from under them on a bend. They slid across the road in a cascade of snow. Neither of them was in the slightest bit hurt and they lay there for a while, surrounded by the woods, laughing.

Then Rita took his head in her hands and began to sing again. This time gently, her pretty voice only for him:

From San Diego up to Maine,
in every mine and mill,
Where working men defend their rights,
it's there you'll find Joe Hill,
it's there you'll find Joe Hill!

And now her granddaughter sang the same song, flawlessly, and not a single music teacher in the land would surely have a word of criticism to say whereas for Konrad Simonsen, with his own memories and associations, it evoked an unsettling blend of suppressed emotion and grim reality. For a brief moment, Bo Widerberg's striking American and Swedish landscapes once again filled his mind, only to be superseded by a very recent photograph of sandy spruce plantations on Denmark's west coast, sent to him by Klavs Arnold after they'd located the holiday camp. Simonsen found himself gripped by a feeling of rage, not knowing where it came from, perhaps directed towards the girl onstage whose voice was so full, or her grandmother who had let the air out of his bicycle tyre, or Lucy Davison whose body lay in that sandy earth. Perhaps even towards them all.

Teresa Metz Andersen's final song, 'We Shall Overcome', disqualified her once and for all from the role of protest singer. Her performance was exquisite, demonstrating all too clearly that the closest she'd ever been to a cotton field was her well-fitting Patrizia Pepe tunic. She bowed demurely when she had finished, relinquishing the stage to the next young genius in line.

In the interval he thought about leaving and yet decided to stay, drinking a cup of weak coffee in a quiet corner of the foyer on his own, from where he could survey the crowd. Now and then his eyes darted this way or that, but mostly he felt calm and settled.

Returning inside, he discovered someone had opened his programme and placed it face down on his seat. He picked it up and stared at the hastily scribbled though clearly legible address, the date and time written in the top right corner, and with that he changed his mind and left, taking the programme with him.

On Monday morning Konrad Simonsen and Klavs Arnold commenced the search for Lucy Davison's body at Esbjerg's town hall, where an accommodating, albeit unexpressive deputy chief executive of the local authority provided them with two bespoke environmental maps from the planning department and permitted them to inspect the grounds of the former Vesterhavsgården with a view to isolating possible sources of pollution – a pretext Klavs Arnold found utterly superfluous, but for which Konrad Simonsen was grateful. The last thing he wanted at this stage was to have the tabloids tugging at his coat tails, and he knew from bitter experience how little it took before reporters suddenly materialised with their barrages of awkward, time-consuming questions.

For three hours they trudged round grounds that were criss-crossed with paths wide and narrow, trampled by the feet of countless children and maintained throughout generations. There was a group booked in at the camp, and now and again an inquisitive little face would pop up in the most unexpected of places, until eventually tiring of spying and deciding to let them get on with it.

Occasionally, when Klavs Arnold felt inclined, they chatted; otherwise they exchanged few words.

Simonsen's mind had turned inwards. He concentrated solely on the ground as if the girl in her grave might reveal herself to him if only he stared at it with sufficient intensity. His partner was evidently more used to being outdoors and consistently knew exactly where they were in relation to the main cabin and the gravel tracks surrounding the area. As time progressed and they found themselves retracing their footsteps for the third or fourth time, Simonsen gradually began to recognise various parts of the grounds.

'We can rule out anywhere near the bigger pines. The roots would have made it impossible to dig there, so we'd be wasting our time,' said Arnold.

'How much does a pine tree grow in forty years?'

'It depends what sort it is, but ten centimetres a year in general.'

'How do you know that?'

'I looked it up on the internet this morning while you were still snoring.'

Simonsen had slept in the spare room at Arnold's place and been woken for breakfast with the children, the object of curious looks from two boys, aged about seven or eight, who quizzed him with all sorts of questions when they weren't feeling too shy. Their dad was busy doing their packed lunches for school. *Is it true you've been on TV? Do you decide over our daddy? Haven't you got your own car?* Klavs Arnold returned to the table and chased them off to their school bags and bikes. Only then did Simonsen settle down to eat.

Later, after another half-hour of studying the ground, Arnold spoke again.

'Open, sandy areas less than fifty metres from the main cabin. That's my guess.'

'That doesn't exactly narrow it down.'

'True.'

Simonsen had his own suggestion.

'How about underneath one of the cabins? They're all built on posts, so it could be done without that much difficulty, unless you wanted to creep all the way in.'

'No, it'd be visible far too long. Open sandy earth is much, much better.'

They sat down under a pair of pine trees and devoured the packed lunches Arnold had made for them. The sun was out, but each passing cloud turned the air cold. Simonsen peered above the trees in search of the next patch of blue. High up in the sky, flocks of migrating birds flew south, long formations that changed shape unpredictably while always perfectly co-ordinated, as though steered by a single brain.

He got to his feet and they carried on.

And then, all at once, three hours of more or less random searching paid off. It was Klavs Arnold who noticed it first. Almost at the far corner of the grounds, by the drystone wall next to the track leading off to the main road, he stopped suddenly, like a predatory animal sensing its prey, and there, among the crowberries, peat and moss, above a little cluster of bell heather whose sad, lilac flowers, swayed this way and that in the breeze, Konrad Simonsen saw it, too: the stone in the wall, jutting out irregularly, reflecting the light mattly and in a way that seemed all too wrong. Both men bent down, and Klavs Arnold scraped at the stone with his finger.

'Candle wax.'

It didn't take them long before they found the bag, wrapped up in a clear, heavy-duty plastic sack and stuffed into a cavity in the wall, only a few metres from the stone covered in candle wax. They put on gloves and Klavs Arnold took photos.

'Do we need forensics?'

Simonsen shook his head.

'No, just be careful, that's all.'

'I always am, with this kind of thing.'

And so he was. It took a while before the bag was opened and its contents consigned one by one to evidence bags: a box of tea lights, three glass cylinders to protect the flames against the wind, a roll of plastic bags, a Bible and a small cushion. Some twenty metres away, in a thicket of raspberry bushes, they came upon a bundle of flower stalks held together by a red elastic band. Klavs Arnold commented expertly:

'They'd be more than a year old, probably two or three. My guess is we'll find more if we search through the thicket here. The wind's always in the west here. It'll have blown his flowers in this direction.'

Simonsen jabbed a finger at the ground in front of the candle-wax stone.

'Do you think this is where she is?'

'No, I think this is as far as he dared to go. He could kneel down here and pray and not be seen from the cabins or the track. But have we got a choice?'

'Not as far as I can see.'

* * *

The JCB was frustratingly slow, consuming the sandy earth shovel by shovel, one load after another drawn a few metres back, then meticulously swung out and deposited on the heap mounting behind them. Each time the blade of the shovel scraped another ten centimetres of soil away, the two men peered into the ground and held their breath for a moment, heads bowed at the edge of the hole, hoping and not hoping that the remains of Lucy Davison would emerge in front of them. The taxing experience lasted almost a couple of hours, without any other result than fraying their nerves. Eventually, they halted the work and left the operator to fill up the hole again on his own.

Simonsen was sufficiently realistic to acknowledge that his options were ebbing away. The discovery of Jørgen Kramer Nielsen's shrine was in no way earth-shattering. The holiday camp's guestbook from 1969, on his desk that Tuesday morning when he clocked in at Police HQ, without him having the faintest idea how it had got there, wasn't exactly a huge step forward either. True, the Gang of Six had dutifully written in their names, on Sunday 15 June 1969, and further investigation did reveal that no other guests had stayed at the place during the same week, but none of this information brought him the slightest bit closer to finding Lucy Davison's last resting place. Therefore it did not provide him with any basis on which he could justifiably put off confronting the four suspects. Moreover, there were three compelling arguments for going ahead with that procedure: the Countess, Arne Pedersen and Pauline Berg. He had solemnly given his word to Arne Pedersen that he would commence questioning with the minimum of delay, and it seemed to him that the time had come to make good on his promise.

However, support for continuing along the same track came suddenly from unexpected quarters. Simonsen had called yet another meeting and had this time skipped the introductory status report, reasoning that it wasn't going to tell anyone anything they didn't already know. Reluctantly, he announced that he had reached the decision they had been waiting for.

'We're going to bring them in now. First Hanne Brummersted, then Pia and Jesper Mikkelsen. One at a time, if possible. Finally Helena Brage Hansen, providing we can get her to Denmark. I spoke to her brother yesterday and asked him to call and have a word with her.'

Pedersen's voiced the general reaction.

'About time, but better late than never.'

The Countess and Pauline Berg gave their agreement. Klavs Arnold, however, begged to differ.

'Big mistake, if you ask me. Where's Plan B? What do we do when they refuse to come in?'

The man from Jutland looked like someone who could do with a week's holiday. Not only had he been criss-crossing the country for meetings and searches, he was also in the middle of moving house, not to mention having to look after all his kids.

The Countess responded:

'What makes you think they'd do that?'

'What makes you think they wouldn't? They'd be wasting their money on a good solicitor, because even a bad one's going to tear us to pieces. We've got nothing... nothing at all.'

There was something refreshingly direct about Klavs Arnold, Simonsen thought to himself. Despite his being new to the group, what he had to say was given full weight by the other members.

The Countess, however, wasn't convinced.

'If we're supposed to hold off on questioning suspects until sufficient evidence is gathered, we'd never get anyone put away, would we? What do you all reckon? Not you, Simon, we know where you stand. It's wide open again now, isn't it?'

Pauline Berg sighed.

'Oh, for fuck's sake, can't we agree on anything?'

Simonsen stared at her wearily. Her changing moods were getting to be a pain, though by now he'd at least learned to decode how she was feeling: if she swore a lot, it was a pretty good indication she was either in one of her... phases... or else well on her way to one. Earlier in the day he'd made an agreement with her and the woman from her annoying group – he couldn't remember her name offhand – to meet with Arthur Elvang the following day over at the Department of Forensic Medicine, as he had promised them that day in the rain out at Melby Overdrev. Truth be told, he'd been hoping she'd lose interest by now, but his hopes were dashed. And here she was, swearing her head off, when she wasn't in a sulk. He wondered if the two things might be connected – the appointment with Elvang and her sour mood. It seemed unlikely, but then again you never knew with Pauline. He glanced round the room and cut in authoritatively:

'We're bringing them in.'

Klavs Arnold accepted the decision without adverse comment. He wasn't the moaning kind. The choice was made, for better or worse, and only time would tell.

What Simonsen had to do now was decide who was going to conduct the interviews. Pedersen would have to be ruled out, having too much on his plate as it was. That left the Countess, Pauline Berg and Klavs Arnold, unless he wanted to bring in others from beyond the inner circle, something he was rarely inclined to do.

Had he been obliged to choose between them a month ago the matter would have been simple, but word had begun to circulate around HQ that Homicide's convalescent man-in-charge had a double killing on his hands. What had started out as a light-duty job wrapping up a report about a postman falling down the stairs had gradually morphed into every ambitious crime investigator's dream. Getting to be a part of clearing up a forty-year-old murder case wasn't the sort of thing that came round more than once in a blue moon. The Countess had even given him a couple of hints as to who she'd like to be brought in once they got round to questioning, mentioning the matter casually on several occasions without his needing to respond, even though her intentions were clear. Arne Pedersen had tried to rearrange his commitments in an effort to clear himself some space, albeit in vain.

It was not without excitement, then, that Simonsen's audience awaited his word. For his own part, it was something to which he'd given a good deal of thought already, striving to use solely his professional judgement. His decision was not for discussion.

'The Countess and I will deal with Hanne Brummersted and Helena Brage Hansen, if we can get her down here from Norway. Klavs and I are going to Aalborg the day after tomorrow, we need more of a hold on Pia and Jesper Mikkelsen. If we can question the two of them separately, the Countess and I will take care of Pia Mikkelsen and I'll handle Jesper Mikkelsen on my own, unless Arne finds the time.'

Pauline protested vociferously:

'That's not fair! I've been on this investigation from day one, and what do I get when the fun starts? Sod all, is what. *And* I'm slogging away at home reading all sorts of books on the dreary sixties.'

Simonsen endeavoured to calm her down.

'Pauline, it's not like that at all. It's crucial you keep yourself one hundred per cent abreast of the investigation in case anything untoward happens and one of us has to be pulled out. What's more, if there's going to be a second round I may want to switch you and the Countess. You could even step in for me.'

Pauline's obscene gesture told him in no uncertain terms what she thought of that. Klavs Arnold brought her back to earth.

'Calm down and hold your horses, Pauline. Simon's got a point, the way he's suggesting we do this, so let's discuss it like adults, shall we?'

The Countess grinned, though Simonsen himself stared at the man in bewilderment. Suggesting? Discuss? There was nothing more to talk about, he'd already told them how it was going to be.

'Er, Klavs, you've not been a part of these deliberations. As yet, I know nothing about your interview techniques, and this isn't a case where I want to experiment. What's more, you still don't know any of us well enough to understand how best to play off each other in an interview situation.'

Again, Arnold took this on the chin.

'No problem. I'd have made the same selection myself. And it does free up Pauline and me to dig a bit deeper into Hanne Brummersted, if you agree? And of course Pauline's going to Aalborg, too, you just forgot to say.'

'Did I? Oh...'

Arnold's argument was hard to counter. The Aalborg couple, and Jesper Mikkelsen in particular, were heavily involved in the nightclub business centred on the area around Jomfru Ane Gade in the middle of the city. It seemed they owned fifty per cent of the Rainbow Six club, a popular dancing and drinking place for young people from all over northern Jutland, but they were possibly involved in other ways, too, drugs and vice perhaps... that was what they needed to get up there and find out. And in that case they'd be daft not to have Pauline Berg with them, given the fact that she could so easily blend in to the nightclub environment, in rather stark contrast to Simonsen and Arnold himself.

Or that was Klavs Arnold's take on the matter.

Simonsen climbed down: yes, quite right... he'd forgotten to mention that Pauline would be going to Aalborg, too.

Her attitude was immediately transformed: from sullen to smiles in one second. Simonsen found himself wondering if now and then she took advantage of her illness, or whatever it was, to play the sulky schoolgirl. He resolved to have a word with her once the opportunity arose.

The Countess turned to Klavs Arnold.

'What was that about digging deeper into Hanne Brummersted? And why her especially?'

'She was in Sweden with Jørgen Kramer Nielsen, and of the four she's got most to lose.'

The Countess came back at him straight away.

'How come? The Aalborg couple own a thriving business with a takeover in the millions of kroner.'

'They can sell their records from their living room without hardly ever needing to get out and meet people. But our consultant doctor's got her image to think of, not to mention the respect of her daughters, maybe even her job, so she's hardly going to want to see herself on the front page of the tabloids. The effect it'd have on her two board positions alone would be disastrous.'

'Perhaps, but I think you're underestimating what the Mikkelsens have to gain. That is, assuming they weren't involved in killing either the girl or their former classmate.'

'Gain? Where's the gain in this?'

'Everything so far tells me they're stuck in a dead-end relationship. What's keeping them together?'

Klavs Arnold yielded.

'So you reckon they'd talk if they got the chance? To make amends, clear up in the past and present? It's not a bad take, I'll buy that.'

Simonsen probed further:

'Perhaps Jørgen Kramer Nielsen broke some kind of covenant or pact that the others have upheld. Perhaps they are in touch, all four of them.'

'Guesswork,' Klavs Arnold retorted.

Pauline Berg shook her head in resignation, rather than annoyance.

'If, and perhaps, and a few tentative maybes for good measure! I don't get why we don't just send that postcard we got from the UK over to Kurt Melsing and get a DNA-analysis done, see if we get a match to our doctor woman. There's got to be a fifty per cent chance she licked the stamp.'

They all fell silent and gawped at her as if she'd just flown round the room. Pauline's former uncertainty bubbled up.

'What are you looking at me like that for? Was it a stupid thing to say? Can't they do that after so many years? Or did we do it already? I might not be up-to-date, I've not had the chance to catch up the last few days... Anyway, I'm sorry. I can see now we've got nothing to compare it with, and Hanne Brummersted's not going to agree to a test, is she? Apologies, go on.'

The Countess was the one to break their silence. She turned to Klavs Arnold.

'There's your Plan B.'

Simonsen beamed.

'Brilliant, Pauline. Absolutely brilliant.'

Again, however, the Countess said what no one wanted to hear.

'But is it at all possible to get DNA after forty years?'

Simonsen's smile became even wider.

'I've no idea.'

'Then why are you laughing?'

'Because if I don't know, Hanne Brummersted won't either.'

'That's true. As a way of talking her round it might work. It'd be useless in court, though, unless she agreed of her own accord to have a sample taken for comparison.'

'Wrong, Countess. We get hold of a sample we can prove is from her, preferably without her knowledge, and then we get her DNA. That would stick all the way.'

'Rubbish. No judge would ever accept that.'

'Not in this country, no. But what about Sweden or the UK? Inadmissibility of evidence relates to jurisdiction not the organic matter itself.'

'All right, so we're being clever. Probably too clever by half.'

'Perhaps, but if she did lick that stamp, our good doctor could find herself in a rather nasty position. And if she didn't, there's still a pretty decent chance she's forgotten whether she did or not.'

That evening the Countess took up the positive results of their discussion. At least on the personal level, for the professional side of things stayed behind in the office. It was what she preferred in her own home, and Simonsen respected her for it – as well as for the fact that she could easily break her own rule if she found it suited her.

They were standing in the kitchen. Simonsen was chopping cabbage, a discipline at which he now excelled. The Countess was slicing beetroot, while Anna Mia sat on a chair exuding moral support.

'That was really good of you, giving Pauline that pat on the back today,' the Countess commented. 'She was glad of it, I can tell you. It was just what she needed.'

'She deserved it. Funny no one thought of it before, though, about DNA on the stamp.'

'I'm glad she was the one who did. It hasn't been easy for her after Klavs Arnold came in. Quite apart from everything else she's got to deal with.'

'Klavs Arnold's not against her.'

'I know, and he's slotted in very easily himself, but I think she feels she's the weakest link, even if she isn't the last one in any more.'

'She is, too,' retorted Simonsen.

'Well, I suppose so, but she needed the boost.'

'Why haven't you given her one before, then? A pat on the back doesn't cost much.'

'Now you're being stupid, Konrad Simonsen.'

Anna Mia joined forces, munching on her second carrot and jabbing what was left of the vegetable at her father accusingly.

'Happy workers work better. All the studies agree.'

'No, they show that workers who work well are happy workers. But that doesn't fit in with the touchy-feely modern workplace, so instead they changed it round and switched cause and effect. And in so doing created thousands of superfluous administrative positions to weigh and measure and keep on feeding the myth.'

The Countess laid her head on his shoulder.

'You don't mean that, and you're not fooling us for a second. We know you too well. Anyway, how many cubic metres of cabbage do you think we can actually eat?'

'I enjoy chopping. It runs away with me, that's all.'

'Pauline hasn't been doing too well of late. After you took her off that problem page research she started ploughing through everything she can find about the sixties on the internet, as well as just about every book she can get her hands on. In the evenings, off duty.'

'So I gathered from what she said. But her being taken off Helena Brage Hansen's column research had nothing to do with her not knowing about the sixties. It was more a matter of Pauline not being able to glean a thing about someone else's personality.'

The Countess ignored him and carried on regardless.

'She's upset, too, about having to ask if she could be involved when you invited Madame to look at your gallery, which, by the way, will have to go back to Kramer Nielsen's estate very soon. She felt she was being overlooked. But she'll be coming back, as it happens. Her therapist has told her she ought to.'

'Fine by me. But you could have brought her home any time to see my... to look at those posters.'

'That wouldn't be the same, would it, silly? Sometimes you've got no idea how you affect people, have you?'

Anna Mia stole another carrot and pitched in:

'Sometimes meaning never. Word is you patted a dog handler on the back. A colleague in Glostrup's going round bragging about it, did you know?'

The Countess followed up:

'Even the executives love it when you praise them. Not to mention Arne. He beams like a little kid whenever you get your act together to give him a word of encouragement.'

Simonsen shrugged indifferently, prompting the Countess to throw up her arms in despair, turning to Anna Mia, who shook her head and said:

'He'll never learn. Can't you peel some more carrots? We're running out.'

'You can have some cabbage.'

Simonsen looked at the Countess.

'You're talking about all the others. What about when I give you a pat on the back?' He sounded surprisingly serious all of a sudden.

She put her arms round him by way of reply and hugged him tightly. Anna Mia whistled.

'Did we hear wedding bells?'

'You mean, is your father going to make an honest woman of me? Well, he hasn't actually asked yet.'

The Countess sounded cheerful and breezy about it. And yet both women's antennae were out, and ultra-sensitive to Simonsen's reaction. His answer, however, was frank and to the point.

'How about when I retire? Will you still want me then? Lounging about the house while you're at work?'

She hugged him again.

'I'd love it. You could do up the basement, mow the lawns and do the weeding. Maybe even find time to mend that socket in the outhouse like you've been promising to do for the last fortnight. And don't forget, I'll be older too. I want to sit in a rocking chair by the fire and knit you a woolly hat, a nice warm one to cover your ears and hide the fact you'll have no hair left.'

Anna Mia cheered.

'All you've got to do is say the magic word, Dad, and it looks like you can stay on here for ever.'

The Countess turned her head, though still resting it against Simonsen's chest. She flashed Anna Mia a playful smile.

'I could knit a little jumper, too, for your third grandchild.'

Konrad Simonsen spun round and stared at his daughter. Or rather, his daughter's stomach. The Countess let go of him and followed his gaze. Anna Mia got to her feet, displeased with the turn the conversation had suddenly taken.

'That's for me to decide, thank you very much. Let me set the table.'

Finn B. Hansen, Helena Brage Hansen's elder brother, had come to Copenhagen, more specifically to Konrad Simonsen's office. The tape recorder he'd brought with him lay on the desk between them, a clumsy, prehistoric monstrosity but nonetheless in full working order.

'I hope you won't tell Helena I recorded her on tape. If you ever need to speak to her, that is.'

'I won't. It'll be between the two of us.'

'I'll be taking the tape with me when I leave. And I shall destroy it afterwards.'

'It's your tape.'

'Indeed. Just so we're in agreement.'

'Why did you record her?'

'Because I thought that if by some chance she did happen to reveal where that poor girl was buried... in case I forgot...'

'I understand.'

'But let's just start the tape, shall we? The beginning's private and isn't relevant to you, so I'll skip that bit.'

'All right.'

Hansen repeated himself, rather more firmly than necessary, Simonsen thought:

'I'm only going to let you hear what's relevant. No more than that, and I won't be moved as far as that's concerned.'

'Of course.'

He pressed a button and Simonsen listened carefully to the voices on the tape:

'Helena, there's something I have to tell you. The criminal department of the Copenhagen police are looking into a trip you and some of your classmates made a long time ago to Esbjerg.'

There was a long pause before she answered.

'I see.'

Two small words, and yet easily sufficient to hear the tremor in her voice.

'Do you remember it at all, Helena? A trip to Esbjerg?'

Again, she hesitated.

'Helena, are you there?'

'No.'

'What do you mean, no?'

'Esbjerg. I don't remember that at all.'

'They've got photos of you. Old photos with you in them. You stayed at a Scout camp, a cabin Dad had let you use. You were revising for exams. And you were part of a group.'

'What group? I've never been to any Scout camp. I've never even been to Esbjerg. I'm not on any photos, and I certainly didn't kill anyone!'

'Kill anyone? Why do you say that?'

'Because it's true.'

'I think it would be a good idea for you to come to Copenhagen, Helena, don't you?'

'I don't want to go to Copenhagen. I'm a Norwegian citizen. No one can make me.'

'A girl died there. A girl your age at the time. Seventeen.'

'I don't want to know.'

'Helena, you can't just ignore this.'

'Yes, I can. Denmark no longer exists for me.'

'I'm afraid it does. And I think you really must…'

Finn B. Hansen stopped the tape:

'She hung up on me.'

Simonsen looked at the tape recorder. Hansen followed his gaze.

'I won't give it to you.'

'No, I understand that.'

'It wouldn't help you in any case.'

'Why not?'

'As evidence it's completely useless, of course. And if you pressure her, she'll break down and then you won't be able to make any contact at all with her after that. Believe me, I know what I'm talking about. I've seen it lots of times, when we were young. It's not what any of us wants.'

'No, that wouldn't be beneficial, I can see that. So what you're saying is that I should leave her alone, is that it?'

'I think so, yes.'

'She said she hadn't killed anyone before you even mentioned anything about Lucy... Lucy Davison, that is, the missing girl from the UK. You're aware of what that indicates to us, obviously.'

Hansen nodded solemnly, and when he spoke again he was almost begging.

'Can't you try her classmates first?'

'Perhaps.'

'Will you be seeking extradition?'

'We'd prefer not to, so only as a last resort.'

'I hope it won't be necessary. Her mental health is poor enough as it is.'

Simonsen regretted the matter, but he would have no option if she maintained the stance she had already taken.

'I'm afraid I'll have to keep your tape, but you realise that, of course?'

'Of course. I just hoped it wouldn't be necessary.'

Konrad Simonsen would have preferred to have skipped the visit to the University of Copenhagen's Department of Forensic Medicine and had avoided thinking about the matter until now.

Annoyed, he pulled open the bottom drawer of his desk and lifted out the stack of documents that resided there, proceeding with sighs of displeasure to leaf hastily through some of the pages. As he had expected, Juli Denissen's unfortunate death out at Melby Overdrev had been twisted and turned in order to look like the result of a conspiracy between the Frederikssund Police and the emergency services, which contradicted all ordinary common sense. It was a shambles of a report, concluded by ten – not nine or eleven, but ten – questions sowing doubt on Juli Denissen's having died from natural causes. Simonsen ran through the list and found it beyond ridiculous. Nonetheless, he took a deep breath and phoned the chief constable in

Frederikssund, who with little trouble was able to furnish him with perfectly reasonable answers to most of the questions.

Why was it never established how the woman and her daughter had got to Melby Overdrev? The answer here was simple: it was. Juli Denissen had borrowed her friend's car and had moreover been witnessed by two different motorists on account of her overcautious slow driving, attributable to the fact that she had only just passed her driving test a few days previously. *How could the jogger in the woods who found the woman's body call the emergency services when there was no mobile coverage at Melby Overdrev?* He could because his own provider's coverage, as opposed to that of more popular companies, was in fact more than adequate in that location.

Only one question puzzled Simonsen. It was to do with why Juli Denissen had walked almost two kilometres over the grasslands away from the car park. It seemed odd considering the fact she had a two-year-old child with her. Odd, but then no more than that. All he could do was accept that she had done so. And that the question was of little interest in light of her having died of a brain haemorrhage. He glanced at his watch, still feeling annoyed; more annoyed, in fact, than he had done before. He had been thinking he might walk over to the Department of Forensic Medicine, but he hadn't got time now and would have to take the car. He dumped the pile of documents back in the drawer, kicked it shut and left.

He was lucky to find a parking space on Trepkasgade and arrived at the department ten minutes before the appointed time for his meeting with Arthur Elvang. On the steps of the main entrance, three people were waiting for him. He nodded a greeting to Pauline Berg, who smiled and was visibly glad to see him, then exchanged a rather offish handshake with the woman he had first met out on Melby Overdrev and whose name suddenly came back to him: Linette Krontoft. She looked like someone who ought to have stayed in bed: her face was blotched and bloated, her eyes glassy as if she'd been out all night on a bender. Her handshake was limp. He wiped his hand on his sleeve and hoped he wasn't going to catch anything. Then, finally, he turned to the man who accompanied Krontoft.

He was in his thirties, slimly built and of average height, with plain features. He put his hand out with exaggerated conviviality.

'You must be Simon. I'm August and I'm part of the group trying to find out why Juli died.'

Simonsen's greeting was rather more reserved. He looked the man up and down without speaking. August went on somewhat hectically, as if sensing a question unasked.

'I live in Helsinge, actually, but I run a cheese shop in Frederiksværk. Just by the station, left-hand side as the train comes in from Hillerød, between the florist's and the sandwich bar. You can't miss it.'

The thought occurred to Simonsen that he had indeed missed it, and had been doing quite all right despite that fact, and indeed hoped the happy state of affairs would continue, but he said nothing. His silence prompted the man to explain further:

'Juli worked in the shop for me a couple of days a week. She only lived three hundred metres down the road, so it was just the jo...'

He pressed a conspiratorial finger to his lips before charmlessly adding:

'On the sly, of course, so don't let on to the taxman. But for a time I knew her quite well... I mean, very well, indeed, if you get my drift.'

He winked suggestively, and Simonsen found himself thinking he'd seldom met a person he found so immediately objectionable. He glanced at the wedding ring on the cheese-monger's finger:

'*Juli and August*, how funny. You must have had a good laugh about that the first time you met. *Juli and August*, such a nice match. I don't suppose your wife would have thought so, though? Still, there'll be plenty of opportunities to ask her if the case is reopened – which, however, I doubt.'

The man blushed and stepped back behind Linette Krontoft as though to hide himself. If that was the intention, it wasn't a bad place to choose. But then all of a sudden Simonsen froze. The cheesemonger's windcheater was open and the top buttons of his shirt had been left undone, presumably to demonstrate his masculinity to the world by suggesting he didn't feel the cold. Around his neck was a fish on a silver chain. The cross, the fish and the Chi-Rho Christogram, three signs of Christianity... Madame's words of warning in the gallery about listening to the Christian man he didn't like rang in his ears. Perhaps his meeting here wouldn't be a waste of time after all. He smiled to himself, and poked a finger towards Linette Krontoft.

'The agreement was that two people could attend this meeting, and that's what I told the professor. Now there's three of you, so if that doesn't suit him you're the one who leaves, and without a fuss. Understood?'

She looked a bit nonplussed, but agreed nevertheless.

The room in which Professor Arthur Elvang received his visitors was bare to the point of emptiness. The walls had just been painted white and the floorboards had obviously very recently been planed and varnished. The place smelled of pinewood and decorating. The furnishings were as sparse as could be and in marked contrast to the newness of the rest of the room. Five classroom desks, the old-fashioned wooden kind with desk and seat all in one, as Simonsen remembered them from his own schooldays, had been arranged in a semi-circle around a larger, more regular desk of recent date. On this latter piece of furniture lay a stack of papers, neatly gathered and placed in meticulous alignment with its foremost edge. Next to them was a seemingly cylindrical object of some thirty centimetres in height covered up by a black cloth that prevented further investigation. Behind the desk sat the professor himself.

He greeted them aloofly in turn and gestured for them to sit down. They edged their way with difficulty on to their seats. Simonsen and Linette Krontoft in particular found it all a bit of a squeeze. He wondered where Elvang had dug up such antiques, but thought a good guess would be the rearmost corner of a storage room in the furthest depths of the department's basement. Once they were all seated, the professor began.

Simonsen was in no doubt whatsoever that the purpose of all this was to humiliate them: it was the professor's little joke, a sarcastic comment on the matter at hand. Nonetheless, he had feared Elvang making no effort at all to appear convincing to his select audience. Now, however, he could see this was not the case. On the contrary, the professor introduced himself by rattling off a selection of his many titles, as well as a number of executive positions on company boards of directors. Most of it was new to Simonsen and he found himself thinking that the old man to his credit had never appeared snobbish or so overly pleased with himself as to broadcast unnecessarily his many academic and professional attainments. However, the no-doubt severely abridged curriculum vitae he now outlined certainly had the desired effect, Linette Krontoft raising a respectful finger in the air and dutifully waiting to speak until the professor indicated that she might.

'Would the professor mind if we recorded his appraisal of the case on a Dictaphone? We know some people who would very much appreciate listening to what he has to say.'

Simonsen interrupted immediately in an attempt to avert the danger, but to no avail, the professor putting him in his place by stating that they were free to record as much as they liked. Permission granted, Linette Krontoft extracted herself from behind her seating arrangement and placed her Dicta-phone on the professor's desk, whereupon his assessment of Juli Denissen's autopsy report could begin. Elvang's tinny voice enunciated:

'Juli Denissen, twenty-four years old, deceased tenth of July two thousand and eight at Melby Overdrev, district of Halsnæs, post-mortem performed eleventh and twelfth July, Department of Forensic Medicine, Hillerød General Hospital, consultant Hans Arne Tholstrup.'

He screwed up his eyes and squinted at the report, to Simonsen's pleasure explaining that normally in the country's eastern region all post-mortems were done by the Rigshospitalet in the capital, but in particularly busy periods the hospital at Hillerød would also be used. This was one of the ten concerns the group had raised.

Elvang looked up and endeavoured in vain to focus through the lenses of his glasses on each member of his audience in turn, then solemnly continued:

'The validity of this autopsy report is beyond question.'

With that he nodded a couple of times as though confirming the fact to himself before going on with his assessment while leafing through his papers.

'A number of samples were taken. Vaginal, anal, oral. From the pharynx and the cavum oris, which is to say palate and oral cavity. Moreover, biopsies of the skin, liver, kidneys and thyroid, as well as samples of blood and hair, were taken – the simple reason for all this being that two students were involved in the procedure as part of their training. At any rate, we may conclude that the deceased was examined very thoroughly indeed, much more so than would normally be the case. Subsequent analyses, however, reveal no signs whatsoever of poisoning or anything else, shall we say, untoward.'

302

He peered questioningly at something in the report – at what exactly, Simonsen was unable to see – then shook his head as though in annoyance. It was a sure sign, in Simonsen's experience, that someone, somewhere along the line, had made an error. None of the others seemed to notice this indication of the professor's irritation, and his conclusion was emphatic.

'Quite categorically, then, the woman was not poisoned. Moreover there is no poison or any other chemical substance capable of triggering what she died of, which is to say a severe subarachnoid haemorrhage, that is a bleeding into the space between the brain and its protective membrane.'

He then provided a detailed account of how the haemorrhage in the woman's brain had caused pressure to build up on her respiratory centre, leading to her being unable to breathe. After that, he spent some time explaining that approximately one per cent of the population was born with such aneurysms – blood-filled bulges in the wall of the brain's blood vessels – and that these abnormities could rupture due to physical or mental strain, for instance while playing sport or during sexual intercourse.

'The symptoms are severe headache, a stiff neck, nausea and vomiting, and often subsequent loss of consciousness or death. In this case, death occurred very swiftly, perhaps in the space of a minute, two at most, the reason being that the bleeding was unusually massive, which although not normally the case, is certainly not unusual.'

Again, he looked up and scanned his audience.

'I asked for autopsy photographs from the hospital in Hillerød, and after the woman's skull was opened and a portion of her brain removed, the haemorrhage itself is plainly visible. Not knowing if you would be comfortable with these images, I brought along a more anonymous example for you to see instead.'

He indicated the cylinder on the desk with the black cloth over it.

'Which would you prefer? The original photographs of Juli Denissen, or the specimen here?'

Simonsen smiled to himself. The professor had obviously decided to pay him back for having tidied his lawn for him. When the others were too hesitant to reply, Elvang made the decision on their behalf and pulled the cloth from the specimen with a flourish. The head in the jar was split down the middle, permitting a view of the interior of the brain. Simonsen couldn't help gloating secretly as he watched the unsavoury cheesemonger pale to the colour of Brie. The women present swallowed visibly. The professor plucked a biro from the pocket of his white coat and used it as a pointer as he explained to them exactly what they were looking at.

'At the time of his death, this man was twenty years old. He died in 1903, the cause being a massive cerebral haemorrhage which...'

His summary of the process of death took almost fifteen minutes and was pure sensationalism, the sole purpose being to illustrate how Juli Denissen's death too was due to natural causes.

When he was done he peered wearily at his audience.

'Any questions?'

His attitude was clearly not inviting, but nonetheless the cheesemonger ventured a query

'From when this eurysm, or whatever, burst, to when Juli was dead... would she have had time to think or feel anything?'

Professor Arthur Elvang stared at him through thick lenses.

'How on earth would I know? I've never died of a brain haemorrhage, and have no idea what it feels like.'

The old man had a point, they could see that, and for a brief optimistic moment Simonsen thought they were finished. The matter could be closed, the group – or whatever they called themselves – could be dissolved, and, most importantly, Pauline Berg would realise that her private involvement in Juli Denissen's death had been nothing but a diversion.

He was allowed to content himself with this illusion for about five seconds. Just as he was about to rise and thank the professor, Linette Krontoft raised another point.

'How do you know Juli was only alive for two minutes after her attack? You said yourself it was very fast.'

'We can ascertain as much by measuring the adrenalin, both that in the bloodstream and that which accumulated in her brain. Adrenalin leaves the blood rather quickly when oxygenated, but the bleeding in the brain receives no oxygen since it doesn't circulate in the bloodstream. Tests can be done on it, allowing us to estimate fairly accurately the length of time between haemorrhage and death, and our calculations indicate two minutes at most.'

'But why did she have adrenalin in her bloodstream at all? Is that normal?'

The question came from Pauline Berg. Elvang replied:

'Quite normal. Adrenalin is released when a person is afraid, as I'm sure you know. Normally adrenalin content is measured in the urine. Juli Denissen's result indicates 11.55 micromoles of adrenalin per litre of urine, which is tremendously high, more than seventy-five times greater than the median and as high as anything I've seen. We can deduce that she must have suffered a state of extreme alarm. Most conceivably, that's what triggered the rupture of her aneurysm. That said, however, she would almost certainly have died from the congenital condition sooner or later.'

'But what made her so afraid?'

The cheesemonger weighed in:

'She's right, no one gets scared on purpose.'

Elvang stared wearily at Simonsen, who sensed he had to intervene.

'Obviously that's not a medical issue. Besides, there's no way of saying one way or the other; any number of things could have given her a fright.'

'But something scared her, we've just heard she was in a state of alarm,' said Pauline Berg, looking animated now.

'Yes, but it could have been anything, for goodness' sake. Some thought that suddenly occurred to her and made her upset... perhaps her daughter came across an adder in the grass, or maybe it was a sudden crack of thunder... we'll never know.'

Simonsen noted the resigned exchange of glances between Linette Krontoft and the cheesemonger, both of them seemingly accepting his point. The professor's run-through of the facts appeared to have done the job. Only Pauline remained unconvinced. He gave her a look of despair, only for her to meet his gaze without wavering, repeating her objection:

'There must have been something, Simon. Something frightened the life out of her. But what?'

He shook his head and thought to himself that at least they'd got rid of her group. Then he considered what the cheesemonger had said. *No one gets scared on purpose.* It was the only intelligent thing he had uttered, if indeed it could be called intelligent. *No one gets scared on purpose.* What the hell was he supposed to do with that?

Hanne Brummersted, consultant of the Department of Clinical Genetics, Herlev Hospital, greeted the Countess and Simonsen at her place of work, in a meeting room not unlike the one Simonsen was familiar with from the Rigshospitalet. Here the two officers ran into a wall of memory loss.

Hanne Brummersted couldn't recall ever having been to Esbjerg. She didn't remember any of her classmates, and had no memory of any girl from the UK. She didn't know if she'd been to Sweden, but even if she had, she certainly had no recollection of any tent, nor of any postcard for that matter. She'd also completely forgotten that she'd had to resit her maths exam in her final year of gymnasium school, and similarly couldn't think of why she might have missed the exam proper. She had no idea if she'd ever been in touch with any of her former classmates after they went their separate ways, but she believed not. She didn't know who Jørgen Kramer Nielsen was, and hadn't the foggiest notion of why he, too, might have failed to turn up for the same exam.

Thus, she rattled off her list of everything she couldn't remember, a long and well-rehearsed monologue that indicated quite clearly that she'd been prepared for this very situation for a good many years indeed. And when asked by the Countess if there was anything else she'd forgotten, she merely replied, without a hint of irony, that she couldn't remember.

Simonsen placed the four photos from the Vesterhavsgården on the table in front of her.

'You're in all of these. Does that jog your memory in any way?'

'I can't deny I was there. I just don't remember it, that's all.'

She spoke to him as if explaining something difficult to a child.

'If you'd care to look at these photographs, perhaps you might recall.'

'That won't be necessary. It won't help.'

'Does the name Lucy Davison mean anything to you? Lucy Selma Davison?'

'Not in the slightest.'

'That's the name of the English girl you're with in the photos.'

'If you say so. I have no recollection of any English girl.'

'That's funny, because you and your friends killed her and buried her body.'

'I have no recollection of that, and what's more I don't believe you.'

'You killed Jørgen Kramer Nielsen, too. You broke his neck.'

'I did not kill Jørgen Kramer Nielsen, whoever he may be.'

Simonsen pointed out the discrepancy between her not remembering if she'd killed Lucy Davison, and yet being perfectly adamant that she had not killed Jørgen Kramer Nielsen. To which she calmly and with detachment replied that memory was a highly complex phenomenon. And what did he think he was trying to achieve?

'Tell me about your childhood.'

'I most certainly will not.'

The Countess stepped in, visibly seething.

'You most certainly will. Unless you want us to call a patrol car and have a couple of uniformed officers drag you out of here in handcuffs.'

Simonsen and the Countess both noted the momentary tremor in the woman's upper lip before she turned back to Simonsen.

'My childhood was quite ordinary. I grew up in Vallensbæk. My father was a baker and my mother helped out in the shop. We lived in a flat. Two children, me and my older brother.'

'What school did you go to?'

'Gammel Vallensbæk Skole.'

'What was the name of your class teacher?'

'We had two. Miss Juncker from Years 1 to 6, then after that Miss Guldbrandsen.'

'Were you bright at school?'

'Fairly.'

'After Year 9 you went on to the gymnasium school, is that right?'

'Yes.'

'Brøndbyøster Gymnasium, maths and science stream.'

'Yes, but I don't remember anything from that time.'

'Only from your comprehensive school?'

'That's correct.'

'So when does your memory kick in again?'

'At medical school.'

'And the gymnasium is a blank?'

'That's very accurately put, yes.'

'You were involved in a group calling yourselves the Lonely Hearts Club, popularly referred to as the Hearts for short.'

'I don't remember that.'

'But you do realise how unlikely it sounds that you should remember nothing at all from that time?'

'It can't be helped. I remember nothing. I think I smoked a lot of cannabis in those days. But my memory's rather vague about that, too, I'm afraid.'

Simonsen got to his feet in frustration.

'Very convenient. You've done a good job thinking all this through, and now you're sitting there wondering what I'm going to do about it, isn't that right?'

He went over to the window and looked out, pretending to be giving the matter some thought. He opened the window and lit a cigarette. It tasted like soap, strong and unpleasant. Brummersted protested immediately.

'You're not allowed to smoke in here.'

'Too late, I already am.'

He saw her suddenly thrown into turmoil by his refusal to co-operate, then after a moment she decided she didn't want any unnecessary confrontation. She opened a drawer, took out an ashtray and placed it in front of her before lighting a cigarette of her own. Simonsen sat down again.

'We'll smoke one only, after that you'll have to wait,' said Brummersted.

'I'll smoke as many as I like,' Simonsen replied. 'Now look at this photo.'

She did as he said.

'So what's your question?' she asked after a moment.

The Countess answered.

'There is no question.'

'So we're finished, are we?'

'Not by a long chalk. I think you're scared.'

The woman said nothing. The Countess continued:

'Deep down, you know perfectly well it doesn't matter how much prestige you've got, how fancy your education and your job, how many scholarly associations you're a member of, how many friends you've got in high places – because none of it's going to help you with this one iota. The only thing you've got to cling to is the flimsy claim that you can't remember.'

'I'm not scared in the slightest.'

'And I don't believe you. I think you're very scared indeed that word of your convenient loss of memory is going to get out and people are going to know.'

'And how would that happen? You've no right to…'

'Ah, touched on a soft spot, did we? Your voice is trembling. But just like we can't do much about your not being able to remember, you've got no influence on what the papers say.'

'You wouldn't dare.'

This time it was the Countess who got to her feet. She picked up the ashtray and dropped it out of the window.

'What a stink. Anyway, where were we? Oh, yes. You think we're nice, decent people who'd never dream of tipping off our friends in the gutter press about a juicy little scandal involving a well-respected consultant. Well, I'm telling you, we're not. The question is, of course, whether it might jog your memory a bit?'

'Are you threatening me?'

'As a matter of fact, I am.'

Hanne Brummersted clenched her teeth and stared into space. Eventually, she spoke.

'I don't remember.'

The Countess altered tack.

'Lucy Davison was seventeen years old. Doesn't that affect you in any way?'

'I've no idea who you're talking about.'

'Both her parents are still alive. They live in Liverpool. For years they travelled around Scandinavia trying to find their daughter. Praying to God and saving up so they could come back and search for her again. Now they're too old, and their only hope is that their daughter's remains can be returned home before they die.'

'Someone ought to tell them God apparently decided to leave their daughter somewhere other than where it suited them.'

The Countess's eyes flashed with rage. She leaned close to the other woman's face, stared her in the eye and said in a voice as quiet and as cold as ice:

'I'm going to make you cry for that. I'll make sure of it.'

CHAPTER 10

'Can you please take me to people who know something about Jesper and Pia Mikkelsen?'

Simonsen's voice was firm if somewhat weary. He was seated in a conference room he'd borrowed at Aalborg's Hotel Budolfi, from where he could see out over the waters of the Limfjord through the window on one side, while on his other sat two officers of the Aalborg Politi. The policemen had gone on for half an hour about the city's nightlife, a matter with which they seemed very familiar, though without their seemingly encyclopaedic knowledge encompassing even the smallest crumb of information on what interested Simonsen, which was the Mikkelsen couple. Next to him, lounging in an armchair, was Pauline Berg, who now chipped in.

'It's not your fault. You didn't ask to get sent over to us, and you can't help it if you've never heard of the couple we want to know about. But the thing is we've been promised we could speak to some people who have, and obviously they sent us the wrong ones.'

She could have added that it was no wonder Aalborg, the country's fourth-largest city, comprising some 125,000 inhabitants, was having a hard time trying to combat problems of violence, drugs and prostitution, but she refrained. Instead, she paused before she painted them a very unflattering picture.

'So, basically, I think it would be a good idea if you got back to your station and told your superiors you're a non-starter. And then you can say from us that if someone doesn't get their finger out sharpish, they can look forward to a word of encouragement from the National Police Commissioner who I'm sure...'

Simonsen intervened.

'Thanks, Pauline, that'll do. I think we've all got the idea.'

He thanked the two officers half-heartedly for their time and showed them the door. As they were leaving, one of them hesitated.

'If you're out on the town questioning, it'd be a good idea to take some back-up along. Were you thinking of going tonight?'

'Yes, we were, as a matter of fact, and thanks for the offer. If we need any help we'll get in touch. What we want for the moment, though, is some background on Jesper and Pia Mikkelsen.'

'If you want us to organise a raid on Rainbow Six, it'll be tomorrow at the earliest, maybe Saturday. The place'll be heaving then, though. Thursday tends to be fairly quiet.'

Pauline Berg removed her legs from the armrest of her chair and sighed heavily.

'There's no need for a raid for what we want. Can't you get it into your heads, the only thing we need from you lot is some reliable information?'

The officers left. Simonsen found himself thinking he'd gone about this all the wrong way. Willing co-operation and support from local police was crucial. No one cared much for arrogant Copenhageners thinking they ran the country. He put it down to being tired and promised himself to phone the duty sergeant at Aalborg East where the two officers were from and apologise for his behaviour. He looked at Pauline and corrected himself: he would apologise for his colleague's behaviour. He studied her for a second.

'How are you feeling anyway?'

He'd meant to ask her on the plane over, had decided even before leaving that it would be a good opportunity. But as things turned out they'd ended up sitting several rows apart. Now would be as good a time as any, he thought. It would still be a while before Klavs Arnold got there. He was on his way from Esbjerg by car and surely wouldn't arrive until after lunch.

Pauline lifted her head and looked at Simonsen, and for a moment he thought she wasn't going to answer. But then she spoke, and when she did her words were measured.

'Not that good, I'm afraid. But thanks for asking.'

There was an uncomfortable silence. He stared out of the window. On the dock, a crane was unloading a container from a ship. A man in a hi-vis jacket waved his arms, though Simonsen couldn't see what for. After a moment she spoke again.

'At night I keep dreaming she's calling out to me.'

He froze and shook his head imperceptibly.

'I wish you'd let that... case... go.'

'I'd like to. At least, sometimes I would. Other times I'm convinced there's something not right. Something that's never come to light, never been investigated.'

Neither of them uttered the name, as if both of them wished to avoid it. And yet they knew what they were talking about: the Juli Denissen case, that wasn't a case at all. The dead woman Pauline Berg still couldn't put out of her mind.

Simonsen wished he hadn't asked. Pauline went on, despondently:

'That case is going to haunt me for a long time to come, I can feel it. I can't let go of it, even though I want to. But if it's any consolation to you, I'm on my own with it now. Nobody else sees the point any more.'

'I was thinking more about how you we were feeling generally.'

'I know. And the answer is: not good a lot of the time. The last few weeks at work I've been scared stiff I'm going to burst out crying any minute. Just like that, for no reason. I feel like crying now.'

'It wouldn't matter if you did.'

She laughed, but her eyes were serious.

'Hypocrite. You can't stand women crying.'

It was true. He smiled at her and thought the exact opposite of what he'd thought two seconds before: that now and again they understood each other.

'I'm reading a lot of stuff from the sixties,' she said, 'and watching films from the era. I was at the library on Saturday going through newspapers from nineteen sixty-nine on the microfiche down in the basement. There was this striplight that kept flickering all the time, it was annoying the shit out of me.'

'Is that because I took you off Helena Brage Hansen's problem pages?'

'No, not really.'

She stared into space before going on.

'When I do a thing, I tend to go all the way. Sometimes I take things to extremes. It's the same with men, but you wouldn't want to hear about that, would you?'

'Yes, I would.'

What the hell else was he supposed to say? Of course he didn't.

'I know I'm being a pain. But I'm going to tell you now, my life's like some terrible dream, a dark and heavy storm, and I can't wake up from it. I can never sleep at night, a few minutes at a time is all I can manage unless I take pills, and the more I take, the more I need. I can't concentrate either. I can't remember things. And then there's the feeling of being scared, it's there all the time. Sometimes I can cope with it, other times it's bad. I don't think it's ever going to leave me again.'

She paused, adding without self-pity:

'I can't help it.'

'No, of course not. No one gets scared on purpose.'

She seemed not to hear him.

'I think sometime... I mean, all that nostalgia you're piling up inside yourself... but what about me, two thousand and eight, here and now?'

Simonsen folded his arms and considered her, cursing himself inside.

She began to cry. Nonetheless, her voice remained quite calm.

'Leave me alone for a bit. I just need to sit here on my own. I'll see you at lunch.'

As he closed the door behind him he wondered if he should take her some tissues. But on the other hand... she'd said she wanted to be on her own. He felt in need of a cigarette, and spineless because of it, but at the same time invigorated. It was an odd combination. No one gets scared on purpose. That's what the cheesemonger had said at the Department of Forensic Medicine. Now, suddenly, he knew what it meant.

'We can take Helena's fear away, Lucy. It's been there, eating away at her for almost forty years. She'll welcome us with open arms when we come for her. You and I are going to Norway. That's what we'll do. It's where you've been wanting to go all along. I should have listened to you before, my lovely diamond girl.'

It was the first time he had spoken to her. It felt good.

After lunch a new officer arrived from the Aalborg police, one considerably better informed about Jesper and Pia Mikkelsen than her two predecessors. She was attached to a special unit charged with various supervisory tasks relating to young people at risk, in the the city of Aalborg as well as the police district as a whole. As such, she had a good grasp of what was going on in the city's nightlife, in particular the bars, nightclubs and discos of Jomfru Ane Gade, the city-centre street on which most of Aalborg's carousing took place, among them Rainbow Six, the club owned in part by Jesper and Pia Mikkelsen. Moreover, she had done her homework and came well prepared.

The Mikkelsens had married in 1973, moving to Aalborg in 1978, the same year they opened their second-hand record shop. In 1986 they had purchased a villa in the affluent suburb of Hasseris, where they still lived, and in 1993 had furthermore bought themselves a small, but exclusive holiday home at Gammel Skagen, a summer playground for the jet set and other well-to-do people at the country's northernmost tip. Neither of the Mikkelsens had any sort of criminal record, and apart from the occasional domestic disturbance that had never resulted in any charges being brought, the couple had had no dealings with police whatsoever. In 1994 they had acquired a fifty per cent share in the Rainbow Six nightclub, as well as a flat above the premises, in which Jesper Mikkelsen had made an office for himself, the rest being used as storage for the couple's record business. In their private as well as commercial affairs, the couple appeared to keep their individual finances apart, likewise filing separately to the tax authorities.

Pia Mikkelsen returned often to the capital, visiting her brother or his grown-up children. Apparently, she was fond of the Austrian singer and entertainer Hansi Hinterseer, and liked to catch him in concert at least twice a year. Jesper Mikkelsen had no hobbies to speak of, or at least none known to police. However, he was seen often, usually on Thursday, Friday and Saturday nights, at his club or elsewhere in the city's nightlife, not infrequently in the company of young girls of somewhat tender age. Whether anything illegal was going on in that respect was hard to tell, and would be even harder to prove, so Mikkelsen was by no means an object of special interest to the police, who had no shortage of other, more important things to be getting on with.

Most of this information was known to the Homicide Department already, and yet Konrad Simonsen had allowed the female officer to find her stride. At her latter remark, however, Pauline bristled.

'If the guy's abusing young girls, it's hardly unimportant.'

Klavs Arnold agreed. He was facing front on a chair he'd turned backwards, his head leaning against the wall, and had looked like he was falling asleep. The officer clarified:

'No, of course not, if that were the case. But there's nothing at all to indicate any abuse defined by criminal law. Nothing in the slightest. I'm not even sure there's a sexual motive to his hanging around with these girls. If there is, though, they're all above age and either consenting or, more likely, procured. But like I said, we've got plenty of other things to allocate resources to.'

Simonsen noted a slight hesitation in the officer's description of Jesper Mikkelsen's escapades – if that was the word.

'So you don't think he's exploiting these girls in any way?'

Her reply was indirect.

'I hear all sorts of stories about all kinds of depravity. They come in all the time. A lot of them are horrendous, and terrifyingly similar. But I've never once heard anything like that in connection with Jesper Mikkelsen and I've been on the scene getting on seven years. I'd be surprised if word hadn't reached me he was...'

Her voice trailed off.

'Are there drugs in this club of his?'

'Bound to be, like everywhere else. But the place has CCTV and the manager and staff aren't turning any blind eyes. I don't think either of them's involved in drugs, definitely not. But there were rumours at one point, probably based on the fact that Jesper Mikkelsen goes round with a minder, preferably two, whenever he's on the town at night. In the daytime as well, sometimes.'

Klavs Arnold woke up.

'Minders? How do you mean?'

'Gorillas. Big blokes with muscle. Biker types, only without the bikes.'

'Professionals?'

'Nothing like.'

'Are they armed?'

'I don't think so. Or rather, no, they're not. Knuckledusters at most, maybe.'

Their discussion continued for another half-hour or so without leading anywhere in particular. Afterwards, Klavs Arnold went up to his room for a lie-down.

'What do you want to do now?' Pauline asked her boss.

Simonsen didn't know yet. Perhaps go for a little drive to begin with. Pauline said she'd go with him. Much to his annoyance.

* * *

Rainbow Six was in the centre of town on Gabrielsgade, leading off Jomfru Ane Gade. Simonsen, Pauline Berg and Klavs Arnold stared across the street at the frontage. It was just past eleven at night, and the weather was cold. Pauline Berg shivered. She'd already uttered a succession of mildly impatient noises, all of which Simonsen had ignored. He looked across at the discotheque's entrance. A vulgar portal had at some point been erected, jutting halfway out on to the pavement and incorporating a neon sign in the shape of a rainbow, each colour flashing in turn with a fraction of a second in between. It was hideous, but no doubt did its job of catching the eye. Somewhat further back was the entrance door itself, in front of it two bouncers bathed in a bluish light akin to that of an emergency vehicle. It lent the men a sickly, almost poisonous appearance. Both of them were dressd in black, the word *Security* printed in large white letters on the back of their T-shirts.

Youngsters werc arriving in clusters, patiently joining the queue and waiting for the bouncers to let them in. Simonsen noted how the occasional guest would be waved past the line and into the club without being checked. Everyone else had their bags searched and their ID carefully inspected before being allowed in. Twice, guests were turned away, the first time when two girls tried to jump the queue, only to be promptly dismissed by a gesticulating doorman. The second instance was more serious and might easily have led to unpleasantness. Three lads were turned away, part of a group of eight or ten young men Simonsen had immediately spotted as potential troublemakers. The club enforced a dress code, and hoodies, baseball caps and tracksuit bottoms were apparently banned. A raucous argument ensued, the two bouncers on the door quickly being aided by four colleagues from inside, prompting the lads to beat a retreat and head off somewhere else instead.

'They're young, aren't they?' asked Arnold.

Pauline Berg explained: the club's clientele differed depending on whether it was Thursday, Friday or Saturday. There was an age limit that varied: on Thursdays it was seventeen, on Fridays twenty and on Saturdays twenty-three. Since most clubbers wanted to party with people their own age or older, not many of this evening's guests would be older than seventeen.

'Can't I join the queue now? My feet are absolutely freezing,' she said by way of conclusion.

Simonsen accepted: she may as well go in now. After she left them he commented drily to Klavs Arnold:

'I thought you said she'd blend in? She no more blends in than we do.'

'How was I to know it was teenage night?'

'All right, I'll let you off this time. Are you armed, by the way?'

'Yeah.'

'If the muscle at the door wants to frisk you, flash them your ID and make yourself known. I don't want any trouble. We stick out like a sore thumb as it is, so it's hardly going to matter much if we tell them where we're from.'

Simonsen's idea had been for them discreetly to gain an impression of the place before going upstairs and confronting Jesper Mikkelsen. If he was in the club, that is, which they had no way of knowing. However, that part of the plan had pretty much gone down the drain now. He stuck to his running order nonetheless, and ten minutes after Pauline had been let in, he crossed the street and prepared for his first visit to a discotheque in thirty years. Klavs Arnold followed on behind.

The doormen were apparently already clued up and they were immediately waved forward before they got a chance to join the queue.

'What do you want?' the youngest of them asked Klavs Arnold.

'In.'

The man conferred with his colleague, who turned to give them the once over before jerking a thumb towards the door and letting them pass.

They stepped into a dimly lit space with a tall black counter on the left-hand side, behind which a woman took entrance money: eighty kroner a head, Simonsen noted. Once a person had paid, he or she was given a stamp on the wrist. He paid for them both, but declined the stamp with a shake of his head. Klavs Arnold checked their coats into the cloakroom while Simonsen studied a framed certificate from the fire services that hung on the wall. The premises was approved for a maximum of 150 persons. The cloakroom attendant squinted at him with concern, more so when Simonsen held Arnold back and they stood for a moment leaning against the black-painted counter while studying the kids as they went up and down a broad but short flight of steps leading to the toilets. Mainly these were girls wanting to freshen up their lip gloss or mascara.

They moved on, stepping through an arched opening into a large space half-filled with revelling kids. The girls were in super-short skirts over bare legs, their feet planted in high-heeled shoes most of them had difficulty walking in. The lads had wax in their hair and were wearing jeans and button-down shirts, preferably with some cheap bling glittering about their chests. The interior was drab: brown wallpaper with a golden floral pattern, soft lighting from a number of chandeliers hanging from the ceiling. One side of the space was a lounge area with leather-covered furniture and heavy wooden tables. Klavs Arnold made a beeline and found them a sofa that was free at the far end of the room. They sat down and soon had the table to themselves, a pair of teenage lads quickly leaving them to it. The dance floor loomed in front of them like the darkest of caverns. A DJ they couldn't see, but whose inane patter between records they had no diffi-culty hearing, made sure the music was almost continuous, though the noise level was thankfully a lot lower than Simonsen had feared, tolerable even. A handful of youngsters writhed about on the dance floor, some with partners, some without. Every now and again they were enveloped in white smoke that had a peculiar, rather sickly smell Simonsen was unable to put his finger on.

A bouncer the size of a barn came over to them. He was wearing a white tuxedo and was polite enough, even if the look of animosity in his eyes was plain to see.

'Is there anything you gentlemen would like?'

Everyone else it seemed had to get their own drinks at the bar over at the opposite side if they wanted anything, but the two older men were apparently worthy of better service. Arnold waved him away.

'Yeah, we'd like to be left alone, if that's all right?'

The man withdrew, his expression stony.

'Can you see any door that might lead upstairs?' Simonsen asked.

Klavs Arnold jabbed a thumb over his shoulder. The door was wallpapered and the join barely visible. Simonsen smiled, picking up a drinks menu, a laminated sheet of black paper with white lettering that lay next to the lamp lit by an artificial candle. He wanted to see if they served anything non-alcoholic. At least half the kids there looked like they were under eighteen. He ran his eyes down the list, without a clue as to what sort of beverage the various exotic names might denote. Klavs Arnold came to his aid.

'None of these teenagers will be forking out a hundred kroner for a *Mai Tai* or *Caipirinha* when they can get a *Tequila Sunrise* or a *Sex on the Beach* for half that. They won't drink anything if it isn't fancy and colourful and hasn't got a funny name...'

Simonsen stopped him by nodding towards the entrance, where Jesper Mikkelsen had just come in. With a young girl for company. Arnold fell silent and they watched the club owner lead his partner to the bar before they both came towards the lounge area, she with a garish blue drink in a tall glass with a straw in it, he with a small draught beer. Simonsen thought the man looked older than he had been expecting, older and wearier. The oddly matched couple passed through the room. Klavs Arnold took out his mobile phone and filmed them without concealing what he was doing. Mikkelsen sent him a brief look of puzzlement, but otherwise ignored them. The couple stopped at the door in the wall immediately behind where Simonsen and Arnold were seated. The girl received a peck on the cheek before Mikkelsen went out through the door with his beer in hand.

The girl was left on her own and stood there looking almost forlorn. Simonsen studied her. Her short-sleeved dress was black and short without being vulgar. It was loose-fitting, with big pockets at the front that gave the garment volume. Her hair, too, hung loose, though thick with hairspray. She was barely more than sixteen. Simonsen watched her as she went back to the bar. Her heels were too high, and she wobbled as she walked. Or perhaps she was intoxicated, it was hard to tell. She sat down on a bar stool at the counter, and Konrad Simonsen nodded to himself as he noted how Pauline slid in and settled beside her.

'Smoky eyes, glitter on the cheeks, the trashy bimbo look,' said Arnold.

Simonsen replied distractedly:

'I'm beginning to find you a bit suspect, you sound like you're used to places like this.'

'I worked a brief spell as a doorman in Esbjerg once. It's almost like coming home again.'

'Policeman, doorman, fitness instructor. How many jobs have you had all at once anyway?'

The answer never came. The bouncer who had approached them before returned with a colleague of much the same proportions. Their previous politeness had evaporated, though the animosity in the eyes remained.

'Right, you come with us. Now!'

The second man opened the door in the wall and stood aside until Simonsen and Klavs Arnold had been ushered through, then followed on behind, giving Simonsen a brutal shove between the shoulder blades and grunting something incomprehensible in the process. The two policemen were prodded up a flight of stairs wide enough for only one person at a time, the first man leading the way, the second bringing up the rear. The stairs opened on to a short corridor, at the end of which they were bundled through a door.

The room in which they found themselves was not large, comparable to a small living room at best. It was without windows, lit only by two bright strip lights on the ceiling. The walls on three sides were lined with a metal shelving system that was stuffed with ring binders in various colours. Behind a desk at the opposite end sat Jesper Mikkelsen. He looked at his guests with disdain. In front of him, his beer remained untouched.

Simonsen hardly registered the five seconds that followed. Klavs Arnold stepped forward, enquiringly almost, as if he hadn't really grasped what was going on, and was immediately flanked by the two security men. Then, in one swift movement he swivelled round and smashed a fist into the face of the man on his left, audibly fracturing his nose, at the same time seamlessly delivering a backwards kick to the groin of the man on his right. He slumped to the floor and rolled over in pain. Before Simonsen could emit even a gasp of surprise, Arnold delivered a second kick that swept the legs from under the first man, whose hands had yet to be lifted to the bloody mess that was his nose before he too lay in a heap on the floor.

'You sit still. Don't move.'

Arnold had his gun out now, as though it had somehow been conjured into his hand, as Simonsen later recalled. The barrel was pointing at Jesper Mikkelsen's chest and the tiny metallic click as he unlocked the safety catch rang in Simonsen's ears. Klavs Arnold repeated his command, calmly, ominously, left hand supporting his extended right arm:

'Just relax, no sudden movements. And get that hand out of the drawer. Slowly!'

Jesper Mikkelsen did as he was told. His raised his arm's and placed both hands on his head, as if anticipating Arnold's next instruction. Klavs Arnold stepped up to his side, dragging him out from behind the desk by his tie, frisking him quickly for any concealed weapon, then forcing him to get down between his two groaning minders. Arnold secured his service pistol and slid it back into its shoulder holster.

Simonsen stepped behind the desk and looked into the open drawer. In it was a mobile phone. He checked the display: Jesper Mikkelsen had managed to press the number of the Aalborg police. At the same moment, there was a knock on the door. Arnold opened it and Pauline came in, followed by the young girl from the bar. She stared in dismay as she saw Mikkelsen on the floor. She got down beside him and began to cry. Pauline Berg surveyed the scene before summing things up:

'Well, this looks like trouble.'

Simonsen sorted things out. The two injured men were quickly dealt with, he and Jesper Mikkelsen agreeing that mistakes had been made on both sides and it would be in everyone's best interest if the episode were dismissed. The minders hobbled from the room, Simonsen scowling at Klavs Arnold as they went. The man from Jutland looked at the floor, realising he was in for a serious dressing-down on account of his overreaction. Pauline encouraged the girl to talk. Hesitantly, she put them in the picture.

Eighteen months previously she'd been in dire straits, dropping out of school after Year 8 and then running away from home. After a couple of brief sojourns abroad she'd ended up in Aalborg, moving in with her boyfriend, a drug abuser. From there it all spiralled out of control. The boyfriend's habit was expensive, and before long she was picking up trade a couple of times a week on Gøglergade and surrounding streets, as well as taking the odd shift at a massage parlour in Nørresundby when she wasn't out of her head on dope. In November she'd been admitted to Aalborg Sygehus with alcohol poisoning, and it was here she first came into contact with Jesper Mikkelsen, albeit to begin with turning down his offer of support. Three weeks later she was back in the hospital, this time following a half-hearted suicide bid. Mikkelsen came to see her, and after a long talk she had accepted the couple's help.

Two ring binders on the shelf supported the girl's story. She hadn't been the first, by any means. Jesper and Pia Mikkelsen had come to the aid of many more besides her. Simonsen and Klavs Arnold each leafed through the contents. Young girls, mostly from the region's smaller towns, who'd hit bottom in Aalborg or else were well on their way. Where necessary, the couple got them admitted to a private rehab centre in Viborg, subsequently finding them somewhere decent to live and getting them started back at school or working, often going back to square one and beginning from scratch when the girls fell back into their former ways. But once they'd picked a girl out, the couple were apparently prepared to go to any lengths to ensure that they made a difference, and no expense seemed to be spared to that end. Klavs Arnold put down his ring binder. A moment later, Simonsen did likewise, turning at once to Jesper Mikkelsen.

'I'm impressed.'

The nightclub owner said nothing. Simonsen went on:

'The Vesterhavsgården holiday cabin. June 1969. Revising for the exams.'

Mikkelsen returned Simonsen's gaze without a sign of apprehension.

'Tomorrow morning, eight o'clock. Here, in my office, with my wife and solicitor.'

'Lucy Davison. I've got photographs of you and your wife with Lucy Davison.'

Jesper Mikkelsen said nothing. Simonsen changed the venue for their meeting to Aalborg Politistation and told Mikkelsen they'd find their own way out.

Pia and Jesper Mikkelsen arrived for questioning at eight the next morning as agreed, bringing with them a solicitor who kicked off by announcing that he wished to make a statement on his clients' behalf. Simonsen and the Countess waited with keen anticipation. Perhaps the Countess's early-morning flight had not been in vain, but in that respect they were disappointed. The solicitor produced a sheet of paper and began to read from it.

'"Pia Mikkelsen and Jesper Mikkelsen wish not to make any statement to police. Should they at any subsequent point in time be detained – either individually or together – in connection with this matter, it is their clear wish that I, their solicitor, be contacted immediately and be present before any questions are put to them."'

Simonsen responded with astonishment:

'But we haven't even told them what this is about yet.'

His protest was ignored, the solicitor continuing in a lifeless monotone:

'"My clients wish to inform the police that Lucy Davison, the English girl they met on their revision trip in nineteen sixty-nine, continued her journey by bus to Varde on the afternoon of Wednesday the eighteenth of June of the same year. Since that time they have not seen her, and they have no further comment to make on the matter." Are my clients detained?'

The Countess shook her head.

'No, but we'd very much like to…'

The solicitor got to his feet. The Mikkelsen couple followed suit.

'In that case we shall leave.'

As indeed they did.

Pauline was glad to be asked if she'd like to see the posters again, and they'd driven straight from the airport to Søllerød. Praising his officers wasn't something Konrad Simonsen found easy to do. He always felt like an actor having to speak a line he'd forgotten. He gave up trying and followed Pauline as she walked slowly round the exhibition. She was silent, allowing herself plenty of time to study each poster in turn, like a buyer at a proper gallery.

In some odd way Simonsen felt the images belonged to him and was stricken by modesty, a feeling he immediately tried to suppress.

'You said yesterday you were reading up on the sixties. What have you discovered?' he asked.

'Nothing hard and fast, but a lot of stuff I didn't know before.'

'Such as?'

'Like how brilliant your music was. Your books were boring, though.'

Your music, *your* books. Simonsen accepted ownership, thinking to himself that he probably wouldn't have done only a month ago. Pauline Berg lingered at the poster she'd just been looking at, staring down at the spot where ten days ago she had suffered a panic attack. After a while she spoke.

'When I felt my throat tightening here, I thought it was Juli Denissen being strangled. But now I know it was Lucy Davison.'

She sounded serene, as if presenting some banal, albeit relevant fact. Simonsen said nothing. He didn't know what to say and responded to her only with a shrug, causing her to look away and proceed to the next image, commenting as she went:

'I know what poster you had on your bedroom wall when you were young.'

'No, you don't.'

He tried without success to make eye contact with her again.

'Marilyn Monroe with flaxen hair, purple mouth and blue eyeshadow. Andy Warhol, nineteen sixty-seven.'

Simonsen flinched. Not only did he remember the poster well, he vividly recalled wanting to buy it, though for some reason, probably lack of funds, he never did.

'Very close indeed, I must say.'

'You thought I was going to say Che Guevara, didn't you? The doctor who ended up an inept guerrilla.'

'That's what I guessed.'

'What poster did you have, then?'

'Nothing typical of the age, I'm afraid. Not that I recall… or, wait a minute, I did have one at the time of the Common Market referendum. It wasn't exactly art, though. It just said *EF NEJ TAK* in big red letters.'

'That wasn't the sixties, though. Wasn't it in nineteen seventy-two, that referendum?'

'I was a late starter.'

The conversation faded as she concentrated on the picture in front of her, Simonsen finding himself unable to think of something to say to fill the void. The pause, however, was short-lived.

'*Nej tak* was typical, though. Everything was *Nej tak*. *Nej tak* to this, *Nej tak* to that. Anyway, I'd have thought you'd vote yes to joining Europe.'

'I did, as a matter of fact. But I was against for a while. And the poster was put up by a girl I knew then.'

'Rita?'

He couldn't recall having mentioned her name, but supposed he must have done. Unless Pauline had been talking to the Countess. He decided not to worry about it, it didn't matter.

'That's right.'

'And she voted no?'

'She didn't vote.'

They fell silent again. By now Pauline only needed to look at three more posters and the tour would soon be over. When she was finished, she returned to one of the first images.

'There's something I can't stand. It's the way you all brag about it. As if in your view no other generation's worth tuppence. Everything else gets weighed and measured against your hallowed nineteen sixties and nothing else ever comes up to scratch.'

She spoke without aggression, a simple statement of fact. Simonsen grinned.

'In three hundred years' time we'll be the only generation remembered, unless some major upheaval occurs in the next twenty. And note, I said *the only one*. We were out on our own, and quite without precedent.'

If he'd been hoping to provoke her, it didn't work. Pauline's reply sounded resigned.

'That's exactly what I mean. I can't stand it.'

'We were the first generation in the history of Denmark never to have experienced war or hunger. I really hope others will follow on, but I'm not optimistic it'll happen.'

At last she turned to face him, and he saw there were tears in her eyes. For a brief moment he was afraid she was about to have one of her attacks. But then he realised she was simply moved by what she'd been looking at and apparently had no desire to hide her emotion as she spoke:

'I understand why you want to find her, and I'm glad you let me stop by. It feels good seeing it all again, and of course especially because... because I didn't get scared.'

'Did you think you would?'

It was a stupid question, and she didn't answer.

They sat down on a pair of chairs Simonsen had pinched from one of the Countess's many rooms. He stared absently at the exercise bike next to them and distractedly batted the nearest pedal with his hand, causing it to spin seamlessly round while Pauline dried her eyes.

'A colleague from Aalborg phoned and confirmed Pia and Jesper Mikkelsen's story, so there seems to be little doubt now,' he said after a while.

'They pick up young girls in trouble and help them get back on their feet again, is that it?'

'It looks like it.'

'What about Jesper Mikkelsen's minders?'

'A simple matter of protection. Not everyone thinks the girls he and his wife come to the aid of deserve a new start in life.'

Pauline nodded. It was just about what she'd worked out for herself.

'But they won't talk about Lucy. Do you think they killed Jørgen Kramer Nielsen?'

'Maybe,' Simonsen said. 'I don't know. But one of the four did, I'm certain of it.'

'We need to talk to the woman in Norway.'

'Helena Brage Hansen. Yes, we do.'

Their second interview with Hanne Brummersted took place at Copenhagen's Police HQ on Friday 7 November 2008 at five in the afternoon, this time without the kid gloves. Both the Countess and Simonsen himself were curious to find out if she'd come on her own or with a solicitor. Simonsen guessed the latter, the Countess the former, and she it was who came out on top: Brummersted was alone. Tight-lipped, she took a seat and awaited their questions. While by no means looking like she was enjoying the situation, she certainly didn't seem to be on the verge of breakdown either. Simonsen began by holding up a clear plastic evidence bag in front of her.

'Can you guess what this is?'

'A cigarette end.'

'Exactly. More specifically, *your* cigarette end.'

It didn't take her many seconds to work out where he was going.

'You've no right! That cigarette end belongs to me. It's against the law.'

'You're wrong. And what's more, you're too late. This is the analysis of the DNA we've taken from your cigarette end, and here's the corresponding analysis of the saliva extracted from the stamp on Lucy Davison's postcard to her parents, sent by you in ninteen sixty-nine.'

'Do you really think you can scare me with this? You've no permission to extract my DNA profile. Can you show me a warrant?'

'We haven't got one. But you can see the results of the analyses. You're a doctor, I'm sure you know something about these things.'

He placed two documents in front of her.

'I've no wish to see them. You've got no permission, and in that case they're as good as non-existent.'

'Oh, but they most certainly do exist. Perhaps you'd care to note where the analyses were conducted?'

She glanced down and exclaimed with surprise:

'Sweden!'

'That's right. More exactly, Lund University, which has an excellent laboratory, as good as any we have here, and now the Swedes would very much like to have a word with you. The legal experts are discussing the matter as we speak, but all indications are that our neighbours will be wanting you extradited. Murder cases, as I'm sure you're aware, are exempted from any time-ban.'

Hanne Brummersted said nothing. They could see she was digesting the information, most of which was complete fabrication, trying to work out a suitable move. Unfortunately for them, she found one.

'I'm willing to go to Sweden, and if it can be proved I licked that stamp, then I suppose I must have done. I can think of all sorts of perfectly natural explanations, but then I'm not the investigator here, am I? As I told you last time we met, I can't remember anything. That's what I'm saying to you now, and it's what I'll tell the Swedes.'

'Orsa post office is a five-hundred-kilometre drive from here. Not exactly a trip you're likely to forget.'

'Don't jump to conclusions. My DNA links me to the stamp, not to Orsa, unless I licked something there as well.'

'Would you care to enlighten us with some of your *perfectly natural explanations* as to how this might have occurred? We can only think of one, you see.'

'No, I wouldn't. That would be highly speculative, and speculation is your department, not mine.'

Simonsen sensed his arsenal rapidly depleting, without Brummersted in any way as yet having been hit. Twice he had bent the truth, now he resorted to another lie.

'The UK police took fingerprints off that postcard at the time. There were quite a number, as was to be expected, but all of them could be accounted for. Apart from one. We'd like to take your fingerprints now, if you don't mind.'

Again, Hanne Brummersted gave the matter some consideration before answering.

'Of course. Anything to oblige.'

'There are also some prints on the staircase at Johannes Lindevej in Hvidovre we're unable to identify.'

'I've no idea what you're talking about.'

'Are you quite sure about that? Doesn't it ring a bell? Jørgen Kramer Nielsen lived at that address until February this year, when you killed him.'

'That's not true. I've never killed anyone.'

'You're a strong woman, and a woman with a knowledge of anatomy. A headlock from behind, a quick snap, and you could shove his body down the stairs.'

'I never killed anyone, and my fingerprints are neither on that postcard nor that staircase.'

She raised her hand to pre-empt interruption before continuing:

'And before you start getting your hopes up that I contradicted myself saying my fingerprints aren't on the postcard when I already said I can't remember, I'd like to remind you of the fact that you just accused me of murder. Anyone can make a slip-up in that situation.'

Simonsen ventured a number of other questions, all of which were likewise skilfully parried. The Countess took over.

'We're playing a game, aren't we, Hanne? You're lying; you know you're lying; we know you're lying; and you know that we know you're lying. And don't pretend you don't understand, because you do.'

'I understand perfectly well, and I'm not lying. There are great chunks of my life about which I have absolutely no recollection, I admit that. But I did not kill anyone. And don't get chummy with me. It's *Doctor* Brummersted to you.'

'What kind of upbringing are you giving your children, Doctor Brummersted?'

'My children aren't relevant to this.'

'My guess is as normal as possible. Nice and secure, lots of love, decent, healthy values: don't tell lies, be good to other people, be responsible for your own actions, recognise your mistakes and learn from them. Would I be right?'

'Like I said, my children aren't relevant to this discussion.'

'And yet all the time here you are, lugging your terrible secret around with you, unable to unburden yourself, no matter what. You're the exact opposite of what you're teaching your children. Every single day is a lie. Your morals, your ethics, your common sense, even the feelings you're gradually beginning to share with your eldest, all of it's a great big lie.'

'My children aren't relevant here.'

Her voice trembled: all three of them were aware of it. The Countess pressed on.

'You'll never be able to explain to them, and when the truth gets out, as it will, the price you'll pay will be unbearable. You'll lose them and the only chance you still have to right the wrongs of the past is passing you by at this very moment.'

The Countess allowed a long and pregnant pause. Without result.

'The choice is simple. Either you tell us now what happened on that revision trip or else you can let us drag it out of you, then later you can try and make your children understand why you chose to remain silent.'

A muscle beneath one of Hanne Brummersted's eyes began to twitch, but apart from that she failed to react.

'Hell is getting used to hell.'

Brummersted collected herself.

'You've been wanting to say that for a while, haven't you? I must admit, it does sound rather good, but the reality of the matter is, it's nonsense. Absolute values can't be compared, I'd have thought you'd have known that.'

'I'm not doubting your intelligence, only your morals.'

'If you're not doubting my intelligence, then why on earth do you think I'd be here without a solicitor if I did kill Jørgen Kramer Nielsen?'

'We'll ask the questions. We told you that last time, too. Now, you were telling us about your morals.'

'No, I wasn't as a matter of fact, but let me do so anyway. All through my adult life I've worked hard, every single day, without a let-up. And you're asking me how I bring up my children? Well, I tell them people should keep their promises... that I've sworn an oath...'

At last, a crack in her voice. A little hiccup, then another, and finally tears, rolling down her cheeks. Her mascara followed suit. Simonsen prepared himself to take over. Promises – he wanted to know more about those. But before he had the chance she'd already got the better of them and left them floundering like a pair of novices. She turned her tearful face to the video camera Simonsen had ostentatiously rigged up to put pressure on her, and then said to the Countess:

'Last time we met you threatened me by saying you'd leak this story to the press unless I admitted certain things I couldn't remember. Regrettably, that didn't make it on to your tape recording, did it? You also promised that you would make me cry. Well, you've succeeded. Are we finished now?'

The address Konrad Simonsen had been given at the concert in Frederiksværk turned out to belong to a multi-storey car park. The man at the gate was friendly enough. He checked Simonsen's name and business and said:

'She's expecting you. Hang on a minute, I'll see if I can find her.'

He studied a bank of flickering monitors to his left.

'She's up on level four. Let me try and give her a call. Can't promise anything, though. We've been having all sorts of trouble with the signal, it disappears all the time after they pulled the building next door down. Work that one out if you can.'

Simonsen stopped him.

'It doesn't matter, I'll just go up.'

The man hesitated, seeming rather sceptical for a moment, then replied:

'If you can't find her, come back down again. We've been told to help you if you ever turn up. Orders, you could say.'

'She gives the orders around here, does she?'

'I'll say. She owns the place. The lift's over to your right, just follow the signs.'

'I think I'll walk. Get the exercise.'

'Fine by me. But mind the cars, now. People tend to forget.'

Much to his satisfaction, Konrad Simonsen walked up to level four keeping a decent pace and without losing his breath. Reaching the landing, he ventured forward into the parking area proper, finding the place apparently empty and gradually beginning to feel somewhat at odds with himself. He stopped and glanced around. Daylight slanted in through the openings in the outer walls, flooding the barren structure, lending the prefabricated concrete elements a grainy, almost surreal quality. Here and there, a zinc pipe broke the visual monotony, and the cars and other vehicles that were dotted about the place sparkled like jewels in a forsaken, silent world. Rita was nowhere to be seen. Only after a depressingly long wander around the level, during which he began to consider going back down to the security guard at the gate, did he finally catch sight of her, standing behind a black Passat, filling in a ticket in a little white book, like a conscientious meter maid. He had all the time in the world simply to look at her.

Time had not been kind to her. She looked gaunt, tight-lipped as though to demonstrate to the world that she wasn't complaining. The once rebellious curls of her hair had been tamed and hung tired and listless. Not even her eyes had aged with grace. They'd seen what there was to see and didn't care to strain themselves for what could only be a pale imitation. Her army-green poncho, reaching to her ankles, made her look older than she was, and combined with the grey bag slung across her shoulder made her resemble a rather shabby army officer.

Simonsen felt his heart sink. The girl of his youth was gone. She had existed only inside him, frozen in time, a precious illusion now cancelled out by a woman he no longer know. Cautiously, he stepped back and glanced around in search of the exit. Immediately, she looked up and saw him. And when she did, the miracle happened: her smile swept away the years as though they had never passed, and Rita was suddenly there in front of him.

'Hi, Konrad, I'm so glad you came.'

The same husky, sensual voice he remembered from the past. Words from his youth abruptly tumbled out.

'Hi, Lovely Rita. Are you free to take tea with me?'

They laughed, not realising how tight they held each other until a car came past and the driver sent them a smile. Simonsen asked her out for dinner.

'If you've got time, that is?'

'I've got lots of time. To be honest, I don't do much, I just like to go about and savour the feel of this place, smell the petrol fumes, write out tickets, little things of no importance. I could get other people to do it.'

'Yes, I've heard the place is all yours.'

'Half of it's yours, Konrad. I realise that.'

He put his hand to her mouth and pressed a finger to his own lips, silencing her gently, but firmly.

'Are you sure? I've already spoken to my accountant, and it's...'

He repeated the gesture, and she acquiesced. After a moment she asked:

'Haven't you ever told anyone about what happened back then?'

'No.'

'Me neither, but there have been times when I've really wanted to. How about you?'

'Only once. Just recently, as a matter of fact.'

'Your wife or partner? Your children, perhaps?'

It was obvious she was angling.

'Neither, but let's not talk about that. There are so many other things to discuss.'

'No, of course... though I'd like to... talk about that, too, I mean.'

He said nothing.

The Countess probed when he got home. He didn't want to lie, and she wasn't the sort to be fobbed off with half-truths.

'She wanted to give you half her multi-storey? Why would she want to do that?'

'That was the gist of it, I think, yes. I gave her some money once, so she could go to America. She was in a tight spot. I never knew the exact details.'

'How much did you give her?'

'I can't remember, but a lot.'

'Where did you get it from?'

'I used to do the pools, everyone did.'

'And you won the famous jackpot, did you?'

'Something like that.'

'You're a very generous and highly fortunate man, Simon. Are you going to be seeing her again?'

'No, and we're agreed on it. We realised that during dinner.'

They had laughed a lot while they were out together. And said they had to see each other again, knowing full well it wouldn't happen.

'Did you ever get to San Francisco?' he asked.

'First I met Ryan in New York. His father was a stockbroker and loaded. He helped me invest my money, most of it in IBM stock. It was a shrewd investment. Later, Ryan and I travelled west. I was pregnant by then. We stayed for a while in Tiburon, an area of San Francisco, living the life on Ryan's dad's money while I got bigger. It was a good time. I thought about you a lot, of course, but I couldn't write, as you know, and then... well, gradually you just faded away. It wasn't until I came back home to Denmark that you became part of me again. From a distance, I mean, whenever you were in the media.'

'When did you come back?'

'Much later, in ninety-three.'

'Tell me about it.'

'We got involved in the Rainbow Family... you know, the Peoples Temple and Jim Jones?'

He wasn't sure he did, though the latter name rang a bell.

'I think so. There was that mass suicide, wasn't there?'

'That's right, but not until later, obviously. Anyway, they had a lot of good things going on when we started. Demos, people working for the cause, a lot of social projects. Racially we were very mixed as well, and in a way it was what I'd always dreamed of. But then gradually I began finding out there were things happening that I didn't like, religious stuff, sex, misuse of authority. These things kept coming to light and just piling up. I wanted out, but Ryan wanted to stay.'

She fell silent.

'That can't have been easy?'

'My father-in-law, as I called him, even though Ryan and I weren't married, used to come over to the camp, trying to persuade us to leave. I think he'd probably hired half the bodyguards in California. He hated Peoples Temple. But Jim Jones didn't keep us there by force. Still, I ended up going back to New York, where I gave birth to our daughter. Unfortunately, Ryan stayed. All the way to Guyana.'

The rest was predictable. Simonsen listened politely as she told him about settling back in Sleepy Hollow under the wing of her father-in-law; her daughter growing up and eventually having a child of her own; the rising value of her own stock investment – tales from a life without drama, rich in American dollars. Only her return home interested him.

'Why did you come back?'

'I missed Denmark. I always did. And then... well, there's this rather negative tradition in my family on the female side. Do you remember how much I adored my grandmother, but didn't get on with my mother at all?'

'I do, yes.'

'Well, that's how my daughter feels, too, and her daughter after her. Teresa's living with me now. She's been here for two years and her Danish is already fluent.'

'I didn't think it was that easy to get in these days, with all those reunification rules.'

'My family's well connected, including in Washington. To start with, she was from a diplomatic family, an embassy child, no questions asked about whose. Now, though, she's got a regular residence permit. She's a lovely girl. But you've seen her yourself. She's amazing, don't you think?'

'Yes, indeed. Amazing.'

Rita picked up the bill.

It was Sunday, the ninth day of the last month of autumn, and the Countess had gone motherly on him.

'The roads can be slippery in the mornings in November, all the more so in the north.'

Simonsen was about to protest. The advance into November had completely escaped his attention. He checked the date on his watch and his words caught in his throat. She went on mollycoddling him.

'I've gathered the printouts of all your internet bookings together and put them in the glove compartment, in case there's any problem at the hotels.'

'I'm not staying at hotels, it's hostels, B&Bs and the like. Small places.'

'Well, at the small places, then. Now, drive carefully, and if you're feeling tired, pull in.'

'We've been through all this.'

But there was no let-up, not even as he got into the car, ready to go.

'Have you got your pills?'

'Yes, I've got my pills.'

'Promise to call me every day?'

'I promise. Every single day. Just give me a kiss so I can get going before the rush hour starts.'

'It's Sunday, there is no rush hour, you know that. Anyway, have a good trip, the two of you.'

He smiled. She was referring to the picture on the back seat. After much deliberation he'd chosen the one that had made Pauline Berg cry, which happened to be one of his favourites, too. He'd had it framed. The picture he'd originally saved for himself was returned to the collection, and now all seventeen would be going back to Jørgen Kramer Nielsen's estate while he was away. The Countess had promised him that she would arrange this.

'How about that kiss?' he said.

She gave him a peck and off he went.

Not until he'd crossed the Øresund Bridge did he feel his journey had started. From Malmö, he followed the coast north to Gothenburg, cutting inland and stopping at the Vänern for his jog. After that, he drove along the western shores of the great lake as far as Karlstad, forging on in an easterly direction and eventually checking in to his lodgings in Gävle north of Stockholm in late afternoon. He'd decided to do a relatively long drive the next day. It seemed right to get as many kilometres on the clock as possible to begin with. Besides, he knew the Swedish forests quickly became monotonous when viewed through the windscreen of a car: endless ribbons of road, straight as a die, and nothing but trees on both sides, kilometre upon kilometre without sign of human habitation and only the pinprick of light far ahead at the apex of the road, for ever out of reach, no matter how far one drove. That night, he slept like a log.

The next day he followed the Gulf of Bothnia, passing through Sundsvall and Umeå, the deciduous trees gone, the spruce gradually becoming sparser and more stunted. Twice he saw eagles. The second time, he stopped the car and sat for a long time watching their majestic, soaring flight high above his head. Arriving almost at the head of the gulf, he stopped for the night in a small town where he'd booked himself into a B&B.

He spoke to her frequently. Just the odd word to begin with, breaking the tedium of his journey, then gradually longer utterances about the landscape and how far they'd got. Pulling in for breaks, he would lift her out of the car and put her down next to him. In those situations, especially, he felt they were together.

'I love you, Lucy. Nothing can change that, it's no use denying it. We would have met in Copenhagen, I'm sure. Bumped into each other in a shop, or on the street, on the S-train, or maybe in a park. Yes, parks are good, a park would have suited us. You with your rucksack and that shy smile, me with the courage to follow you, without even thinking, no two ways about it. We could have hitchhiked our way here. A week, a fortnight, what difference would it have made? We had so much time to spend, we'd have got here eventually. But they killed you. They took away your future, and mine, too.'

The more sentimental the better. Tears welled in his eyes, and he revelled in it.

On the third day, they veered north-east, Lapland. Passing the Arctic Circle he said:

'You made it, Lucy. You'll have to wait for summer to see your midnight sun, though, and be prepared for a long, dark winter first. I wish I could do something about that, but I can't.'

At Karesuando they stopped and saw Sweden's northernmost church before following the road along the border of Finland. The scenery was magnificent and breathtaking: steadfast, slender birch lining rushing rivers; a vast wilderness where no human would be seen for kilometres on end; an immense and humbling sky. They reached Treriksröset before nightfall. Ever the informative tourist guide, he entertained his imaginary passenger:

'Here you can stand with one leg in Norway, one in Sweden and one in Finland, and all at the same time, as my old geography teacher once told us, though none of us dared to laugh, I might add. Let's see if he was right, shall we?'

The next day, they got up early and drove the last part of the way, up through Norway, the road winding in and out through splendid fjords. As they turned off and drove the final stretch towards Hammerfest, he tried to scale down her expectations.

'They've pledged an oath never to speak of you. I'm certain of that. None of my colleagues understands how powerful such a pledge can become, but I do. To begin with, you remember every word. Gradually, it becomes a voice inside, with only the meaning recalled. Year by year, it becomes more and more entrenched in the mind. Eventually, it's become a part of you. Something that can't be changed. Neither good nor bad, but impossible to break, the same way as you can't do anything about your name, you're stuck with it whether you like it or not. Now we must help one of them overcome her fear, so I can find out where they buried you and make sure you get home again. But if we work together, I'm sure things will work out just fine.'

After that, he spoke to her no more.

Helena Brage Hansen looked exactly like she did in the photos Simonsen was familiar with, apart from the fact that her hair was now white and she wore glasses. He waylaid her outside her home on the Thursday. It was mid-morning and she came wheeling her bike up the hill. He got out of the car and waited for her. He introduced himself, and she answered calmly:

'I've been expecting this, but I've got nothing to say to you. I'm afraid you've come all this way for nothing.'

'It was a lovely drive.'

'I'm sure. But I'm sorry, we've got nothing to talk about.'

'I'm not just here to talk. I'm also here because I was hoping you'd be able to help me with something else.'

He showed her the poster in its frame. She stood and looked at it for a long time, enough for his arms to tire. Then, after a while, she spoke.

'Oh, goodness.'

That was all. A tiny, sorrowful exclamation. Simonsen sensed it would be best to avoid mention of the photographer and the additional circumstances. Perhaps she knew already, or perhaps it would spoil this first, tentative opening.

'Would you help me find a place to hang her up? I don't know anyone here. Preferably in a room with many windows.'

'Is that why you've come?'

'Yes, and to speak with you, though I haven't envisaged you'd be willing to tell me anything.'

'Wait.'

Shortly afterwards she returned, wearing a jacket and carrying a rucksack. He followed her out of the town, up a winding path that led them on to the hillside and quickly had him panting for breath. They passed a few reindeer along the way, the grazing animals barely pausing to look up, and she exchanged a brief word of greeting with an elderly man at a wooden rack of stockfish. She walked briskly. For a time he struggled to keep up with her, eventually falling back and finding his own pace. He was carrying the framed poster; it was unwieldy and held him up.

'You're going too fast,' he called out.

She slowed down to accommodate him. They hiked through the stunning landscape for perhaps half an hour. Barren, grey-black rock, broken here and there by sparse expanses of moss and lichen, or glistening white snow. Soon, they were high above the town. The view was stupendous and almost hurt his eyes, so much did he stare. Eventually, they came to three crofts settled snuggly in a dip in the hillside. She went to the largest of them, going inside without a knock and leading him up some stairs. The room they entered was bright and pleasant, tastefully decorated. At the far end, a man sat huddled at a computer, writing. He turned abruptly, rose cheerfully to his feet and greeted her with a kiss, whereupon they immediately began to converse in sign language. The man stepped forward and extended his hand silently to Konrad Simonsen. They shook, and Helena Brage Hansen explained:

'Kaare's a journalist, financial affairs. He works freelance, specialising in Switzerland. He's travelled all over the world. These days, though, he'll hardly bother to go into town.'

'I can well understand it. This is an amazing place.'

'Yes, it's lovely now, but in a month's time the weather makes it too gloomy for me.'

Together they found a space for Lucy Davison. It took them a while. All three had their opinions, but eventually they agreed on Kaare's proposal. He fetched some tools and before long the picture was up and hanging on the wall.

'What's he saying?' Simonsen asked as the man signed at him.

'He wants you to taste his blueberry aquavit.'

'I'd like to, but just a taste. I had a heart attack not long ago, so there are certain pleasures I have to forego.'

She translated for him.

'Kaare says blueberry schnapps is good for the heart.'

It was all very cordial, and hours passed. Kaare's home was a place in which Simonsen quickly felt comfortable. At some point, almost casually, Helena Brage Hansen said:

'I've booked two seats on the plane for Copenhagen at ten-thirty in the morning, but there'll be a couple of transfers. If you pick me up early I can help you make arrangements to get your car back to Denmark.'

No more was said on the matter, and it was mid-afternoon by the time they made tracks. Simonsen noted her farewell to the man was not the sort that indicated she was expecting to be gone for long.

The next day she was quiet, albeit neither distraught nor nervous. On their way to the airport few words were exchanged between them, and it was only once they were on the plane that he asked her:

'What are you intending to do when we get to Copenhagen?'

'Check in to the hotel and sleep, I think.'

'And tomorrow?'

'Speak to the other five.'

'Mouritz Malmborg and Jørgen Kramer Nielsen are dead.'

'Oh. Well, I suppose it was only to be expected. Statistically, I mean.'

'What are you going to say to them?'

'I'll arrange a meeting.'

'Do you know where they live?'

'No, but you do.'

'Yes. Where will you meet?'

'Vesterhavsgården.'

'You remember the name?'

'I remember every second, and the others do, too.'

'You made each other a promise.'

'Yes, but we shouldn't have done. We should never have done that. And this is what ought to have happened a very long time ago. If it had, we might have had lives worth living.'

Simonsen refrained from passing comment, but a short while later he said:

'Jørgen Kramer Nielsen was murdered.'

Her reaction was subdued. He thought she might have taken a sedative.

'I think one of you four who remain killed him. Or had him killed.'

'I don't think so.'

'Why not?'

'I don't know.'

'Were you their leader?'

'You could say. Until Lucy came along. She took over as easy as anything.'

'Did you and the others kill her?'

'That's for you to decide later.'

'I'm asking you now.'

'Yes, we did.'

CHAPTER 11

Konrad Simonsen set up a meeting with the priest on the Saturday, the day after he arrived home from Norway, prompting the Countess to comment:

'Don't you think you should relax a bit? Surely it can wait until next week? You've got a drive ahead of you, remember.'

She was right. Of course it could wait. It probably wasn't even necessary. The meeting had no real bearing on the investigation, or anything at all, most likely. And yet, much to his bemusement, he had found himself calling the man and arranging an appointment. The priest, for his part, didn't seem in the slightest bit surprised. He hadn't asked what it was about, had simply fitted Simonsen in, if not in so many words.

'What do you want to talk to him about anyway?' the Countess wanted to know.

She had an unerring ability to pinpoint the matters on which he himself was uncertain. Sometimes it was good, clarifying things for him; other times it was annoying and he felt himself oddly laid bare. Like now. He tried to be honest.

'I don't know, really. I just want to talk to him, perhaps tell him how far I've got with Lucy. That we're going over to dig up her remains tomorrow.'

After they'd landed at Copenhagen, Helena Brage Hansen had booked herself into a hotel in Christianshavn. They had parted company for a few hours, after which she had contacted him again and briefly informed him that she and the others would be arriving at the Vesterhavsgården camp the following day. The others – Jesper and Pia Mikkelsen and Hanne Brummersted – he hadn't even contacted, merely asking if they'd be there without the presence of solicitors or any other third party, which Helena assured him would be the case. He got Klavs Arnold activated right away, clearing the place of any children's groups that might have been booked in.

'You sound very confident about it,' the Countess said.

He was. Tomorrow Lucy would be found. *After nearly forty years in the sand.* The thought was so full of pathos he hastened to continue:

'I'm going to tell the priest I've nicked one of his posters. Or whoever it is who's going to own them now.'

There was something else he wanted to talk to the priest about. Something he wanted to confess. That was the word he used in his mind: *confess*. It was the way he felt obliged to think about it, if he could think about it at all. And yet this confession had no bearing on his investigation. Truth be told, it was hardly a matter for a priest at all. But he was a person Konrad Simonsen was comfortable talking to, even about difficult matters.

'Sounds like a good idea,' the Countess said.

It was indeed, he thought. She let the matter drop. If he was quick about it he could go for his run before dinner.

The Countess had made an effort in the kitchen, which he appreciated even if her culinary skills were rather limited. Prawn cocktail with avocado and a homemade thousand island dressing, followed by veal with sautéed vegetables and four consciously apportioned small potatoes each. Unusually, she'd bought a non-alcoholic wine to go with it. They raised their glasses and tasted the grape like a pair of master sommeliers, Simonsen electing not to comment adversely: it was the thought that mattered. The Countess, however, passed judgement herself.

'It tastes like stale fruit juice. I'll open a proper bottle, you'll just have to jog an extra kilometre tomorrow. How's it going with that anyway? Did you run the whole way today?'

He shook his head. He still had a bit to go, but he was getting there. Then, as they sat with their wine, he said:

'I should never have looked Rita up like that. It was a mistake, a big mistake.'

He drank another sip, before explaining.

'When I think about her now, it's all negative. The time before we broke up was... weird. I'm annoyed about that multi-storey, as well. I mean, if she really needed to invest in something, couldn't she have put her money in...'

His voice trailed away, then he added pensively:

'Perhaps I'm just angry with her for getting older.'

'You're older yourself.'

'Which is why I can't afford to have all my dreams falling apart on me. And if everything goes according to plan I'll be seeing Lucy, too… the way she is today. It can't be helped. Has she gone, by the way?'

He nodded towards the annexe. The Countess confirmed it. The posters had been removed while he was away.

The priest had given him an address on a side street in Valby, not far from the Søndermarken park. He took the S-train and walked from Valby station. The place turned out to be a coffee bar, the old-fashioned kind where a cup of coffee cost five kroner, a refill three, sugar and cream at no extra cost. It was about the only thing they sold in the place, tiny premises with just enough room for a few tables and the counter itself, behind which a woman who looked to be about the same age as the building served his beverage from a classic Madam Blå coffee pot, guaranteed freshly brewed. She took his money and he sat down at the nearest table and sipped what for the sake of his dodgy heart ought to have been tea, though he sensed it would have been sacrilege to have asked for such a thing here. He was the only customer, and having brought nothing with him to read he simply sat and stared out of the window. The sun was out, though it was windy: the street looked pleasant and quiet. His mind was empty of thought, but after a bit he began to wonder if he'd got the time wrong.

Eventually, however, the priest came hurrying in, apologising for the delay and sitting down at the table. The old woman brought him a cup of coffee without being asked. Simonsen surmised he was probably a regular. He asked, by way of conversation:

'Do you come here often?'

He indicated the priest's coffee cup, suddenly feeling intrusive.

'I know two people who live in the area and visit whenever I've got the time. I usually come in here for a coffee. It's the only place I actually drink coffee, usually I'm a tea-drinker, but this has become something of a tradition.'

'I see.'

Simonsen found the situation awkward and the lull that followed all too prolonged. The priest seemed to sense his unease and began to tell him about the people he'd been to see. Lonely people, people who'd been left behind somehow and who now lived their lives in the past. What did you want to see me about? – the perfectly natural question that would make Simonsen feel self-conscious – never arose. When the priest finished talking, Simonsen took over. He told him about Helmer Hammer, the executive from the Prime Minister's Office, carefully avoiding any mention of the man's name. The priest listened with interest, clearly enjoying their conversation. Simonsen went on:

'Anyway, when this top civil servant told us your church wished to purchase Lucy's posters, we in the Homicide Department of course began to look for an explanation. We could imagine all sorts, to be honest, growing increasingly more sinister. That's what my job's like, you see. Everything, no matter what, has to be viewed with a certain amount of scepticism. It's ingrained in us, I'm afraid.'

The priest nodded his understanding. Obviously, the police couldn't just accept any old story. Simonsen told him how Pauline Berg – he referred to her as *one of my junior staff* – had tired of all their theorising and simply grabbed the phone and called this *officialis* from the British diocese who was trying to obtain the pictures of Lucy Davison. She asked the man straight out for an explanation, which was promptly provided. The priest responded with a smile.

'Our organisation Missing Children in Liverpool will be inheriting one and a half million kroner from Jørgen, as you know. That's a considerable sum of money, which will do a world of good. At the moment, Missing Children's Liverpool branch has its premises in a dilapidated building off Romer Road in the city's Kensington area. What's more, they've been very short of space. Now, however, they've bought themselves some roomier offices on Rydal Avenue in Formby, which at present they're doing up. I thought it would be the ideal place for Lucy's pictures, so I phoned our *officialis*, as you refer to him. We know each other personally, he used to be in charge of Missing Children in Liverpool himself, as a matter of fact, and... well, I managed to persuade him.'

Simonsen put his elbows on the table and leaned forward.

'Lucy...'

The priest followed his example, folding his hands and resting his chin on them. His eyes were kind, his gaze firm.

'Lucy, indeed.'

'Tomorrow we'll finally discover what happened to her. In Esbjerg, all those years ago.'

'I hope so. Tell me, do you like onion soup?'

Simonsen laughed.

'That's the most elegant change of subject I've heard in a very long time. And yes, I love onion soup.'

The priest led the way. It wasn't far, he said. They turned down a quiet residential street, then took a right up a long driveway. The priest explained:

'My brother's a chef and works in a canteen here. Smashing place, don't you think?'

Simonsen glanced around at what looked like storage halls, a number of nicely renovated old buildings and modern modular prefabs – an oddly harmonious cluster. It was like stepping into a village. A busy village, with people scuttling about between the various buildings, on their own or several at a time, despite its being the weekend. They passed a coachload of tourists being shown around by a guide rattling off information in English. Simonsen took hold of the priest's sleeve and held him back.

'What on earth is this place?'

'Nordisk Film. Didn't you see the sign?'

Simonsen shook his head.

'And I thought I knew this city. I even used to live here in Valby. And yet I've never been here, ever.'

'It is tucked a bit out of the way. Perhaps that's what makes the place so charming. Did you know Nordisk Film is the world's oldest surviving film company? I'll tell you the history in a minute, but let's have our soup first, shall we? Just wait here, I'll be back in a minute.'

He went through a door, returning shortly afterwards carrying two precariously balanced bowls of soup. He handed one to Simonsen and the two men proceeded slowly through a narrow passage between two buildings, the priest still leading the way. Emerging, they came to a lawn on which three small huts had been erected in a row. They reminded Simonsen of children's playhouses, the kind that came with their own sandpit. Each hut had its own name, etched into a wooden nameplate above the door: *Faith*, *Hope* and *Charity*. Simonsen was allowed to choose and pointed to the one in the middle.

'Let's take *Hope*. What are they used for anyway?'

'Mostly they're for scriptwriters, if they need a couple of hours to themselves.'

The two men edged their way inside and found room in the cramped space, Simonsen seating himself on the only chair, the priest on a bench next to him. They slurped their onion soup while the priest told him about Ole Olsen, the film company's founder – businessman, entrepreneur, art collector and all-round character.

Simonsen listened with interest. Then without warning he said:

354

'I've kept one of the Lucy posters. Missing Children in Liverpool will have to make do with seventeen, but there were eighteen in all.'

He had feared the reaction. The priest would be well within his rights to report him for theft, but there was no cause for concern:

'Well, nine plus nine is usually eighteen, I can see that. But I think seventeen will suffice in this case, don't you?'

He'd known, of course. Nine posters on one wall, nine on the other. He'd told Simonsen himself that he'd stood on top of the ladder staring into Jørgen Kramer Nielsen's mirror room. Simonsen told him about his trip to Hammerfest and the new home the poster had found in Kaare's study up on the fell. The priest found it to be an excellent choice and asked him about the trip in general. He'd once been to Tromsø in his younger days. The conversation moved on and the missing picture was relegated to the past. Hesitantly Simonsen told him about Rita, to see how it felt. The priest listened with few comments.

'There's a story from that time that I'd like to tell you,' said Simonsen.

'By all means. Go ahead.'

'I think I'd like to wait, if you don't mind. I'm... not quite ready yet. I think that's what they say, isn't it? But some other time, if you're still up for it?'

'Certainly, no problem.'

They parted on the street outside the film studios. Simonsen, who had not asked a single question relating to his investigation, angled at the last minute:

'I'd actually brought along four photographs of the students Lucy and Jørgen Kramer Nielsen were with in Esbjerg. I didn't get round to showing them to you.'

'No matter. I don't know any of them.'

'One of them killed Jørgen.'

'You're an extremely capable investigator. I trust and rely on your judgement.'

They shook hands. On his way back to the station, Simonsen found himself in good spirits. He was glad he'd taken the time out, even more so for what he'd been told. He was so immersed in thought he walked straight past the station, stopping only when the squeal of an incoming S-train prompted him to turn back. Jesper Mikkelsen, Pia Mikkelsen, Hanne Brummersted, Helena Brage Hansen. *I trust and rely on your judgement.* Rather an odd thing to say, if complimentary. He crossed the street to the steps leading down to the trains and felt confident he would live up to that judgement. He had already made significant progress, he thought, and… well, yes, he was an extremely capable investigator.

The time was just over half-past eight in the morning. It was Sunday 16 November and a punchy wind battered the spruce and hastened ragged clouds across the sky from the west. The day had hardly started and it was freezing cold. Simonsen shivered and glanced at Pauline by his side. She wasn't wrapped up, but didn't seem overly bothered by the fact either.

'How come you chose me and Arne to come with you?' she asked.

The day before, as they'd driven over to Esbjerg, she'd asked the same question, and again that afternoon at the hotel. On both occasions he'd fobbed her off: *No reason in particular,* he'd said, then changed the subject. Later, when Pauline had gone to bed and he and Arne Pedersen had adjourned to the bar, each with a fizzing glass of mineral water, Pedersen had put the question to him again, only for Simonsen to sidestep the matter once more.

He answered Pauline with a touch of annoyance.

'That's the third time. It doesn't matter, surely?'

'It does to me, Simon.'

She wormed her hand under his arm, but he shook her off.

'The Countess is disqualified because of her poor relationship with Hanne Brummersted, even if she would have been my first choice.'

'Was she miffed?'

'I can't allow personal considerations to sway my professional judgement, so she'll have to live with it. Anyway it's not an issue, she's a professional too. You're here because I wanted a woman involved.'

None of which was true. He'd passed over the Countess for personal reasons. It was unprofessional, he readily conceded, but that was how it was. He didn't want her there when he found Lucy. In fact, he had seriously considered coming over on his own, though had eventually dismissed the idea. He needed someone besides himself to study the reactions of the four individuals who in a short time would once more be assembled after almost forty years apart. Not their reactions to Lucy Davison, but to Jørgen Kramer Nielsen.

'And why Arne and not Klavs?' Pauline wanted to know next.

'Because Klavs is moving to Copenhagen today. Among other things.'

'I'm pleased to hear it.'

He wasn't sure quite what she was pleased to hear, but he mumbled a reply nevertheless and gazed out at the surroundings. They were sheltering behind a woodshed next to the main entrance to the Scout hut, gusts of wind tugging at the smaller construction's roofing felt and whistling around its eaves. The weather had worsened, he thought, despite the forecast predicting a calm spell. Pauline stamped her feet a few times on the sandy earth.

'I thought it was to give me and Arne the chance to work together again,' she said after a bit.

'Well, it wasn't.'

'I think Arne thinks that too.'

He turned his head to look at her.

'Can't you just concentrate on something other than yourself, for the next few hours at least?'

Sometimes he forgot how needy she could be. Especially if she'd been normal for a while, back to the way she'd been a year and a half ago. When she regressed her voice changed. It sounded as if she were quoting from a book, a passage she didn't care for but had been asked to read aloud.

'When you sat with me that night at my flat and I was asleep, didn't you want to get into bed with me?'

'For crying out loud, Pauline! No, and you know perfectly well I didn't. But right now I'd like to send you home.'

He snorted with contempt and instantly regretted his reaction. It was obvious she was trying to provoke, and he shouldn't have bothered answering her at all, that would have been by far the best thing to do. He channelled his annoyance elsewhere.

'Where the hell's Arne got to anyway?'

'He had to go for a whizz.'

'I know what he said. And I also know we're surrounded by about ten thousand pine trees he could have gone behind, if that was what it was.'

Again, Pauline slipped her hand under his arm. A conciliatory gesture, accompanied by a comment about not being a man herself and not knowing. She gave his arm a little squeeze, then removed her hand before he did it for her. The conversation died as soon as they heard the car.

A blue Citroën came up the driveway and pulled up in the car park, the gravel crunching beneath its tyres. It was Hanne Brummersted. The agreement had been for Arne Pedersen to receive her. Simonsen nudged Pauline forward.

'If Arne's not here, you'll have to…'

At the same moment, Pedersen came round the corner of the main cabin. Simonsen stopped talking and watched as Pedersen led the woman inside and into the communal living room, where Helena Brage Hansen was already seated. It was the room she and her classmates had used most back in 1969. After a short while, Pedersen came out.

'She seems relaxed about it. We won't be having any problems with her.'

'What's that supposed to mean, relaxed about it?'

Pedersen muttered a few brief words of explanation without Simonsen being any the wiser.

'How did the reunion go off?'

'Cautious, non-committal.'

'Are they talking?'

'How would I know? You never taught me to look through walls.'

'What I meant, obviously, was do you *think* they're talking?'

Arne Pedersen hesitated. Pauline Berg shook her head as if dismissing the bickering of two errant schoolboys. Then she walked the ten metres or so over to the window and peered in for a second before returning.

'No, they're not talking. The doctor one's just sitting staring into space. The little thin one's typing something on her phone.'

Pedersen was infuriated.

'Don't you even know their names?'

Pauline clenched her fists, almost as if she was about to strike out. Of course she knew their names. Perhaps he wanted to test her? Was that it? She paused and growled the two women's names. Simonsen's phone vibrated in his inside pocket. With difficulty he opened the text message. It was from Helena Brage Hansen. He read it, informing Berg and Pedersen of its content:

'The Mikkelsen couple won't be here for another half-hour. They're running late.'

Arne Pedersen had found a back room they could access from the main cabin's rear entrance, a room with heating. He went off, rolling his eyes at Simonsen as he did, with a telling nod in Pauline's direction. She watched him go, turning to Simonsen once he was gone, suddenly with sweetness in her voice:

'Let's take a walk round the grounds.'

He dragged his feet while she chatted gaily.

'I was out on the town on Friday and met this guy in a bar. Do you know what he said? He said I'd got child-bearing hips. What do you reckon? Is that any way to score a girl? Child-bearing hips!'

Simonsen didn't reckon anything at all and could only muster an inkling of a polite smile in response to her incredulous laughter. Then, abruptly, she changed the subject.

'What did Kramer Nielsen's priest say when you interviewed him yesterday?'

'It wasn't an interview. Have you been talking to the Countess?'

'I phoned when you were out with him. If it wasn't an interview, what was it?'

Simonsen's own view was that it might best be described as a prologue, preparing him to reveal something he had kept secret for many years. If the opportunity even arose.

'Can't you go back to Arne?' he said. 'I'd like to be on my own for a minute.'

She left him alone, without protest and without taking offence. The woman was clearly frustrated. He stared after her, disappearing into his own thoughts.

He didn't remember exactly when it was, but it must have been around midsummer, because when the film ended and they left the cinema it was still light. Maybe it was the Grand Teatret on Mikkel Bryggers Gade, but he wasn't sure about that either. And yet he recalled the film so vividly: *Easy Rider*. Peter Fonda and Dennis Hopper crossing America from West to East.

On their way out she'd stopped at an amusement machine, one of those where you steer a claw to grab a prize. It was as if she ground to a halt, standing there amid the throng of filmgoers, feeding the machine with coins, coming up with three cuddly toys for herself. But her success left her strangely unmoved. Then all at once it came pouring out.

She wanted to go away. To America. They should leave immediately, start afresh, just the two of them. That was what they'd do – go to America, far away from Denmark. She could play music, sing. He could... get a job somewhere. They'd be transformed, and life would be good, she felt sure of it. In America, not Denmark.

Thinking back on it now, it seemed to him she'd been quite unflappable and rational about it, and yet exalted and manic at the same time. She couldn't have been, but that's how he remembered it.

She dropped her last coin into the machine without success, not even trying. And then she said:

'I'm taking some cash to Germany next week. I'm going to steal it and take off.'

He said nothing, merely shook his head, realising she meant it. They went back to his flat, leaving her cuddly toys behind on top of the machine.

The next day he called in sick, the only time in his career he'd ever skived off. They holed up together in his home and he spent the entire first day trying to persuade her to give up her hopeless venture. After that he went to a bookshop and bought six exercise books, and for the next four days she wrote it all down: names, people, dates, places, conversations – everything she could recall, down to the minutest detail. The times she'd run cash... How much? Who gave it to her? Where did she deliver it? To whom? Who kept the books? And so on. In hindsight it was his first interrogation. His first and most difficult. When she'd finished he read her statement through carefully, putting additional questions to her and writing down her answers in the exercise books. She co-operated willingly, albeit disillusioned, and without holding back on any fact.

He found it a lesson he would never forget: the importance of the interrogator penetrating into the soul of his witness, understanding and accepting their feelings, ultimately putting himself in their place. Oddly enough, it was Rita who, in one of their occasional breaks, first passed comment on his skills:

'You're good at this, Konrad.'

It was an objective statement of fact, yet tinged with sadness. The distance between them when he wasn't questioning her was marked. They slept apart.

When they were done, he went to Kasper Planck, who had helped them once before and might do so again. Who else was there? He knew no one.

Tremblingly uncertain, he waylaid the man outside the Store Kongensgade Politistation.

They went for a walk on Larsens Plads by the Kvæsthusbroen, back and forth, circling about on the same cobbles while Simonsen explained his predicament. Planck accepted the exercise books with a grunt of annoyance, like a schoolteacher receiving an essay handed in late. Two days later they met up again at the same place, this time seated on a bench in drizzling rain. Planck had brought an umbrella, but only for himself. He began by asking Simonsen a core question:

'What about you? Are you going to America too?'

'No.'

He had mulled over the dilemma, lain awake half the night thinking about it, weighing the pros and cons, but now the answer came to him at once. And he knew, as soon as he uttered the word, that it was true.

'I didn't think you would be.'

Planck's assessment was immediately borne out. He gave back the exercise books along with some documents: three typed sheets of additional questions, one – and only one – visa application for the United States, and a form whereby Konrad Simonsen applied to be transferred to the Criminal Investigation Department.

'I'll be docking you eight days' holiday. I won't have people skiving off,' was Planck's only comment.

'Eight days? I've only been away five.'

'The other three's to teach you a lesson.'

And that was that. Planck told him what to do, a plan Simonsen followed to the letter. At the bookshop he bought two more exercise books in which Rita wrote down her answers to Planck's additional questions. She filled in her visa application and gave him her passport. At some point it dawned on her she would be going on her own, but they never discussed the matter.

At the Bellahøj Politistation he handed in half the exercise books and Rita's documents to PET, represented by an ageing assistant with horn-rimmed glasses and an inscrutable expression. The man spent a couple of minutes leafing through the material. The visa application was passed without comment, warranting merely a near-imperceptible nod, and Simonsen was given another appointment the following week. A bit like going to the dentist's.

He gave her her passport and visa at the Grønjordskollegium halls one gorgeous summer evening, well suited to melancholy. She cried a little and asked in a tiny voice:

'Will you sleep with me?'

It was in the air: for the last time. He declined. She asked:

363

'What now?'

'Now we need money.'

He'd been walking about for a bit and found himself at the far end of the parking area, hardly realising how he'd got there. He swivelled round as a BMW swung in and pulled up in front of the Scout cabin. Pia Mikkelsen got out of the back, followed by her husband, who emerged from behind the wheel. The solicitor was not present. Simonsen turned away in the opposite direction without bothering to say hello. After a short detour he returned to the top of the driveway, where Arne and Pauline were waiting for him. Wearily, he looked them both in the eye for a moment before collecting himself and leading the way through the front door.

The four friends of old had seated themselves in armchairs as far apart from each other as possible. Even the Mikkelsen couple were distanced from one another. Helena Brage Hansen sat disinterestedly leafing through a magazine on the table in front of her, while the others stared into space. The air was thick with the solemnity of the occasion. Behind them, a breakfast buffet had been provided, and Konrad Simonsen sent a kind thought to the staff of Esbjerg Kommune. Then he took the floor, bidding them welcome in a breezy tone that seemed almost like a provocation.

'Good morning, everyone, and thank you indeed for coming. I can tell by your faces that you're all aware how serious a matter we have to deal with here today. The good news is that I'm certain once you've had the opportunity to relieve your consciences, you'll all be feeling rather more comfortable. Especially after you've decided to take a trip down memory lane back to the old school…'

Helena Brage Hansen interrupted his flow, her words like a well-directed whiplash.

'Put that magazine away, Hanne, and pay attention.'

The consultant immediately obeyed orders, blushing. Simonsen continued:

'I see little has changed. For the moment, however, I have nothing more to say. It's your turn now. I'm sure you've lots to talk about, am I right?'

As expected, it was Helena Brage Hansen who spoke first:

'I think we need ten minutes to ourselves to begin with. I hope you'll allow us that?'

He didn't have much choice, and a moment later was once more standing outside with Arne Pedersen and Pauline Berg, sheltering from the wind behind the woodshed. The gusts had eased and two military helicopters passed almost directly above their heads. They looked up spontaneously and in unison. When they were gone, Pedersen said:

'Why did you provoke them like that? Was it wise?'

'It was quite intentional.'

'I realise that, but why?'

'I don't want them to think I'm their cheerful uncle. We've got two killings to clear up. It's not a holiday.'

Pauline Berg chipped in with support for Pedersen.

'Why would they think that? You're running the risk of alienating them and then they won't talk to us.'

'No, I'm not. They've come all this way knowing full well they can't go home again before they tell us what happened and where Lucy's remains are. Psychologically, they wouldn't be able to cope with that, not after they've been struggling to accept the thought for two days. I'm convinced it'll be a major relief to them, or at least to three of them.'

Pedersen changed tack.

'I agree with that analysis. But when you say three, is that because you think the one who killed Jørgen Kramer Nielsen has other interests?'

'Yes, and I want it all. The lot. It's got to come out, today.'

'Sounds realistic to me. What do you think they're doing in there?'

Pauline shrugged. Simonsen said:

'They're going back on the promise they made each other forty years ago.'

Then, after a pause:

'Make sure to focus on the two you've been assigned. All the time, without interruption.'

The agreement was for Pauline to observe Helena Brage Hansen and, in particular, Hanne Brummersted, while Arne was to watch the Mikkelsen couple. Body language: an involuntary posture, a revealing glance, a suggestive slip of the tongue, a nervous twitch. The postman's killer would be unable to keep up appearances, Simonsen was convinced of it.

Helena Brage Hansen appeared in the doorway and called them back in.

The mood was heavy. The three women were quietly crying, and Jesper Mikkelsen sat motionless in his chair. He collected himself after a moment and addressed Simonsen directly.

'We'll tell you everything, but we need your help, too. We imagine you might start by putting questions to us and then perhaps we can tell you more as we go on. It's not...'

His voice cracked and he looked away for a second before completing the sentence:

'... easy for us.'

It sounded reasonable. Simonsen refrained from sitting down and jabbed a finger at the man instead, without so much as attempting to sound accommodating.

'In that case, we can start with you showing me where you people buried Lucy Davison.'

'There's no need to show you. We buried her in the campfire pit.'

'Now!'

Mikkelsen did as he was told, rising to his feet, while the women remained behind. Simonsen followed him. The man wasn't weeping, but every now and then he expelled a little sob and was plainly unable to speak. The procession, however, was more than a mere demonstration of Simonsen's authority: the fire pit had quite conceivably been moved in the years that had passed.

They walked perhaps twenty metres along a path, arriving abruptly at their destination. Mikkelsen pointed to the middle, where ash and charred logs lay in a heap, wreathed by a circle of stones.

'Is that where she is?'

He nodded.

'And you're quite sure? The campfire might have been somewhere else then.'

Mikkelsen looked around and stammered a reply:

'I – I'm sure.'

'How far down did you dig?'

He held a hand above his head, and Simonsen estimated two to three metres.

They went back. The women were still sobbing, though both Hanne Brummersted and Helena Brage Hansen had taken a bread roll from the buffet. Jesper Mikkelsen poured himself a glass of orange juice before returning to his chair. Simonsen addressed them all.

'Right, just so everyone knows: you can turn on the waterworks as much as you want, but you will tell the truth and every little bit of it, so I strongly advise you to pull yourselves together. It'll make things easier. Now, let's start at the beginning, shall we? You were all in the same class at the Brøndbyøster Gymnasium from nineteen sixty-seven to sixty-nine, and there you formed a club you called the Lonely Hearts Club. The other students in the class called you the Hearts for short. Did you refer to yourselves in that way, too?'

367

Helena Brage Hansen answered:

'Yes, we were the ones who shortened it, as it happens. The long form was a bit unwieldy.'

'And you, Helena, were the club's founder, is that right?'

'Yes.'

'Who was in it from your class?'

'The four of us here, Jørgen and Mouritz.'

Her voice sounded frail and pitiful. Simonsen went on without any sympathy:

'When you went back, did you tell him what had happened?'

'No, of course not.'

He continued speaking to Helena Brage Hansen.

'All right, back to the Hearts. Why was this club formed?'

'So those of us who were left out could enjoy a sense of community, too.'

'Left out of what?'

'The class, the parties, the talk... all the movements, however loose they were – the hippies and the provos, the singing and the guitar-playing, the concerts, the general day and age... everything.'

'So you were bullied?'

'No one thought of it like that at the time. But suffice to say that while our so-called classmates preached love and togetherness, they could be nasty and mean. We've all of us got our own stories and memories, things we're stuck with the rest of our lives.'

Simonsen wheeled round and pointed at Hanne Brummersted:

'Tell me yours.'

The shock effect he had hoped for failed to materialise, the consultant merely doing as she was instructed, muttering her story bleakly and without delay.

'In the first year I was part of the main group for a while. I even came to school without a bra on once. It happened to be the day we had our class photo taken. Someone wrote a letter and

368

complained. Nearly everyone in the class signed it. It was before pornography was made legal, that wasn't until a couple of years later. They sent it to the Ministry of Justice for a laugh, accusing me of debauchery. They even got a reply they put up on the noticeboard and sent a copy home to my parents. For a time after that they called me *Nia*. It stood for *nipples in agony*, but at least then they weren't calling me *Chub*, *Fat-face* or *The Virgin Blubber*. There was a lot more unpleasantness besides that, but the thing that hurt most was when they gave me a frying pan for my eighteenth birthday. I cried nearly the whole day, even though by then I had the others for support.'

She indicated her three former classmates.

It was hard for Simonsen not to feel pity.

'So the reason you formed the Hearts was to counter all that?'

Pia Mikkelsen answered without having been asked.

'The worst thing was that to begin with we used to be in on the teasing, too, trying to make ourselves popular. I actually signed that letter Hanne just mentioned, but then in the third year I finally had the guts to tell the ones who gave her that frying pan what I thought of them. But there's no doubt the Hearts was a defensive move, a place to go, because no one else wanted us.'

The three others nodded, and even Helena Brage Hansen was in agreement. She added:

'It wasn't just appearance that mattered, though that was definitely important. You had to think, do and feel the same as them. Anyone who didn't was going to have a hard time of it, even from the younger teachers. It was unfair and very... wrong.'

Simonsen believed he'd got the gist. It wasn't that far from what he'd imagined, though as witnesses they were hardly reliable, having a clear interest in exaggerating and putting themselves forward as victims.

He continued:

'On Friday, the thirteenth of June nineteen sixty-nine you'd got your last oral exam but one out of the way and would soon graduate. All that was left was Maths the week after, on Friday the twentieth. Who wants to go on?'

Jesper Mikkelsen spoke up.

'It was a long-standing arrangement that we'd revise together for Maths. Not that any of us was in danger of failing, because we weren't. But it was our most important subject and the grade meant something in terms of getting on to our favoured courses at university and college. Hanne wanted to be a doctor, so she needed at least eight on the old scale, preferably more...'

Simonsen cut in:

'You remember that, so many years on?'

'I remember every minute of that trip. There hasn't been a day gone by without my thinking about it. I remember what I dreamed at night, and how much our train tickets cost.'

'All right, go on.'

'Helena had the use of this place through her dad. The Scouts only used it at weekends and never in holiday seasons. We didn't even need to pay for it. The idea was for Jørgen to be a kind of teacher to us, he was really good at Maths. He and Pia had worked out this really tight revision schedule, so it was no picnic. We arrived on the Sunday evening, that'd be the fifteenth of June, and from Esbjerg to Nørballe we got the bus.'

He paused.

'Go on.'

'Can't someone else?'

'I said, go on.'

'On the Monday we revised as planned for half the day. We were all very concentrated about it and were soon ahead of schedule... so then Jørgen and Mouritz went into Esbjerg to get some shopping in while the rest of us worked on assignments. Integrals, I remember. The Scouts had bikes here, so they borrowed two of them.'

'What about Mouritz, wasn't he supposed to be revising, as well?'

'He didn't really need the grade. He was going into his dad's firm, and it didn't matter much what results he got. Besides, Jørgen needed a hand with the shopping.'

'There was a grocery store close by. How come they didn't go there instead?'

'It was a lot more expensive, Helena knew that, and we didn't have much money.'

'OK, so what happened then?'

He let Jesper Mikkelsen off the hook and pointed to Helena Brage Hansen instead. She took a deep breath and carried on in a quiet voice.

'They got back just after three with an English girl they'd met in Esbjerg. Jørgen had given her a ride on the back of his bike. It was Lucy.'

'Lucy Selma Davison?'

'Lucy Selma Davison, that's right. But of course we just knew her as Lucy.'

'Of course,' Simonsen echoed. No one else spoke.

'Does anyone feel the need for a break?'

They'd only been going for ten minutes, and yet everyone wanted the pause. Pauline and Arne each sent him a look of surprise. He ignored their silent protests and indicated that he wanted them to stay put. He himself stepped outside.

The weather had changed, it was calmer now, the layer of cloud breaking up from the east. It looked like the sun was coming out. He ambled down to the campfire site and stood for a minute with his hands folded, annoyed with himself for not being able to remember a single prayer. He lingered nonetheless.

Back at the cabin he chose Pia Mikkelsen to carry on. She hadn't said much up to then and he wanted everyone to contribute.

It took her a while to get started, but there was no help to be had, either from Simonsen or any of the others, and her looks of appeal were in vain. Eventually, she collected herself.

'We were all of us in awe of her, that was obvious from the start. She was everything we weren't. Pretty, beautiful you could say, free and impulsive, English – from Liverpool, even – but most importantly she wanted to be with us. She was kind, and interested in all of us. It wasn't what we were used to. Mouritz, for example, could hardly utter a word to her, he was so nervous. All he did was blush. Having to speak English didn't make things any easier for him, especially having to speak to her... with her looks... if you understand what I mean?'

Simonsen nodded.

'We sat out on the lawn. Or rather, not all of us, I don't think ...'

'Jørgen and Helena were making dinner. Fried pork with parsley sauce and potatoes.'

Jesper Mikkelsen and his memory for detail.

'That's right, yes. But then he started talking about his dad's firm, and what he was going to do after the holidays – as far as he was able in English, of course. He kept grinding to a halt, it was embarrassing, even more so than usual. But then Lucy laid her head in his lap, just like that, without saying anything. That didn't help him one bit. I think he gave up after that. But it was like, exactly what he needed. He was so happy about it.'

Helena Brage Hansen took over.

'Before we knew it, everything was revolving around her. No one was bothered about Maths any more, the exam didn't seem to matter, only Lucy. It was almost as if she'd consumed us. Not because she wanted to, but because we did. It wasn't like we had any formal arrangement or anything, but it tended to be me who had the deciding opinion if we couldn't agree, only now we were all following this English girl who'd suddenly appeared out of the blue. She suggested we go for a walk before dinner and so we did, all of us together. We held hands. That was new to us. I know it sounds very innocent, but for us it was... I don't know... exciting. A lot more interesting than fried pork and parsley sauce.'

Simonsen asked:

'Did you talk about how long she was going to stay?'

'Not as far as I remember. But she did put her tent up, so it was obvious she was staying the night, at least.'

'Why didn't she sleep inside? You had lots of room.'

Helena Brage Hansen shook her head. Everyone looked at Jesper Mikkelsen.

'She wanted to sleep outside, it was the fresh air.'

Rather surprisingly for Simonsen, Hanne Brummersted continued of her own accord.

'Obviously, we didn't get any more revision done that day. In the evening she played the mouth organ and sang for us round the campfire. Now and then we sang together, all of us, and she taught us a couple of songs we didn't know, lullabies, I think. At some point, not that late, she went off to bed. I think she was tired after the crossing. We tried to do a bit of revision afterwards, but no one could concentrate, so instead we decided to call it a day and get up early the next morning. I don't recall anyone saying as much, but I think we all realised we weren't going to get much done. Not once Lucy woke up anyway.'

Pia Mikkelsen cut in:

'I much preferred to be with Lucy than to do Maths, and I'm sure the boys felt that way, too. It was pretty obvious to everyone.'

'We all felt like that,' Hanne Brummersted added, somewhat curtly, Simonsen thought, after having been interrupted.

'Did you talk about her after she turned in for the night? Does anyone remember that?' he asked.

They shook their heads. Even Jesper Mikkelsen had to pass, but couldn't stop himself from firing back:

'Why are you asking us that? It can't be important, surely?'

Simonsen's reply was sharp.

'I ask, you answer. And why I ask is no concern of yours. You concentrate on telling the truth as best you can. Now it's the next day, or so I assume. Tuesday the seventeenth of June. It might jog your memories to know that the weather in Esbjerg that day was typical Danish summer: occasional cloud, scattered showers in between the sunshine, nineteen degrees Celsius, a bit lower at the coasts. All in all, not the kind of weather to run around half-naked in. I'd like you to carry on.'

He pointed at Hanne Brummersted.

'We all got up early and did revision until mid-morning. Lucy didn't wake up until late. She had some breakfast and then she had a bath. I went with her and told her what to do. There was a kind of meter, you had to put a ten-øre coin in for the hot water, so we collected what we had. Not that she was scrounging or anything, she just didn't have any change on her. Anyway, she had a bath and we carried on revising, but when she came out... that was when it started... she came into the dining room...'

Hanne Brummersted burst into tears.

'I'm all right... it's just difficult, that's all,' she said after a moment, struggling to get the words out between sobs. 'She was naked. She just stood there with her pyjamas and underwear rolled up in a wet towel, like it was the most natural thing in the world. She asked what we were thinking of doing.'

'Was she trying to provoke you? Perhaps test you in some way? Was it a joke?'

'Not at all. It didn't mean anything to her, but we all stared as if she'd suddenly grown another head. And the boys... it must have been beyond their wildest dreams.'

'We'd all thought about it, I'm certain,' Jesper Mikkelsen cut in. 'But only in our wildest dreams, as you say.'

'Well, there she was anyway, and when she realised we were looking at her... or gawping, more like... ogling even... she just laughed, and... I can't remember her exact words, but we had to learn to be less modest, *not to be shy*, I think she said. And all of a sudden that was what the day was going to be about.'

'And she decided that?'

'We all did. We wanted to, just as much as she did.'

Helena Brage Hansen interrupted and went on:

'We were unsure of ourselves, but at the same time it was tremendously exciting, and arousing in a sexual way. Now we had the chance to make up for everything our classmates had made sure never came our way, the way we looked at it, at least. It probably wasn't like that at all. None of us had any real experience of sex, practically none at all, and we would never have been that... I don't know, immodest, of our own accord. Lucy was the catalyst, but for her it was different, of course. More fun than sex.'

Simonsen pointed to Hanne Brummersted again.

'Didn't she realise the effect she was having on you?'

'We thought she was a part of all the things we'd heard about. The free love, the hippie orgies, group sex. Things that were probably all just blown up by the newspapers to titillate their readers and boost their circulation. We were very naive. She was seventeen years old, for goodness sake, and couldn't have had any idea what she was igniting inside us. None of us had a clue, and we certainly didn't know when to stop.'

'You took off your clothes. I've seen a photo Jørgen Kramer Nielsen took.'

'It wasn't something that happened right away. It was a line to cross, we had to work up the courage, especially the girls. None of us could compete with Lucy. Eventually, though, we were all naked together, walking about and trying to be proud of our bodies. The boys were, well, aroused, to begin with, but she just laughed about that, and we did, too, after a while. Gradually, there was a more natural feel about it. At one point the postman came with a parcel, a cake from Mouritz's mum. We heard him coming up the drive on his moped, and we all went out to meet him just as we were, in the nude.'

'But there was no sexual activity?'

'Not at that point, only later. It was in the air that something had to happen. Everyone felt that, I think. Apart from Lucy, perhaps.'

'So later on, things happened. Is that right?'

'We decided we needed some beer. Lucy said we should club together and put in some of her own money. The rest of us did likewise and the boys went off to the grocery store. When they got back we lit the campfire and started drinking. It was late afternoon by then.'

'Still without clothes on?'

'No, not at that point. It was too cold. But then Troels turned up. He had Down's. Back then we'd have said he was retarded, a mongol. Lucy called him *Happy Troels*. Helena had seen him before and knew he was harmless, so we let him stay and even gave him a beer. Afterwards we made sure he stuck to fizzy drinks because we weren't sure what'd happen if he got drunk. Later on, they whistled from the farm next door for him to come back. Imagine, they whistled like he was a dog, but off he went back home and we went inside. We'd had a few beers by then, without really being drunk, and we decided to play strip poker, even if... well, it wasn't that exciting seeing as how we'd been going about with no clothes on most of the day anyway. So that all petered out. But then Lucy knew a game she taught us.'

Hanne Brummersted paused and glanced around. Simonsen got the feeling she'd been opening up in the expectation of someone else taking over.

'Go on,' he said.

She obeyed, though with ill-concealed reluctance.

'It was a game of five dice. Mostly it was down to luck, but you had to throw the dice in the air and catch them again according to a series of increasingly difficult rules. She called it *knucklebones*. If you lost, you had to do something the previous player picked for you. And, of course, it got more and more daring each time you lost.'

'What sort of things?'

'Sexual things, increasingly intimate. To begin with, you lost the rest of your clothes, but after that it got more erotic, a lot more erotic... I don't suppose we need go into detail.'

'We most certainly do need to go into detail. Besides, you're a doctor. I'm sure you can be detached about it.'

The look she gave him was one of sadness rather than anger.

'At first all we did was touch each other, one on one, depending on who lost. The others watched, and then it just escalated, getting more intense all the time. At some point Troels came back and wanted to join in. When he saw what we were doing he took his pants off and sat there with an erection, masturbating himself. Then it was my turn to lose and I had to make him ejaculate, with my hands. It was a mistake, a big mistake. After that, he left and we carried on. It all got out of hand. We were doing all sorts of things we shouldn't have, opening up for each other, fondling, groping, kissing, licking.'

'Was Lucy directing all this?'

'No, not at all. She just thought it was funny. She played along like the rest of us, only she hardly ever lost, she was very dexterous with the dice, much better than us. I remember she took her clothes off, though she didn't have to.'

'So she didn't get involved physically, as it were?'

'Hardly at all. She kissed me when we were both naked, and she had to fondle Jørgen's penis while the rest of us counted to twenty. But by that time it was nothing. Pia and Jesper had already had intercourse by then, and after that it was Mouritz and me. I was a virgin, so I bled. It hurt, too, but I just clenched my teeth.'

Simonsen turned to Helena Brage Hansen.

'It sounds like some of you, at least, wanted it to stop. I've read the agony column you edited in the Scouting magazine. You come across as a mature, sensible girl who would have known how far to go and when to say stop. Why didn't you step in? Or at least leave?'

Her reply came promptly:

'A lot of it was probably to do with the alcohol, though that wasn't the most important reason. We all carried on in the hope that Lucy would lose, too, and really lose. The boys had their obvious reasons, and we girls because we'd already gone so far, some of us all the way, we thought it was her turn.'

'Did her turn come round?'

'No, it didn't.'

'Was she cheating?'

'No, she was just too good.'

'So how did it end? Perhaps you gave fortune a helping hand?'

'No, we didn't. Pia felt ill and was sick, and by then the boys were... well, spent. We'd run out of beer, too, so we just went to bed.'

'You went to bed?'

'Yes.'

'What about Lucy?'

'She went back to her tent.'

'And nothing more happened?'

'Not until the next morning.'

'All right, go on.'

'We were the first ones up again. Lucy was still asleep. We all felt terrible. We were embarrassed about what had happened and couldn't look each other in the eye, so we immersed ourselves in Maths and just wanted to go home, I suppose. I think we were angry with Lucy, too, because in a way she'd started it all off and yet she'd never really got involved herself. That's how I felt about it, at any rate.'

Simonsen noted the nods of agreement.

'And then Troels came back. It was obvious what he wanted. He had his hands down his trousers, and so on. At first we were going to send him home, but then we got the idea of sending him down to Lucy instead.'

'Oh, dear.'

'I'm afraid so. We said now she could have a taste of her own medicine, and went to the windows and watched as he crawled into her tent. Obviously, there wasn't that much we could see, and after a while he crawled out again and went away.'

'And you were hoping he was going to rape her?'

'No, not like that. We just thought she could take care of *Happy Troels* the way we, or rather Hanne, had done the night before. But then when nothing happened, we went back to our Maths and hangovers, moral as well as physical. It wasn't until after lunch we began to suspect something wasn't quite right. We called for her, and when she didn't appear we eventually went down to the tent and looked inside. And that's when we discovered she was dead. He'd strangled her.'

'Six people don't get the same idea all at once. Which of you suggested sending Troels off to Lucy?'

'I can't remember. All I know is we were all in agreement.'

Jesper Mikkelsen's memory was rather better:

'I did,' he said, almost inaudibly.

The rest of the interview was predictable and, if possible, even sadder. Pia Mikkelsen hit the nail on the head.

'We panicked. It was pure panic. The obvious thing to do was call the police and tell them what had happened, but we didn't even consider it. The mere thought of our parents finding out what we'd done was unbearable, not to mention what would happen to us. We decided to bury her and I said we should do it under the campfire. I thought if they sent dogs out looking for her they wouldn't be able to detect her there if we buried her deep enough. The boys worked like mad, while we girls packed her tent and rucksack. We couldn't find room for her Afghan coat, so we lit a fire and burned it.'

'Where was her body while all this was going on?'

'We carried her out of the tent, then covered her up with a sheet and put some stones down on the edges so it wouldn't blow away.'

'Did she have any clothes on?'

'Only her knickers. We took them off her and put them in her rucksack. We thought she'd decompose in time, but the clothes wouldn't.'

'What were you going to do with her things?'

Jesper Mikkelsen cut in:

'We washed semen off her thigh as well. Troels had ejaculated on her, but she hadn't been raped, only killed.'

Simonsen turned on him like a clap of thunder, but Mikkelsen managed to nip his rage in the bud.

'I'm sorry, I didn't mean it like that. What I meant was only that she at least hadn't been raped.'

Simonsen was appeased. He turned back to Pia Mikkelsen.

'What about her things?'

'At first we talked about dumping them in the sea, but we soon gave up on that idea. Then we remembered she'd written a postcard she hadn't got round to sending. We found it and it said she was going to head up to Norway to see the midnight sun, and then Helena got the idea of taking her things to Sweden and sending the postcard from there. We had her rucksack and tent with us on the train back to Copenhagen.'

'Who drove to Sweden?'

'Hanne and Jørgen.'

Simonsen turned to Hanne Brummersted.

'Why you two?'

'Me, because I had a driving licence, and Jørgen to help. He volunteered.'

'Wouldn't it have been better to go on your own? He couldn't help you drive.'

'I can see that now, but at the time it seemed best if there were two of us.'

'Whose car did you take? And what about your exam?'

'I told my older brother I'd got myself pregnant and borrowed money from him for an abortion. We hired a car, and to my parents I said the exam had been put back a week and that I was going to Esbjerg again to revise. Later, I told them I'd got it all mixed up, then took the resit in August.'

'And they believed you?'

'No, they thought I was pregnant and had gone off to have an abortion. That was I wanted them to think. Don't ask me what excuse Jørgen made up, because I don't know. I did the driving and he slept. We hardly said a word. At some point we sent the postcard and drove on, eventually stopping where it was all forest. We went into the trees and put the tent up. After that we drove home.'

'There was some money in her wallet.'

'We put some Swedish notes in there. I can't remember how much it was, only that we had gloves on all the time so as not to leave any fingerprints. Clingy yellow latex, they felt horrible.'

Simonsen indicated he wanted Jesper Mikkelsen to tell the rest.

'When the grave was dug we dropped her body down and covered it up again. The remains of the fire and her Afghan coat went in there, too. We stamped the earth down with a wooden post, but it was very sandy, so it wasn't that big a problem. Finally, we put the stones back round the site and lit a huge fire to get some ash.'

'And that was it? Into the grave with her and back to the Maths books?'

'We didn't want to go back early, so we stayed on. I don't think anyone did any revision, though.'

'So the day after wasn't much fun, was it?'

'None of the days after has been much fun.'

'You still haven't told me about your pledge. The oath, or whatever you called it.'

'Pledge. We called it our pledge. It was Helena's idea, We gathered around the campfire...'

Simonsen growled:

'Lucy Davison's grave! It wasn't a campfire.'

'I'm sorry. We gathered around Lucy's grave and repeated over and over: *Never, ever speak of it. Never, ever speak of it.* We carried on for ages.'

There was a long pause. They had reached the end of their journey and all eyes were on Konrad Simonsen. Hanne Brummersted and Pia Mikkelsen had started crying again. Eventually, Helena Brage Hansen broke the silence:

'What's going to happen to us now?'

'You'll be questioned individually in Copenhagen. After that, the public prosecutor and I will decide what to do with you. Perhaps nothing. Regrettably, that seems the likely outcome. But if you're referring to here and now, then... well, it's probably easier to show you.'

He got up and went outside, and when he came back he was holding four shovels in his hands.

It took them the best part of three hours. Simonsen showed no pity. Short breaks were allowed for food, water and rest, so no one was made to suffer physically, but apart from that he tolerated nothing but labour. They accepted the conditions and toiled as instructed. Arne Pedersen and Pauline Berg, who had said nothing for hours, withdrew and watched the scene from a distance. At first, the loose, sandy earth meant that the sides continually gave way, making the hole more of a crater than anything else, but eventually it took shape and narrowed, allowing room for two shovels only at a time. They took turns. Simonsen had hoped for sunshine as they worked. It was how he had imagined it. But the sky darkened and the weather changed once again. In early afternoon, as the light slowly dissolved away into the dismal blanket of cloud, the sand suddenly turned black. He gathered the shovels and handed them a bucket. They continued to dig, though now with their hands. It was Jesper Mikkelsen who found her. He straightened his back without a word, the tip of a white thighbone protruding from the grave at his feet.

Simonsen stopped them:

'That's enough. Forensics will take care of the rest. Now all we need to do is to find out which of you killed Jørgen Kramer Nielsen.'

CHAPTER 12

'None of them!'

The conclusion was plain for all to see, but Arne Pedersen and Pauline Berg left it to Simonsen to utter the words. They could only speak for their own two witnesses, Hanne Brummersted and Helena Brage Hansen in Pauline's case, the Mikkelsen couple in Arne's. That couldn't be true, thought Simonsen, getting up from his chair and frustratedly pacing back and forth as far as the limited space allowed. The Countess studied him with concern. Arne and Pauline, both seated on the sofa, looked away and waited as Simonsen wondered if he'd made a mistake including them in the Esbjerg meeting. Of all his colleagues, Arne was the least well informed on the case, busy as he was with his funding issues, accounts and the like. And as for Pauline, well, she wasn't exactly easy to work with in the best of circumstances and now all she could come up with was nothing. Two duds, or at the very least one, the one who'd messed up, whoever that might be. Simonsen sat down again with a single, unconstructive thought in his head: *What a sodding day*.

The Countess ventured a query.

'What do we do now, Simon?'

'Run me through it again.'

He prodded a finger at Arne, who spluttered a protest:

'You mean, repeat myself?'

'Yes, it's all in the word *again*. So once more, from the beginning.'

Pauline shook her head.

'This is stupid. We told you everything already five minutes ago.'

Simonsen growled at her:

'If you think this investigation's stupid, you know what you can do.'

He pointed towards the door.

'Go somewhere else and cause trouble. You're not my headache anyway until next year and I can easily do without you until then.'

The Countess intervened: 'All right, Simon, that'll do.' Pauline remained seated and sullen as Arne proceeded once more to summarise his observations from two days before in Esbjerg. From the beginning, as per orders.

Pia and Jesper Mikkelsen had been under extreme psychological pressure for long periods during Simonsen's rounds of questioning. At the same time, neither of them seemed to be concealing a second agenda – Arne didn't know quite what else to call it – concerning Jørgen Kramer Nielsen, either individually or as a couple. Throughout the day they'd hardly communicated with each other, no surreptitious glances had been exchanged at any point, in fact they'd barely seemed aware of each other's presence. But most importantly, neither had shown any sign of apprehension at the mention of the postman's name. Arne gave a couple of concrete examples from his notes before concluding almost apologetically:

'Unless they're the world's best actors, better than any suspect I've ever seen, then neither of them killed your postman, Simon. And they didn't get anyone else to do it for them either.'

Simonsen grimaced like a miser presented with a bill. Arne stuck to his guns:

'I know it's not what you want to hear, Simon. But they didn't kill anyone.'

Simonsen's eyes flashed. The Countess was quick to intervene:

'Apart from Lucy Davison, of course.'

Pauline's account of Hanne Brummersted's and Helena Brage Hansen's reactions was depressingly similar. Neither Brummersted nor Brage Hansen had anything to do with Kramer Nielsen's murder in Hvidovre. Simonsen shook his head again in annoyance, a clear sign that he didn't believe a word. He collected himself and probed further into Pauline's observations of Hanne Brummersted. The consultant doctor had long been his prime suspect.

'What was her *exact* reaction when I said the only thing we needed was to find out who killed him?'

'She didn't react at all. She was just completely stunned by having seen the remains of the body.'

'What about when I mentioned the pledge they made? And that one of them had broken it?'

'She didn't know what you meant. I didn't, either, to be honest. I don't think anyone did.'

He decided to start again from another angle. Maybe that was what was needed. He clapped his hands together and exclaimed in a more optimistic tone:

'All right, let's forget about their reactions for a minute and look at the overall picture. Who made the biggest impression on you that day?'

He looked at Pauline, then at Arne, then back again, as if to coax an answer from one of them. Eventually, Pauline replied:

'You did. Especially when you made them dig the body up. That was totally uncalled for and very cruel.'

'They killed a young girl.'

'A young girl you've been slobbering over for months, a girl you obviously decided to avenge at the first possible opportunity. And anyway, they didn't kill her, that daft lad did.'

Simonsen gasped for breath and sensed himself about to erupt in rage. Only by a gargantuan effort did he manage to contain his first urge to yell into Pauline's face with all his might. The brief respite made him even more livid when he realised neither the Countess nor Arne had put her in her place. It could only mean one thing: that they agreed with her, but hadn't the guts to say so themselves.

He was about to walk out, leave them all. Depart from his office in anger and let them sit there with their useless logic, to rot in their own ineptitude. And yet he opted for an even better solution, or so he thought. He began to issue orders.

'Arne, you check their alibis again. I know it's been done, but I want them scrutinised and I don't care if it's the fifth, sixth or tenth time. And I want you to be responsible for getting written permission from all four of them, allowing us to search their homes and any other property they happen to own. Voluntarily... even if you have to twist their arms off in the process. And make sure we get experienced officers conducting those searches. Inform Norwegian police for the sake of good relations, but send three of our own to Hammerfest as soon as you've got Helena Brage Hansen's signature.'

Arne accepted this with a weary nod. Simonsen turned to Pauline then, his voice icy.

'You make sure all four of them remain in Copenhagen and are available to me for at least the rest of this week. I intend to question them from A to Z until one of them breaks. They can get their arses over here to HQ as soon as and whenever I say. And if they don't, they'll have what they did to Lucy Davison splashed all over the tabloids with their own photos in there to boot. And if they're in any doubt about that threat, just remind them how pretty Lucy was, then ask if they think she'll sell copy. And if that doesn't convince them, I'll personally have the public prosecutor bring charges against them for manslaughter, group rape, indecent acts with a corpse and unauthorised burial of a human being in unconsecrated ground.'

Pauline retorted:

'For whose benefit?'

Simonsen slammed his fist down on the coffee table.

'Mine! And you, Countess, get me some solid medical opinions on Troels Holst, our man with Down's. I want to know if he could react the way they claim. As far as I'm informed, people with Down's tend to be peaceful and harmless, and this is the first instance I've ever heard of where someone like that... a person suffering from that disorder... supposedly killed someone.

And I want the information from at least two independent sources.'

He clapped his hands together again.

'Let's get cracking.'

Pauline and Arne got to their feet and shuffled off without comment. The Countess remained seated. Simonsen flopped down on the sofa, falling silent. Oddly, he found himself thinking about Pauline, recently the object of his fury, and yet the way he thought about her now was different, albeit he was unable to put his finger on quite how. He shook his head, as if to rid his mind of whatever was puzzling him, and when that didn't help he turned to the Countess.

'I stood there when the forensics guys uncovered Lucy, and when they took their photographs and laid her bone by bone into one of those boxes. When they lifted up her skull I found her... becoming. That's what I thought to myself: that she was still beautiful. Her teeth were so regular and white, and the shape of her head... she was just so... whole and perfect.'

The Countess smiled to herself, and threw out a casual invitation in the same dreamy tone.

'Should we go out for dinner tonight? Somewhere cosy, in Helsingør, perhaps? I could do with it.'

Simonsen decided to conduct all interviews with what was now the Gang of Four on his own. An hour or more with each, and with half an hour in between so they didn't get the chance to collude on their way in or out. The bulk of his suspicion was still aimed at Hanne Brummersted, the hospital consultant who had been so arrogant and dismissive the last time they'd questioned her on her own. Now the arrogance was gone; her eyes were tearful and she looked like she hadn't slept.

'Don't you think it's about time you got it off your chest? We *know* you were in touch with Jørgen Kramer Nielsen. It's all over his diary.'

She shook her head in despair.

'It must be wrong. I haven't seen him since the trip to Sweden. Not once... at least, not to my knowledge.'

Simonsen was upon her like a cobra.

'To your knowledge? What's that supposed to mean?'

He sensed the tension mount explosively, but her explanation was worthless. Maybe sometime in the late nineties, 1997 perhaps, she wasn't sure, but she might have seen him in IKEA in Gentofte. She'd avoided him and had deliberately gone the other way. He hadn't seen her, she felt sure of it.

'Why would he mention you in his diary, then? How do you explain that?'

She couldn't. She wished she could, but no, it was inexplicable to her. At no point did she seem to realise Simonsen was lying.

With Helena Brage Hansen he was rather more cautious. He didn't want her to break down the way her brother had told him she was liable to do at the slightest provocation. He put his questions to her calmly, as if the game were up and he had nothing personal against her.

'Jørgen Kramer Nielsen came to see you in Norway. When was the first time he was there?'

'No, you're wrong. He was never in Norway. At least, not to see me.'

'So you went to see him in Copenhagen?'

'No, I didn't, no such thing. We haven't been in touch since... since *then*.'

'Phone records don't lie, Helena.'

'Then there must be some mistake. Please check again. We never phoned each other. Never once.'

With the Mikkelsen couple he tried to play one off against the other. Jesper Mikkelsen wept for most of the duration, wringing a handkerchief that became increasingly wretched the longer they went on. Simonsen noted with irritation the way he kept dabbing at his tears. He thought about Lucy, and the small measure of pity he'd felt evaporated instantly.

'Stop blubbering, man. Find yourself a decent solicitor instead.'

'I didn't think you wanted us to.'

'No, but you'd better. Did you really think your wife was going to cover up for you for ever? How naive can you be? Especially in view of the way your relationship's been going over the years.'

Mikkelsen burst into tears again, struggling to utter his words through the sobs.

'Then punish me for killing Jørgen, even though I didn't. I deserve to go to prison.'

Pia Mikkelsen was the only one who offered a measure of resistance.

'Can't you people get it into your heads? I had nothing to do with Jørgen whatsoever.'

'But you're the only one who was in touch with him.'

'I most certainly was not. That's a lie.'

Simonsen slammed the flat of his hand down on the table and yelled. And then she was crying, too.

That evening he and the Countess had dinner at a little Italian place in Helsingør's town centre. Anna Mia joined them, the Countess having called and asked her. Or maybe it was vice versa, Simonsen never really found out.

The food was good without being spectacular, and reasonably priced, too, as the Countess noted when eventually they sat with their tea and coffee. Anna Mia didn't get it.

'I don't understand you, Nathalie. You're absolutely loaded with dosh and normally you're not bothered how much you spend, but every time we got out for a meal you look at the bill as if every penny counted. Did your parents starve you when you were a kid, or what?'

The Countess laughed. No, she'd wanted for nothing. Anna Mia persisted:

'Maybe it doesn't always have to be you who pays every time we're out. Dad could, for a change... or me, for that matter.'

The afterthought was a bit hesitant.

'I thought you were saving up,' said the Countess.

'I am, but there's a long way to go yet.'

Simonsen suddenly paid attention. He'd been staring out of the window without really listening. Pauline Berg was inside him again, a voice, an emotion... impossible to explain, but he found it happening increasingly.

'What was that you said about saving up?' he asked his daughter.

Anna Mia shook her head in resignation.

'It doesn't matter. There's no point anyway with property prices the way they are in Copenhagen. Flats, I mean. I'll never get anywhere near being able to put something down for a mortgage.'

'Aren't you happy where you are?' he said, a note of concern in his voice.

The Countess shook her head with a little smile.

'Simon...'

She made it sound like he should stop contesting the law of gravity. He acquiesced. She was right, of course, he shouldn't interfere. Anna Mia explained it to him.

'I'm getting older, too, Dad. But it's not feasible, especially if I want to live in the centre, Frederiksberg or Valby. Sometimes I think I should move to Jutland. Aarhus, perhaps, or Aalborg. The prices over there are more reasonable.'

The Countess came to her aid.

'That sounds like a good idea. Live somewhere else for a few years, Copenhagen's not everything. We could drive over one day and look at some places, if you want. I love doing that.'

'That'd be brilliant.'

Anna Mia sounded happy. Simonsen was not. He spun out a couple of inarticulate arguments in favour of the capital: Copenhagen would be best in career terms, and besides, her friends were all here. What's more, she had to bear in mind the greater distances involved in Jutland. The region was bigger, much bigger than she was used to, for which reason she would have to work a car into her budget, meaning there wouldn't be much gained anyway. Probably the opposite, all things considered. No doubt about it.

The Countess again offered her help.

'You can buy my car cheap, I'll get another. We'd be able to see you a bit more then, though it wouldn't be the same as when you're living here, of course.'

The ensuing pause lasted all of five seconds, and then Simonsen had another idea. He still had his own flat, which basically he hardly ever used. Anna Mia put a hand on his arm at the suggestion.

'But it's yours, Dad. And you're so fond of Valby, I know you are.'

He might well have been, but he'd hardly been there more than three or four times in the past couple of months, apart from picking up his mail. Besides, it had been on his mind for a good while now that something had to change, and this was as good a time as any. It was worth considering, at least. At some point, in the near future.

The Countess thought it was a splendid idea. She knew a solicitor who was brilliant at that sort of thing. Anna Mia could buy the place cheap, the Countess could chip in and help, and Simonsen himself would then have enough in his account to buy something else if he ever found he couldn't stick living with her any more. She waved away all protests. There were no two ways about it. It was an investment, and she'd be saving money on the car, too, if Anna Mia didn't need it.

They hadn't touched a drop of alcohol during the meal, but now she ordered three glasses of Calvados, enlivened by the excitement. Anna Mia conceded that Aalborg was perhaps rather too far away after all, and agreed it would be fantastic if they really could work this out. The Countess raised her glass.

'Of course we can. I'll get the solicitor to come round tomorrow evening. *Skål!*'

The two women chinked glasses. Anna Mia turned to her father.

'It's really kind of you, Dad. And thanks for having a drink with us, too. I know you don't normally. But it's like sealing the bargain, isn't it?'

They toasted and drank up.

The second and third round of questioning yielded as little as the first. Simonsen huffed and puffed, begged and pleaded, and used every trick in the book, and a couple more besides, but all to no avail. Jørgen Kramer Nielsen's killer remained unforthcoming. The searches he initiated, the surveillance and phone taps, permission for which was so infuriatingly difficult to secure, brought no result either. None of the four suspects had been in contact with any of the others, apart from the Mikkelsen couple, of course, and none had made phone calls that could in any way be considered suspicious. After three days' slog, Simonsen was left with a big, fat zero.

These were days when he felt everyone was conspiring against him, with the Countess as ringleader. Even Klavs Arnold, who had been on his side right from day one, seemed to have changed tack. When Thursday came round Simonsen took the bull by the horns, gathering his inner circle to hammer it home once and for all: they may reject his theory that one of the Hearts was responsible for Kramer Nielsen's untimely death, but he was still heading up the investigation, and he alone decided how it was to proceed.

He repeated himself for effect and felt almost gleeful at the sight of their weary-eyed expressions as he hammered home his message.

'Lonely Hearts, Lonely Hearts, Lonely Hearts. That's where we need to look. One of them did away with Jørgen Kramer Nielsen. They may even all be in on it. Somewhere there's a connection, and we have to find it. I want bright ideas, and I want them fast.'

His voice boomed out, to be met only by the blank wall of a rare consensus. Klavs Arnold was frank with him.

'You're wrong, and you won't admit it. The main thing preventing us from finding Jørgen Kramer Nielsen's killer at the moment is you being so stubborn.'

Arne Pedersen was more diplomatic.

'I'm sorry, I just don't think there *is* a connection, not any more.'

He contended that the searches they'd conducted had been a waste of *resources*. Naturally, that was the word Arne used: *resources*. Not *time* or *effort*. It was the way executives viewed people, Simonsen thought to himself. He listened, feeling somewhat detached, as Arne listed the negative results, going on to confirm Helena Brage Hansen's and Jesper Mikkelsen's alibis from the period the killing in Hvidovre had been deemed to have taken place. Eventually, Arne Pedersen concluded:

'I've watched and reviewed all your interviews and have done my utmost in each case to go into things with an open mind. But all I can see is that it holds up. In the case of the unfortunate incident concerning Lucy Davison, they've put everything on the table. Every detail has been satisfactorily accounted for. There are no loose ends.'

'It's not about Esbjerg, it's about Hvidovre.'

'I know that, and in my honest opinion, none of them had anything whatsoever to do with what happened there. And that's supported by the fact that we've yet to find the slightest, even remotely recent piece of evidence linking any of the four together or to Kramer Nielsen himself. And the reason for that is that there *is* no link, not to mention a conspiracy.'

The Countess twisted the blade.

'You're barking up the wrong tree, Simon. It's as simple as that. Every time we've confronted them with Kramer Nielsen's death they've provided us with logically consistent answers without hesitation or any kind of beating about the bush, and even you must admit you've been turning the screws on them. Perhaps excessively so at that.'

'What about Hanne Brummersted? You suspected her yourself for quite some time, if I remember rightly?'

'Suspected, yes, past tense. It's no secret I don't much care for the woman, but she didn't kill Jørgen Kramer Nielsen. And while I remember it, I've got a report for you about people with Down's Syndrome and their control of sexual urges.'

He was about to cut her off. That could wait, this was neither the time nor the place. But with an efficient flourish he immediately found infuriating she produced a printout and proceeded to go through its main points with pedantic insistence.

People with Down's did indeed suffer from lack of self-control, though to varying degrees. In particular, they often found difficulty correctly interpreting human behaviour and language, communicative situations in general. Sexually, they could be considered promiscuous, and indecent exposure including public masturbation was not uncommon, a fact attributed to sexual confusion and disorientation. This could furthermore lead to inappropriate, offensive or physically violent behaviour. So, yes, there was a definite possibility that Troels Holst had killed Lucy Davison. Not because he intended to, but because he lost control of himself and the situation.

Simonsen grunted a word of thanks and endeavoured to pick up the thread.

'Does this mean that you seriously consider we just happen to be dealing with the murder of a man who demonstrably colluded with others in causing the death of a young woman, and yet there is no link between the two occurrences? Think how unusual murder thankfully still is in this country, and then tell me you believe in this utterly incredible coincidence.'

His words were wasted. It was what they believed. Unanimously so.

'Somewhere, there's a detail we've missed. It's there. Somewhere.'

There was a shaking of heads. No missing detail. Anywhere.

'I'd like to help you, but I don't know what to do.'

It was Pauline who said it and she sounded like she meant it. He didn't know how to reply to her.

He spent the next day pondering different theories, each more unlikely than the next. Only one seemed to open up some small measure of possibility, enough for him to want to put it to others anyway, in this case Arne Pedersen, whom he waylaid in the corridor.

'Listen, Arne. Suppose Kramer Nielsen was ill. Suppose he knew he was dying. As long as he was alive he wasn't going to break that precious pledge of theirs, but on the other hand his Catholic faith is tearing away at him, urging him to make a clean breast of it so he can be ready to meet his maker. Maybe he wrote a letter, to be opened after his death, outlining how Lucy Davison died. Hanne Brummersted happens to find out about his illness via her medical connections. She goes to sees him, to make him think better of it before it's too late. How does that sound?'

'Like an equation with too many unknown quantities. *Was* he ill?'

'We should be able to find out easily enough.'

Two wasted hours and a handful of phone calls later, Simonsen was forced to concede that there was nothing at all to indicate that the postman had been at death's door. The priest had no information to that effect, the postmaster likewise, the man hardly having had a day off sick. Kramer Nielsen's GP and the regional hospitals had nothing, and the list of the deceased's personal effects contained no medicine other than a jar of aspirin, and even that was unopened. In short, whichever way he turned he drew a blank, and the theory died a death accordingly. Simonsen reminded himself he ought to inform Arne Pedersen, and then forgot all about it again.

There was more substance to Pauline's input. She didn't hide the fact that she inclined towards the majority line, as she referred to it, and yet she had taken his call for bright ideas seriously. Arriving in his office one morning, he found her lying flat out on the sofa in his annexe waiting for him. He commented on her choice of clothing, suddenly recalling it had been a problem for her – and for him – some months previously. Since then he hadn't given the matter a thought, but now he noticed again:

'You're wearing your old clothes, the ones you had on before...'

He hesitated and could have kicked himself. She finished the sentence for him.

'Before I was abducted and tortured. Yeah, so what?'

'Nothing. It just made me wonder if you were beginning to feel better, that's all.'

She shook her head.

'I'm feeling like I always do. It's up and down. But I don't want to talk about it. Not today.'

He respected her for it, apologised and kicked himself again for apologising.

'Two points, Simon,' she said. 'First, what if one of them from the Esbjerg trip used to go back once in a while, like Kramer Nielsen did, and then maybe at some point found the bag he'd hidden?'

'It was well concealed, but not impossible, by any means.'

'And second, I can't see that we've cross-checked there for your suspects' fingerprints.'

'*Our* suspects.' It was a point he had to stress. *His* suspects were *Homicide's* suspects, and thereby *theirs*. Apart from that, he praised her and made a note. Pauline's face lit up. Apparently, she was having one of *those* days. He went on:

'They were all of them affected by what happened on that trip, and it's no exaggeration to say it marked them for life.'

'I agree.'

'Jørgen Kramer Nielsen with his photos and his maths. Hanne Brummersted with all her work in diagnostics and genetic aspects of Down's...'

His voice trailed off.

'Go on, I'm with you.'

'We're leaving out Mouritz Malmborg. We've forgotten about him completely. How was he affected by Lucy Davison's death? More importantly, have we even looked into how he died?'

Simonsen scribbled down another note with a pensive grunt and gave her credit once more. He wondered if that was why she was so tenacious with her theories. Much more so than the rest of them put together. Was it all to garner praise? If so, she was the complete opposite of himself. He would ask the Countess about it as soon as he got the chance.

By mid-morning, however, both loose ends came together. No fingerprints from any of the others had been found on Jørgen Kramer Nielsen's bag or any other of his personal effects, and if Mouritz Malmborg's death had been orchestrated, the rather intricate performance had involved an Italian lorry driver falling asleep at the wheel and two totalled lamp posts. Konrad Simonsen went home for his jog.

* * *

Anna Mia was all ready in her running gear, full of beans. The weather was perfect: chilly, though not too cold, no wind and just a slight drizzle that would keep them feeling fresh. This was the day he was going to *run* all the way from start to finish. It would be a triumph. He was ready for it, and he wanted to share the moment with his daughter.

They ran. She chatted, while he saved his breath.

'It's really nice of you to let me come with you. How close are you now to your goal, do you think? Not having to walk, I mean.'

He pinched his index finger and thumb together, leaving a little gap. She understood and stopped talking. It lasted a hundred metres or so.

'You don't need to answer, but I think it's good you found that girl.'

'Thanks.'

'Now they're all saying you'll clear up that case about the postman, too.'

'Really.'

'But that's stupid, I know. You're not a magician.'

'No.'

He had begun to perspire, and the pleasant sensation of controlled exercise on which he had increasingly become dependent spread through his body and mind. They passed along the well-to-do residential roads at a silent jog, shortly afterwards rounding his midway mark for only the third time without pause. Soon the pain set in, his lungs crying out to him.

'How are you doing? All right?' his daughter asked.

He didn't reply. She took this to be an invitation to carry on talking:

'If you don't clear up that murder, it won't matter. You don't need to live up to some stupid image other people have of you, you know. Anyway, only a couple of kilometres to go now. Less, maybe. You're doing really well today.'

It was hard for him to think clearly. He wanted the word *kilo-metre* abolished, and outlawing corporal punishment of one's offspring seemed suddenly to have been too hasty a measure by half, but apart from that he was unable to attain any form of coherence as he gasped and heaved for air. He dragged himself along the next stretch of road, and as he turned left he knew that if he looked up and saw how far he still had to go, he wouldn't make it. And then he noticed the car come gliding slowly towards him, and he had all the time in the world to stare: a Wartburg Convertible from 1969, fully restored, of course. He halted abruptly.

'Concentrate, Rita.'

They had got an early start and sat themselves down on a bench next to a bus stop on the city's Rådhuspladsen, facing Vester Voldgade. It was a good place to practise. She was no good at cars. He knew all the makes and models, but she needed to recognise only one. Nonetheless, it was proving more difficult than it sounded. Not least because he wouldn't tell her why. She enquired cautiously, sounding cowed as she had done all week:

'But why is this important, Konrad? I'm useless with cars.'

He snarled at her. It just *was*, that was all, and if she could swan around Europe delivering cash to suspicious individuals for some cause of which she was utterly oblivious, then she could also damn' well pull herself together and pick out a single make of car when he asked her to. She indulged him and turned her attention back to the morning rush-hour traffic, though it was obvious her lack of knowledge of the subject curbed her motiv-ation. She was exceptionally poor at this task he had given her, hazarding wayward guesses, picking out Datsuns and Chryslers that looked nothing remotely like a Wartburg Convertible. He threw up his arms in exasperation, turning his eyes to the heavens and the bronze statue of the two Viking lur blowers that looked down on them from their pedestal on the square. She apologised, her voice timid as a little girl's:

'I'm doing my best.'

She tried again, and for the first time succeeded. He praised her, issuing words of encouragement: now she was getting the hang of it. And yet two more passed by without her noticing. He had set aside the whole day, but was now beginning to wonder if it would be enough. Gradually, however, she became more practised, and by late morning she was rather good at it. He asked if she was packed and prepared. She nodded. Tomorrow, she'd be saying goodbye to her old friends: they were meeting up in Kongens Have, and she hoped he'd come, too. Then, the day after, she would board the jumbo that would take her from Copenhagen to New York. She nodded in the direction of a Wartburg Convertible as it passed by. Everything was ready: suitcases, tickets, passport and visa. Everything except money.

'I'm going to miss you.'

She sounded like she meant it. He told her he'd never in all his life met a girl like her. *In all his life...* what a ridiculous thing to say now in hindsight; he'd been in his early twenties at the time. She tried to sound optimistic.

'But you've got to come over and see me soon. You promise, don't you?'

Naturally, he promised. She could count on it.

He was less emotional about it than she was. Somewhere inside, he felt relieved to see her go, though at the same time he knew he loved her in a way, enough at least to feel torn apart by the thought of her sinking to the bottom in America without the means – the money – to take care of herself.

He hadn't for a moment doubted his own plan once the idea had occurred to him. Moreover, he told himself, it was as good as foolproof – though he knew better than most that the country's prisons were full of people who had believed their crimes to be without risk of detection.

Their rehearsal now took in the parking spaces around Nørreport Station and the streets behind the Grønttorvet in the direction of Nansensgade, where they biked around, and she identified four Wartburg Convertibles without hesitation.

Her baptism of fire came the following day. They waited outside a telephone box at one end of a slumbering street. The location was ideal. A few shoppers idled past, and some children were playing. That's how he remembered it.

His instructions to her were clear as the car came into sight and passed by. He nodded towards it discreetly, satisfying himself that she'd noticed.

'Stay in the phone box. If you see the red Wartburg Convertible come back into the street here, you call. Let it ring three times, then put the receiver down and walk home.'

He went into the phone box, dropped a coin into the slot, dialling a number twice, each time allowing it to ring. There was no answer. He hung up and instructed her again:

'Tell me the phone number.'

She told him.

'Tell me again.'

She repeated it.

'Now, remember. The red Wartburg. You call the number. Let it ring three times, hang up and walk home.'

He repeated the words again, and she likewise. Twice more. And then he left.

Thirty-five years later on a residential street in Søllerød, he stoically accepted defeat. His lungs heaved like a pair of bellows, striving to deliver oxygen to his sorry organism as he stood bent double, head down, hands on knees. But there was nothing wrong with his mind.

'It's OK, Dad. You did your best, and in a couple of weeks you'll be running all the way, no problem. You gave your all today, you can't ask for more than that. It'll come, believe me.'

Though his body protested, he chose to run the rest of the way home.

On Saturday 29 November 2008, a day of resplendent late-autumnal colour, Denmark bade farewell to Lucy Davison. It was a difficult day for Konrad Simonsen.

The Countess endeavoured to cheer him up and help make him look presentable. The suit was a present she'd bought him, and this was its first outing. She'd dragged him to a tailor's in the centre of town, a small and exclusive place that looked like a museum exhibition. He had his measurements taken by an elderly gentleman who prodded a stiff digit into his stomach and generally made him feel like a shop dummy. The tailoring process had involved three return visits before the tailor and the Countess were satisfied. No one asked his opinion and the bill was a secret, too, but today he was happy he'd gone to the trouble. The alternative was his uniform, which more than likely fitted him like a tent after he'd lost so much weight.

'Are you sure it's all right to take flowers?'

'Yes, positive.'

'But I didn't know her.'

'That doesn't mean you can't take flowers.'

'Do you think there'll be others with flowers?'

'No.'

'Won't it be embarrassing?'

'No.'

The Deputy Commissioner and a laconic individual from the Ministry of Foreign Affairs made up the official delegation, Konrad Simonsen was there in a private capacity. A DNA test had recently established the victim's identity once and for all. Despite their advanced age, George and Margaret Davison had insisted on making the journey to Copenhagen to accompany their daughter on her final journey. The Danish government had with all possible speed sent off a formal invitation and procured a coffin. The hearse drove slowly out to the aircraft and waited.

'What a nice thought, to bring flowers,' the Deputy Commissioner said.

Simonsen felt awkward, and doubtful his rudimentary English would hold up in the face of Liverpudlian dialect.

'Do me a favour and translate if the parents say anything to me.'

'Of course, Simon.'

'Or answer on my behalf.'

The man from the ministry muttered under his breath in English: *'Welcome to Denmark, kingdom of bilingual bizzies.'*

The Deputy Commissioner hissed at him:

'That's quite enough arrogance, thank you.'

She turned to Simonsen.

'Perhaps you should go and put the flowers on her coffin.'

Passengers were now boarding the aircraft. The pilot took his place beside the Deputy Commissioner and shortly afterwards the car carrying Lucy Davison's parents pulled up. Her father was very elderly and poorly sighted, her mother hunched yet somewhat more animated. Simonsen greeted them both and offered his condolences according to the book, then withdrew a couple of paces, hoping it would all soon be over. But what only took a few short minutes felt like an eternity to him, and he feared the worst when the Deputy Commissioner stepped up to him with Margaret Davison on her arm.

'You don't need to say anything, Simon, just listen.'

For a long moment, the old woman considered him with intense blue eyes, clasping his hand in a tight and bony grip before speaking, her voice thin and brittle as parchment:

'God bless you. Mr Simonsen. God bless you.'

The able among them carried Lucy Davison's coffin the short distance from the hearse to the conveyor belt that would take her into the hold. Simonsen felt consternation: would her bones end up in a jumble at the rear of the casket, or had the forensic technicians gathered her together in a plastic bag? He didn't know, and for a moment feared the sudden clatter that would occur if her mortal remains started to slide. Fortunately, he had no reason to fear, and only his own flowers succumbed to the laws of gravity, the coffin tipping gently back and forth for a second at the top of the ramp, as if unable to decide whether to return to England or remain in Denmark. It looked too light by half, he thought to himself.

The Countess picked him up. To begin with he said little, all of a sudden having thought of Pauline Berg and been gripped by a sense of some connection resolved, a truth that had been staring them in the face. It had happened several times during these past few days. He felt like a mathematician suddenly realising he had found the solution to some difficult problem, without yet having done the calculations.

'Are you all right?' the Countess asked. 'You're even more absent than usual. Was it that bad?'

He replied wearily:

'No, it's Kramer Nielsen getting at me again.'

'Sometimes, you know, success just doesn't come. It's part of life, you ought to know by now.'

'I do. And why everyone keeps lecturing me about it, I've no idea.'

'Well, excuse *me*. Who's *everyone* anyway, besides me?'

'Anna Mia, yesterday, when we were out jogging.'

'Simon, Anna Mia's your daughter, not *everyone...*'

He cut her off in annoyance.

'Sorry, just an expression, that's all.'

'It doesn't matter. But what about Kramer Nielsen? Is it because none of us agrees with you? It doesn't normally bother you.'

'No, of course not. That little difference of opinion is quite clear-cut: I'm right and you're wrong. No, it's something else. I've got a guilty conscience and I don't know why. As long as it was

Lucy Davison we were concerned about, I was totally involved every second of the way – sometimes too involved, perhaps. But now it's only Kramer Nielsen... there, you see, *only*. That's it in a nutshell. Jørgen Kramer Nielsen, the eternal loser, even in death. All his adult life there wasn't a soul who cared about him, and now he's dead... well, to tell you the truth, I couldn't really be bothered to find out who killed him so I let myself be diverted. I'm going to have to go back to square one with him, start from the beginning again, retrace my tracks.'

'Didn't you just tell us all Esbjerg and Hvidovre are linked? And that we're stupid for not realising it?'

'Of course there's a link, but that doesn't necessarily mean I'm able to find it. And I never said anyone was *stupid*.'

'No, I know you didn't. It's just that you're so sure of yourself it gets up people's noses sometimes.'

'It's not my fault I'm right.'

They drove for a while in silence.

'Are we having an argument?' he said finally.

'No. But as soon as we get home you're going out for a jog.'

It sounded like a good idea.

He went over to Valby on the Sunday evening, thinking he would sleep in his own bed one last time. After all, he'd lived there more than twenty years. But somehow it didn't feel like home any more when he walked through the door. He hovered about in the living room, like a stranger, wondering what furniture he should take with him and what would have to go. He hadn't a clue: other thoughts encroached, thoughts about Pauline Berg, as if she wouldn't let go of him. He cursed her under his breath. Ever since he'd got to the bottom of things with Rita and Lucy – he had, surely? – it was like suddenly he'd made room for her. He tried to focus his mind on the sideboard, a monstrosity of a thing handed down from his great-grandmother. He opened one of its cupboards, only to find himself daydreaming again, Pauline's pretty, petulant face staring back at him in his mind's eye.

He couldn't sleep either. Eventually, at a quarter-past two in the morning, he capitulated. He got up and dressed, then put on his warm oilskin coat, scarf and woollen hat. It was bitterly cold outside, though without a breath of wind. The air pinched at his cheeks as he stepped out on to the empty street with a shudder. He wandered, strangely serene. The buildings seemed anonymous, alike in the semi-darkness, and he felt himself merge comfortably into the surroundings. From a modest drinking establishment came the sound of song, no drunken bawling as might be expected at this hour, but a gentle bass line accompanied by a rather out-of-tune piano. He paused, casting an inquisitive glance through the door without being able to see much, and soon, after he'd passed, the song died away and silence returned. It was a long wander.

On his way back, in a side street off Pile Allé, he found himself caught up in an incident against his will. A few short metres ahead of him, a gateway suddenly opened and a caretaker in grey overalls heavy-handedly propelled a sparrow of a man half his own size out on to the street. He had him by the scruff of the neck, showering him with abuse for whatever reason. Simonsen stopped. The caretaker let go of his victim, dropping him on the kerb on the other side of the road, where he rolled over in a heap, presumably drunk.

'What's going on here? You can't leave him there like that in this weather.'

The caretaker rose to his full height and wheeled round. *Why didn't he mind his own business? Or maybe he fancied a punch on the nose?* Simonsen produced his ID, noting how the man still debated with himself as to whether to stand down or not.

'You can have a try, and I'll give you three months inside in return, as well as putting you on your back.'

407

The man calmed down a bit and growled at him:

'I was down in the basement checking the boiler. Bloody thing went out again, didn't it? There he was, crashed out in the stairwell... nearly fell over him. Bloody homeless, they're all over the place if you're not careful. I can't have them on my property, it could put me in all sorts of trouble.'

'Clear off before I take you in.'

The man did as he was told and Simonsen turned his attention to the man on the pavement. A low-life, one of those for whom there was no use any more, in clothes that were sorely inadequate for the time of year. Simonsen took off his coat and wrapped him up, then called for a patrol car.

He was familiar with the statistics. Increasing numbers with not enough money to pay the rent and no other option but the street; twice as many now as five years ago. The credit crunch had undoubtedly speeded up the process. He sighed and stepped back. The man reeked.

And then suddenly, in the space of ten golden seconds, everything came together.

For whose benefit? That's what she'd said, and it was why he couldn't get her out of his mind. Not because he was mixing her up with other women, not at all. It was because of those words she'd said at that last meeting when he'd lost his rag. *Cui bono? For whose benefit?* It was the oldest question in the book, the starting point of any police investigation. *Thank you, Pauline. Thank you!*

The patrol car arrived swiftly. Simonsen asked them to drive him over to HQ first. It was stupid, really: it would have taken him fifteen minutes at most to go back and pick up his own car. But he couldn't wait. The two officers rolled down all the windows and lugged the sleeping tramp on to the back seat.

'Is this your coat?' one of them asked.

Simonsen nodded.

'We've got a bin liner in the boot, if you want.'

It was a decent thought: he'd be able to take it with him and have it dry-cleaned without touching the thing. On the other hand, he hadn't worn it for a year, so what the hell?

'It's all right, he can keep it.'

He hastened his way through HQ to his office, unlocked the door, switched on the light and found the folder on the shelf. His fingers fumbled their way through the contents before pulling out the printout he'd got himself so worked up about. He scanned the few lines he was looking for and felt his face light up in a smile.

Cui bono?

That day, Simonsen didn't come in until mid-morning. He made for his office, gathering all the folders from the Kramer Nielsen case and spreading them out along the length of the deep window sill. Nineteen in all. They took up the entire space. He mused briefly on the fact that no matter what Homicide did, paper was a sure result. He paced about, ambled almost, gazing up at the ceiling or down at the floor, spirits high.

Pauline knocked on his door an hour later, by which time he was seated at his desk with a staple gun, firing at the coffee cup he'd positioned on the floor. The place was littered with staples. She stared at him in disbelief.

'What are you doing?'

'Working.'

He fired another shot. A hit.

'The secret is to find the right angle and then pull the trigger slowly, so you're never quite sure when it's going to go off. All rather self-evident. But there's two other things. Can you guess what they are?'

He fired again. Another hit.

'That was twenty-six out of one hundred and sixteen, so I must be doing something right. What do you reckon?'

'Arne wants you to help him out with a memo.'

'You don't say. A memo. How important-sounding. Why doesn't he come and ask me himself?'

'Because he's busy working on it, that's why.'

'I'm busy, too. As you can see.'

Another hit. Third in a row.

'The other two things are *persistence* and *luck*. *Persistence* and *luck*.'

'Are you coming, or what?'

'Yes, I'm coming. Do you think you could get me a couple of boxes of ammo from the store while Arne and I fine-tune his memo?'

'Seriously?'

'No, but you can get me the address of that nervous friend of yours, the girl who stole – or rather *didn't* steal – Jørgen Kramer Nielsen's mobile phone. I'd like to speak to her again.'

'You mean her private address?'

'No, that's probably overdoing it. Her e-mail will do.'

'Why don't you phone her?'

'E-mail's better in her case, it'll give her time to think about her answers without being scared I'm going to come after her on account of that mobile.'

He dumped his weapon on the desk in front of him and went with Pauline Berg. She seemed to be in a good mood, too. *Having a good spell*, as she might say. He took the opportunity to have a jab at her:

'Do you fancy sweeping some staples up off my floor afterwards?'

'In your dreams.'

'How about running zigzag? I could do with something more exciting to aim at than a coffee cup.'

'Now you're talking.'

He found Arne Pedersen slouched behind his computer, unproductive, staring emptily into space. Simonsen slapped him on the back. *Don't worry, help's at hand.* One little memo would hardly

410

be a match for two grown men like them. Arne snapped back to reality.

'I've never known a case to need so much mopping up as this school shooting. We got the actual events cleared up fast enough, but now they've got me writing at least five reports about what we can do to prevent it happening again. The fact of the matter is, we can do very little. I can't say that, though, can I?'

Simonsen agreed. Preventing school shootings was clearly not the job of the Homicide Department. Arne went on wearily:

'It's not so much this memo, even if I have ground to a halt and could do with a hand. The thing is, I was sitting here thinking about something.'

'Go on, we've got plenty of time.'

'In that classroom at Marmorgades Skole, after they'd taken the three bodies away, the floor was covered in tiny shards from the window. They kept crunching under my feet as I walked around.'

'I can imagine that.'

'I just kept circling about the room, thinking about what a terrible thing it is when kids are ostracised like that, how deeply it can affect the soul of the victim and give rise to the worst imaginable catastrophes. I knew full well, even then, that Robert Steen Hertz had been victimised and left out. His physical appearance was quite enough on its own to suggest the fact. And then again with the Hearts in Esbjerg. If the kids in that class had just shown them even the slightest positive interest, that girl from England would never have been killed.'

Simonsen could well understand him. It was a neat comparison, certainly one that was worth contemplating. Arne glanced at him distrustfully, expecting a note of dissent perhaps, but there was none.

Nevertheless, he left the subject and returned to the matter of his memo.

* * *

Simonsen's high spirits carried over into his home life. Full of himself, he lectured the Countess and his daughter about the virtues of persistence and luck.

'How I wish I'd inherited some of your genius, Dad. But what is it you've found out about this postman of yours? Or haven't you?'

The Countess chipped in. Of course he'd found something out. He'd been going around with that silly grin on his face for three whole days now.

She turned and looked at him.

'Where have you been all day, anyway? The last person to see you at HS was Pauline. She said you were playing stupid games in your office and looked like you'd gone soft in the head.'

'National Centre of Forensic Services in Vanløse. I was with Kurt Melsing most of the day and will be tomorrow, as well. The things you learn out there. Do you know, they've got this machine... you can put anything you want in it and it'll tell you the chemical make-up of it. A gaschromo-something-or-other, they call it. You put, say, a rubber eraser in it and it'll spit out a whole lot of complicated-looking graphs that apparently aren't nearly as complicated as they look, because they've all got regular chemical designations with numbers attached. Then what they do is, they feed a computer with these designations and hey, presto, it'll tell you you've got a rubber eraser. It's marvellous, and all for as little as just under a million kroner.'

'All right, I'm with you. You're not going to tell us. But you might at least say when we can expect to be informed of whatever it is you've come up with.'

'Yes, Dad, I'm dying to know, too.'

'Patience, ladies. Everything comes to she who waits, and if you wait long enough they'll make you Queen of Sweden, as the saying goes. I know there are two of you but Sweden's a big place, a vast country. There'll be enough of it for both of you. One of you can have the north, the other the south. You can even swap around once in a while.'

412

Anna Mia gave up.

'And you can be King Daft-Arse and I can find myself another dad. Come on, Nathalie, let's leave him on his own. He doesn't deserve us.'

Word spread quickly at Police HQ. Simonsen had solved the postman murder. Everyone, it seemed, had it on good authority, from someone who knew someone else who was one hundred per cent reliable. Only a few short months previously, not a single soul could have cared less about Jørgen Kramer Nielsen's death; now it was just the opposite. The Countess could hardly get her work done for people poking their heads round the door on some stupid pretext, each excuse lamer than the last, and while they were there, what was it they'd heard about that killing out in Hvidovre? Eventually, she put a note on her door saying she didn't have a clue about the matter, and when that didn't help she called it a day and went home. Even the Deputy Commissioner stopped by Simonsen's own office, for no reason in particular other than to hear how he was getting on. She could be Queen of Sweden, too, he thought to himself, and what a divided country that was turning out to be.

'Promise me I'll be the first to be informed when you're ready,' she said.

'Cross my heart.'

'Not that I normally need to know things the second they happen, but HS is buzzing, and... well, you know.'

'I know,' said Simonsen, without the faintest idea what she was on about.

That same evening he called a meeting for the next morning at eight, knowing full well he was leaving it late and that eight o'clock was early, two facts he thought might just cancel each other out. In the morning they were all there on the dot. He

413

himself arrived a couple of minutes late, carrying a box full of pastries from the baker's and a bag of peeled carrots.

He stood in the middle of the room with the air of a televangelist.

'Very nice of you all to come. As I'm sure most of you know, since my heart attack I've been forced to change my habits rather drastically, and part of my new regimen consists of a daily jog. The first time out was more literally a *walk*, but gradually...'

He spent ten minutes telling them about his triumph: yesterday, for the first time, he had managed to run the entire way! Which called for pastries and organic carrots all round.

Some time passed before everyone had settled. Eventually, Klavs Arnold said:

'Was that it?'

'Well, it's not my birthday, but I've got a packet of raisins in my lunch box if you're still hungry.'

They trickled away to avoid further embarrassment, bumping into a seething Deputy Commissioner in the corridor outside. Arne Pedersen stopped her to explain. Simonsen offered her a carrot.

The next day was more serious. They were all there again, realising that yesterday's stunt would not be repeated, if only because Simonsen clearly was in a more solemn mood. He began by handing round a report. It was rather a comprehensive report, and a quick leaf through its pages revealed that its subject matter was by no means easily fathomed. The Countess frowned and asked:

'What *is* this, Simon? A dissertation in physics, or what? What sort of person would understand this?'

He ignored her and commenced more formally.

'First off, I'd like to thank you all for the hard work and effort you've put into this case. Sometimes more in spite of than because of me, for which I would like to apologise. Now to the matter at hand. I know it's rather symbolic, but it was extremely important to Melsing

414

that he provide us with a most thorough analysis in this instance. I'm afraid that might slightly have affected the readability of the thing.'

Pauline chipped in:

'Slightly? It might as well be Greek.'

'Not at all. It's mathematics and mechanics, with a bit of anatomy and physiology thrown in for good measure. Newton and Hippocrates, you could say. But perhaps we ought to start with the conclusion. After all, it's the most important bit.'

He flicked through to the end and quoted:

'"*Assuming the premises of our calculations to be correct, what this means is that the position of the deceased's body on the stairs may beyond reasonable doubt be taken to be the result of accident.*"'

'You mean Kramer Nielsen just fell down the stairs? Is that it?' the Countess exclaimed in astonishment.

'Jørgen Kramer Nielsen fell and broke his neck. There's no doubt about it now.'

Arne cut in:

'That bloody idiot.'

'It's not his fault he wasn't murdered. It could happen to anyone.'

'Not him – Hans Ulrik Gormsen. His mother-in-law, too, for that matter.'

'Yes, but think of the *positive* results the investigation's yielded. You can't say our efforts have been in vain. Perhaps I should run through the main points so you get the general idea. So, Melsing drew up the report himself, separating Kramer Nielsen's fall into eleven different stages, each accompanied by illustrations and the complex differential equation they use to work out how the relevant forces impacted on the position of the body during each phase of the fall. The blue arrows are velocity vectors for each object or part of the body viewed in partial isolation. Basically it's all spatial geometry using the staircase as its system of co-ordinates. The various parts of Kramer Nielsen's body considered individually can be seen in attachment six.'

415

Arne Pedersen capitulated and closed his folder. Klavs Arnold, however, wasn't so quickly thrown.

'What are all these figures above each... what did you call it... complex differential equation? The ones in the curly brackets.'

'Well spotted, Klavs. They're crucial. What it is is an overview of the estimated or measured parameter values. You can see how the various parameters and values are matched at the different stages of the fall in attachment eleven's attachment four. But to give an example, the coefficient of kinetic friction between the carpet and the deceased is calculated to be one point two with a degree of uncertainty of nought point eight per cent. That's at eighteen degrees centigrade.'

The Countess wasn't convinced.

'I'm sorry, but this all looks like a gigantic cover-up, if you ask me.'

'Well, in a way that's exactly what it is. The report's conclusion is correct given the premises, but Melsing also wanted to... protect a young intern of his who unfortunately messed up with the software application used in all the previous calculations. Since then, Melsing has been off on a course learning how to use it himself, including, most importantly for us, what they call *reverse engineering modus*. Whereas the intern proceeded very much by trial and error using different points of departure in order to achieve predetermined results, what Melsing did was to feed in the final result and then ask the software to work out the relevant points of departure. It may sound like a technicality, but it actually turns out to be crucial. Providing us with the results in such mathematical detail as he does is his way of covering our backs in case anyone in accounts starts to kick up a fuss. We've spent a lot of resources on the basis of the intern's initial mistake.'

The Countess went from indignation to a warm smile.

'I'm not sure if I'm the right person to say this, but I'm going to anyway: well done, Simon. You solved both cases, after all.'

Her words met with agreement all round. Case solved was case solved. It was as simple as that, no matter what the circumstances.

Simonsen looked at his watch:

'Thank you, everyone. However, there is one thing that remains to be said. A few days ago I stood here playing the clown for you. I hope you enjoyed the performance, but now it's time to stop. *Lonely Hearts, Lonely Hearts, Lonely Hearts.* That's what I said. But I was wrong and you were right. There *was* no link. I can only apologise for my stubborn persistence in the face of that fact, and… well, let me just thank you all once again for your patience.'

As if she'd yet to cotton on, Pauline said:

'Is that it, then?'

'Not quite, but close. I've promised to inform our Deputy Commissioner. By rights, she ought to have been the first to know, so all lips sealed until I get back. If she accepts Melsing's report, that'll be the end of it.'

'I can't see her not accepting it,' the Countess said. 'What do you reckon, Arne? You're the one who knows her best.'

'Definitely. No two ways about it. What possible objection could she have?'

CHAPTER 13

It was 12 December, a Friday, the weather calm and dismally grey. It had been a night of violence in Copenhagen: three people had been wounded, one seriously, in a shootout involving bikers and members of an immigrant gang, while out in Amager a young man had been stabbed to death in a club. And yet, things were about to get worse. Much worse. During the morning, a pregnant young financial adviser to one of the big banks was murdered as she left home on her way to work. The perpetrator was a forty-four-year-old psychiatric outpatient, released from treatment the previous evening with a handful of pills and a prescription in his pocket. Not because he didn't need help – plainly he did – but because no more beds were available, a chronic shortage now in its fifteenth year. The killing had been utterly without reason or premeditation. Moreover, it was an attack of the most brutal nature, the victim having been kicked to death. Curiously, this had taken place on Hambros Allé in affluent Hellerup. Normally, such incidents were confined to less privileged areas – housing estates comfortably remote from city centres, in the peripheral regions of the hinterland – only very seldom in areas whose inhabitants could afford private treatment for psychiatric illness. Certainly not in Gentofte Kommune, inside whose boundaries, clustered together within a radius of only a few hundred metres, resided assorted members of parliament, no less than three television presenters and two chief editors of national newspapers. The killing was hands-down the morning's top story. A grave government minister appeared on television, genuinely affected by the incident. His daughter lived on the same street.

'Do you mind if I switch it off?' Simonsen said to Pauline, who was sitting sprawled at the opposite end of the sofa in his little annexe.

'Be my guest. I can do without him going on.'

He pressed the remote.

'I hear you and the Countess are taking some holiday,' she said. 'Are you going anywhere?'

'I might. I'm not sure yet.'

'Oh, well, I hope you have a nice time. What are we supposed to be doing today anyway?'

'Melsing and I have got an appointment with the Deputy Commissioner in an hour to go through the Kramer Nielsen case for Hans Ulrik Gormsen and his mother-in-law from the Legal Affairs Committee. You can come with us, if you want.'

'Do you need me?' she asked, sounding disinterested.

'Not really. But I don't want you feeling left out. You're the only one besides me who's been with the case from day one.'

'Will you be going through all those figures again?'

'Of course. You don't have to decide yet, though. Just come along, if you feel like it.'

She didn't.

The presentation went off according to plan: none of their audience understood a word.

Kurt Melsing passed handouts around and held forth on the HOMS software application and his complex differential equations with their various physical and physiological parameters, eventually leading on to levels of significance and a statistically well-founded conclusion: Jørgen Kramer Nielsen's death was due to an accidental fall on the stairs outside the door to his flat. Only politeness prevented his exclusive audience of three from fleeing the building as he droned on.

Simonsen was affability itself.

'Would you like us to go through it again? It can be rather opaque the first time around.'

No one took him up on the kind offer, and instead he turned to Hans Ulrik Gormsen.

'Perhaps you'd like to comment from your side?'

His politician mother-in-law thought this to be a splendid idea and stared in anticipation at the former police officer who had initiated the whole matter as he rummaged hectically through the pages of his handout, only to declare red-faced:

'Well, it seems obvious to me that the man fell down his own stairs. That's what the calculations show. No doubt about it, none whatsoever. The science is quite clear about that.'

The woman beamed. Her son-in-law was a most gifted communicator. Simonsen took back the handouts.

On the Saturday, Konrad Simonsen moved out of his flat in Valby. He'd been dreading the day, but his sadness at leaving the place turned to gladness once he realised how excited Anna Mia was about her new home. The move itself didn't take long at all, the Countess having hired a firm of professionals, and in no time the place was cleared and his stuff shifted into storage in his former gallery at the house in Søllerød.

Sunday afternoon he stopped by Police HQ, spending an hour clearing up the odds and ends of his investigation so he'd be ready to start on something new once he got back from his holiday. He finished a couple of reports he'd been putting off, making sure the case was archived in the proper manner. After that, he left together with Klavs Arnold, who'd come in to get his new office sorted out. Simonsen offered him a lift to Farum.

'We just have to stop off in Valby first, I need to give my daughter some keys.'

Arnold accepted willingly, having only the vaguest notion of where Farum and Valby might be on a map.

Arnold went up the stairs to the flat with him, eager to say hello to his superior's daughter. Simonsen led the way, only to discover the door was open. Inside, someone was hammering. They went in and followed the racket into the kitchen. Half the units had been ripped out and lay in bits in a heap on the floor. A pair of legs in blue jeans and sneakers poked out from under a cupboard. They weren't Anna Mia's.

'Can you get me that jemmy, sweetie? It's on the window sill.

A hand reached back. Konrad Simonsen placed a wrench in it.

'No, that's not it. It's blue and looks like... well, a jemmy.'

Simonsen picked up a screwdriver but the man apparently decided to fetch the tool himself and crawled out backwards to get it.

The two men stared at each other. Klavs Arnold glanced around at the mess. 'I hope you know what you're doing,' he said.

The man was in his twenties, tall, with tousled, dark brown hair and bright blue eyes. He was wearing a lumberjack shirt and claimed his name was Oliver.

Simonsen put out a reluctant hand and received a firm handshake in return.

'Anna Mia's probably just popped out to the shop. I'm sure she'll be back in a minute,' Oliver said, sheepishly.

'What's this *sweetie* business?' asked Simonsen.

Oliver explained. He was a carpenter by trade, which satisfied Klavs Arnold. He lived in Rødovre and had known Anna Mia, *your daughter*, since the summer, and together with a friend of his he ran his own little building firm. His words emerged in a nervous stutter, and Konrad Simonsen decided he liked him. He handed over the keys, before cautiously stepping over the pile of broken wood on the floor and making his way out. In the doorway he stopped.

'Oh, and one last thing. Treat her nicely or I'll be down on you with all the might of the constabulary. But I suppose you know that already?'

Oliver smiled and nodded. Klavs Arnold chipped in with his Jutland accent:

'It's a hiding to nothing. Make sure you do a good job on that kitchen.'

Konrad Simonsen proposed in a flower bed on Sunday afternoon, in a tangle of last year's perennials. He went down on his knees on the soggy ground before the Countess, who true to weekend habit was out in the garden clearing autumn leaves. At the same instant, he forgot the speech he'd been carefully rehearsing, but realising there was no going back he improvised, eventually popping the question and feeling like time stood still in the split second it took for her to say yes.

'Simon, I thought you'd never ask. Better late than never, though. Come on, let's celebrate.'

'I've got you a present as well,' he mumbled.

He'd placed each of the pictures on a chair and turned them towards the light, presenting them as best he could. Two rubbings of ancient rock carvings from Nordkalotten. Helena Brage Hansen's deaf friend Kaare had shown him how, by rubbing the roots of a certain kind of moss hard against a sheet of paper, you could make the carvings appear in the loveliest ochre. Subsequently, he'd had them framed.

The Countess enthused about them.

'What do they depict, do you know?'

'People celebrating the return of the sun. At least, that's what Kaare said.'

In the evening they sat and watched TV. Suddenly, with a sense of purpose in his voice, he announced:

'I'm going to Liverpool on Thursday. I want to be there for Lucy Davison's funeral. The service is at St Mary's Church in Walton, I've found it on the map. There's an early flight, so I should be able to make it there and back in one day.'

She didn't answer, and for a moment he thought she wasn't pleased with him for wanting to go on his own, though he conceded that would have been unlike her. But then, cryptically, and as if speaking only to herself, she said: 'You gave me such a lovely present before. Perhaps I can give you one in return, if there are any tickets left. Wait here, Simon, I'll be back in a tick.'

A tick turned out to be an hour and a half. He was dozing and she had to wake him up.

'Sorted,' she said. 'We're going on a little getaway together, to celebrate, so your departure's put forward a day.'

He yawned and shook his head in an effort to dispel sleep.

'What do you mean?'

'We're going to a football match on Wednesday night.'

'In Liverpool?'

'Yes, and you can start looking forward to it.'

'But I don't like football.'

'You'll like this. It's a lot more than football, believe me.'

However, all was not entirely well. Amid the sweet nothings and tender caresses that abounded in the wake of their engagement, and a newfound belief in a bright and better future, was a single source of irritation that wouldn't go away. The Countess probed into the Kramer Nielsen case, pointing to little cracks in the logic that she failed to comprehend, forcing him to account for each in turn, only to find that for each satisfactory answer he provided, two new questions arose. He felt like she was interrogating him, which was more or less exactly what she was doing, albeit flippantly and in a tone that indicated to him that she no longer believed a word he was telling her. Eventually, he had to come clean.

'OK, so Melsing and I haven't told the whole truth.'

'You don't say,' she said, sarcasm dripping from every syllable. 'I'd never have guessed.'

'I'll give you the full story in due course.'

'And when might that be? I wonder.'

'Everything comes to she who waits...'

She cut him off with annoyance:

'Oh, don't start that again, Simon.'

Konrad Simonsen was not one to be easily impressed but Anfield took his breath away. From the very first, he was fascinated: the swell of the songs he didn't understand, the supporters' euphoric pride in their team and the stadium, the sense of belonging in everyone around them. There was no humility about it, and yet it was quite without arrogance or aggression.

'What do you think?'

'It's amazing. Magnificent.'

The Countess swept out an arm as though it all belonged to her:

'*This is Anfield.*'

'Why do you say that?'

'I'll tell you about that later. All I can say is, I've been looking forward to showing you this. I knew you'd like it.'

'It's overwhelming. Do they sing all the time?'

'As good as. Liverpudlians like their songs. There was a band from here once, they got to be quite famous.'

He missed the reference entirely. By now she was pointing to the area behind the goal.

'That section over there's called the Kop. They decide what to sing and when.'

'What's our bit called?'

'I'm not sure, to be honest. Oh, yes, we're the Paddock, but we're not as famous as the Kop.'

'How long have you known about this?'

'It's not exactly a secret.'

'No, of course not, stupid question. What I mean is, I wish I'd realised before.'

'I know how you feel. My dad always said: "*You haven't lived until you've seen the Pyramids, made love under a full moon and seen Liverpool play at Anfield Road.*"'

Suddenly, she roared with the crowd. Simonsen looked around the stadium: a heaving ocean of red and white scarves raised above tens of thousands of heads in joyous praise. The actual match he found less interesting.

'It all makes sense when you're here. Has anyone scored?'

'Not yet. You won't be in any doubt when Liverpool do, though.'

He nodded, twisting round again to look up at the packed tiers of the stand above.

'So, have you seen the Pyramids and made love under a full moon?' he asked, turning back to look at her with a gleam in his eye.

'No, but this is the ninth time I've been to Anfield.'

Lucy Davison's funeral failed to stir up much feeling in Konrad Simonsen. He'd already said goodbye to her at the airport in Copenhagen and found it hard to engage in further farewells. Not even when her remains were taken to the grave accompanied by prayers and blessings and once more laid in the ground was he able to summon emotion. The ceremony was tasteful and the church filled with parishioners, but he kept himself apart at the back and made sure he was among the first to leave once it was over, recognised by no one and without awakening the slightest interest in his presence. Afterwards, he stood waiting on the corner across the road, and for the first time in what seemed like an age he wanted a cigarette. A short while passed before he caught sight of the man. He crossed back over, hastening up alongside him.

'We meet again.'

The priest turned, his face lighting up instantly as if he'd run into an old friend.

'What a nice surprise. Yes, indeed.'

'*A coming together of two people*, isn't that what you called it?'

'Ah, yes. A coming together.'

'Have you got time for a chat? I've got lots to tell and something I'd like to ask you.'

'All the time in the world. Shall we find a pub?'

'Why not just walk? The weather's nice.'

'Anywhere in particular?'

Simonsen didn't know the city at all, so he had no preference. They agreed just to wander, and did so for a while in silence. Eventually, Simonsen spoke:

'There's a story I've been wanting to tell you. I almost did, when we met in Valby, but this is better.'

'I'm all ears.'

'It's got nothing to do with our... with the investigation. To tell you the truth, it's a private matter, and I'm not sure exactly why I want to talk to you about it rather than anyone else. It's just the way it's turned out.'

'I'm all ears, regardless.'

'Back in nineteen seventy-three I had a girlfriend who'd got herself into a spot of trouble. We were an odd match. I was in the police and she was a left-wing activist.'

He told the story of how, following the Olympic Games massacre in Munich, Rita desperately wanted to break with the political association she'd got herself mixed up in. It wasn't entirely accurate, insofar as she didn't actually say as much until the following year, but explaining it this way added cohesion, and it made no difference in terms of what he needed to convey.

'She wanted to go to the States and start again. Only she didn't have any money and her ideas for getting hold of some were... well, naive, and would have involved putting herself at risk.'

'Such is the way when we need money fast.'

'Don't I know! Unfortunately, or fortunately, depending on how you look at it, my own ideas on the matter were neither naive nor particularly risky. You won't have been old enough at the time, but there were a lot of struggles going on back then in the early seventies.'

He recounted the strikes, many politically motivated, others simply in favour of higher wages, others still to demonstrate solidarity with striking workers elsewhere, though in many instances it seemed like the actual purpose was known only to the organisers.

'They called them lightning strikes, or *wild* strikes, and that's exactly what they were, though not illegal, even if that's sometimes claimed.'

'There was no compulsory labour, not even then.'

'No, thank goodness.'

Many of these strikes were partly or wholly beyond the control of the established trade unions. They were led by desultory groupings of radicals, thrown together ad hoc. Simonsen named a few examples of ones he could remember. And yet it had also been a time of solidarity, strikers often being helped along financially by what was referred to as *the man with the cardboard box*.

'The cardboard box being full of money?' the priest enquired.

'Exactly. A lot of money.'

It all went on very discreetly, otherwise the donor, usually another trade union, ran the risk of heavy penalties. No one ever knew anything, Simonsen explained, apart from the fact that some person or persons unknown had been rather charitable all of a sudden. He went on:

'Oddly enough, this money was actually always delivered in a cardboard box, never a carrier bag or a rucksack, but a cardboard box.'

'See, hear and speak no evil?'

'You could say.'

The priest nodded and listened with interest. Simonsen continued with his story. The recipient of the cardboard box would preferably be the senior shop steward for whatever area was on strike. There were no accounts, for obvious reasons, and no involvement by the banks, and thereby no risk of banknotes being traced. Those involved trusted each other, and had to.

'Anyway, to cut a long story short, it didn't take a genius to work out who'd have large sums of money stashed away in the bedroom dresser at the end of the month. Quite literally, as it happens.'

'I understand.'

'The shop steward I'd picked out lived on his own. In a fourth-floor flat in Nørrebro.'

Simonsen had stolen a bike from outside the Hovedbanegården, the city's central station, and now he pedalled off, away from Rita and the telephone box. Two hundred metres along the street he turned in through a gateway and got off, wheeling the bike into the courtyard and parking it in the bicycle rack, confident that this was behaviour that would not awake suspicion. Systematically, he glanced around. The yard was deserted, and in the windows at the back of the premises he detected no signs of activity. With purpose in his stride, and without hurrying, he went up to the door leading to the rear stairway, opened it and stepped inside. He stood for a moment as planned, having imagined nerves would require him to pause here and collect himself. To his own surprise, however, he realised he wasn't in the slightest bit anxious. Nonetheless, he stuck to his plan and slowly counted to thirty before making his way up the stairs to the fourth floor.

He put his ear to the kitchen doors on both sides of the stairway, first one, then the other, listening and hearing nothing. He took his tools from his little rucksack, though only the lock pick proved necessary, the lock a simple and commonplace older variety that took him less than a minute to open. He stepped into a narrow kitchen. Yesterday's dirty dishes had been left in the sink. The flat was small, comprising besides the kitchen only a living room, a hall and a single bedroom. As soon as he'd satisfied himself he was on his own, he opened the front door, jammed a matchstick in the lock and closed it again gently. Now he'd have plenty of time to make his getaway if the owner suddenly came back in his Wartburg Convertible and Rita, for whatever reason, failed to phone. Thus, he began systematically to search the place, quickly and with efficiency, taking care not to disturb anything unduly.

The shop steward had hidden the money away in the second drawer of the bedroom dresser, wads of banknotes stashed away in nine long socks at the bottom of the drawer. Simonsen checked the contents of one: used notes in large denominations. It could hardly have been better. He stuffed the haul into his rucksack, closed the drawer and left.

The priest summed up without any air of condemnation:
'So you stole the money from the drawer?'

'The lot, almost three hundred thousand kroner, an absolute fortune in those days. It'd be ten times the amount today. And, just as I'd thought, it was never reported. It was all dealt with internally, and it can't have been much fun for that poor shop steward. That was what worried me most, more than the fact that I'd taken something that didn't belong to me. On the whole, though, if I'm to tell the truth, what I'd done didn't really bother me that much. I was too busy trying to get the money transferred so my girlfriend could get it paid to her in the States. It was no easy matter, it took some time.'

'Well, I can't say I condone what you did. It was wrong, especially in view of the fact that you were in the police. But then you realised that yourself a long time ago?'

'Yes, I did. And put it all well and truly to the back of my mind. It's been there ever since, until now. So many things have happened in my life of late that seem to have brought it bobbing back up to the surface again. Not least this Lucy Davison case. Such a senseless killing... so without meaning... and yet her death has affected so many people for life. It's as if we could just as well throw a dice and determine our fate that way. If I'd been found out that day back in nineteen seventy-three, my whole life would have been drastically different.'

'I'm not sure things are quite as meaningless as you make out, though naturally I can't provide explanations for everything, nowhere near. But when you stole that money, Lucy Davison had already been in the ground more than four years. Perhaps the reason you weren't found out then was because you were needed to find her again all this time after. Who knows?'

'That sounds even more frightening.'

'You think so? I don't. And I don't think you need to feel particularly weighed down by what you did back then, either. You've led a law-abiding life since, I assume.'

'Of course.'

'All I can say is that I've heard much worse. It's not up to me to forgive, but in the big picture your crime is rather trivial.'

'A scruple, isn't that what you call it? A minor sin?'

The priest laughed:

'Indeed, let's call it that, shall we?'

Simonsen smiled.

'I needed to tell another person. Not even my girlfriend at the time, Rita, knew for certain what I'd done. But these past months I've found it increasingly difficult to keep it inside. I'm glad I've told you.'

'Me, too.'

'Don't get me wrong, it's not because I want us to swap secrets or anything.'

'The thought hadn't occurred to me.'

They walked on for a while without speaking, each preparing for the next act they both knew would come. All of a sudden they came to Anfield. Simonsen jabbed a finger towards the ground.

'I was there yesterday and heard them sing.'

'Really? I did happen to see on the news this morning that the English army had just won the war.'

'Oh, it wasn't war, not at all. I've never experienced anything quite like it. Not the football – I wouldn't know about that – but the atmosphere. We stayed behind in our seats for a bit while the crowds were leaving. I just needed to sit there and… take it all in. Eventually we were asked to move along by one of the stewards.'

'I tend to just skim the results in the paper. It's quicker that way.'

To his surprise, Simonsen felt offended.

'It's not the same.'

'No, of course not, but they're football mad in this city and I like to tease them a bit every now and again. The truth is I've seen a few matches there myself.'

'I wish I could sing with them.'

'It comes with time.'

'You mean, you know the songs?'

'A couple. The most important one, certainly. I might let you hear it later on. But it wasn't football you wanted to talk about, was it?'

'No, quite. Do you want to know how I discovered the truth? It's a bit funny, actually.'

'The truth, indeed. No mean feat. Tell me, by all means.'

It was hard for him to know quite where to start. After his epiphany on his nocturnal wander that night in Valby, the pieces had all simply fallen neatly into place, though the order in which they came to him was the opposite of the actual chronology of events. He told the priest about the woman officer who'd accidentally removed Jørgen Kramer Nielsen's mobile phone from the scene. He'd contacted her again recently and realised there was an important detail that ought to have puzzled him at the time, but which for some reason had escaped his attention.

'You closed Kramer Nielsen's eyes when you found him, didn't you?'

'Yes, I did.'

'It could have happened by chance, but we would have expected his eyes to be open, regardless of whether he was killed or just fell. But they weren't.'

'I never gave it a thought until now. It seemed the natural thing to do, that's all.'

'*Cui bono?* For whose benefit? That was what set me off, that expression. The answer was so obvious all of a sudden: for *my* benefit.'

He'd found Lucy, and now finally she'd come home. It was a satisfactory conclusion, and it pleased him more than anyone. Moreover, the priest was contented, too. Simonsen had come to see the man at his side in a whole new light. He had studied the transcripts of his interview with the priest and his bishop again from a fresh vantage point, and been impressed. Not once had the priest told a lie, not once had he compromised his vow of secrecy, but at the same time he had allowed the police to believe

431

exactly what they wanted to believe: that he had been led into revealing that he knew Lucy Davison and that she was dead. Simonsen explained the finer points and concluded with a smile.

'On the other hand, what would one expect of a man who won his seminary's annual debating competition twice in a row?'

'You've been doing your homework.'

'I certainly have.'

'Perhaps there was a convergence of interests during that interview.'

'Definitely. We didn't know that, but you did. Do you know the story about Mefisto from *Ekstra Bladet*?'

The priest knew it well. Simonsen told him anyway. Erling Olsen, a keenly intelligent scholar, also known as *The Owl*, was Minister of Housing in Prime Minister Anker Jørgensen's government in the seventies. At the same time, Olsen was penning highly insightful and scathingly satirical political copy in a national tabloid *Ekstra Bladet* under the pseudonym of Mefisto. No one knew Mefisto's true identity, only that it was obvious it had to be someone very high up in the political eche- lons. Legend had it that the prime minister eventually narrowed the field down and confronted Olsen at a cabinet meeting, asking him straight out if he was behind the articles, to which Olsen supposedly had replied rather indignantly: *Why would I do a thing like that?* And with that the matter was effectively closed.

'I never thought for a moment that you would lie to me directly,' Simonsen went on. 'So when you said you didn't move Jørgen Kramer Nielsen's body, I believed you. Until one night I realised that you'd never actually said that at all. I asked you in your garden if you'd moved the body or altered its position in any way, and you said: *Why on earth would I do that?* You could see your neighbour was obviously dead and that there was nothing you could do. Which was true, there wasn't. But while I believed you to have told me you never moved the body, the truth is you never actually said one way or the other. What you said led me to believe what I wished to believe. Our former housing minister would have complimented you.'

'How astute. It sounds like you know more than I do,' said the priest, his voice a mutter.

Simonsen laughed.

'Come now, there's no need to be modest. I think the time has come for us to tick some boxes, see how much of what we know tallies. Jørgen Kramer Nielsen lay dead on the stairs when you got back from your holiday. He'd fallen and broken his neck, not down the short flight that starts by his own door, but down the longer one that ends at yours. Seeing your upstairs neighbour lying dead like that, you realised the chances of ever finding Lucy Davison and having her remains laid to rest in consecrated ground were now slim indeed. The thought tormented you, as it had tormented Kramer Nielsen, but you were both bound by an oath that couldn't be broken. You, however, had an idea. You decided to move him up on to the little landing before calling the ambulance, and as you did so Kramer Nielsen's mobile fell out of his pocket, only you didn't notice that. By changing the position of the body you hoped the police would realise something didn't add up and look into the matter in such detail as to discover the secret he'd been keeping all those years. What's more, you were right, that's exactly what happened. There's only one thing I don't understand, though: how come you didn't carry him all the way up to his own door, rather than leaving him at the bottom of the second, albeit shorter flight?'

'How reassuring you don't know everything.'

'Now you're avoiding the issue. In actual fact, you were very, very lucky. If our investigation hadn't kicked off in such chaotic manner, our technicians would have discovered the truth within days.'

'You do seem to rely a lot on luck, good and bad.'

'Let's say it's just my way of looking at things. If you prefer, we could call it divine providence.'

'*Divine providence*, I like that.'

'So we agree. As it turned out, we believed the lack of physical evidence from the short flight of stairs was down to time elapsed and the cleaning that had been done in the interim. Later, we found skin cells in the carpet of the long flight, in the exact places we'd expect to find them, clearing you of suspicion of killing him, though I never seriously thought you did.'

They came to a crossing. For the umpteenth time, Simonsen nearly got himself run over, looking left instead of right before stepping out. The priest grabbed his shoulder and held him back.

Simonsen collected himself for a moment, before going on:

'There's something that puzzles me. The first time I questioned you, I thought I'd caught you out with regards to your confessing to your bishop. Now I'm uncertain.'

'You needn't be. I was completely unprepared for that. I fell right in. I must say, it was a very clever trap you laid for me there.'

'A coming together.'

The priest smiled.

'Indeed, a coming together.'

Again they walked in silence, the streets continually changing character: rows of small, terraced houses, as any tourist in a northern English town would expect to see, giving way to imposing edifices of the nineteenth century, unpretentious rows of local shops in whose doorways the proprietors often stood waiting for passing trade, towers of steel and glass striving for the sky. A mix of run-down and pleasant.

Eventually, the priest spoke again:

'What will happen now?'

'Nothing.'

'Nothing? Isn't that getting off rather lightly?'

It was indeed. According to paragraph 125 of the criminal code, what he had done carried a sentence of up to two years' imprisonment, or a very considerable fine at minimum. This was the reason Simonsen and Kurt Melsing had gone to such pains.

'I'm glad you moved him, and officially it doesn't make much odds whether he fell down one flight or the other. On that, my technical colleague and I are in complete agreement. He's prepared a report stating that Kramer Nielsen's fall occurred on the shorter flight of stairs, and the funny thing is his exposition is all still perfectly correct.'

'How strange.'

Simonsen told him about the FBI's software.

'The conclusion, then, is that if the premises hold up, the fall could have taken place quite naturally on the shorter flight, too.'

'But the premises don't quite, do they?'

'A very astute reader with the requisite skills in mathematics and physics might conceivably wonder about a single detail. You're an educated man, perhaps you know about the empirical physical constant denoted by the letter g?'

'The gravitational constant, if it's a capital G. Small g denotes free-fall acceleration, popularly known as gravity. Nine point eight one metres per second per second, if I remember rightly.'

'Gravity, that's right. Very good. And that's just one of dozens of parameters in the software that can be varied. Maybe they think one day we'll be solving crimes on the moon, who knows? But it turns out that by increasing gravity by only thirty per cent, Jørgen Kramer Nielsen's fall down the top stairs comes out as natural in relation to the position in which he was discovered, and, well, you know better than I do, climbing those stairs must feel like heavy going sometimes, or am I wrong?'

'I've never thought about it, to be honest, but now you mention it, yes, it does. Hasn't anyone asked questions yet?'

'Not yet, and I'm sure it's not going to happen either. No one can be bothered reading anything other than the conclusion. The actual body of the thing is too complicated, mind-numbingly to be frank, so Jørgen Kramer Nielsen's death has been well and truly buried in the maths, you could say. Funny, really: all his

435

adult life he carried this dreadful secret around and sought refuge in mathematics to keep his demons at arm's length, and now the actual circumstances of his death are hidden away in calculus.'

Simonsen held up a pre-emptive hand.

'I know you can't answer, and this isn't an interrogation. It just struck me how ironic life can be. I should mention, though, that there's one person to whom I do intend to tell the truth at some point, but she can keep a secret. Probably just as well as you.'

They passed by a church and the priest stopped to look up for a moment. There was a wistful note in his voice.

'I'm fond of mathematics and physics, and rhetoric, too, for that matter, though that's something else entirely. But there's one thing I can never understand when it comes to people who subscribe to the natural sciences, and that is, they're never in doubt about their own infallibility. Particularly when it comes to logic – if something hangs together logically, then it must be true and all other forms of inquiry and ways of seeing must therefore be wrong. It's a very peculiar form of hubris: if something's true, it's logical; if it's logical, it's true.'

Simonsen didn't know quite what to say and so chose to say nothing. The priest asked him a question.

'You've tied a very nice, *logical* ribbon around your investigation, I must admit. But tell me: considering what you know about me, however little that might be, do you really think that, arriving home from holiday to find a dead body on my stairs, my immediate thought would be to seek to exploit the circumstance and manipulate the police into finding a second body? I know what your logic tells you, but is it what your knowledge of human nature says, too?'

Simonsen continued walking without replying for a while, eventually conceding:

'No, it isn't. So what did you do? I know you moved him, that's beyond doubt.'

'Yes, I did. But I don't think you'd understand why.'

'Try me.'

This time it was the priest's turn to contemplate before answering.

'Jørgen's body lay at the bottom of the lower stairs, as you so rightly say, in the dimmest of light. I closed his eyes, sat with him and said a little prayer. But then, as I was about to go inside to my own flat and call the ambulance, I happened to look up. The most wonderful light was streaming in through the window on the upper landing: yellow, green, red, blue, a rainbow filtered through the stained glass of the panes. It was as if it were crying out to us, and I stood there almost in awe for quite some time. Then I carried him up into the light, as I felt compelled to do. And when I put him down I was filled with a most wondrous sense of peace and joy such as I'd never known before. I knew then that I'd done the right thing.'

Simonsen thought for a moment, before admitting that this was more plausible by a long way.

There was no more to say about it. And yet they continued walking. Like an LP that went on turning with the needle in the run-out groove, the music finished.

'Road, street, place, avenue, way, drive,' Simonsen mused after a while. 'I wouldn't be able to find my way back if I had a month to try.'

'You're forgetting park, lane, grove, hey, croft and close. It's confusing, I know.'

'What's the difference?'

'No idea.'

On Croxteth Lane the priest said:

'We could come over again when Missing Children get their new premises on Rydal Avenue finished. You'll be able to see your posters again. I think that would be rather nice.'

Konrad Simonsen thought it was a good idea.

'Perhaps we could go to a football match. I really must do that again.'

'That's what everyone says who's been to Anfield. I did, too, after my first time.'

'By the way, do you know when the sun is at its highest in northern Norway?' Simonsen asked, changing the subject all of a sudden.

'Midsummer, when the tilt of the earth towards the sun is at its greatest. It's the same throughout the northern hemisphere.'

They talked about Simonsen's trip to Hammerfest. As they had done in Valby.

'Will you say a prayer for Lucy on Midsummer's Eve?'

'I will indeed. You can, too.'

'I don't know any prayers.'

'Make one up. Often, they're the best.'

They found themselves in a park, ambling along crooked paths lined with angular, half-bare trees.

'You promised you'd sing for me.'

The priest looked at him and nodded. He took a breath, and then began to sing in a loud and confident tenor. Passers-by smiled at them, and the priest repeated the final lines:

Walk on, walk on, with hope in your heart,
And you'll never walk alone!
You'll never walk alone.

Konrad Simonsen joined in. He sang poorly, hitting only an occasional note. But it didn't matter. Two were better than one. Now they were a choir.

A NOTE ON THE AUTHORS

Lotte and Søren Hammer are a sister and brother from Denmark. Younger sister Lotte worked as a nurse after finishing her training in 1977 and her brother Søren was a trained teacher and a lecturer at the Copenhagen University College of Engineering. After Søren moved into the house where Lotte lived with her family in 2004 they began writing crime novels together. To date they have written six books in the series. *The Hanging* is the first, *The Girl in the Ice* is the second, and *The Vanished* is the third.

A NOTE ON THE TRANSLATOR

Martin Aitken is an award-winning translator of Danish literature. His many books include novels by Helle Helle, Jussi Adler-Olsen, Peter Høeg, and Kim Leine.